Migration and the Global Landscapes of Religion

Bloomsbury Studies in Religion, Space and Place

Series editors: Paul-François Tremlett, John Eade and Katy Soar

Religions, spiritualities and mysticisms are deeply implicated in processes of place-making. These include political and geopolitical spaces, local and national spaces, urban spaces, global and virtual spaces, contested spaces, spaces of performance, spaces of memory and spaces of confinement. At the leading edge of theoretical, methodological and interdisciplinary innovation in the study of religion, Bloomsbury Studies in Religion, Space and Place brings together and gives shape to the study of such processes.

These places are not defined simply by the material or the physical but also by the sensual and the psychological, by the ways in which spaces are gendered, classified, stratified, moved through, seen, touched, heard, interpreted and occupied. Places are constituted through embodied practices that direct critical and analytical attention to the spatial production of insides, outsides, bodies, landscapes, cities, sovereignties, publics and interiorities.

Christianity in Brazil
Sílvia Fernandes

Global Trajectories of Brazilian Religion
Edited by Martijn Oosterbaan, Linda van de Kamp and Joana Bahia

Ideologies and Infrastructures of Religious Urbanization in Africa
Edited by David Garbin, Simon Coleman and Gareth Millington

Religion and the Global City
Edited by David Garbin and Anna Strhan

Religious Pluralism and the City
Edited by Helmuth Berking, Silke Steets and Jochen Schwenk

Singapore, Spirituality, and the Space of the State
Joanne Punzo Waghorne

Struggles for Hindu Sacred Space in the Netherlands
Priya Swamy

Towards a New Theory of Religion and Social Change
Paul-François Tremlett

Urban Religious Events
Edited by Paul Bramadat, Mar Griera, Julia Martinez-Ariño and Marian Burchardt

Migration and the Global Landscapes of Religion

Making Congolese Moral Worlds in Diaspora and Homeland

David Garbin

BLOOMSBURY ACADEMIC

LONDON • NEW YORK • OXFORD • NEW DELHI • SYDNEY

BLOOMSBURY ACADEMIC
Bloomsbury Publishing Plc
50 Bedford Square, London, WC1B 3DP, UK
1385 Broadway, New York, NY 10018, USA
29 Earlsfort Terrace, Dublin 2, Ireland

BLOOMSBURY, BLOOMSBURY ACADEMIC and the Diana logo are trademarks of
Bloomsbury Publishing Plc

First published in Great Britain 2023
This paperback edition published 2025

A catalogue record for this book is available from the British Library.

A catalogue record for this book is available from the Library of Congress.

ISBN: HB: 978-1-4742-8337-3
PB: 978-1-3503-8711-9
ePDF: 978-1-4742-8335-9
eBook: 978-1-4742-8336-6

Series: Bloomsbury Studies in Religion, Space and Place

Typeset by Deanta Global Publishing Services, Chennai, India

To find out more about our authors and books visit www.bloomsbury.com and
sign up for our newsletters

Contents

Figures

Acknowledgements

I am greatly indebted to many people who have supported and inspired me while writing this manuscript. I would especially like to thank Paul-François Tremlett as well as Lily McMahon at Bloomsbury Academic for their patience, help and encouragement in producing this book. The research would never have come about without my involvement in the project 'The religious lives of migrant minorities: a transnational and multi-sited perspective', a project of the Social Science Research Council (SSRC) funded by the Ford Foundation. I am grateful to the participants and coordinators of the project, including Josh de Wind, Manuel Vásquez, Peggy Levitt, Thomas Hansen, José Casanova, Ann David, Kim Knott and Samadi Sadouni – with a special thanks to John Eade, the London field site coordinator, who has always been so generous with his time and support. Funding for the research upon which Chapters 5–7 are partly based was provided by the British Academy as part of two separate grants ('Religion and development in Central Africa: a pilot study of the Kimbanguist church in the DRC' and the 'Religious urbanisation and infrastructural lives in African megacities: moral economies of development in Kinshasa and Lagos'). I am grateful to the American Academy of Religion's small grant programme and the 'Global Prayers' network (in particular Stephan Lanz and Jochen Becker) for funding the fieldwork in Atlanta. I would also like to thank Susanne Rau and Jörg Rüpke from the 'Religion and Urbanity' research group at the Max Weber Centre for Advanced Cultural and Social Studies (University of Erfurt, Germany), who have hosted me for a few (pre-Covid) months, allowing me to work on the manuscript. A big thank you to all the fellows there, in particular Marian Burchardt and Emiliano Urciuoli.

Without the input and support from the Congolese community, it would have been impossible for me to complete this research. I am grateful to all of the interviewees and research participants for the time they spent with me and the personal, often intimate experiences they shared with me. I would like to thank in particular the members of the Kimbanguist church across the diaspora and in the DRC, especially Papa Guy, José, Marc, JP, Aubin, Joël, Cyril, Vanessa, Antoinette, Tetys, Becken, Maman Rose (RIP), FAKI members and many others *qui se reconnaîtront*. I am also grateful to all my Congolese friends in

London and those who have generously provided time, advice and support, including Norbert, Papa Pambu, Frankos, JJ Bola, Letitia, Sylvestre, Salem, Charles, Guérick (RIP), Fred, Victoria and many others. I would also like to thank colleagues at the University of Kinshasa, in particular José Mangalu and Floribert Ntungila-Nkama.

A special thanks also to colleagues, academic friends and those with whom I crossed (research) paths over the years and from whom I learned much: Marie Godin, Claude Sumata, Aurélien Mokoko Gampiot, Xavier Moyet, Simon Coleman, Anne Mélice, Gareth Millington, Dimitra Pahis, Martyn Barrett, Enrico Masi, Ramon Sarró, Caroline Knowles, Anna Strhan, Katrien Pype, Nimrod Luz, Yannick Fer, Gwendoline Malogne-Fer, Fabien Truong, Michaela Benson and Irene Becci. Thanks also to Kent colleagues: Sophia Labadi, Miri Song, Vince Miller, Trude Sundberg, Johnny Ilan, Mike Calnan, Daisy Esiebo, Dawn Lyon, Balihar Sanghera, Phil Hubbard and the undergraduate and postgraduate students with whom I had fruitful seminar discussions about this research.

Finally, I am eternally grateful for the support of friends and family. Thanks to Lorena for her continuous support and especially to Inès and Lorenzo for providing a constant source of joy – I dedicate this to them.

Introduction

Papa Gérard[1] is a Congolese living in London who, while born in the Democratic Republic of Congo (DRC), grew up in France and, as a French passport holder, exercised his EU right to 'Freedom of Movement' to come to the UK in the early 2000s, almost a couple of decades before the Brexit rupture. Papa Gérard's trajectory is just one among many of the Congolese in the UK who have come from the DRC as asylum seekers or migrants via a number of routes through European and/or African countries, sometimes transiting several years in countries like Morocco or South Africa.

I open the book with Papa Gérard not only as a tribute to his contributions to my research on 'diasporic religion' among Congolese in London – as an important gatekeeper who has become a trusted friend – but also because he allowed me to travel with him to the Congo to take part in a ritual related to a sad, intimate, yet also highly social event – the death of his father. In the current literature on diaspora and migrant communities, while a lot has been written about cultural, social and religious 'life', death and death rituals have received scant scholarly attention. Yet for the Congolese, like for many other African communities, rituals surrounding death, in particular *matangas* (funeral wake parties or commemorations), rely on a 'shared labour of loss' (De Boeck 2014: 316) and are often lively performances of social life. They are events that link individuals with extended kin and friendship networks, the past with the present and, for those in diaspora, the country of origin with the country of settlement. In Atlanta, where I also conducted fieldwork, a member of the Congolese community once told me: 'Everybody goes to *matangas* – they are bigger than weddings, if you travel anywhere around the diaspora, to measure the size of a Congolese community, the best way to do so is to attend a *matanga*.'

While *matangas* among Congolese in diaspora are always well attended, they can also reflect the fragmented, hybrid and polyvalent nature of what Avtar Brah (1996) once called the 'diaspora condition'. When Congolese families and kinship groups are dispersed globally, like it is often the case, multiple *matangas* can be organized simultaneously in several continents, with connections between kin established via phone or social media. But there may also be tensions and conflicts, especially regarding the financing of *matangas* in the homeland where they can be quite costly, with those in diaspora sometimes complaining that they have to bear all the costs and that family members in the homeland are unaware of their financial hardship.

The question of burial also raises many issues related to belonging, ancestrality and territoriality. Being buried in the DRC may represent an ultimate 'return' journey for those in diaspora, but, for many, the insecurity and dysfunctionality of the Congolese state is reflected in the decaying of public cemeteries in the capital Kinshasa: often ran down, overgrown, inadequately maintained and where, I was told, the theft of stones and artefacts is rife, or where people live (and love) on top of graves.[2] Being buried in such cemeteries 'is like dying twice' as Papa Gérard put it to me once. Adding to this, the cost of shipping the body from Europe to Kinshasa, where the majority of Congolese migrants are from, can be prohibitive.

The father of Papa Gérard was not, in fact, buried in Kinshasa, but in the small cemetery of Nkamba, the holy city of the Kimbanguist church, situated in the Kongo Central province,[3] 120 kilometres southwest of the Congolese capital. The deceased was a respected figure of the Kimbanguist church, an Afro-Christian church which developed initially as a prophetic revival movement in the 1920s, led by Simon Kimbangu, who was born and buried in Nkamba. Simon Kimbangu belonged to the large Kongo ethnic group and had been educated in a Baptist Missionary Society station near Nkamba, and in 1921, he began to preach and heal in Nkamba and its surroundings. Only several months after the start of his ministry of faith healing, which brought thousands of pilgrims to Nkamba, Kimbangu was arrested by the Belgian army as his prophetic (*ngunza*) status was seen as a major threat to the colonial order. During Kimbangu's time in jail (where he died in 1951, after a thirty-year-imprisonment), the movement was forced to go underground as many Kimbanguist families were being deported and scattered across the Belgian Congo.

In postcolonial times, Papa Gérard's father helped establish Kimbanguist structures among Congolese in France and returned to the Congo in the DRC to fulfil important ecclesial functions within the church in Kinshasa. His status and reputation explain why his family and, in particular his elder son Papa Gérard, have managed to convince the spiritual leader of the church (grandson of the Prophet-founder Kimbangu) to bury him on 'holy grounds', a privilege reserved for a select few. In addition, Papa Gérard himself, as a talented member of the Kimbanguist brass band and a youth leader within the church in London, is a well-known figure across the whole Kimbanguist diaspora. He is reputed for his role in educating and evangelizing second-generation Kimbanguists, protecting them from what many Kimbanguist leaders and parents see as the moral urban 'void' of London.

* * *

The vignette of the *matanga* and burial of Gérard's father point to some key elements of the story of Christianity – or better put perhaps, 'Christianities' – in the DRC and the Congolese diaspora. In many respects, it is a story of maintaining connections, with people and places, including, in this case, ancestral territories, a story about providing symbolic, social and spiritual resources, an important component of the work – for Kimbanguists, sacred labour (*misala*) – of both Papa Gérard and his father. But this starting vignette illustrates only one aspect of the wider, pluralized configuration I want to explore in this book. Through a study of this configuration of 'urban Christianities' in Congo and in the Congolese diaspora, one of my central aims will be to examine the entanglement of religion and migration in the making of moral worlds, in particular in the context of global societies where migrants reconstruct a sense of home and temporality, where they socially and spiritually map and remap their collective and family lives.

Despite their growing numbers and presence in cities throughout Europe and North America, from London, Paris and Brussels to Atlanta and Montreal, the Congolese diaspora has not received sustained scholarly attention. I focus on religion, particularly Christianity, because, as we shall see, it plays a vital role in navigating the challenges posed by the mobility of Congolese and the ongoing connections but also disconnections with the homeland. Because of the central roles it plays, focusing on religion affords us an enlightening window into the texture of everyday life for the Congolese, from family and kinship relations to the politics of the urban and the (trans)national, from the body to the production of meaningful spaces to belong and dwell. This story of Congolese Christianities, like the story of many other 'faiths in motion', religions *sans frontières*, takes place (and makes space) across several scales, and it is not without frictions.

Congolese moral worlds in a context of plurality

In the context of the Congolese diaspora, my research mainly focussed on London and Atlanta. While Atlanta and London constitute two very distinct sites and urban regimes, they may be both considered somehow *peripheral* within the wider Congolese diaspora. Located within predominantly Anglophone societies,[4] they constitute more recent sites of settlement than Brussels or Paris, which represent stronger community and symbolic centres and where there is a well-established Congolese urban presence through often vibrant commercial or cultural activities like in the *quartiers* of 'Matonge' in Brussels[5] or Château Rouge in Paris 18th District. That said, Atlanta and London's Congolese presence reflect, both in their own ways, the increasing complexity of contemporary global migratory flows (de Haas, Castles and Miller 2019) and, as I discuss in the next chapter, they are both characteristic of the changing ethnic and religious landscapes of many 'super-diverse' urban, multicultural societies (Vertovec 2007). Including London and Atlanta enables us to explore how the Congolese draw from their religious and cultural resources to build new individual and collective identities beyond the Francophone diasporic field.

What will also be evident throughout this book is that for Congolese living in London, Atlanta, Brussels or Paris, the Congo – as the *mboka*, the homeland – continues to be a relevant space of material, financial, social, emotional and spiritual investment. Hence, while I give special attention in this book to how religious cultures, identities, material and immaterial infrastructures shape life in diasporic contexts, I also want to show how these dynamics impact the homeland in a wide range of ways, in particular by filling the gaps of a retreating and dysfunctional postcolonial state – for instance, in deploying and enacting various 'visions' of development and charitable interventions.

Here, the question of morality is central. At the level of the individual, such a focus on morality has often implied construing virtue as much more than a ritualized and/or interiorized manifestation of belief and faith. Thus, largely inspired by Foucauldian-oriented notions of the 'ethical self', anthropological studies, in particular studies of Islamic piety movements (Mahmood 2005, Hirschkind 2006), have explored how the cultivation of personal virtue is *productive*, connected to the remaking of the self as an embodied, reflexive subject, a form of moral agency (and moral distinction) combining idioms of power, discipline and control. Among the scholarship on contemporary Christianity, this 'piety turn', as Khan (2022) coined it, is also recognizable in the work of O'Neill (2015) on Pentecostalism in post-Civil War Guatemala. In his ethnography, O'Neill shows how Pentecostalism operates as a 'soft security' regime through which former gang members (many of whom are deportees from the United States) are disciplined into becoming new, self-governing subjects.[6] This regime reflects a wider context where the welfare of citizens, including the inculcation of their civic habitus, has been increasingly privatized, with religious institutions coming to fill the vacuum left by the (neoliberal) crisis of Guatemalan civil society. Salvation and redemption through piety is here valued not only because it offers routes to rebuild self-esteem and display moral distinction but also because it provides an 'ethics of escape' (2015: 160) increasingly needed for survival in a structurally uneven, violent and precarious urban society. The remoralization of individuals 'reorders the city as well as its souls' (2015: 192), integrating the pious to various 'programmes' of physical, emotional, spiritual and bodily reform, sometimes with some degree of coercion (as the case with the Pentecostal rehabilitation clinics).

While transnational migration among the Congolese and everyday urban life in the Congo involve different dynamics than those in post-Civil War Guatemala, it often poses similar challenges of insecurity, danger and impurity that are dealt with the (self)imposition of 'pastoral power' (Foucault 2007). In African contexts, Marshall (2009) similarly evokes the centrality of 'techniques of the self' in the making of 'born-again' identities among Nigerian Pentecostals. While this process of remoralization hinges on the adoption of embodied religious conduct (praying and fasting), bodily asceticism and an inner life of constant self-examination, the Pentecostal 'programmatic' vision also aspires to transform the political and public culture. Marshall's work suggests the importance of looking at religious intervention through remoralization across the public/private boundary. While recognizing the 'microphysics' of power behind subjectivizing forms of piety, I also want to consider, in this book, how the politics of moral presence and transformation both shape and are shaped by lived social spaces at multiple scales. For it is not just nation-states that engage in governmentality; diasporas too deploy power to 'conduct their conduct' as they negotiate insertion in different contexts. Accordingly, I understand moral landscapes as contested and ambivalent terrains: environments of action and transmission and of identity, visibility and recognition (in particular in the diasporic context) that are charged with meaning, but also as spaces of religious and spiritual intervention and investment. As we shall see throughout the book, particularly in Chapters 3 and 7, these sites are connected to various modes of urban presence, including strategies of territorialization (through urbanization, symbolization and re-semantization) – key to forms of moral 'regeneration' at multiple scales. This moralization, as we shall also see, is closely tied to a sense of permanent struggle between evil and divine forces, especially among Pentecostals who tend to problematize 'older' spiritual imaginaries linked to ancestrality and generate ambivalence about the social and familial spheres within which the 'born-again' individual is spatially and temporally embedded.

Because of the plurality within Congolese Christianity, the making and remaking of these moral worlds, these moral landscapes, is justified and performed in a number of ways. In this book, I focus on three key religious 'movements' in the homeland context and the diaspora: (i) the Catholic Church, which in the Congo developed a broad and hierarchically arranged array of institutions, including parishes, schools and hospitals, as part of the process of colonization; (ii) Pentecostalism, an evangelical and 'pneumacentric' Protestantism, which, although fragmented into hundreds of *églises de réveil* of various sizes and scales, became a crucial, perhaps dominant, way of 'being Christian' in the 1990s with the collapse of the Mobutu autocratic/kleptocratic regime; and (iii) Kimbanguism, which, as I already indicated, grew out of the encounter of Kongo prophetic tradition with missionary Protestantism. We shall see that Christianity – at least in these three expressions – provides key networks, symbols, worldviews and material as well as moral resources that enable the Congolese to navigate the challenges of mobility, settlement and identity formation, creating multiple landscapes of belonging.

A great deal of attention has been paid in recent years to the pivotal role of Pentecostalism both in African and diasporic contexts, to the extent that it seems to dominate the scholarship on Christianity in Africa and the African diaspora (Adogame 2013, Butticci 2016, Lindhardt 2015). Yet, despite the spectacular Pentecostalization of African (urban) societies and the significant influence of a Pentecostal agenda of remoralization, African Independent Churches (AICs), like the Kimbanguist or Angolan Tokoist prophetic churches (as well as Nigerian-originated 'white garment' Aladura churches), have maintained an important role and even expanded at various scales. The Kimbanguist church is now one of the largest AICs, with a strong presence in Central Africa, mainly in what Kimbanguists call the 'three Kongos' (Democratic Republic of Congo (DRC), Congo-Brazzaville and Angola) and among Congolese in diaspora, in particular in Europe and North America. The case of transnational Kimbanguism in postcolonial times is particularly relevant to our understanding of how a process of 'globalization from below' can operate through the circulation and mobility of religious actors, beliefs, ideas and materialities within migratory networks and diasporic spaces (Levitt 2002, Vásquez and Marquardt 2003).

That said, the book is also about religious localization and place-making, about how migrants and religious actors carve out spaces of livelihood drawing from their religious resources. I approach this localization not through the study of single congregations, but of the ways in which churches like the Kimbanguist church are embedded in a pluralized religious landscape, within which differentiated worldviews, rituals and attitudes produce and reproduce meaningful boundaries for individuals and groups to (re)locate themselves. As we shall see in the next chapter, boundaries between these groups – Pentecostals, Kimbanguists but also Catholics – are not always clear-cut, and the salience of differences in discourses, rituals and worldviews may be contingent on particular contexts of action and interaction. This flexibility is also reflected by contradictions and changes as we shall see throughout this book.

Outline of the book

This book is primarily a study of a complex religious landscape and its deployment across several scales in diasporic and homeland environments through the constitution and reconstitution of 'moral worlds', providing meaning, resources and constraints to migrants and their families. In that sense, the content and structure of the book also reflect the need to explore how a range of religious dynamics – practices, subjectivities, boundary-making processes or moralizing strategies – overlap with other meaningful spaces and categories of social action and interaction. This is why I thought it was important to see how religious frames and modes of reading can be applied to practices and social worlds that could be seen as located outside the religious sphere (politics, domestic relations and urbanity/urban life, for instance). In addition, it was important to see how religious actors can navigate a plurality of social figurations beyond the simplistic secular/religious divide implied by linear models of disenchantment that assume rationality, advanced technology and urbanization are mutually reinforcing elements of the inevitable triumph of the secular modern.

To address the plurilocal and multiscalar character of Congolese modes of religiosities and diasporic dynamics and the interplay of migration and place-making, I have divided the book into seven chapters, which, although each can be read separately, are organized sequentially. The first chapter discusses questions of religious pluralization as well as the empirical contexts and multi-sited approach of the study. The book then progresses from questions of migration, mobility and settlement (Chapter 2) to themes related to visibility, territorialization and mediation (Chapter 3) before addressing questions of political mobilization across different generations of the Congolese diaspora (Chapter 4). Chapter 5 engages with the world of *linkages* between the diaspora and homeland through a study of the moral economies of remittances, while Chapters 6 and 7 are concerned with the impact of religion in the homeland in terms of developmental intervention and urbanization.

In the following chapter (Chapter 1), I build upon the introductory discussion on death rituals to highlight the diversity of attitudes to ancestrality and to conceptually frame the emergence of a pluralized, global religious landscape among Congolese Christians. I then introduce the idea of the diaspora environment as a specific arena of interaction, affordances and modes of belongings, before discussing my ethnographic engagement with the different study sites in London, Atlanta, and the homeland and the ways these sites constitute urban/spatial regimes constraining or facilitating various forms of religious territorialization.

In Chapter 2, I explore how 'spiritual infrastructures' create affordances for Congolese migrants to unblock paths and manage movement and also how they include resources to address immobility while providing meaning against increasingly restricting migration regimes. We will see that spiritual infrastructures may play multiple and even contradictory roles, allowing migrants to perform empowering forms of moral citizenship, even as they reproduce power asymmetries linked to religious authority and hierarchy, sometimes 'imported' from the homeland.

Chapter 3 is concerned with what I have called the *modalities of presence* of Congolese churches in global cities like London or Atlanta, which have become urban landscapes where forces of secularization and desecularization often combine in uneven ways. This chapter will characterize the range of (re) territorializing strategies adopted by Congolese churches, including spatial conversion and expansion, public processions and pilgrimages. In relocating themselves in new – highly ambivalent – environments, often deemed morally risky but also full of potential, Congolese diasporic religious actors negotiate regimes of visibility and invisibility to perform what is essentially place-making practices (even if transient and unrecognized), often linked to the notions of moral citizenship explored in Chapter 2. The chapter will also argue that an understanding of these modalities of presence needs to consider the multiscalarity of place-making, a territorialization which includes but is not limited to physical sites of 'anchoring' like places of worship. Thus the chapter will also examine the deployment of digital public spheres and mediascapes as ways of mapping, connecting and (re)grounding the sacred.

Chapter 4 expands the exploration of these multiscalar processes, by focusing on the political diasporic engagement of a range of actors – including religious actors – in a context of political crisis in the homeland. We will see how the fight to 'liberate' the Congo can be construed as part of a wider spiritual battle, which relocates the homeland within prophetic or biblical chronotopes. In the second half of this chapter, I draw upon an ethnography of anti-Kabila[8] street protests in London to discuss the limitations of the religious field in sustaining widespread and impactful political action in diaspora, by focusing mainly on the role and experiences of young Congolese activists. Reflecting the importance of a 'right to the city' (Lefebvre 1996), these activists are keen to connect urban presence – in particular, presence at the heart of the city – to political claims, bringing together questions of (postcolonial) race dynamics, global injustice and media invisibility. In doing so, I show how they craft an alternative public sphere – social, urban and digital – to voice claims that cannot be expressed within the space of Congolese churches.

In Chapter 5, "Painful choices': The moral economies of remittances", I relocate questions of politics and transnational social relations to the kinship sphere. I focus on the key practices of remittance-sending to explore the affective circuits between homeland and diaspora spaces. Remittances as 'global money' (Singh 2016) can be considered 'currency of care', but they carry a deep sense of ambivalence, involving both proximity and distance, an ambivalence reflecting some of the contradictions of the 'diaspora condition' discussed at the start of this introductory chapter. We will see that this particular moral economy of financial connections (and disconnections) can be shaped by religious tropes linked, for instance, to reinterpreted notions of indebtedness and dependency.

Chapter 6, centred on narratives and interventions of 'development' in the homeland, examines how everyday urban life, in particular in Kinshasa, is constructed in moral terms. Despite its challenges and contradictions, the diasporic environment is often remapped in positive ways, as part and parcel of a 'search for coherence' (Strhan 2015), visibility and legitimacy; while, in the homeland, charitable and development interventions are performed and justified against the backdrop of a postcolonial society deemed largely corrupt with a dysfunctional, retreating state. Drawing upon the case studies of Catholic, Pentecostal and Kimbanguist educational and health infrastructures, I discuss a range of development narratives to highlight divergences in visions and strategies. I do so without neglecting convergences, for instance, regarding the connection made between the occult and witchcraft with affliction, as well as the imperatives to build moral citizens. I suggest that these convergences within pluralistic and tensile religious, cultural and social fields stem from an inculcated 'collective habitus'.

In the final empirical chapter, Chapter 7, I continue exploring religious developmental dynamics, turning more specifically to the *spatial* aspects of religious-driven changes. The chapter will address how the construction of health and education infrastructures discussed in Chapter 6, as well as the holy city of Nkamba, contributes to a process of religious urbanization. This process enacts religious visions of an 'alter-city' – an urban and infrastructural ideal, a promise to address the gaps of a postcolonial present – constructed in opposition to what is perceived as the chaos and immorality of the megacity Kinshasa. The main argument of the chapter is that religious urbanization does not solely and simply constitute a by-product of religious expansion/transformation. It operates as a kind of 'spatial fix', through the materialization of redemptive or remoralizing imaginaries across multiple scales and is an efficacious way in which the Congolese actively build, understand and dwell in their cities.

In the concluding chapter, I return to the question of performance and its role in revealing how various categories of social life are articulated in the making of Congolese moral worlds. I discuss the metaphor of mapping – which appears recurrently in this book – as a way to frame an ambivalent urbanity as a site of intervention and projection. I also go back to the themes of differentiation and plurality emphasizing the configuration of a global landscape of Congolese 'Christianities' shaped by a range of power-geometries. Last, I re-examine one of the key arguments of the book, that despite the existence of contestations, in particular over the moral legitimacy and political vision of religious actors (both in homeland and diaspora contexts), religious life provides affordances and resources while modes of territorialization of space (and time) allow religious actors to maintain or even expand their influence on public and private domains.

While the book covers a range of strategies, practices and experiences related to the construction (and contestation) of moral worlds across religious boundaries, I do not claim to have covered all configurations of 'Congolese Christianities'. For instance, within the religious sphere which could be loosely defined as 'Protestant-oriented', I mostly focus on Kimbanguist[9] and Pentecostal actors. My aim here is neither to minimize the impact of Protestant missionary interventions in the Congolese/African context nor to minimize the contemporary role of mainstream Protestant churches and movements (including non-Pentecostal evangelicals). Nevertheless, my focus on Catholics, Kimbanguists and Pentecostal *églises de réveil* can be explained by the important role they play or have maintained over the years, including in diaspora (where the role of mainstream Protestant churches is not really significant among

Congolese). Equally, while the study sites (London, Atlanta and the homeland – Kinshasa and Nkamba) contribute only partly to the overall story of the (re) territorialization of contemporary forms of Congolese Christianities gone global, it is hoped that such a multi-sited engagement may reveal not only a rich commonality of experience but also the contingent, situated nature of the making and remaking of moral worlds, contributing, in turn, to an understanding of the role of religion in shaping transnational relations, diasporic cultures and migration networks.

1

Locating Congolese Christianities
Diaspora and homeland contexts

The example of death rituals and discourses about death and ancestrality discussed in the introduction aptly illustrate the continuities and ruptures within and among various forms of Congolese Christianity. When I accompanied Papa Gérard to Nkamba's cemetery, it was to replace his father's temporary gravestone and erect a small mausoleum. After the work has been completed, a small celebration took place, involving members of his kinship group who had travelled from Kinshasa and also some Kimbanguists based in Nkamba from the same ethno-linguistic group/region (Equateur). Food was shared, and prayers were said. One of the participants, a female Kimbanguist pastor who led the prayers, threw food – fish and rice – and sprinkled soda widely on the mausoleum and the adjoining graves for several minutes. 'The dead are not dead' the pastor said, adding that 'if the *bakoko* [ancestors] are not fed they can get angry and jealous, and then they get their revenge spiritually'.

This belief in the power of the ancestors (including the power to harm spiritually and to curse) is generally shared by Congolese Kimbanguists, Catholics and Pentecostals alike. During the many Masses I attended in the Congolese Catholic chaplaincy in London, the support of the *bakoko* was always requested in the opening prayers – a symbol of the Africanization of Congo Catholicism – *le rite Zairois* – brought about in the wake of the Second Vatican Council – the renaming of the country 'Zaire' being the decision of the autocrat president Mobutu in power between 1965 and 1997. The ancestors 'have opened the path for us, they have prepared the way, we need their presence when we praise the Lord', the chaplaincy Abbé once told me.

Recognizing the agency of ancestors is one thing, but needing their presence and asking for their support is another. For Congolese Pentecostals, this is usually where the line is drawn and most of them will regard the feeding ritual in Nkamba's cemetery as pure idolatry, bordering on witchcraft. For certain

Congolese Pentecostal churches in diaspora, even the 'simple' act of sending money to kin in the Congo to organize *matangas* has become highly problematic. This is the case for one of the churches I studied – the Combat Spirituel church ('Ministère du Combat Spirituel', commonly known as 'Maman Olangi church', after one of its founders), for whom ancestrality is *inherently* detrimental to the spiritual liberation of individuals.

In a Maman Olangi church service I attended in Atlanta, sending money for homeland *matangas* was described as a source of (evil) bondage to the world of ancestors, blocking the horizons and progress of the born-again individual. This association with ancestor worship was actually problematized after the death of the Olangi couple (Maman Olangi died a few months after her husband, 'Papa Olangi') in 2018 and revealed some contradictions in Pentecostal attitudes to death. Indeed, after their death, the church leaders and kin of the Olangis decided to erect a large mausoleum to honour the memory and celebrate the legacy of leadership of the couple who funded the Combat Spirituel church and established it as one of the most successful churches in Congo. However, this mausoleum was perceived in Congolese Pentecostal circles as a shrine encouraging 'unChristian' worshipping practices, reflecting the enormous devotion the Olangi couple generated among their followers when they were alive. Here, we see the tension in Pentecostalism between the centrality of the gifts of the Holy Spirit, often manifested in the personal charisma of the pastor, and its iconoclasm, that is, its rejection of the institutions, images and rituals associated with Catholicism (and 'traditional' African religions).

A pluralized religious landscape

This mausoleum is located within one of the church compounds on the periphery of Kinshasa – a compound that also includes a school and a clinic. This incursion of the church in the domains of education and health reflects the increasing 'developmental' role of Pentecostal actors, which should be understood as postcolonial incarnations of earlier forms of Christian missionary cultures, when 'conversion to Christianity and conversion to modernity were essentially collapsed together' (Burchardt 2015: 51, see also Comaroff and Comaroff 1997; Van der Veer 1996). As we shall see, despite the Pentecostalization of Congolese society, Kimbanguists and Catholics have also invested (or remained invested) in these key sectors of education and health. These interventions in the 'secular' public demonstrate how important it is to make sense of plurality within this religious landscape in the Congo and the diaspora. Comparing and contrasting the theologies, views of morality and modus operandi of various transnational religious networks within this plural landscape will help us capture the complex interplay of religion, migration and the making of moral landscapes in an age of globalization.

Ethnographies of African migrant churches have been essential to our understanding of the social, religious and cultural worlds of the 'new African diaspora' (Koser 2003), in particular of the ways in which migrant/transnational religion can be reterritorialized in (secular) host societies, facilitating or hindering the process of integration. Some scholars have explored the importance of boundaries and the dynamics of distinction, explicitly drawing upon a Bourdieusian theorization to explain the functioning, logics and fragmentation of religious fields and subfields. For instance, as part of the collection *Bourdieu in Africa*, Ukah (2016b) shows how Pentecostal pastors in urban South Africa adopt powerful rhetorical strategies valorizing their 'authentic' missionary role and superior spiritual legitimacy, while delegitimizing the relevance of established churches and other Christian actors. These pastors seek to establish their dominance within the religious field by deconstructing and reimagining it on their own terms – without however radically changing the 'structuring structures' (Bourdieu 1992: 164) which have historically governed it. As I shall show, Congolese Pentecostals have produced a wide range of claims constructing and legitimizing a moral and (perhaps more importantly) spiritual superiority. Just like Pentecostals, Catholics are also eager to draw boundaries around their own aesthetic/ritual regime and their collective civic role and history, emphasizing their church's role in the constituting of a Congolese national identity.

Given the intense struggle over charismatic authority/recognition and over the definition of the boundaries of a legitimate (Christian) symbolic order (see Pype 2012), the Bourdieusian notion of field can be a useful analytical model to make sense of the dynamics operating within the landscape of Congolese 'diasporic Christianities' and also in the homeland context, in particular in Kinshasa. However, there are also potential limitations, as Echtler and Ukah (2016) note when discussing, in the context of African religiosity, the relevance of Bourdieu's conceptualization of social space and his understanding of the social characteristics and functions of religious power, largely inspired by Weber's sociology of religion (Rey 2007). Echtler and Ukah (2016: 16) make the point that prioritizing an analysis of the 'field of forces imposed on actors as well as a field of struggles between actors' and of the incessant competition over symbolic profit

– despite the objectified disinterestedness of actors governing the field – risks overstressing the reality and stability of congregational/ritualistic particularities legitimized as (de)valorizing differences. In turn, this would neglect or minimize the commonality of experiences and worldviews as well as the role of hybrid practices and boundary-crossing (Janson 2021, McGuire 2008, Gez et al. 2021).

As Rey and Stepick (2015) suggest in their study of Haitian religion in Miami, it is actually possible to address common experiential features within a Bourdieusian framework. They show that within the Haitian diasporic religious field, distinction mechanisms operate – sometimes at the intersection of class and religion – between the three major Haitian-based religious traditions – Catholicism, Protestantism/Pentecostalism and Vodou. However, despite social and theological differences, Rey and Stepick argue that a unifying 'religious *collusio*' – akin to a 'collective habitus' – is the key force influencing and regulating the landscape of diasporic religion among Haitians in Miami. The *collusio*, which 'forms the basis of practical mutual understanding' shaping judgement and action, according to Bourdieu (2000: 45), is here related to the powerful role of spiritual imaginaries locating Haitians in diaspora within a wider time-space and connecting them, socially, symbolically and culturally, to their homeland. The religious *collusio* is also defined in relation to the range of affordances enabled by diasporic religion for Haitian migrants in the marginalizing backdrop of the United States. The religious *collusio* is here inflected by the dynamics of national and race/ethnic identity and by the challenges of the diasporic condition as a horizon where matrices of belonging involve both reflexivity and contestation.

Several parallels are observable with the Congolese religious field. As mentioned earlier, the belief in ancestral powers, and that affliction and misfortune can be linked to spiritual attacks, is generally shared by all religious actors studied in this book. In addition, and as we will see particularly in the next chapter, what I call 'spiritual infrastructures' operate in moral and affective domains across religious boundaries with a remarkable capacity to provide direction and meaning to migrants and to orient and channel their mobility, as well as that of the capital, values and goods that circulate between home and host countries.

Despite the universal aspiration (and transnational reach) of the Congolese Christianities explored in this book, another key aspect of a Congolese religious (Christian) *collusio*, especially in diaspora, is the view that a sense of *Congolité* or 'Congoliness' is performed through religious life. It situates the Congolese within a specific chronotope from which they draw meaning in the postcolonial and 'post-Mobutu' periods and construct projections for change, spiritual liberation or development. My examination of diasporic politics (in Chapter 4) will show that, while this 'Congoliness', when expressed publicly, is produced in clear differentiation with other African (diasporic) groups, it remains highly hybrid, an assemblage of identities and ethnic/nationalistic, religious references functioning at multiple socio-spatial and historical scales.

While these shared characteristics form the contour of Congolese diasporic religion and to some extent the field of 'urban Christianities' in the DRC (see Garbin and Mokoko Gampiot 2022), a full understanding of the religious landscape needs to account for the meaning and relevance of internal differences within each of these Christianities, which is where a Bourdieusian approach can again be helpful, being mindful not to over-emphasize intra-processes of competition. If we take the 'subfield' of Pentecostalism, Katsaura observed among Nigerian Pentecostals how a 'politics of denominational specialization and distinction' enabling a spiritual division of labour of sorts can coexist with 'inter-denominationalism and affinity' (Garbin and Mokoko Gampiot 2022: 4), expressed by filiation, mutual recognition and collaboration between pastors or by the mobility of churchgoers across denominational boundaries for special events, like large 'crusades' or prayer meetings. Similarly, Rey (2019) argues that the existence of pluralized landscapes of churches – each with their own 'profile', in a way complementing each other – is seen as highly desirable by the African Pentecostals she has studied in Switzerland.

Division of labour and specialization, in the Durkheimian tradition, is conducive to societal and moral integration and operates through interdependent relations – organic solidarity. The concept of 'figuration' developed by Norbert Elias (2000) also brings interdependency to the fore and is a useful tool to make sense of the pluralized and differentiated nature of a religious field beyond the idiom of competition. A figuration (or configuration) is, for Elias, a social space shaped by the dynamics and networks of power but within which actors always coexist in interdependent relations. While these interdependencies maintain stability and involve the persistence of internal social patterns, the overall figurations evolve on par with the transformation of relations. In addition, changes also occurring at certain points and junctions of the figuration, at the level of individual actors or within groups, may have consequences for other groups or actors, through the web of interdependent relations. In other words, interdependency may act as a diffusor of change along networks linking actors and groups. The way change affects the internal equilibrium of the figuration and how difference is internally constructed vary. For instance, one may read the Pentecostalization of Congolese society as a general 'figurational' transformation (initially spread and circulated by interdependent actors) having an impact on specific actors in particular ways. What happened in the case of the Kimbanguist church with the *milimo* phenomenon is a good illustration of this.

The *milimo* story refers to the emergence among Kimbanguists, especially female members, of alternative spiritual and embodied practices linked to divination and spirit (*molimo*, plur. *milimo*) possession, which were radically contrasting with Kimbanguist theology and *techniques du corps* – based on restraint and control. As a circulating form of charisma, it also challenged the centralized authority of the spiritual leader and anointed Kimbanguist leaders. The spiritual effervescence that took hold of several Kimbanguist parishes, including in the diaspora (see Garbin 2010), can in great part be attributed to the influence of Charismatic Christianity and the dominant presence and visibility of Pentecostal actors in the religious field. To publicly reaffirm a strong sense of differentiation and in a context of an internal struggle for leadership, Kimbanguist clergy officially banned the practice, seen as a depersonalization of charisma from established hierarchies. However, with the risk of losing the faithful to Pentecostal churches, the *milimo* spiritual practices have implicitly remained tolerated, as long as they take place in the privacy of the home.

I want to argue here that a full understanding of a changing, competitive fragmented religious landscape requires taking into account the webs of interdependent relations between religious actors, while recognizing that, in some contexts, differences are relevant (and marked). In other circumstances, commonalities of a religious *collusio* can be shared across boundaries. We can, for example, recognize that the differentiated 'aesthetic regimes' (Butticci 2016) of Catholics, Pentecostals and Kimbanguists in relation to materiality and embodiment play a key role in boundary-making and modes of belonging, while not losing sight of the fact that these groups all share a 'longing for real presence' (Butticci 2016: 9), relying on strategies of urban visibility and, more importantly, territorialization through place-making and mediation. There are variations, however, in the meaning these strategies take on according to their contexts – homeland or diaspora – of deployment and operationalization, even if, as we shall also see, the 'spiritual infrastructures' constructed by these groups may bridge homeland and diasporic concerns about remoralization and social transformation.

Diaspora and transnational (dis)connections

In many ways, this diaspora environment constitutes a specific arena of action, interaction and affordances, with Congolese migrants reflecting on their religious practices and identities, and interpreting the meaning of collective presence in new 'host' settings, a presence often constructed in moral terms or in relation to dynamics of incorporation and exclusion – themselves inflected by race and ethnicity. Moreover, each diasporic setting studied in this book – London and Atlanta – also has its own urban/spatial regime constraining or facilitating the 'regrounding' of religious practices and habitus.

The widespread use of the concept of *diaspora* across a range of disciplines reflects a growing engagement with the complexity of modes of belongings, home-making and cross-border processes for individuals and communities living their lives away from their 'homelands'. The affinity between religion and diaspora has often been explored in relation to tropes of exile, the shared experience of suffering and the sacralization of homeland spaces and traditions. However, there have been attempts to move away from this 'classical' model largely based on the paradigmatic Jewish experience. For instance, in relation to 'new African diasporas' (Koser 2003), there has been an emphasis on a range of experiences and subjectivities beyond the idea of a catastrophic, forced migration linked to slavery and the symbolism of the middle passage – the foundational moment of what Paul Gilroy (1993) calls the 'Black Atlantic' as a 'counterproject of modernity'. This emphasis ties in with a revitalized attention to the diaspora as a social space of cultural creations and recreations of new hybrid identities, practices and symbols emerging out of the 'deterritorialized combination of local referents' (Vásquez and Garbin 2016) and shaped by fluid affective circuits of belonging and 'homing desires' (Brah 1996, Clifford 1994). These alternative approaches have been heavily influenced by cultural theorists like Stuart Hall, for whom diaspora is 'defined, not by essence or purity, but by a recognition of a necessary heterogeneity and diversity; by a conception of "identity" which lives with and through, not despite, difference' (Hall 1990: 235).

The experience of hybridity and multifocality, as well as the preponderance of 'routes' over 'roots' (Gilroy 1993), can coexist with the deployment of exilic imaginations and repertoires of return to (the idea of) a sacralized, authentic homeland, which can be given powerful credence through religious and/or political tropes. For instance, in his pioneering ethnography of the Lady of Charity shrine built by Cuban immigrants in Miami, Tweed (1997) explores how a politics of nostalgia to a pre-revolutionary, in many ways romanticized, homeland can be framed religiously through sacred place-making, linking remapping of urban space to a sense of diasporic *longing*. The experience of 'diasporic religion' is here 'translocative', involving diasporic mimesis through the materialization of homeland memories as well as symbolic connections and crossings between homeland and a (partly) territorialized host society. Diasporic religion is also 'transtemporal', as Miami Cubans inhabit a fluid temporal space within which constructed past and imagined future shape the social experience of the present (Tweed 1997: 94). The Lady of Charity shrine has become a 'heterotopian' space for diasporic home-making alongside individual, more intimate rituals, allowing for alternative and contested modes of diasporic identification. This nuanced reading of diasporic religion suggests that migrants can mobilize categories of belonging associated with 'authentic'/ totalizing visions of a resacralized or remoralized homeland, while engaging in multiple and hybrid practices. This is the flexible approach I adopt in this book.[1]

In a later work, Tweed built upon his analysis of 'diasporic religion' to theorize contemporary religious dynamics under globalization, using aquatic metaphors to stress the 'hydrodynamic' fluidity of 'sacroscapes' and the affordances of religion to 'make homes and cross boundaries'. However, while Tweed's theory challenges fixed conceptions of religion as tied to a particular people or place, an over-reliance on aquatic metaphors risks minimizing the dynamics of closure, exclusion, containment or friction. In fact, processes of deterritorialization and reterritorialization that accompany the globalization of religion are shaped by a range of power asymmetries, which could be internal or external to diasporic groups. Disconnections, tensions and blockages may occur as a result of constraining regimes of mobility, for instance, or uneven access to material and immaterial resources between actors and groups across the migration divide (especially when churches have developed transnationally and rely on networked cartographies linking periphery and centre, such as Kimbanguists or Pentecostal Olangistes).

The focus on transnationalism and, in particular, transnational relations is here important as it complements any understanding of diaspora from a globalization perspective and has the potential to allow for a recognition of both connections and disconnections.

While both 'transnationalism' and 'diaspora' point to the bifocal and multifocal/triadic experience of migrants and minorities challenging the hypothesis of a unidirectional movement towards assimilation to the receiving country's hegemonic culture and societal norms, each term characterizes different dynamics of mobility practices and modes of belonging. The concept of 'transnationalism' puts a stronger emphasis on connections, networks, exchanges and flows between spaces across nation-state boundaries, while the notion of diaspora also operates transtemporally, joining multiple spaces through a work of imagination and memory that link past, present and future.

Transnationalism usually considers the embeddedness of minorities and migrants within a plurality of deterritorialized spaces of flows through which migrants 'forge and sustain multi-stranded social relations that link together societies of origin and settlement', as described by Basch, Glick Schiller and Szanton Blanc (1994) in their pioneering study of transnationalism among Haitians and Grenadians in the United States. Migrant transnational religions produce alternative cartographies of practice and belonging whose moral and physical territorialities may be contained within national boundaries but may also transcend or supersede them (Levitt, 2001a). The intensity, scope, frequency and volume of material and immaterial flows within these spaces may vary. As we shall see in Chapter 5, remittances constitute one example of this transnational circulation, as they represent an important form of 'global money' which can not only be converted into symbolic and religious capital but also reveal tensions over established or new hierarchies. Examining remittances through the prism of affective politics between kin will show how they are imbued with moral attributes that Congolese often read through religious/spiritual frames.

Another aspect of transnational relations central to many Congolese in the United Kingdom and the United States relates to the use of media to bridge the gap between homeland and diasporic peripheries (and between diasporic communities) or to create and sustain mediascapes and virtual worlds transcending local attachments. But we will see that taking into consideration the space of transnational (or translocal) flows between homeland and diasporas or between diasporic communities also throws light on the tensions between offline and online, as well as on the frictions and obstructions occurring at multiple scales, and finally on the power of certain actors (like political diasporic activists) to alter or even block the flows and circulation of people and things.

As Johnson (2007: 9) remarks, transnationalism is often used to reveal the range of social or institutional cross-border linkages between spaces, but it is rarely used by the actors themselves to make sense of their positionality or to make collective claims. Diaspora, on the other hand, can be 'a discursive marker of a person's conscious extension toward a given space or imaginal representation' (Johnson 2007: 9), and, as we shall see in the book, it is recurrently used in all sorts of ways to make specific claims over presence, visibility or political change. For instance, in the context of protracted conflict, political instability and growing injustices in the DRC, the notion of diaspora becomes a 'stance' (Brubaker 2005), a powerful discursive and performative tool for constructing the shared aesthetics of a 'community of suffering'.

While Congolese diasporic actors, including religious actors, may in some contexts draw upon a 'collective habitus' combining pan-African references to spiritual warfare or prophetic nationalism, as we discussed earlier, there are clear divergences in the ways these diasporic religious politics are understood, embodied and performed. In other words, the emic use of the term can here function as a performance of unity and coherence, concealing the divisions and fragmentations that this study will attempt to uncover in relation to politics and multiple domains of the diasporic lives of Congolese in the United Kingdom and the United States. In a sense, our Congolese example will suggest that at the heart of the diasporic experience lies the performance of fragmented moral communities and collective aesthetics. As such, as Brubaker (2005) argues, 'diaspora' should perhaps be better understood as a 'category of practice [. . .] used to make claims, to articulate projects, to formulate expectations, to mobilize energies, to appeal to loyalties'. In other words, the term 'does not so much describe the world as seek to remake it' (2005: 12).

Diaspora and homeland: Multi-sited approach

The book is a result of several years of research[2] as part of a range of projects which took me along the religious – Kimbanguist, Pentecostal and Catholic – networks of the Congolese diaspora in the United Kingdom, the United States and the DRC. In the sections that follow, I want to reflect on this multi-sitedness, providing some context on the socio-spatial positionality of each of these religious actors and urban/spatial regimes.

London: Congolese in the 'super-diverse' global city

My entry into the field of African diaspora Christianities took place in London and illustrates some of the ways in which Pentecostalism has (re)territorialized itself within the plural landscape of global cities. As I was scouting for possible access into Pentecostal migrant churches as part of a project on religion, migration and transnationalism,[3] I came across a large event organized in the West Ham football stadium by a well-known Pentecostal church, the Universal Church of the Kingdom of God (UCKG), one of the fastest growing Pentecostal churches globally. Founded in Brazil, the church is present in more than 100 countries throughout the world and is known for its strategy of appropriating buildings (in particular, shops, halls or even cinemas, in the

UK context) in the zones of important foot traffic, to set up church branches renamed 'Help Centres'.

The UCKG advertised the (free) event I attended, called 'Signs', through billboards, TV ads on Christian Satellite channels and a free newspaper, distributed in a rather spectacular fashion: from a double-decker bus, blaring what seemed to be Christian pop songs, going through the streets of multicultural inner London. The well-designed, coloured brochure announcing the prayer gathering was handed out to me as the bus was going through the East End where I was living at the time. The brochure also advertised the activities of the Help Centres (twelve in London), with stories of individuals who had dealt successfully with affliction, illnesses or deeply personal issues, such as addiction, broken marriages, difficult relationships or financial problems. The newspaper under-communicated the identity of UCKG, with 'church' appearing only in the small prints and containing almost no reference to 'religion', or 'God'. This practice reflects one of the strategies of the church, that is to 'blend' on the surface with the secular space, to use non-threatening 'hooks' such as the Help Centres, to attract new members to their services or a large event like 'Signs'.

The day of the event, the 37,000 seat capacity stadium was far from being full, perhaps 6,000 or 7,000 people were in attendance that day, occupying one side of the stadium, to pray, sing and listen to sermons, encouraged to give donations for health and prosperity. I was seated among a mostly Black audience, next to Francine, an Angolan woman, who had sought refuge in the Congo during the civil war in Angola (and thus spoke French) before coming to London in the early 2000s. She was not a member of the UCKG, unlike Angelina, her friend, and also Angolan, who had brought her to the prayer meeting. As I was asking Francine about her religious life, the description of her church intrigued me: a French-speaking parish of a large Pentecostal church (KICC, Kingsway International Christian Centre) led by a charismatic Nigerian pastor and located very close to my own neighbourhood, in Hackney. A few weeks later, she invited me to a service of 'KICC-French Connection', as the parish was called, in a two-storey converted industrial warehouse building. The parish, whose members were mostly Francophone Africans, predominantly from the DRC with a handful of Togolese, Ivorians and Congolese from Congo-Brazzaville, is where I conducted my first observations of Pentecostal Sunday services. The services were led in English by a Nigerian pastor[4] and simultaneously translated into French by a young enthusiastic member born in Congo-Brazzaville, but who grew up in France and, like Papa Gérard, exercised his EU Freedom of Movement rights to come to the UK in the early 2000s.

The aims of these first observations and interviews among members of KICC-FC were initially to learn about the linkages between the experience of migration and religious life in urban, multicultural contexts as well as the dynamics of religious place-making. The membership of the KICC-French connection, mostly Congolese, reflected the overall landscape of Francophone African communities in London. As I gradually expanded my focus to cover the larger field of Congolese churches in the global city, I snowballed my way across not only Congolese Pentecostal churches but also Kimbanguist and Catholic communities. Over the years, I also established links with secular/charity associations and participated in dozens of community events, meetings, celebrations, *matangas* and so on, mostly in London. I also collaborated closely with a community group supporting Congolese families and asylum seekers in East London, contributing to the organization of workshops on identity and heritage as well as museum visits with young people – including a visit to the Royal Museum for Central Africa in Tervuren, Brussels.[5] Throughout my years of fieldwork in London, my principal ethnographic, long-standing social 'bases' were three Kimbanguists church parishes in East and North London and a group of activists and young people I regularly met, especially during and after the period of street protests organized during the tense period of elections in DRC in 2011–2 that I analyse in Chapter 4. In addition to the countless Sundays spent among Kimbanguists, I also attended services in Pentecostal churches and Masses with members of the *Aumonerie Congolaise de Londres* – the Congolese Catholic chaplaincy established in 2005.

The politicization of the Congolese diaspora that I discuss in Chapter 4 can be traced back to the activities of the anti-Mobutu opposition in Paris, Brussels and later London, which gradually hosted an increasing number of students and political activists fleeing Mobutu's regime as it was considered safer than Brussels or Paris, where Mobutu circles were active. With a growing internal discontent and the changing global geopolitical climate, Mobutu, seen as a supporter of US/ Western interests in Central Africa during the Cold War, had little choice but to introduce a partial multipartyism in 1990. This paved the way for a National Conference (1991–2) attended by civil society actors and newly created political parties, some with the involvement of Congolese from the diaspora.

Despite this new context of multipartyism (ironically coined 'multi-Mobutism' by regime opponents) and the organization of a National Conference, political instability and unrest went on during the turbulent decade of the 1990s. In 1997, the rebellion led by Laurent Désiré Kabila with the backing of Rwanda and Uganda eventually succeeded in overthrowing Mobutu, but it was followed by a war, after the invasion of Rwandan and Ugandan troops in the East of the country. The bulk of the Congolese migration to Europe occurred during this very instable period, during the 1990s and early 2000s, and the United Kingdom, Canada, the United States and Germany soon emerged as new destination countries beyond the early Francophone confines of the Congolese diaspora. After a long transition period (2001-2006), which began with the assassination of L.-D. Kabila in 2001, the politicization of the diaspora took on a more radical form with the deterioration of the state, the ongoing conflict in the east and the inability of the government led by Joseph Kabila, the son of L.-D. Kabila and president between 2001 and 2019, to improve the economic situation, especially in the capital Kinshasa from where the great majority of the Congolese migrants originate.

While Congolese are present in most of the largest British cities, such as Manchester, Birmingham and Glasgow, the Congolese community in the UK is mostly based in London in particular in the boroughs of Haringey, Newham or Croydon. The size of the 'community' is hard to assess – figures vary between 20,000 and 40,000 (Trapido 2017: 10) – and this may be due to the challenges of statistically capturing its internal diversity. The Congolese are indeed one of the many minority communities that have contributed to the 'super-diverse' landscape of London, as famously defined by Vertovec (2007): a group with no 'historical' colonial ties to the UK (though this is disputed by some of my research participants, as we shall discuss) and internally heterogeneous, in particular in terms of migration/citizenship status; in other words, an increasingly 'diverse diversity'. The membership of the Kimbanguist church reflects this internal diversity, with the co-presence of Congolese with British, French, Belgium and Portuguese citizenship, asylum seekers and those with refugee status or residence permit, as well as undocumented individuals. There is also a growing group of second-generation British Congolese born and/or raised in the UK, many of whom have never been to the Congo.

The trajectories of London Kimbanguists also mirror the increasing complexity of migratory routes taken by London-based Congolese (Flahaux et al. 2013), with almost none of the Kimbanguists I know having come to the UK directly from the DRC – most having transited through or sojourned in a wide range of countries including Angola, Spain, Portugal, France, Belgium, Turkey, South Africa, Morocco, Germany and the Netherlands. While men formed the bulk of the early migration cohort (Flahaux et al. 2013), the fact that many Congolese women came to the UK as single migrants also illustrates the overall feminization of migration from sub-Saharan Africa, itself a product of the protracted economic crisis, which led a growing number of women to be financially autonomous through self-entrepreneurship or migration strategies.

The Congolese in London work in a variety of occupations, often in low-paid jobs, in post offices, public transports (in particular London buses), hospitals, restaurants, cleaning companies, warehouses, schools or nurseries – with some running their own businesses (for instance, in 'community' catering, media or trade), sometimes in parallel with salaried employment. Congolese in Paris or Brussels often talk negatively of the members of the Congolese diaspora in the UK, who have an image of being 'uneducated' and relying on the 'Système D'[6] culture of hustling prevalent in Kinshasa. However, findings of the MAFE project[7] indicate that while Congolese in Belgium tend to have a higher level of education than those in the UK, the latter have still relatively high levels of education (for instance, 41 per cent of UK-based Congolese have at least a higher education degree).[8] Like other African migrants to North America or Europe (Creese and Wiebe 2012), many Congolese came to the UK already with a university degree but faced processes of downward mobility and de-skilling, unable to find work matching their skills or level of education in a context of entrenched structural discrimination and devaluation of qualifications obtained in the DRC or elsewhere. Examples I encountered included François, who had a medical degree obtained in Turkey but was an ambulance paramedic; Maman Berthe, who had an MA in economics but was cleaning offices for a living; and Papa Joseph, who was pursuing a distance-learning PhD in religious studies in Paris but was also a low-paid kitchen porter in a Central London restaurant, working long hours, in precarious conditions.

Another notable aspect of the London context, which I will discuss in more detail in the next chapter, is the particular reputation Congolese in London had. During the 1980s and 1990s, groups of Congolese in London were engaged in what was known as 'les co-ops' or *mayuya* (scheming), usually linked to non-violent petty crimes such as cheque or benefit fraud (see Tipo-Tipo 1995, Trapido 2017). This fact only seemed to reinforce the negative perceptions Congolese in France and Belgium have of their compatriots in the UK even though the *mayuya* economy also existed there (Trapido 2017).

As we shall see throughout this book, for many Congolese in diaspora, the church represents both a space of mutual support and a mediating institution where not only social but also spiritual infrastructures can be deployed to provide the 'grounding' needed to deal with this type of immoral behaviours. In addition, these spaces can create affective affordances to deal with what could be called 'levelling' regimes – the fact that those with higher credentials may have similar occupations/professional status as those with lower or no education. In this context, church communities also often operate as translocal *political publics* through which symbolic and social capital can be gained and/or converted. For instance, Papa Joseph has cultivated networks among the clergy in the church and Kimbanguists in the diaspora. Thus, in great contrast to his restaurant job, he has been appointed in important roles within the church over the years, allowing him to travel to the DRC, in particular Kinshasa and Nkamba, several times a year and to be a respected figure both in the diaspora and in the homeland contexts.

Atlanta: Congolese in the 'Black Mecca' of the 'New South'

This study also relies on additional data collected as part of projects examining the making of diasporic religious spaces in the United States,[9] in particular in the context of Atlanta, the sprawling metropolis of the increasingly pluralized American 'New South' (Vásquez and Marquardt 2003), where Congolese migrants have settled in growing numbers, especially from the early 2000s. The case of Atlanta is particularly relevant to foreground the moral dimensions of diaspora. As we shall see, the city has witnessed two potent narratives of boundary-making and exclusion/inclusion in terms of racialized and class-mediated collective identities: a recalcitrant narrative of white supremacy and a vibrant story of the struggle for civil rights. Both narratives contain powerful symbols which the Congolese negotiate, appropriate and even blend with their own cultural, religious and moral frames as they carve their spaces of livelihood.

My ability to undertake multi-sited fieldwork and explore the socio-spatial environments of Congolese 'urban Christianities' was facilitated in great part by the existence of a religious transnational architecture linking homeland and Congolese diasporic hubs. Contacts in the Kimbanguist and Maman Olangi churches in London or Kinshasa, for instance, helped me locate research participants and gatekeepers in Atlanta. One of them was Papa Jose, a member of the Kimbanguist church, with whom I spent countless hours driving across exurban landscapes of the sprawling metropolis, where the classical street ethnographic practice of 'hanging out' is all but impossible. Here, we see how a 'particular place', as sociologist Nancy Eiesland (2000) titled her pioneering study of the variegated 'religious ecology' of greater Atlanta, shapes not only the mobility and kinds of relationality that migrants can establish with each other and with the other residents but also the types of fieldwork scholars can undertake. With a sorely inadequate public transportation system, I, like the

Congolese I studied, had to rely very heavily on the car, spending countless hours stuck in bad traffic and limiting the time I could spend 'deep hanging'.

In (and around Atlanta), I visited many Congolese churches and conducted interviews with their members about their experiences of settlement and incorporation into the social and religious landscape of the 'New South'. With its sprawling geography, Atlanta's spatial regime contrasts with the density of most parts of post-industrial inner London, although Atlanta, the 'city too busy to hate' (as coined by Atlanta's Mayor William Hartsfield in 1959), is also, if not a global, at least a 'globalizing' city, home to the world's busiest airport and to major global companies such as Coca Cola, CNN or Delta Airlines. Political and business élites have increasingly promoted this status as an international and dynamic city, especially after the 1996 Atlanta Olympic Games, which also involved large-scale urban redevelopment projects, leading to the removal of low-income African American populations from downtown Atlanta (Keating 2001).

In his seminal social history of Atlanta, Charles Rutheiser (1996) notes the importance of the symbolic politics of place in this city, which started to be represented, in the second half of the nineteenth century, as the capital of the 'New South' by local political and business élites, who envisioned a 'New York or Chicago of the South'. Pivotal in the reimagining of the 'Atlanta spirit' was the idea of an emerging and growing gateway city, a 'resplendent phoenix rising from the ashes' (the city was nearly entirely destroyed during the civil war), combined with the romanticization of a Southern bucolic charm, which would later feed *Gone with the Wind*-type imageries. This representation, still powerful to this day, obscures the unresolved tension between two competing legacies. On the one hand, a violent and pervasive racism (Atlanta became the 'Imperial Capital' of a revived Ku Klux Klan), and on the other hand, the image of a 'Black Mecca' (as coined by W. E. B. Dubois), linked to the gradual emergence of a local African-American political and business élite and middle class (Rutheiser 1996: 3). This reputation was enhanced by the central role that Atlanta's African American community leaders played during the civil rights movement and by the presence of prestigious historically Black universities, such as Morehouse College, founded in 1867.

Despite this image of Atlanta as 'racially progressive', there was an initial massive resistance to the process of desegregation, most notably in the spheres of housing, leisure (public parks, for instance), public transports or schools. As African American families became socially and thus spatially mobile, this resistance quickly gave way to the mass out-migration of white communities towards suburban counties. As Kruse points out in his detailed study of what he calls 'suburban secession' in the Atlanta region: 'at the dawn of the twenty-first century, white flight had spread from the city through the suburbs to a new exurban frontier, with no signs of slowing down' (Kruse 2007: 264). Forsyth, one hour's drive north of downtown Atlanta, is one of the best examples of this link between 'white flight' and the creation of outer-edge cities, which have become real 'Whitopias' (Benjamin 2009).

This socio-spatial context connected to particular suburban politics and race and class in the capital of the 'New South' forms a crucial backdrop against which Congolese migrants give meaning to their presence, their social and symbolic location and their collective migration project and 'integration' in the gateway city. Many Congolese I met live in suburban multicultural neighbourhoods, some comprising large proportions of Black middle-class, lower-middle-class or Latino residents (*les Spanish*, as some Congolese in Atlanta call them). They generally eschew the traditionally Black working-class/low-income areas, in more centrally located zones of the city.

The Congolese community in Atlanta is heterogeneous, fragmented along ethno-linguistic and class lines. It is hard to compare the experience of, say, a newly arrived migrant who has fled the conflict-ridden eastern Congo region and now lives in Clarkston (eastern Atlanta), in subsidized accommodations among other refugees (from East Africa or South East Asia, for instance) with the experience of an American Congolese professional who initially came as a sponsored student and resides in the Black middle-class suburbs (although during community events and in certain contexts, such as in churches, a strong sense of 'community unity' can be performed and played out). Many have also come through the 'Diversity Immigrant Visa (DV) program' lottery, which has become a key migration channel for Africans to come to the United States (Imoagene 2017). The DV Program lottery allows the migration of individuals (and their spouses and young children) who are from countries with traditionally low rates of immigration to the United States. While applicants are randomly selected through a draw, some criteria apply (such as a minimum level of education). As we will discuss, for those who mobilize the cosmic energy of 'spiritual infrastructures' in their quest for mobility, being successful at the 'DV lottery' can be interpreted as a sign of divine intervention or even divine election.

The views of Congolese on Atlanta's multiculturalism and, more specifically, regarding its strong African American identity, are highly diverse. They are shaped by residential trajectories (some had moved from large eastern cities such as New York or Washington, DC) and social mobility, personal experience of everyday ethnic/class diversity and old and new forms of prejudice in a context of segregation and 'white flight'. Discourses collected in Atlanta capture a certain ambivalence in the representations of African American communities, with the existence of competing images, linked on one side of the coin to (Black or white) middle-class respectability, the legacy of the civil rights movement or ideals of Black unity. On the other side, there was concern about the possible influence that a 'Black ghetto culture' may exert on younger generations – an anxiety that is also prevalent in London. As we shall see later in this book, churches, in this context, have become places where a set of conflated African and Christian values can be transmitted, in order to respond to the risks and moral dangers of everyday life in the diasporic and pluralized urban environment.

Despite the social and spatial distance maintained by some Congolese vis-à-vis the urban presence of African Americans, the city's Black history and identity constitute a powerful backdrop against which some religious actors define and reimagine their local inscribing. In Atlanta, the Kimbanguist tropes of Black emancipation, redemption and liberation resonate with the local memory of the civil rights movement and the political struggles of African Americans. This creates a sphere of interpretation, which enables symbolic connections and reconnections across time-spaces and 'diasporic horizons' (Johnson 2007), thus bestowing powerful meaning to the contextual regrounding of a travelling and portable faith like Kimbanguism. For instance, the 'return' of African Americans to Nkamba, one of the key Kimbanguist prophetic beliefs, and a 'divine promise', is evoked in relation to early links forged with the Kimbanguist church by a well-known African American Protestant religious leader (who passed away in 2012, at the age of eighty-seven). He first visited the Congo in the 1950s as a missionary and he is now buried, with his wife, in the sacred and ancestral soil of Nkamba, close to the grave of Papa Gérard's father. Over the years, more visits of African Americans to Nkamba have taken place, facilitated by Kimbanguists based in the United States who have cultivated links with African American religious leaders or activists.

During my fieldwork in the United States, the political debates were often dominated by the election and presidency of Barack Obama. For many Kimbanguists, Obama's election also resonated with a core prophetic belief, a theology of reversal, known through Kimbangu's most renowned 'promise' (*bilaka*) that 'the white man shall become black and the black man shall become white', thus marking the start of a global process of spiritual liberation and redemption. This symbolic proximity between the Prophet Kimbangu and American president Obama is well illustrated by a visual juxtaposition of the

Figure 1 Display of iconic photographs in a Kimbanguist home in Atlanta, juxtaposing the Prophet Kimbangu and Barack Obama. Credit: Author.

two figures I encountered in the house of an Atlantan Kimbanguist, with the iconic photograph of Kimbangu (displayed in most Kimbanguist homes) next to the one of Obama, himself rendered quasi-messianic by the promise of a 'new tomorrow' (Figure 1).

Homeland contexts

Having characterized the contexts abroad in which Congolese have settled, I would like to say, in this final section, a few words about the homeland, with which many of them maintain constant relations via transnational flows and networks and through a diasporic imagination. Given this ongoing connection, which is expressed in everyday (religious and non-religious) life, a substantial portion of this book is devoted to the impact of religion in the homeland context, exploring how religious visions for development, but also (re)moralization and spiritual liberation are deployed and how they cohere with strategies of place-making and urbanization in the contexts of Kinshasa and Nkamba (Chapters 6 and 7). Here again, fieldwork in the homeland, where I conducted observations and interviews with Catholics, Pentecostals (in particular Olangistes) and Kimbanguists, has been facilitated by my insertion in transnational networks allowing me to travel to the Congo on three separate occasions (2007, 2015 and 2018) to spend time with various religious communities.

In the interest of critical reflexivity, I would like to acknowledge that my ethnographic multi-sited practice was shaped in many ways by research participants, not only in terms of logistics (i.e. they facilitated contacts, transportation and even visas to travel[10]) but also through their eagerness for me to capture the 'true' dimensions of their religious lives. This was particularly the case for Kimbanguists in London who insisted that I should visit Nkamba as the 'authentic source' of their beliefs and ritual world. Thus, they made easier my insertion into pilgrimage networks through which I could conduct fieldwork in the Kimbanguist holy city, also get to know Kimbanguists in Kinshasa and visit their parishes and infrastructures. As my involvement in diasporic Congolese circles grew, I could insert myself into a wider range of cross-border networks, in particular the religious networks of Catholics or Pentecostals (Maman Olangi church and the New Jerusalem Church, for instance). My presence in key places like Nkamba or La Cité de Triomphe (the Headquarters of the Maman Olangi church) provided me with 'ethnographic capital', the recognition, trust and legitimacy to be able to go into more places. The accumulation of this ethnographic capital was intensified by the fact that I was interviewed several times about my presence by both Kimbanguist and Olangi media, with video clips circulating transnationally through social media and satellite TV. Sometimes, these clips preceded my trips to new sites, perhaps helping to unblock, so to speak, my ethnographic path. For instance, in Atlanta I got 'recognized' from a clip on Facebook originally shot in Kinshasa. I thus benefited from the transnational digital and organizational religious architecture the Congolese have built, easing my ethnographic cross-border mobility. While, as a white (*mundele*) scholar at an established research university in *Poto* (the West/Europe), I had privileges – especially in terms of mobility – that many of my informants do not have; they were, of course, not passive as they expressed their own interests and exerted agency in many different ways.

Multi-sited research is often seen as key to making sense of migration-related processes and subjectivities in all their social, cultural and affective complexity, as well as understanding the 'fragmented and plurilocally situated transnational networks' (Boccagni 2014: 2) within which migrants and diasporic actors are embedded. In addition, there has been a growing emphasis on the study of processes of transformation of sending communities linked to the transfer of not just capital but also ideas, values or norms between host societies and homeland

(Eckstein and Najam 2013, Levitt 2001b, Lopez 2015). In this sense, and as Chu (2010) indicates in her ethnography of Longyan, an emigration town in Fuzhou, China: 'one could experience displacement while remaining at "home" simply because the boundaries of locality and one's social world had shifted or come under contestation' (2010: 12). Chu's ethnography of a 'local' context in which international migration has become a normative reality is one of the few which have looked at the material impact of migration and remittances on religious life in the homeland (see also the pioneering work of Gardner 1995). She describes the emergence of religious material landscapes linked to new global-local cosmologies in the 'post-Mao context' through the renovation or 'modernization' of temples financially supported by the remittances of 'spiritually indebted' migrants working abroad.

The diasporic groups studied in this book have an uneven level of influence when it comes to the material transformation of the homeland. For instance, the impact and influence of Congolese Catholics migrants are rather limited, given the institutional arrangement of the Catholic ensemble, which is organized top-down, and given the absence of an explicit unified strategy to 'develop' what remains a vast and fragmented spatio-religious landscape in the homeland. Kimbanguists, on the other hand, place a lot of emphasis on developing Nkamba and on investing and channelling a range of resources – not only material and financial but also symbolic and spiritual – to transform their holy city. While they have not sacralized the homeland as Kimbanguists have done, many Congolese Pentecostal actors in diaspora are also embarked, albeit to a lesser extent, on charitable or developmental interventions in the Congo, promoting particular visions of infrastructural and urban changes, as we shall see in Chapters 6 and 7.

Unlike religious or 'sacred' remittances (Garbin 2018) impacting on the homeland in various ways, family remittances raise a number of issues that cut across the three groups studied. For Catholics, Kimbanguists and Pentecostals alike, the practice of sending remittances can be a way to establish a proxy presence in the homeland. It can also be tied to conflicted emotions and relationships of debts and dependence. Multi-sited observations (partly through a 'follow-the-money' approach as remittances travel through transnational networks or even with migrants themselves) have allowed me to explore how the regimes of values may operate in both diaspora and homeland contexts, and how ideas, values and resources move across 'affective transnational circuits' (Cole and Groes 2016). This is particularly important as, even if not directly inflicted by ritualistic religious dynamics, remittances as global money are also a key component of the moral worlds of Congolese both in diaspora and homeland.

While the migrants' role in the homeland can be evident through the transformative impact of family or religious remittances, the homeland may also exert a strong influence on those in diaspora. This combination of centripetal and centrifugal forces is particularly notable in the case of Olangi and Kimbanguist churches, which have cultivated – in different ways – the ideas of strong centres in the homeland which diasporic members are encouraged to visit regularly (and for Kimbanguists, there is the idea of a 'promised' return). This 'centring' coexists with strategies of global expansion through the making of diasporic 'peripheries'. In addition, homeland developments have shaped the evolution of the diasporic landscape in several ways, for instance, leading to collective political mobilization, which I analyse in Chapter 4.

Arguably, the most striking aspect of the religious life of Congolese in diaspora is the numerical and symbolic dominance of Pentecostal churches, reflecting the 'charismatization' of the homeland, a multiform 'Pentecostalization' of the public sphere observable in many other African urban societies (Meyer 2010). While it is beyond the scope of this book to provide a detailed historical analysis of the emergence of Pentecostalism in the DRC, in particular in Kinshasa (see Demart 2017 for a good overview) – it is important to locate the ubiquitous presence of *églises de réveil* in urban Congo (and the Congolese diaspora) within the (post-) Mobutu era, as Pype (2012) has noted.

The trope of the 'void' is here central to an understanding of how these developments emerged out of not only the collapse of Mobutist state infrastructure and national economy but, more generally, the crisis of forms of autocratic sovereignty that dominated the region, relying on the combination of ideological, quasi-religious (in the case of Mobutu[11]) aesthetics of control, buttressed by external (Western) support in the Cold War context. Focusing on post-Cold War Togo, Piot (2010) shows that the Pentecostal revival, the charismatic *réveil*, filled a moral, social and ideological vacuum and heralded an era of redemption, a self-understanding that is at the core of Pentecostal discourses of development and future progress. In the post-Mobutu Congolese context, the much-needed transition to a new ideological and aesthetic horizon is linked to the belief that, during his rule, Mobutu had formed an alliance with the Devil. This belief adds urgency to the project of national and individual purification and remoralization. Even today, this belief is still very powerful in the Congolese collective memory and in the *imaginaire* of churches I have studied – like Combat Spirituel. A pivotal moment of the transition out of the post-Mobutu moral void which many of my Pentecostal interlocutors often cite is the public confession of Sakombi Inongo, one of Mobutu's former right-hand men during a 'national day of redemption', which Kinshasa's Charismatic prayer groups organized in 1992. On that day, Inongo famously confessed in front of thousands of people that 'Mobutism' was a project of bewitchment of the entire Zairean nation and that the government's 'authenticity' (*l'authenticité*)[12] policy and introduction of new national symbols – flags, national anthem and coins – all bore occult signs of Mobutu's personal pact with Satan (Demart 2017: 188).

The dramatic impact of Pentecostal *réveil* in Congolese society is not confined to the religious domain. Indeed, the public cultural sphere became more and more charismatic with, for example, the conversion of hundreds of 'worldly' music bands and theatre groups to strict evangelical Christian forms of performing arts (see Pype 2012). The Catholic Church has managed to maintain an alternative to this powerful charismatization of Congolese society, but the *réveil* has also shaped Catholic liturgy, rendering its ritualization more affective and personalized. Unlike Kimbanguists who sought to suppress the embodied performance of charismatic modes of religiosity, Catholic Charismatics carved out a space of expression and worship within the Catholic structure, with, for instance, the organization of charismatic Masses or prayer sessions as part of parish life, including in the diasporic context.

2

'God stamps the visa first'

Spiritual infrastructures and the paths of mobility and settlement

After a long Sunday service at the Kimbanguist headquarters (*centre d'accueil*) in Kinshasa, I got to talk to Maurice, in his early thirties, who had lived two years in a continental European country before being deported back to the Congo. Recalling the hardship of his experience, Maurice underscores his six-month incarceration in a detention centre before his eventual removal to Kinshasa. His narrative clearly relocated his personal trajectory against the backdrop of a powerfully constraining migration regime. The abrupt end of his stay in Europe meant a rapid deterioration of his social and economic status and the impossibility to accumulate sufficient symbolic and financial capital to get married:

> Before I left Congo, I was anxious but got the blessing from the spiritual leader.... In [country of destination] I was working, but I was not fully registered, since I was waiting for my papers. Three times I had to deal with the police. And the second time, they nearly arrested me: I was cycling at night without a light, my back light was not working. The police stopped me because of the light, but when they saw I was Black, they wanted to check my identity and status with their special computer. ... I prayed and prayed in my head and then they said the machine wasn't working. It was a divine intervention. But the third time, after my application was rejected, they arrested me at home, put me in a detention centre for 6 months. It was like a prison. I was sharing my room with 2 other Africans. We were all like prisoners. Then a transfer to a centre near the airport – for 2 weeks this time. Then they put me on a regular flight back to Kinshasa with a few others. Arriving in Kinshasa, I didn't get arrested at the airport. Again, that was an intervention from Papa. Papa really helped me. Prayer really helped me in [country of destination]. There one lives with the fear, of getting arrested and getting harassed . . . because you are Black and there weren't many Black people where I was. Prayer helped me. I was deported, I got back home. I was ashamed

[*j'ai eu honte*]: 'what, someone comes back from Europe with only the clothes on his back?' That's shameful! I stayed at home [in Kinshasa] without going out for 2 weeks. Then I went to Nkamba to see Papa. Papa said to me 'there is nothing more for you in Europe'. In any case, I'd rather not go back without a visa and stable job. And they have my fingerprints over there. I am going to try to go to Angola or Congo-Brazza. I am 32 and [had I stayed] in Europe, marriage would have been possible for me. But now I have no money I cannot get married. But now European countries deport a lot [*expulsent beaucoup*] these days. More than before.

Maurice met the full force of a migration regime criminalizing those lacking appropriate paperwork, waiting to be 'regularized' or left in a liminal situation after the rejection of their application for stay or asylum. Coming back with 'just the clothes on his back' and staying home 'without going out for two weeks', Maurice experienced deportation as deeply regressive, stigmatizing and shameful. As Vigh (2016: 235) notes, deportation 'transforms hope of social becoming into fear of social unbecoming'. And because migrants are expected to fulfill a range of obligations – in particular sending regular remittances to their kin, as we shall see in Chapter 5 – those who are returned forcibly lose 'the ability to contribute positively to one's affective circuit' (2016: 240), sliding down the hierarchy of social value.

A striking aspect of Maurice's physical as well as social and affective trajectories is what I shall call 'spiritual infrastructures', a dynamic assemblage of conditions, agents, practices, narratives, values, moral resources and mapped orientations which, among other things, enable and sustain mobility while addressing regimes of immobility. These spiritual infrastructures give meaning to both mobility and immobility, especially during moments of crisis, junction or choices. In Maurice's case, these infrastructures encompass blessings, advice (from 'Papa', the Kimbanguist spiritual leader) and prayers operating as a divine protection in a context of constant threats and dangers. The idea of spiritual infrastructures mostly relates here to the empowering dimension of religion and the range of affordances it allows, the main focus of this chapter. While operating as a 'sanctuary' for migrants in the often precarious and uncertain milieu of the host societies, the affordances of religious affiliation or religious network(ing) act as a spiritual 'compass' at various stages of the journey, as suggested by the case of Maurice.

This empowering dimension of religion for migrants as they cross borders and settle in new 'host' contexts is a recurrent theme in the literature on transnational religion, migration and globalization (Adogame 2013, Chu 2010,

Hagan 2008, Tweed 2006, Meyer and Van der Veer 2021). As Hagan (2008) writes in her study of undocumented migration from Latin America to the United States, 'religion permeates the entirety of the migration experience, from decision making and departure through the dangerous undocumented journey from their home communities north to the United States' (2008: 7). Similarly, in her ethnography of Longyan, China, Chu (2010) describes how, in a world of differentiated mobility, high-risk migration to the United States increasingly 'hinge[s] on contingencies beyond human control' (2010: 158). In this context, individuals draw upon a range of spiritual strategies to manage international mobility: consultation of mediums, routine prayers for a visa or for protection during perilous journeys and gift offerings to gods in local temples. People in Longyan also perform ritual activities specifically tailored for the asylum court hearings of their kin overseas, mobilizing gods 'to soften the heart' of American immigration judges thousands of miles away (Chu 2010: 157).

Channelling flows, unblocking paths, managing movement, transit and return, these spiritual infrastructures are at the heart of a moral economy of mobility, as we shall see in this chapter. They also include resources to address the predicaments of immobility and waithood, projecting horizons of hope. In that sense, they provide meaning and legitimacy, in particular for those who see their journeys as embedded within the wider time-spaces of missionization or exilic imaginaries. The idea of diaspora, for instance among Kimbanguists, is often connected to Old Testament tropes of collective pain and suffering, and, in similar ways, predicaments of migration are (re)interpreted with references to the biblical Exodus among Pentecostals.[1] At the same time, in their 'host' settings, as migrants negotiate new (im)moral landscapes, these spiritual infrastructures help create possibilities of exchange and solidarity, allowing the experience of a familiar religiosity – in part entailing linkages with the homeland through the circulation of information, people, objects and capital.

In a world marked by the increasing hardening of borders and the deployment of technologies of surveillance and population control, these translocative arrangements allow migrants to engage in processes of deterritorialization and reterritorialization through a 'regrounding' of values and community norms, which, as we shall see, can reinforce claims for authority and moral righteousness. These spiritual infrastructures not only provide a range of affordances – affective, cognitive, moral and socio-economic – but can also enact constraining boundaries based on the (re)production of hierarchical, moral-theological visions, such as the Pentecostal 'ethics of submission' or prosperity gospel, that bear elective affinities with the dynamics of late capitalism (Marshall 2009: 10).

In addition, spiritual guidance may also prompt deviations or return journeys and restrain mobility and migration, as suggested, for instance, by Maurice's testimony, when the Kimbanguist leader told him that 'there was nothing more for him' in Europe.

While, in many ways, these spiritual infrastructures bridge homeland and diasporic concerns about remoralization and social transformation, they operate in different ways in the country of origin and in the country of settlement. For instance, a totalizing, aspirational discourse of 'development' may find a weaker resonance in diasporic settings than in the homeland, where religious groups have been at the forefront of service provision (in health and education for instance) against the backdrop of what is perceived to be a dysfunctional postcolonial state (see Chapter 6). In diaspora, as we shall see, these spiritual infrastructures may also contribute to alternative forms of (religious) belonging, incorporation and citizenship in a context of minoritization.

Before focusing on these questions of settlement and incorporation, let us explore in more detail how these spiritual infrastructures map affective trajectories and how idioms of spiritual warfare can frame movements across space and time.

Spiritual infrastructures as a resource to address mobility regimes

As we saw, Maurice (like many of my Congolese Christian interlocutors) has mobilized the 'cosmic efficacy of divine support' (Chu 2010: 159) as a personal strategy to address constraining migration regimes and the numerous risks and obstacles he encountered. In his narrative, 'Papa' – the Kimbanguist spiritual leader – spiritually intervened to help him, including preventing his arrest at the airport, presumably by the police or the notorious Agence Nationale de Renseignements (ANR – government intelligence agency), who is said to 'collect' failed asylum seekers returning to the homeland, especially men deemed politically active. The 'word of Papa' has here a particular significance: it counsels, warns, accompanies, reassures and predicts. It is also at times performative in the sense that it directly produces particular kinetic practices, (re)routing people (e.g. to and from Nkamba), like the case of Maman Juju, whom I met in the Kimbanguist holy city.

At the time of our encounter, Maman Juju, while originally from Kinshasa, was living in Nkamba most of the time. Like Maurice, Maman Juju had been deported from Europe and upon her return was told by the spiritual leader to join him in Nkamba, to contribute to the sacred work (*misala*) of the church (i.e. helping with cooking and cleaning during major pilgrimages) and 'to resource herself spiritually', as she put it. Papa, who told her that 'she shouldn't worry as she will eventually return to Europe', had initially encouraged her to migrate, to be 'among the other ambassadors of Kimbanguism in *Poto*'. Like Maurice, Maman Juju spent several months in a detention centre – and was put on a specially chartered flight with other Congolese from all over Europe (she described a chaotic plane journey with handcuffed and screaming returnees, some being violently manhandled). She recalled how she felt humiliated (e.g. during body searches when she had to fully strip), isolated and fearful during her stay in the detention centre, with prayers for only comfort. And because she could not talk directly with the spiritual leader, the pastor of her parish would visit her from time to time, informing Papa of her situation and providing her with some spiritual support. She concluded her narrative by stressing the powerful role played by 'Papa' in shaping her trajectory and allowing her to 'spiritually grow' through challenges:

> Papa knows everything, Papa intervenes positively but also negatively. He puts you to the test and these challenges make you grow spiritually. I became richer spiritually speaking, in the end. These experiences in Europe made me grow spiritually.

Maman Juju's case shows how national and transnational church networks circulate symbolic and social resources issuing from the collective recognized power linked to spiritual leadership. In a context of struggle for moral authority and ecclesial legitimacy, the emergence of the *milimo* among Kimbanguists in London also shows how the challenges of immigration status can be addressed by the deployment and mobilization of empowering spiritual infrastructures. As explained in the previous chapter, what became known as the *milimo* phenomenon – the embodiment by several female mediums of the spirits (*milimo*) of the Prophet Kimbangu and his sons – started in the 1990s and lasted for several years, a period of early settlement and 'moral transition' (Werbner 1990) among Congolese in London. During this period the *milimo* were consulted by the worshippers – during special séances and Sunday services – asking for spiritual help to solve their immigration issues and regularize their status in the UK, as recalled by these two pastors:

> Thanks to the *milimo*, we were successful with the papers. . . . For example, you have been rejected and you need to leave the country, when you see her [the medium], you pray and she would tell you what to do and to pray, to adopt a

good Christian behaviour. Her prayers will help you to get the papers. Nobody in our parish was deported [*expulsé*] because of absence of legal documents, nobody. (Pastor G.)

What people would ask was to get papers. . . . We were all waiting for the decision of the Home Office. They wanted spiritual help . . . they were going to see the spirits of the *Papas* to see if they could get the papers. . . . People would come with the letters of the Home office and she [the medium] would touch the letter and pray. . . . But instead of calling Papa *Mfumu a Mbanza* [Papa Dialungana, spiritual leader at that time] they were asking the *milimo* 'help me with the papers'. (Pastor A.)

While, as Pastor A. suggests, the *milimo* represented forces challenging the centralized Kimbanguist matrix of charismatic power (embodied at the time by the then spiritual leader Papa Dialungana), the widespread view was (and still is) that the *milimo* were enacting a sense of divine protection in the uncertain and precarious context of early settlement (Pastor A. was one of those who subsequently rejected the role played by the *milimo*). The practice of touching and praying over 'Home Office[2] letters' vividly demonstrates the strong belief and hope that spiritual power can influence the bureaucratic authority materialized by a 'documentation regime' that can be including or excluding (see Tuckett 2018). Migrants have to negotiate this inscrutable and impersonal regime, mobilizing resources – financial, social or spiritual – at their disposal. For Kimbanguists, and especially since the reassertion of a centralized institutional/charismatic order (leading, among other things to the 'ban' of the *milimo*), spiritually acting upon material elements of a constraining migration regime is now entirely the monopoly of the spiritual leader and it is frequent to see pilgrims in Nkamba bringing passports and visa letters, asking Papa to intercede (the same way that some would ask him to bless the pictures of husbands/wives-to-be and so on).

For Pentecostals, the spiritual infrastructures constituted by the church – as a space of intense individual and collective devotion – the pastor and the praying community have clear intercessory efficacy. Similarly to Kimbanguists, Pentecostals bring their passports, visa applications or related travel documents to church, harnessing and directing the power of the Holy Spirit to intercede in their bureaucratic journey. Thus, as a leader of the Maman Olangi church whom I met in Kinshasa explains, visas can be 'stamped spiritually by God':

It is normal to pray so that you can travel [*prier pour voyager*], or to get your *mukanda* ['papers']. We do that during intercessory prayer sessions. One can bring a passport or documents to church if you need to. It's God that stamps the visa first, the visa is stamped spiritually by God before being stamped physically. It is the will of God [*la volonté de Dieu*] that controls the hand that will stamp the passport at the embassy. The spiritual can unblock situations.

The importance of the discourse of 'unblocking' suggests the extent to which Pentecostal churches have become a privileged site for the materialization and mediation of aspirations, especially in Kinshasa, a postcolonial megacity experienced (perhaps more rightly, fantasized) as 'a huge machine of evacuation' as coined by De Boeck and Plissart (2004: 45). Across Africa and beyond, Pentecostal urban presence often resonates with notions of 'path clearing' and 'unblocking' of movement, flows or circulation, whether it is obtaining a visa or medical treatment, having consistent electricity (see Chapter 7) or realizing educational ambitions. For Congolese Christians – in particular Pentecostals, but also for Kimbanguists – blockages are expressed through limitations, closures and slowdowns and they often result from spiritual/witchcraft attacks and/or the curse of ancestral 'bondage'.

Fighting the spirit(s) of immobility

A story that Papa Marcel shared as a testimony (*témoignage*) during a Maman Olangi church service in Kinshasa evokes the detrimental impact of these blockages on migration and aspirations to migrate:

> The testimony starts with the information that the family of Papa Marcel is dominated by an elder figure and *chef coutumier* – his grandfather. To keep his power over the kinship group, the grandfather made a sacrificial pact with the Devil, putting a curse on the entire family: that 'no family members shall ever leave the city of their birth' (i.e. Kinshasa). After Marcel joined Combat Spirituel to fight this occult influence, he managed to obtain a visa to travel to Belgium, a success he attributed to the power of prayers. However, on the day of his departure, the person who was supposed to drive him to Kinshasa Ndjili airport did not show up. Marcel had lost a lot of time, but managed to take a taxi-moto. There was another hurdle at the airport this time, when he realized he had forgotten his passport. Luckily, he could ask someone to bring his passport in time for his flight. Despite these obstacles, he made it to Belgium.

> However, when he had to pass immigration control, he encountered yet more problems. 'This is the picture of an old man on the passport, this isn't you!' exclaimed the Belgian immigration officer after examining Papa Marcel's

passport. Papa Marcel looked at his passport and realised that the photo was in fact his grandfather's. He was subsequently deported, put on the next flight home. The interpretation provided by the testimony is that his grandfather had in fact enacted a 'spirit of immobility' which altered the photo of his passport, projecting his own image onto it. Satan used the grandfather because Satan uses *la coutume* – traditional clan authority – to control people and this ancestral bondage had to be 'renounced'. Papa Marcel had to undergo a long deliverance to cut the ties that were trapping him and blocking his movements and progress – a curse of 'limitations'. After an intense year of prayers and fasting he managed to get a second visa to Belgium, to 'exit' [*sortir*] Kinshasa. But this time, he didn't tell anybody, unlike during his first attempt when he said to have been 'vain', having 'boasted' about this visa success. He only contacted family and friends once in Belgium and they were all stunned to learn that he had managed to reach *Poto*.

This testimony highlights how overcoming the power of evil forces is needed to conquer mobility and defeat the spirit of blockage and 'limitations' that Satan imposed, using the traditional/ancestral structure of power to do so. In order to travel – 'to exit' (*sortir*) – not only Marcel had to be delivered from a family curse which was spiritually and physically tying him to Kinshasa, but he also adopted a reformed, virtuous behaviour more in tune with what is expected of a 'good Christian' – to be humble and discrete after his second 'visa success'.

While migration regimes are undoubtedly potent, this type of narrative suggests the overlapping existence of several regimes of mobility which need to be considered to see how 'crossing and dwelling' trajectories can be endowed with religious meaning as part of wider worldviews and theologies of spiritual warfare. Here I want to briefly discuss another testimony which shows how the theme of mobility (afforded, constrained, blocked or as transitory) can be central to these theologies. The testimony is about Maman Betty's journey, recorded in Belgium during a Maman Olangi women's prayer session. Available on the church's YouTube channel, it describes a long and hazardous journey from Kinshasa to Brussels, a journey which lasted several years, punctuated by multiple hurdles, slowdowns and dangerous episodes.

The testimony evokes perilous crossings of the Sahara desert and Mediterranean Sea, precarious transit stays in Algeria and Morocco and even kidnapping by Boko Haram fighters at the Niger–Libya border. While we know from the testimony that some of her kin live in Europe, migration to *Poto* never features, in Maman Betty's narrative, as an explicit aim to this whole journey. Her motivations are not entirely clear; there is the mention of escaping a military posting in the Congo where she was briefly working for the army and we also learn of her desire to start a trade business between Lagos and Kinshasa. What is clear in the testimony, however, is that her story reveals how her journey was continuously shaped by an intense spiritual struggle – the blockages she encountered are all attributed to family curses (not only limiting her mobility but also forcing her, for instance, to be promiscuous with men met along the way), while the Holy Spirit and power of prayer helped her to overcome obstacles. The trip across Africa and Europe is thus presented as a dual, parallel journey: as a quest to become morally autonomous and to reach a redemptive state, but also as an 'evil trajectory' under the influence of a spell she is constantly struggling with. As a female pastor providing commentary during the recorded testimony put it, her journey was a way to 'evangelise for the forces of darkness' and her immoral behaviour a way 'to create messengers for the Devil's church' at every stage of her peregrinations. While the end of the journey, Brussels, which coincides with the death of the kin who had bewitched her, is heralded as a sign of a divine victory, the journey is metonymic of the long process of deliverance itself. As Werbner points out in her ethnography of Pakistani Sufis in the UK, the notion of religious journey not only evokes the sacred migration of the Prophet (*Hijra*) but also relates to a path of self-purification and moral reform, a 'journey within the person' (2003: 41). But in the eyes of Maman Olangi Pentecostals, this process is never fully achieved, and the journey becomes one of permanent vigilance, if not constant struggle against evil influences.

Mapping the vision: Mission and migration

Marcel and Maman Betty's stories link mobility with spiritual struggle, as they invoke overlapping journeys involving the successive, or at times simultaneous, crossing of affective, physical and otherworldly boundaries. They point to the ways in which spiritual infrastructures provide frames of interpretation recasting the power of divine and satanic forces to shape trajectories in a world of differentiated mobility. In this case, the duality of God versus Satan locked in a cosmic struggle helps to make sense of why there is (im)mobility and to provide the psycho-moral guidance and impetus to act upon material and spiritual constraints. Similarly, mobilizing the idea of a Christian identity is a way to claim some form of legitimacy against the increasing closure – the 'walling desires' (Brown 2010) – of migration/border regimes, while fulfilling an evangelical mission. For instance, Pastor Eric, the founder of a small Congolese

Pentecostal church in suburban Atlanta, stressed the importance of what could be described as a form of religious citizenship through the labour of praying and preaching, aimed at securing and expanding the Kingdom of God:

> I believe in the Bible and the Bible says 'wherever you put your feet, you take possession'. So, you can be an American, a White, a Black, you don't support me – I don't care. I believe I take possession, through the preaching and the praying. . . . Abraham and Jesus did not need visas to go to Canaan!

The power of faith allows those who believe in the Bible to 'take possession' and overcome exclusion, hostility and bureaucratic obstacles or, in the case of Pastor Eric, to harness the (limited) opportunities of contemporary mobility regimes. Pastor Eric, who migrated to Atlanta in 1996, had been successful at the 'DV lottery' (diversity visa programme), a success he attributed to a divine intervention. He has been an American citizen for more than a decade and praises the United States as a country 'where rules are strict and respected', describing himself as law abiding. His sense of religious citizenship is also expressed through outreach and charitable work: he collects money among his followers to buy food and drinks, which he distributes from his van to (mostly African American) homeless people in downtown Atlanta, 'sharing the Word of God' with them at the same time.

Pastor's Eric narrative links a divine election to a role of pastor and spiritual leader equipped with God-given gifts of discernment and prophecy and with the power to move across borders. This narrative also shows that, although religious citizenship may stand in tension and supersede national citizenship, they can also become entwined and reinforce each other. Central in this discourse is the idea of spiritually mapping and 'indexing' places, a familiar element of Pentecostal spatial theology (Coleman 2010, Rey 2019). Here, a spiritual landscape brought into being by Pastor Eric's 'revelations' invites intervention. This landscape is constituted of multiple battlefronts, the fight against the Devil requiring a recognition that there exists 'different categories of evil manifestations' territorialized and mapped across the globe as he explains:

> What we do is a new ministry that will take over everywhere. I feel that because people need it. I need people that understand the vision and God's revelations. . . . I had a revelation for France – a vision. The Lord asked me to pray on [*sic*] the people who are Freemasons. . . . I have revelation for Ivory Coast . . . the devil of seduction and *concubinage*. Polygamy. . . . I have revelations on China. . . . They worship the dragon. . . . Whatever places God gives us revelation about, this the place where we will establish the ministry. . . . Everywhere where we have

revelation, via the different categories of evil manifestations, we have to place our ministry right there to fight against . . . God will give the vision. Like a map. And you need therefore to prepare yourself.

Coleman (2010: 199) sees religious mapping as central to a 'charismatic gaze' through which 'the world becomes an object to be owned, or at least controlled, by the believer'. In other words, a geo-religious vision sustains, generates and undergirds a spiritual infrastructure of movements and settlement. Projecting oneself onto this remapped world becomes a form of kinetic practice, which is reinforced by a missionary calling to redeem places and revitalize them. The rhetoric of the 'reverse mission' recurrent in the ways migration to the West is construed by African Pentecostals is often seen as a central component of this spiritual mapping (see Adogame 2013, Kalu 2008, Pasura 2012, Hunt 2002)[3] – a form of 'evangelisation going the opposite direction' as this London-based pastor told me:

> Men [*les hommes*] have rejected God. . . . Men said to themselves: 'ok, we have created science, science will solve all our problems' . . . In the Western world when they used to put God in the first position, everything was different. . . . But because they have rejected God now it's different. . . . God has never forgotten its people. Now evangelisation is going the opposite direction. It's now the Africans, the Asians, who are coming to Europe with God's message . . . Europe has sown, now it's the harvest. Europe is harvesting what they sowed.

The loss of spirituality, the decline of Christian identity and values, in a secular West that has 'rejected God', is expressed first and foremost by the landscapes of immorality shaping an everyday life full of risks. It is also linked to the evolution of what is perceived to be the civic and political frames of immoral governance. This is especially the case when it comes to the legalization of abortion and same-sex marriages as stressed by Pastor Eric who evoked the Devil's 'occupation' of California:

> In California, the Governor agreed for homosexual marriage. It is against the Bible. Now, I believe that, not only that the Devil can occupy one person, but it can also occupy a big place, like California to influence people and make them obey his will. America was built on God's foundation, but now . . . We don't find the same-sex marriage in the Bible.

Missionization in the midst of a secular and sinful world provides meaning and agency to the believer against the uncertainty of the diaspora condition and empowers them with a sense of divine purpose, which can validate claims for legitimacy and moral superiority (Ukah 2016b). However, the tension between the universal tropes of (reverse) missionization and the reality of 'ethnic encapsulation' for many, if not most, African churches in diaspora raises a range of conceptual issues when interrogating the potential for more cosmopolitan forms of religious affiliation and practices (Glick Schiller and Karagiannis 2006).

There is a need here for a nuanced approach that combines an awareness of the ways in which religion often reinforces national and transnational hegemonic projects while also providing resources for migrant mobility, solidarity and rearticulation of the self. We need to consider the overlaps between missionary tropes of planetary territorialization and references to the nation (see Chapter 4), as well as the need for protective 'community' encapsulation in the midst of a morally ambivalent society. While many African Christians see their presence in the West as part of the Great Commission, Jesus Christ's call to 'make disciples of all nations', the idea of the 'reverse' mission of attracting/evangelizing non-Africans is also often discussed in relation to particular attitudes to the 'host' environment. Papa Luc, a pastor from Maman Olangi church I met in Kinshasa (but based in France), commented on what he called the 'myth' of evangelizing Europe, reflecting on his own (contested) decision to adapt to a non-Congolese audience:

> We hear about evangelizing Europe in some Congolese churches. But you could say it's a myth. How do you do this when everything is in Lingala? Some don't really want to adapt to the environment. It is difficult – for the Apostles it was difficult! In my church, I try to adapt, and some don't agree. Adapting the songs, trying to translate, explaining what we preach to guests or non-Congolese who are married to those attending our ministry. After a few sessions, they understand.

At the same time, Papa Luc stressed that travel is valued not only to 'spread the Word of God' but also with a view to gain from it, the return to the homeland being, in many respects, part of a wider trajectory, a wider vision. Here again, 'Europe'/*Poto* remains an ambivalent space, which is presented as morally decadent and where the 'suffering' of migrants can be expressed through testimonies produced in church. Moreover, Papa Luc's discourse demonstrates the mixture of scepticism towards the dominant geopolitical vision of the core-periphery and a desire to address the plight of migrants on the ground with the reaffirmation of the continued importance of the nation-state:

> By traveling, we can spread the Word of God, but Papa and Maman Olangi encouraged us to travel, like they did themselves, to discover the world not to

stay abroad for ever. They used to say 'take the best from elsewhere to return to the Congo, to do better in the Congo'. They taught us about the ills [*les méfaits*] of Europe, its moral decadence – we see this with same-sex marriage [*mariage pour tous*]. Europe is in spiritual chaos. They wanted to challenge the myth that Europe is the country of milk and honey. A lot of us give testimony in church about the suffering of migration, things migrants are going through.

There is a strong parallel here with how travel is framed by diasporic Kimbanguists, for whom migration represents a way to convey the 'universal hope' of a prophetic message. They often evoke a prophecy attributed to Kimbangu (based on Acts 2:17) envisioning the global dispersion of 'young followers with spiritual gifts' as well as the discourse of Papa Diangienda, one of Kimbangu's sons. As the church's leader, Diangienda encouraged members to go abroad to study or gain skills and at the same time become *ambassadeurs du Kimbanguisme* by spreading the name of Kimbangu and, perhaps more importantly, by upholding virtue and righteousness amidst a new tempting environment. Kimbanguists are animated by a sense of mission (see Mokoko Gampiot 2010: 313), and adopting an exemplary moral behaviour to convince others of the value and authenticity of Kimbanguism is an important way to evangelize. However, for some, the absence of non-Congolese (or non-Angolan) Africans, as well as *mindele* ('whites'), in the community of the church is a clear sign of failure – failure often explained by weakened adhesion to Kimbanguist commandments, the 'distractions of Europe' or the existence of internal conflicts.

Spiritual infrastructures and the experience of settlement

While the spiritual infrastructures afforded by deliverance – an often long and intensive process – and missionizing visions are key to unblock and unlock spatial/social mobility, they also point to the role of religious social networks as key resources easing the journey, arrival and settlement. Unlike migrants who can rely on village associations (see Lacroix 2016 on Algerian Hometown Associations – HTAs – in France), for newly arrived Congolese in the United States and United Kingdom, churches and religious groups are among the only emerging community structures where they can find comfort, moral support, help and assistance especially at the start of the migration process. In the case of Kimbanguists, joining the recreated and nascent *lingomba* ('the community of the church') provided a sense of home and was seen as an antidote to loneliness and isolation. Maman Lucie who migrated on her own, initially to study before settling permanently and becoming British, evoked her first months in London, at a time when the Congolese diaspora was still relatively small:

> I arrived here [in London] in 1992. I wasn't really happy. . . . Because at that time there weren't many Africans, like now. It was rare to see an African! I was crying, would call home, 'Mum, I want to go back home!'. . . . It took me six months to find the church. . . . There weren't many Congolese people, so it was difficult. . . . I asked other Congolese, and it was at Manor Park. But during six months I didn't pray. It was very hard. I really felt that something was missing. . . . In the Congo I was used to go [to church] at 9am each Sunday, and go back home at 6pm. Here, I was staying at home, I was feeling lonely [. . .] When I found the church I was very happy. First, they were speaking my language, Lingala. . . . And then, seeing my Congolese brothers, I was very happy.

Papa Hubert, fifty-two, a member of Nouvelle Jerusalem Church in Atlanta, recalled his experience of settlement and his first contact with a religious community – an American Pentecostal church with a 'mixed' congregation. At first, Papa Hubert and his wife were warned to avoid Congolese churches (said to be 'unstable' and conflict-ridden), but the barrier of language was so 'frustrating' that after a short period of time in the American church, they joined the New Jerusalem Church. While language was a key factor in this decision, Papa Hubert also stressed how, in a Congolese church environment, there is 'real support', for instance, in case of bereavement (typically, a moment where intense community support is expected):

> We have a saying: 'one prays better in the language one learned to cry'. We found a Congolese woman, she was going to an American church, a mixed church with Whites, Blacks . . . People from a lot of different countries. When we were in Kinshasa we used to pray in a church called La Borne. Pasteur Vernant, who just died, he is the one who married us. . . . She said she knew La Borne and said that the church is a bit similar. 'I am sure you will like it' she said. . . . We had just arrived in the US we didn't have a car. . . . She could take us to this church. . . . And we liked it, but with the English, we could not understand – going in one ear and out the other. We had to get it translated all the time, it was frustrating. . . . Then we found out about the New Jerusalem Church, they had a shuttle bus and we liked it and we stayed ever since. . . . And you quickly feel the difference between American and Congolese church: when you have a problem for instance and above all a loss in the family. . . . A Congolese who is going to an American church when he is bereaved [*éprouvé*], people from the church may

send you a card. . . . But in a Congolese church, the community will spend time
with you, will visit you at home, there is real support.

Churches like the New Jerusalem act as mediating institutions for new migrants
in the United States – with more established members offering support and
advice to newcomers in terms of housing or Green Card applications. Special
collections are also regularly organized for those in need of financial assistance
– like it was the case during the sub-prime crisis in 2008, when several members
were at risk of defaulting on their mortgage payments. Since the New Jerusalem
Church is one of the better-known Congolese churches among the diaspora in
Atlanta, it operates as a sort of religious transit space, for instance, for groups
of resettled refugees from eastern Congo who would initially attend the church
before joining a Swahili-speaking church – or creating their own church or
religious community.

Historically, the role churches and religious structures played as mediating
institutions has evolved in pace with their own development. At the start of the
migration process for most Congolese (for instance, in the 1990s in the UK and
later in the US context), early Pentecostal prayer groups were typically organized
in the home of a community member and around a charismatic pastor (who
may have been a pastor in the DRC or become one in the UK). With their
formalization, their expansion and their stronger territorial anchoring, these
religious groups, 'routinized' into full-fledged churches or branches of already
established congregations (like Maman Olangi church), could provide a greater
range of resources (for instance, provide temporary accommodation), allowing
for the circulation of information about housing, employment opportunities or
immigration issues. This – often very quick – consolidation of a European/US
presence meant that translocal connections could link up church members in
the DRC to those in diaspora or those within the diaspora space, in particular
in Europe. I met several Kimbanguists who grew up or initially settled in
France, Belgium or Portugal and who took advantage of the EU 'Freedom of
Movement' to find work and stay in the UK. This intra-EU, secondary migration
was facilitated by the existence of networks linking Kimbanguists in London,
Paris, Brussels or Liège and sustained over the years by regular mobility (as
part of brass band concerts, weddings and *matangas* – funeral wakes) and
communications through social media. Churches like the Kimbanguist church
or Combat Spirituel (Maman Olangi), which have expanded transnationally
via branches and parishes established globally and have consolidated their
translocal networks with the regular circulation of congregants (and leaders),

can allow members to accumulate and deploy 'mobility capital' across borders. While increasingly harsher regimes of mobility and stricter immigration regulations have a detrimental impact on the mobility of some (Brexit is now limiting the settlement of EU-born Congolese in the UK), the transnational scope of these churches is often projected as an ideal of global reach and universal encompassment. Both in the Kimbanguist Nkamba-New Jerusalem and in the headquarters of Maman Olangi in Kinshasa, this global scope was made visible by the use of flags (European, US, Canadian and some African) and by processions and speeches of visiting international members during several services I attended.

According to Vásquez (2009: 280), the global portability and transposability of 'pneumatic Christianities' that foreground the embodied and affective experience of the Holy Spirit, is characterized by

> a fluidity and capacity to circulate through flexible transnational church and immigrant networks and to become localised through specific spirits or condensed in material objects, from bodies to money to commodities, which then become associated with dramatic, image-heavy public practices of warfare, purification, prayer and conversion.

This flexibility has allowed the deterritorialization and reterritorialization, the swift 'regrounding' (Garbin 2014), of Congolese Pentecostalism and Kimbanguism in new diasporic settings from the 1990s, in contrast with the more rigid and centralized infrastructures sustaining global Catholicism. It was indeed only in 2007 that the Congolese Catholic chaplaincy was established, following the appointment of a Congolese Abbé from Kinshasa. The greater portability of Charismatic Christianity and the differences in worshipping style between Catholics in *Poto* and in the homeland were often highlighted as reasons why, once in diaspora, many Congolese Catholics initially joined Pentecostal churches:

> When Congolese get here, in London, and go to Catholic churches, it's boring for them, it's not as lively . . . *Eglises de réveil* are successful because they have kept what we have in the Congo, for instance in the Catholic churches. . . . The Catholic Church is, of course, very centralized and it's different with the Congolese pastors of these *églises de réveil* who can create their own churches freely, they are not appointed like Catholic priests. That's also why we have the spread of all these churches here in London. (Member of chaplaincy, 66, male)

In Atlanta, while many Catholics also joined Congolese Pentecostal groups, some attended Mass in American churches. This was the case of Papa Yvan, in his forties, who regularly attended an American Catholic church where Masses in Spanish for Hispanic migrants are also organized. His 22-year-old son (who had recently migrated to the United States) used to go to a Catholic parish in Kinshasa but preferred *l'ambiance* of the Combat Spirituel church in Atlanta – which his mother, Papa Yvan's wife also attends – to the 'coldness' of the American Catholic style of worshipping:

> If Congolese go to the American Catholic Church, the priest speaks in English so they don't really understand. That is why they go more to *églises de réveil* where there is more movement, more singing and where the pastor explains the Bible in our language. . . . I tried to take my son with me to church but he said 'it's *malili*', it's cold! We have this expression: 'in Europe it's cold but in Kinshasa it's hot'. First, he was going with me but once he went with his mum [to Combat Spirituel] and he saw the dancing and all that, he stayed with her.

Papa Yvan's testimony points to the fact that settlement is not just a legal and financial matter. It is also an affective one, which involves the powerful emotions and embodied memories of being/feeling at home. In other words, the materialities offered by spiritual infrastructures are not purely instrumental and functional. Even when dealing with the socio-economic realities, these materialities can carry a strong normative component.

The civic and political role of the Catholic Church in the Congo is reflected in the activities of the London chaplaincy's *Commission Justice et Paix*, through which parish members not only receive support on immigration issues but can also be involved in advocacy campaigns, promoting the rights of refugees and asylum seekers. This is often done across ethnic and community boundaries, for example, through the 'Strangers to Citizens' campaign in support of refugees and asylum seekers organized by a London-wide coalition of FBOs, migrant church groups and civil society actors. In her work on Brazilians in London, Sheringham (2013: 93) describes how leaders of the Brazilian Catholic chaplaincy stress the importance of their civic role and their duty 'to represent the voice of the voiceless', putting a stronger emphasis on the 'rights of irregular migrants' than Brazilian Pentecostals who encourage migrants to regularize their status as a matter of 'respect' for the rules and legal requirements of the host society. Similarly, and in contrast to most Pentecostal and Kimbanguist actors, Congolese Catholic leaders in London were recurrently putting forward the need to connect pastoral work, civic initiatives and political emancipation, while talking of a duty to provide unconditional support 'emulating the social mission of Jesus', as the Abbé put it. From 2006 and the creation of the Congolese chaplaincy, Catholic Congolese migrants arriving in London could gradually insert themselves into a socio-religious space of exchange and solidarity, a site where they could experience a familiar religiosity and take part in church groups mirroring those of their parish back in the Congo, while simultaneously maintaining connections with the homeland through not only the circulation of information but also people, objects and capital. Being Catholic in diasporic context also allows them to be part of wider *oikumene*, with the possibility of integrating into a strong and well-established institution (Levitt 2008) that links them, for instance, to other Catholic migrants through participation in multicultural Masses such as the 'Mass for Migrants' at Westminster Cathedral[4] or pilgrimages to sacred spaces such as the Shrine of Our Lady of Walsingham, in Norfolk, East of England (see Chapter 3).

Moral transition and the 'mayuya' economy

In the *Migration Process*, a classic ethnography of Pakistani migrants in Britain, Pnina Werbner (1990) discusses how the development of mosques and other early community institutions as well as the gradual reconstitution of a ritual world centred, in particular, around the performance of offerings, implied the reconstitution of a 'spatial moral order' in the host context, with the 'locus of valued relations' gradually shifting towards Britain as the diasporic community grew. This 'moral transition', as she coins it, was for Pakistani migrants a signifier of a symbolic claim for permanency in their diasporic home, a claim which, however, did not exclude a continual material and socio-religious investment in Pakistan, based on transnational networks of reciprocity linking migrants to their kinship groups and communities in the homeland. Likewise, among Congolese these linkages with the homeland – especially flows of remittances and gifts (see Chapter 5) – may take on new meanings as relationships are reassessed in the context of changing economic dynamics and according to the evolution of domestic life cycle in the UK. And because '[Pakistani] migrants must reconstitute crucial moral categories of the person' (Werbner 1990: 151), the way they re-enacted their ritual universe in the UK made legible the new diasporic horizon that they had to navigate, shaped by what is seen as permissive and morally uncertain urban life where relationships are more segmented and migrants spatially dispersed.

Applied to the case of Congolese migration, this idea of 'moral transition' encourages us to think about the role spiritual infrastructures plays in the (re)construction of a moral order, in the new social context of arrival and, gradually, settlement. There are clear differences between Congolese Christians and Pakistani Muslims, for whom, as Werbner suggests, the performance of gift-giving is more encompassing and centrally connected to essential questions of honour, religious respectability, spiritual blessings, reciprocity and (gendered) moral personhood at various scales (family, lineage, caste/*zat* village grouping or regionally based networks). While for Pakistanis and Congolese alike religious home-making is seen as essential to the (re)production of a moral order among spatially dispersed migrants, the impact of Pentecostal Christian discourses of rupture with ancestrality as well as the stress on individual spiritual empowerment and on the nuclear family ideal have led many Congolese to reinterpret their 'moral' obligations to members of their extended kinship groups. Moreover, the grammar of rupture and redemption (as a matrix of remoralization), which has become central as the 'sins', excess and occult economies of the Mobutu regime were publicly exposed (and confessed), has taken on an additional meaning in the London context.

As evoked in the previous chapter, London was infamous in the late 1980s and 1990s among Congolese globally as a hub of *mayuya* ('scheming'), where *argent facile* ('easy money') could be accumulated through what was known as 'les co-ops', for example, cheque or benefit fraud (see Tipo-Tipo 1995, Trapido 2017). Many of those involved in *mayuya*, mostly young men (known as *mikilistes*), sustained a quasi-potlach economy of excess and ostentation, distributing cash, buying expensive clothes or luxury cars and displaying their wealth during highly 'performed' visits – *descentes* – in Kinshasa. A lot of the *mayuya* money was also invested in *mabanga*, the financial patronage of famous Congolese musicians and artists, who would then 'sing the names' of generous donators/patrons, the latter enhancing their prestige and status across the diaspora but also back in the DRC (see Trapido 2017). While *mabanga* and the *mikiliste* economy of ostentation contributed to the reputation of London as a fascinating place of riches in the eyes of *Kinois*, a specific imaginary developed in various circles (from churches to popular culture, music and TV drama), connecting London-based *mikilistes* to the power of occult economies ('invisible' and rapid accumulation of wealth is almost always synonymous with witchcraft) and to a universe of immorality and sins mostly because of the association of 'worldly music' to drug/alcohol use, sexual promiscuity and suggestive dancing.

The heyday of this *mikiliste* economy among Congolese in Europe coincided with the emergence of the powerful Pentecostal *réveil* in Kinshasa, which also impacted the nascent diasporic community. Papa T., who was a posted diplomat and one of the early Congolese in London, evokes how in the 1980s, after a calling to become a *berger* ('shepherd'), he started a prayer group to 'spiritually guide' Congolese migrants and asylum seekers, including those involved in the *mayuya* economy:

> As Christians, my family and I prayed at home [in London], and little by little the group grew, with friends and friends of friends. Congolese arriving here, it was easy for them, straight away they could get a house, *allocations sociales* [benefits]. Some with several houses claiming many times. As a diplomat, my colleagues told me not to bother with them – but they too needed a fellowship. Even if they seek asylum, they need a place where they can get together and pray in their language. We ended up renting a hall, and I ended up leading the group after we found out that the [Congolese] pastor who had come from France to be our *berger* had a polygamous wife and he knew it, and ignored it. We thought it was not normal to have such a *berger* because it was a time of repentance. A lot of Congolese in London at the time were involved in many things, the mafia of *mayuya*. I was talking and preaching to them this spirit of repentance. It was very hard at the start because of the age difference, my experience, which was different from theirs. We wanted to help them, so that they would unburden themselves from the weight of sins. They continued the *mayuya* but these teachings did start to have an impact [. . .] Many went through their repentance after they got arrested, some were sent to prison. [. . .] In Kinshasa, music introduced more debauchery [*débauche*], Papa Wemba, Les Enfants de Molokai, La Sape, all the youngsters wanted to follow this, all this delinquency, that led to what we have today with the *kulunas* [street youngsters/petty criminals in Kinshasa]. The *réveil* changed things – sorcerers began to give up their fetishes, prostitutes stopping prostitution, accepting Jesus in their heart. But *la débauche* entered the community here also with music.

The *mayuya* economy gradually declined throughout the 1990s and early 2000s with arrests and criminal convictions in a context of tighter bureaucratic and immigration controls (and more sophisticated technology of identity checks). At the same time, Congolese musicians and artists became increasingly criticized and started to be boycotted by opposition activists in the Congolese diaspora – among them former *mikilistes* who saw them as complicit to the post-Mobutu Kabila regime (see Chapter 4). The moral transition spearheaded in diaspora by pastors and religious actors like Papa T. reoriented the gift economy towards the religious sphere, as popular culture became increasingly 'Pentecostalized', with the emergence of Christian/Charismatic music genre, media and drama groups in the Congo (Pype 2012).

During the same period, among Kimbanguists in London, there were similar concerns about the attraction of *mayuya* 'easy money' and the moral risks of a new urban life for young migrants and asylum seekers. Here again, the most 'senior' religious actors (most only a few years older but with more ecclesial authority gained in the Congo) felt they had the responsibility to 'provide a frame' (*un encadrement*) for those newly arrived, to guide them morally and spiritually, and to reinforce a Kimbanguist life ethic. As mentioned earlier, this moral transition also coincided with the *milimo* phenomenon – also known as *manifestations spirituelles* – which occurred among a group of female worshippers possessed by the spirits (*milimo*) of Kimbangu's sons. We see again the polyvalence of spiritual infrastructures: they provide protection against immoral forms of accumulation and excess, some of them operating through migrant networks, while at the same time disciplining the self, generating pious and productive migrants, as well as solidifying hierarchies in the religious field.

Spirit possession has sometimes been analysed as form of meta-narration of experienced social and cultural transformations (Giles 1995, Sharp 1995, Wilkens 2020), and in that sense, the coming of the *milimo* could be seen as a way to dramatize, to 'emplot' the socio-cultural changes and challenges associated with the migration experience. Many London Kimbanguists I spoke to indicated that the *milimo*'s messages were indeed providing a way to both narrate and negotiate the sense of loss and the 'cultural shock of migration' which, according to Pastor G., contributed directly to a 'lack of respect' for the Kimbanguist doctrine and the church hierarchy:

> There was not enough respect for the Kimbanguist doctrine. There were tensions between people, problems. So, in some ways the *milimo* came to help us. . . . The church was a way for some people to show that they had money, because there was easy money [*argent facile*] at that time! *Chekoula* [cheque fraud] and *booku* [benefit fraud]. . . . So these young people were accumulating money, there was no respect. . . . So the *milimo* came in this context, it was to help us, within the church. . . . The spirit of Papa Simon Kimbangu came, to put some order in the church.

Here again, *mayuya* activities are described as a source of immoral behaviours and disorder in the church – a space losing its sacredness as it is turned into a stage to display the 'easy money' accumulated through petty crime and fraud. According to this particular interpretation of the *manifestations spirituelles*, the *milimo* were divine agents of spiritual and social control with the mission of reviving the faith and the obedience to a strict and 'authentic' Kimbanguist code of conduct (*mibeko*). The *milimo* were 'helping' the moral transition, the reterritorialization of a Kimbanguist ethos and order, while providing a commentary on the morally dangerous and tempting context of migration (see Garbin 2011). While for Pentecostals, the remoralization of the early diasporic community foregrounded the powerful tropes of repentance and redemption, in the wake of the collapse of the Mobutu Zairean state and its 'sinful' elites, for London-based Kimbanguists, the spirits of the 'Papas' were enabling a sense of ancestral 'home' as well as providing hope for the future and divine protection in times of uncertainty resulting from the 'in-betweeness' of the condition of migrants in Britain.

'Integration' and citizenship: Modes of incorporation

Spiritual infrastructures have differential impacts in terms of integration, as more established migrant actors, including pastors, construct narratives that justify their socio-economic success. Through the institutions they lead, they disseminate these narratives among those more recently arrived, setting and modelling the proper behaviours and attitudes that need to be followed to be incorporated into the host societies. In the United States, for example, discourses on citizenship and professional/educational aspirations are part and parcel of a particular stance on 'integration' recurrent in Pentecostal migrant congregations. As shown by Vásquez and Marquardt (2003) in their study of Latino churches in Atlanta, and Sheringham (2013) in her work on Brazilians in London, the fact that migrant Protestant/Pentecostal congregations maintain or develop transnational connections with a range of overlapping social spaces does not exclude a focus on incorporation in the civic sphere of host societies. There is of course a well-established literature on the role played by religious institutions in facilitating migrants' adaptation, starting in particular with Will Herberg's (1955) classic study on American immigrant religion *Protestant, Catholic, Jew*, which more recent works have tried to critically reassess, accounting for the evolution of religious pluralism, differentiated levels of religiosity (Hirschman 2004) or religious forms of cosmopolitanism (see Karagiannis and Glick Schiller 2006, Levitt 2008). Taking into consideration the multiscalar, hybrid engagement of Latino religious communities in Atlanta, Vásquez and Marquardt (2003: 170) describe a quest for incorporation reflecting a desire to make a place for oneself 'at the multicultural table', a particular form of citizenship and participation, which I found to be sometimes inflected with values intrinsic to a Weberian Puritan ethos, for instance, self-discipline, control and frugality.

These discourses can make apparent dynamics of distinction among Congolese, between, on the one hand, those who have 'made the right choices' and 'have more education, a better vision for their self-development', and those, on the other hand, who have chosen the path of 'short-termism', as one pastor put it. This distinction often coincided with class and educational differences (but not always) and served to draw a boundary, for instance, between those who had managed to be socially mobile and joined the Atlantan Black middle class and those who were stuck in the 'black hole' of lower paid jobs and multiple loans so 'that they can rent large houses and buy big cars to show off', as one Congolese interviewee (MBA-educated with a good position in a multinational company) told me when discussing '[Congolese] asylum seekers and refugees who just come here and work' as he put it. These types of differentiating discourses were more prevalent in the US diasporic context, which is more heterogeneous and divided along class, ethnic and educational lines than the Congolese diasporic UK context. Oftentimes, church leaders or established members provide advice to newcomers, encouraging them to adopt an attitude that is both virtuous and productive, more in tune with a Christian/Pentecostal discipline and what they see as the right behaviour to espouse in order 'to get ahead' in American society as this senior member of an Atlanta-based Congolese Pentecostal church remarked:

> Our pastor, when people come he says: 'if you are going to come to this country, you need to learn how to speak English, you need to go to English school – there are free programs, you can't just sit at home talk Lingala all day . . . and then you speak a broken English'. . . . Because like that you are not going to get ahead. . . . People coming here, refugees coming here, quickly finding work, with a short-term vision. Once you are getting into that working mode you get sucked into that system, then it's hard to get out. . . . When people come, I start advising them: 'don't worry about getting a job right now, first learn English, take six months, learn English. After you have learned English then you can go and get a job or if you get a job just get something part-time while you are really focusing on learning English'. Because they are a lot of jobs here where you can work without really speaking English, like working in chicken farms or the farmers' markets. . . . These kinds of places. This is what we are stressing now. And we are finding that a lot of people, those who came here in the last three years, some of them are going to school for nursing, and other things. I think it is because we started reorienting them in a different direction . . . focusing on yourself, developing yourself first – instead of getting into jobs full-time and overtime because once you get into that you will never have time to go to class and learn English.

While the support provided to 'reorient' newcomers reflects a focus on advancement, self-development and training (complemented by a stress on higher education for US-born generations), other pastors linked acquiring citizenship to a greater participation in US society.

It was the case of Pastor M. who talked about a campaign with external – religious and non-religious – actors aimed at encouraging church members to apply for US citizenship, to become citizens with 'a voice' rather than just wage earners with a Green Card:

> The Green Card is nothing in the US. . . . In my church, I started three years ago, a campaign on that. Congolese, because they were earning dollars, they think it's enough with the Green Card, they never thought of getting American citizenship. So, I work there with the Catholics and other NGOs that are helping people to get some stability in this country so we are working on that sense. We have helped more than 10 people to become American, when you are American you can say things . . . you have a voice, for instance in the domain of racism and all that.

In the UK context, British identity and Britishness can be articulated as political claims among young, second-generation Congolese, as we shall see in Chapter 4. However, and in contrast with the US context, there was no equivalent emphasis on the political or civic significance/advantages of acquiring (British) citizenship for newcomers – a least in the discourses of pastors or religious leaders. As Adogame (2013: 135–8) remarks, questions of citizenship and nationality are contingent, complex and contested, often overlapping with issues of moral legitimacy and shaped by religious tropes of home, exile and return. Dynamics of belonging linked to notion(s) of citizenship are themselves inflected by specific collective/historical trajectories and positionalities in differentiated national contexts. For instance, Fumanti (2010, 2017) has documented the importance, in the spiritual infrastructures of Ghanaian Methodists in London, of the notion of 'virtuous citizenship' encompassing religious and community participation (including transnational community engagement) and informed by both Protestant Christian ethics and Akan 'cultural values' of compassion and empathy (ɔtema). In addition, their membership of the British Methodist church repositions London-based Ghanaian Methodists within a larger postcolonial time-space, allowing them to claim a legitimate presence against a societal context of precarity and suspicion. In other words, this multi-layered, alternative form of citizenship becomes a symbolic resource for Ghanaian Methodists, regardless of the 'legality' of their formal (immigration) status, and in spite of the disempowering impact of bureaucratic regimes of citizenship. This virtuous citizenship helps them to 'reconfigure their presence in Britain beyond official discourses on multiculturalism and migration' (Fumanti 2017: 508). Here, religious citizenship does not contradict or supersede the one regulated by the state. Rather, it embeds the host nation in its global colonial history, offering an alternative, expanded notion of belonging in the metropolis.

Parallels can be drawn here with the Kimbanguists, for whom the ideal of an 'exemplary' ethos and code of conduct is mobilized as a symbolic resource to claim moral legitimacy. While Kimbanguists draw on a Kongo ancestrality and locate their more recent collective history within a Belgian (post-)colonial space, those in London often stress a historical connection with Britain through the British-led Baptist Missionary Society, where Simon Kimbangu was educated. But Kimbanguists' understanding of their role and place in Britain is also shaped by powerful prophetic tropes of return articulated with the centripetal dimension of Kimbanguist territoriality revolving around Nkamba. For many London-based Kimbanguists, the 'security' of future salvation in the holy city was contrasted with the insecurity experienced at the margin of the 'host society' in the West, where citizenship for Black/African migrants and minorities is seen as increasingly precarious and unstable:

> Our spiritual leader told us we need to get ready to return to Africa, we need to invest, send money. We need to build our house in Nkamba. There are clear signs. *Mama na likambo* ['the mother of all things'], the real thing is coming. . . . Black people killed every day in the US, xenophobia and racism here, wars, Brexit. One day you are a citizen, the next day you can be deported. All the signs are there. . . . Also Europe is declining, weakening, Africa is growing, and will catch up very soon. (Papa M. Kimbanguist, male, forty-five, from London)

Other interlocutors in the Kimbanguist church and among Catholics and Pentecostals echoed Papa M.'s view that (in the British context) citizenship was increasingly exclusive and restrictive – a view even shared by several second-/third-generation individuals 'British born and raised' who were aware of the limitations that being Black and of African descent impose on their rights as citizens (Garbin and Millington 2018).[5] In a context where practices of securitization and rebordering rely heavily on the postcolonial governance of the Other through tighter immigration regimes and restrictive citizenship (Byrne 2014, Prabhat 2018, Tyler 2013), emotional attachment to Britishness was indeed limited. Instead, a more instrumental view was often put forward revolving around the affordances and advantages of citizenship and formal status (in terms of largely unrestricted travel, for instance) (see Imoagene 2017 for similar findings among the UK-based Nigerian diaspora). However, in particular contexts Britishness can also be articulated to a series of claims, for instance, regarding the political situation in the Congo and the role of the UK in sustaining the conflict in the eastern region through its support to Rwanda, as we shall see in Chapter 4.

While views about the place of minorities in multicultural Britain/London are often shaped by perceptions or experiences of life in French and Belgian societies (often deemed to be 'more racist', see Trapido 2017: 142), there is a strong rejection of 'cultural' elements seen as inherent in British/Western society. These included not only practices considered immoral or opposed to Christian values – drinking, drug use, sexual promiscuity, homosexuality or abortion – but also attitudes towards disciplining children seen as disempowering parents. Maier (2011) notes similar trends in her ethnography of the Redeemed Christian Church of God (RCCG) in London and Lagos (see also Coleman and Maier 2013 and Maguire and Murphy 2012 on Nigerians in Ireland). She describes how Nigerian Pentecostal regimes of child discipline and education are seen at odds with British (state) attitudes deemed lax and restrictive, creating clear frictions in the eyes of Pentecostals concerned about 'rais[ing] their children primarily as citizens of the "Kingdom of God"' (2011: 166) in a context of suspicion of child abuse and maltreatment, stigmatizing UK-based African religious communities. During my research, I did come across several cases of parents sending, or considering sending, their children (especially in their teenage years) back to the Congo, to an educational environment seen as stricter and morally superior. These parents – Kimbanguists and members of Combat Spirituel (Maman Olangi's church) – rely on the transnational infrastructure of these two churches and their networks of schools, which they consider an extension of both a wider religious 'family' and a moral community. However, among Congolese in diaspora, this practice seemed marginal overall. For them, the aim of socializing children into Christian values in diaspora can be best achieved through an 'emphasis on boundary-drawing around Christian familial and congregational space' (Coleman and Maier 2013: 466). At the same time, the landscape of the homeland is (also) morally ambiguous, if not negative, and the prestige of a reliable and recognized education in the West remains resilient and often constructed in opposition to the situation in the Congo, a context of heightened insecurity and dysfunctional infrastructures.

The spiritual infrastructures of diasporic religion are here made legible through the recreating of an encapsulated community around strong boundaries and values. This recreation emerges as a response to address the dilemma over children's moral socialization: it is essential to facilitate a moral transition in diaspora and carve up a protective space amidst a morally risky society – while at the same time anchoring a presence through place-making in order to 'conquer territories for God'.

Conclusion

This chapter has highlighted the significance of religion in the process of migration by focusing on the efficacious role of 'spiritual infrastructures' in, first, providing interpretative frames and creating social affordances for those engaged in cross-border journeys. Religious migrants negotiate powerful closure regimes arrayed against them and through these infrastructures they are able to mobilize spiritual energies and material resources to foster hope, provide orientation and protection and 'unblock' paths of socio-spatial mobility or progress. Perhaps more importantly, diasporic religious dynamics operate as meaning-making canopies, with mobility and immobility both interpreted against a repertoire of sacralized kinetic idioms linked to missionary tropes, moral mappings and/or exilic imaginaries.

We also saw that the spiritual infrastructures of diasporic religion facilitated a process of 'moral transition' and provided legitimacy to modalities of moral or religious citizenship in contexts of settlement. With the emergence of a second generation in the diaspora settings of the United States or Europe, the transmission of moral values (sometimes conflated with what is described as African/Congolese values) and the carving up of permanent protective spaces in the midst of a morally urban society take on vital importance. Just as during the earlier phase of settlement when 'moral transition' reoriented the gift economy of *mayuya* activities towards the religious sphere, the reconstitution of a moral order as part of strategies of incorporation also expresses desire for social and charismatic control. Spiritual infrastructures, thus, play multiple and even contradictory roles, offering resources for migrants to exert contesting agency, while, sometimes simultaneously, reproducing power asymmetries dominant in the countries of origin and settlement.

Strategies of incorporation, such as those described in this chapter, do not preclude the existence of religious transnationalism and the making of global religious publics fostering circulation and mobility (see also Chapters 4 and 5). Moreover, with the Kimbanguist example, we discussed the central role of the trope of return against the increasing ambivalence of dominant modes of citizenship, suggesting the impact of exclusionary dynamics, in particular for those 'born and bred' abroad, in *Poto*. The reterritorialization of migrant faith is, consequently, shaped by a multitude of forces operating at different scales, a process which I will examine further in the next chapter on urban place-making in cityscapes of the Congolese diaspora.

3

Modalities of presence

Territorializing and performing diasporic religion

What is the role of religion in the making of urban diasporic environments? What kinds of modes of belonging and positionalities are enacted through performances of religious presence? While the previous chapter mostly dealt with the individual experience of mobility and the affordances of spiritual infrastructures for migration, incorporation and meaning-making, this chapter focuses on the 'regrounding' of the sacred through collective dynamics of territorialization. Traditionally, the notion of territory has been closely attached to the emergence and politics of nation-state sovereignty (Elden 2013, Moore 2015) and seen as part and parcel of the 'methodological nationalism' that has dominated the social sciences (Wimmer and Glick Schiller 2003). As I discuss in the next chapter, the idea of the nation continues to play a central role in migrants' geo-theologies, as demonstrated by widespread politico-religious tropes of sacred national exceptionalism, redemption and liberation. However, here I understand territory in a non-reductive way, one in which the processes of place-making are not univocally shaped and circumscribed by the nation-state as a monolithic unit. I see religious territorialization as an assemblage of attitudes, practices and strategies enabling the production of religious spatialities that allow diasporic actors to position themselves at multiple scales. These spatialities reveal particular *modalities of presence*, which not only operate through spatial appropriation and place-making, for instance linked to the 'anchoring' of places of worship, but are also expressed through other – interconnected – locative or translocative forms of territorialization. This multiscalar deployment is far from being static: territories are made and remade through movement and flows, opening up the question of 'kinetic visibility', for instance, in the case of pilgrimage or urban processions.

The spiritual infrastructures described in the previous chapter operate as conduits and frameworks of mobility, orientation and reorientation. They allow for the mapping and remapping of individual trajectories, as well as for moral governance and spiritual warfare, while creating a horizon of possibilities. The dynamics of religious territorialization are connected to the making of these cartographies and paths. At the same time, they point to the (re)location and performance of the sacred. Yet, the 'sacred' – as a category of spatialized action and as a mode of relationality – is produced through an engagement with what is seen as a deeply ambiguous urban reality, rendering the collective act of sacralization itself multivocal and laden with ambivalence. When African churches convert warehouses or office buildings within anonymous peripheral areas, when they play God-given, 'inspired', music while parading in the immoral global city or when they establish 'churches without walls' (to quote KICC's media strategy) within an already saturated mediascape, they deploy modalities of presence, which often play on the ambivalence between visibility and invisibility, also suggesting, particularly in the case of 'spirit-oriented' Christianities, a creative and powerful capacity to bridge material and immaterial. Global cities like London or Atlanta are sites where forces of secularization and desecularization converge in intense but uneven ways (see Stevenson et al. 2010, Eade 2012), and as they are (partly) 'territorialized' by diasporic religious groups such as Congolese Christians, they become privileged terrains for those documenting the complex, 'infrasecular' reality of urban religion (della Dora 2016) – landscapes where secular/religious boundaries are at times reinforced, and, at other times, rendered porous.

This chapter will engage with these complex and shifting dimensions of religious territorialization, revealing the tensions between continuity and discontinuities in the ways in which diasporic religious actors relocate themselves in new environments. To do so, I will be drawing upon an analysis of modalities of presence through which boundaries between religious and secular, visibility and invisibility, flow and stasis, permanence and transience are negotiated among Congolese Christians in diaspora. Before focusing on these various forms of place-making – through places of worship, home spaces, processions or religious mediascapes – I would like first to discuss the moral geographies and religious maps produced in a collective quest for urban presence.

Urban space, expansion and sacred 'mapping'

While in the previous chapter we saw how individual religious actors and pastors may mobilize missionizing tropes stressing a desire to 'take possession' and redeem immoral spaces, it is also clear that churches – as organized institutions – have explicit spatial strategies, which they see as part of the fulfilment of the 'Great Commission' of the Apostles 'to go and make disciples of all nations' in the name of Jesus (Mt. 28:18-20). For instance, in its much-cited mission statement the Nigeria-headquartered Redeemed Christian Church of God (RCCG) describes the duty to 'plant churches within five minutes walking distance in every city and town of developing countries and within five minutes driving distance in every city and town of developed countries' (cited by Knibbe 2009: 143, see also Coleman and Vásquez 2015: 38). For a large international church like the RCCG, this grammar of mapping relies on an 'extraordinary temporal and spatial grid' (Coleman and Vásquez 2015: 38) that is eminently multiscalar. This 'grid' allows the church to transcend the local and establish linkages among far-flung diasporic congregations, fulfilling its global vision for expansion and inscribing a 'celestial' horizon of redemption and salvation. The mapping contained in this spatial strategy not only bridges the local, the global and the ethereal but also offers an image of the future while providing a sense of territorial control and ownership (Coleman 2010: 199).

The Kingsway International Christian Centre (KICC), the church I attended during the early stage of fieldwork in London, has also produced an explicit discourse hinging on religious mapping and territorial expansion. Like the RCCG, the idioms of expansion, evangelization and conquest are salient in the KICC grammar of mapping – this is well illustrated by one of the mottos of the church, 'raising champions, taking territories'. Some Congolese (and non-Congolese) KICC members I spoke to referred to the growing number of branches and 'chapels' in London and other major UK urban centres as a clear sign that 'the Spirit was on their side' and was 'working for them'. Some also stressed with pride how, unlike many African-led churches, the KICC has purchased a large piece of land, mortgage-free, where the 'Miracle Centre', the headquarters of the church, was established, in a former industrial building. The Miracle Centre, with its auditorium and multi-function rooms, represented the 'largest church to be created in the UK since the start of Christianity' according to the KICC's website[1] before the church was obliged to relocate in 2007 because the site fell within the London 2012 Olympics redevelopment zone. The KICC then moved to a former cinema in Walthamstow, renamed 'Land of Wonders', and, a few years later in 2012, acquired (also mortgage-free) a 24-acre, partly run-down, former Scout sporting complex, with numerous buildings, near Chatham in Kent, 40 miles outside of London (Cartledge et al. 2019: 192–3). The site was opened and dedicated in 2014 by the General Overseer of the RCCG, Pastor Enoch Adeboye, suggesting the importance of diasporic urban nodes and of mutual recognition within the fragmented and competitive Pentecostal field, where distinction and specialization play a key role (Katsaura 2019). Renamed 'Prayer City', it now comprises offices, multi-purpose buildings, an outdoor children's play area and a large hall ('Prayer Palace', which used to be the largest sports hall of the whole complex) with the capacity to accommodate thousands of worshippers at once. Located a stone's throw from the M2 motorway and accessible mostly by private cars or the church's free shuttle buses, Prayer City is akin to US megachurches, 'sacred archipelagos' of the American post-secular exurban landscape (Wilford 2012). The site also evokes the huge Nigerian Pentecostal enclave 'prayer camps' in suburban Lagos and which, as we shall discuss in Chapter 7, are reimagined as religious 'alter-cities'– models of moral order and infrastructural autonomy defined in opposition to the morally risky and dysfunctional megacity.

In other Congolese Pentecostal churches in the United Kingdom and the United States, the theme of spatial expansion – even at a smaller scale – was discursively used in preaching (and in my discussions with church members and leaders) to comment upon a successful trajectory, seen as a divinely sanctioned collective effort to establish a local 'sanctuary', to borrow the expression used by the pastor of the Combat Spirituel church in Atlanta. As I showed in the previous chapter, the idea of sanctuary suggests how the place of worship can represent a refuge, a place of solidarity and community – a new 'family in Christ' – in the new and often difficult context of settlement, where many have to work several jobs and struggle to regularize their immigration status (and may live in fear of deportation, especially in the United States). Moreover, in these narratives, the future possibility of acquiring – not renting – a larger building resonates with a collective quest for stability, security and autonomy. Here again, mapping, projecting and envisioning a horizon of evangelization link the local territorialization to a global sense of mission.

Resisting immoral urbanity

The diasporic space within which church development, expansion and 'planting' occur is not a neutral backdrop to religious territorialization and religious life in general. London and Atlanta, and by extension British and American societies, are charged with meanings and constitute discursive realities within a wider moral cartography. One of its key components is the perceived 'spiritual chaos' of Western societies caused by practices considered immoral or opposed to

Christian values. Permissiveness and moral insecurity are particularly palpable in city environments – as a Kimbanguist youth leader once said to me: 'London, especially for youngsters, can be a black hole within which you can easily lose yourself.' Scholars of contemporary urban religion, such as Burchardt (2017), Kirby (2017) and Maguire and Murphy (2012), have documented this view of cityscapes as ambivalent sites – sites of opportunity, progress and potential success (in particular for migrants) but also of moral danger, uncertainty, temptation and vigilance.

While religious groups, such as African churches, are fearful of the immoralities of certain forms of urban living, they are not typically threatened or made vulnerable by the urban per se. In fact, some African churches may be playing or aspiring to play influential roles in cities through community participation or civic engagement (Cartledge et al. 2019, DeHanas 2016, Levitt 2008). In African context, as we shall see later in this book, religious actors are eager to promote their own ethical and moral motivations for urban activism, in addition to providing basic urban utilities – housing, health and educational facilities, as the case in megacity Kinshasa, where the state is seen as unable to fulfil its duty of welfare, care and development.

In host societies the more prominent African-led churches are keen to be involved in charitable projects or develop external networks, as a way to re-enact some of the prestige they enjoy in the homeland (Adogame 2013: 192). Nevertheless, not all African churches engage or are able to engage with external communities. While churches such as KICC or the RCCG are involved in charity work, fundraising and local outreach (also understood as part of evangelizing efforts, see Burgess 2009, Cartledge et al. 2019: 202–95), the situation is different for Congolese churches. Smaller and lacking the symbolic capital and the networked structure of large, 'Black majority' churches, Congolese churches have very limited engagement with their immediate urban environment and in general with non-African, non-Christian communities.

Yet, for both large and smaller diasporic African Christian communities, their moral judgements about the experience and potentialities of city life reveal a deeply polysemic and ambivalent urban space. In this regard, the UK and US urban contexts share common features but differ in certain respects. For instance, among Congolese in Atlanta, religious territorialization is inscribed with particular forms of post-secular religiosity through the presence of 'megachurches'. Internationally known churches, such as Creflo Dollar Ministries or Eddie Long's New Birth Ministry, are striking features of the religious cartography of the suburban 'New South' within which they constitute impressive spatial statements. These congregations, with their 'polynucleated' socio-spatial configurations, are perfectly attuned to the fragmented, centreless and differentiated ecology of the American 'post-suburbia' (Wilford 2012). Through their multi-functionality, the use of practices and media common in 'profane' popular culture, these megachurches blur the boundaries between the secular and the religious and provide an attractive hybrid and re-enchanting territoriality for busy suburbanites.[2]

In the narratives of some of the Congolese I interviewed in Atlanta, the presence of these megachurches, their visibility and the (symbolic and physical) 'space' they occupy are powerful signs of the key role played by religion in the American society, the *mboka ya Bible*, the 'land of the Bible', as one Maman Olangi member put it. However, for others, this 'suburban Christianity' (Hsu 2006) associated with megachurches reflected a *chrétien du dimanche*-attitude ('being Christian only on Sundays') that echoed an excessive secular encroachment of a business ethic onto the religious sphere. *Le vrai Dieu ici c'est l'argent*, 'the true God here is money', as an Atlantan Kimbanguist remarked when we discussed the presence of bank facilities and ATMs in some Atlanta megachurches.

In both London and Atlanta, the making of particular spiritual cartographies was also integral to the ways in which Congolese Christians 'situated' themselves in diasporic context. In addition to an emphasis on the 'moral decline' associated with gender and sexual politics, this type of (re)mapping included the presence of 'travelling spirits' (Huwelmeier and Krause 2011) believed to have followed migrants coming from Asia or Africa, and more generally the covert influence of 'occult economies' (Comaroff and Comaroff 1999) and secret societies (Illuminati, Freemasonry, Rosicrucianism). Because of the ubiquity of evil forces, permanent vigilance is thus required, even in the 'land of the Bible', although at times, like during the celebrations of Halloween, specific spiritual protective practices are intensely needed.

The evil wind of Halloween

Halloween celebrations are here worthy of discussion insofar as they reveal religious attitudes to the consumerism of 'occult themes' as part of a wider moral geography but also since they tend to be important social and community/family events. They raise a number of questions about belonging and (the limits) of 'integration' in particular host society contexts (Maguire and Murphy 2012). Halloween celebrations, iconic of American culture, are very visible in the (sub)urban fabric of Atlanta (and it seems, starting earlier than in the UK), with elaborated displays already noticeable from the first week of October in many houses and gardens of 'subdivision' neighbourhoods where Congolese reside. During that time, a pastor's sermon heard in a small Congolese Pentecostal in Atlanta criticized the consumerism associated with the 'Halloween season', a celebration, which for him is 'mixing the living and the dead' and distracting from celebrating Jesus 'who had died for us but now living among us through the Holy Spirit'. Unsurprisingly, both in the United Kingdom and the United States, several Congolese parents I spoke to mentioned having their children opt out of Halloween school events, especially when involving costumes or activities associated with witchcraft, ghosts and so on. Decorating the house and the distribution of sweets are also out of the question – 'it would be like opening the door of your home for the Devil to enter', as a Kimbanguist put it. In addition, many churches seek to provide an alternative space to combat what is seen as the iconography of a 'demonic tradition' through the organization of prayer events or night vigils. It was the case, for instance, of the Maman Olangi church, for which the trope of a spiritual warfare was particularly heightened during the period of Halloween. The celebrations were described by its Atlanta pastor as an 'evil wind' blowing across the cityscape, particularly targeting children and youth, in need of spiritual protection – through intense prayers, retreats and fasting:

> In this city [Atlanta], we organize retreats and intense prayers to fight the Devil, present around us, for example during Halloween. There is an evil wind, which blows on that day, the day of Halloween, so we need to protect our children. Things . . . and people get sacrificed for the Devil. In Europe, even if people are atheist, they don't follow the Devil openly like here during Halloween. But when you do it openly. . . . As the Bible says: 'on the last day I will spread my Spirit everywhere. Your children will prophesy, old people will have dreams'. But the Devil also says that on the last day, children will become evil . . . and this is what happens. How many people are using drugs in this city? People killing each other. This is the work of the Devil. The Devil uses youth in this city. On the other hand, God also uses young people. It is a fight, it is a spiritual fight. (Interview with Maman Olangi church pastor, Atlanta)

In their ethnography of African diasporas in Ireland, Maguire and Murphy (2012) also report the organization of this type of church event – in particular 'Hallelujah Night' on the night of Halloween. Similarly, Kirby (2017) describes Halloween night vigils organized by African Pentecostals in Hong Kong to mobilize the 'armies of God', as part of a wider 'aspirational project of urban critique and regeneration' (2017: 76). The 'programmatic born-again vision', a mode of governmentality and social control at different scales discussed by Marshall (2009), is here integral to discourses produced by African Christians about space, especially urban space, and in this context, the project of 'recharismatization' is often seen as a quest to 'redeem cityscapes' (Coleman and Maier 2013). This quest reveals the need to control (and purify) morally transgressive and spiritually dangerous urban environments through the production of a 'disciplinary cartography' (Orsi 1999: 53) which can be shaped by particular temporalities, like Halloween.

We see again the moral ambivalence of the city: African Christians, equipped with the conviction that the Holy Spirit will allow them to prosper in health and wealth, may see London or Atlanta as sites of potential progress, interconnections, opportunities and 'social catapulting' (Van Dijk 2010). However, the global city is also construed as the quintessential site of spiritual warfare, a battleground between divine and demonic forces. Creating alternative spaces to mobilize spiritual energies during Halloween involves creating some distance (rather, perhaps, than a direct confrontation) with a perceived secular host society, a practice Congolese may share with other non-African evangelicals/Pentecostals. In suburban Atlanta, large evangelical churches organize 'Trunk or Treat' alternative celebrations that take place within the enclosed, protective and safe space of the church parking lot where children and families can walk from car to car to collect sweets and small gifts from the opened decorated trunks/boots. However, most Congolese I talked to were not aware of the practice and/or rejected it outright as another sign that American-based Christianity was excessively accommodating to the forces of secularity.

Resistance to the 'evil wind' of satanic forces associated with Halloween could be seen as part of what Coleman (2019) calls an 'ideological encompassment'. For Coleman, while this process points to the 'continued salience of [West] African categories of evil powers', it also indicates the importance of 'asserting a moral claim over newly occupied social, cultural, and religious environments' (2019: 115). Not unlike the 'virtuous citizenship' discussed in the previous chapter, this moral claim becomes a symbolic resource to assert some superiority in the context of a lack of recognition; and expressed through prayers and rituals, it empowers believers to act as full-fledged participants of the urban reality within which they are emplaced. These 'alternative forms of Christianized citizenship' (Coleman 2019: 127) are especially important to consider when sacred place-making often occurs at the socio-spatial (and symbolic) margins of the (global) city.

Precarious place-making? Spatial conversion at the margins of the 'global city'

While expansionist visions through church planting and the construction of large structures are central to the territorial strategy of African churches, many of them understate their presence in the urban or suburban landscapes of multicultural cities like London, Atlanta, Paris, Berlin or Brussels. In other words, they show 'a complete lack of visual authority' (Dilger, Kasmani and Mattes 2018: 97). These churches often occupy former warehouses, shops, offices, workshops, garages and railway arches. Moreover, they are sometimes concentrated in specific portions of the cities, such as industrial districts or peripheral brownfield areas. For instance, one of the London parishes of the Kimbanguist church is located in Edmonton (Haringey, North London) in the midst of a bland landscape of garages, small factories and warehouses and dominated by an imposing Coca-Cola manufacturing plant. On Sunday, this industrial park turns into a thriving 'religious district' (McRoberts 2003) where dozens of churches, mostly African Pentecostal churches, rent or even sub-let vacant buildings such as garages and warehouses. On that day, the usual noise of industrial activity, trucks and delivery vans are replaced by another kind of sonic landscape, with the sounds of musical instruments, preaching, songs, praises and prayers, emanating from quasi-invisible places of worship. These elements of aural sacrality seem to be 'leaking' from the windows and walls of a myriad of these warehouse churches which sometimes betray their presence by modest external surfacing signs, posters or banners like above the door of the Kimbanguist church, where the Kimbanguist flag flutters. The sacred flag bearing the Kimbanguist symbols and colours indicates that the church, even if sandwiched between a Polish 'cash and carry' and a Turkish meat wholesaler, 'is a consecrated house of God' as the parish pastor told me. On Sundays, the Kimbanguist *ambiance* of brass band and choir songs and the collective effervescence and *communitas* of religious worship represent very directly a counter-story to the surrounding dull urban *milieu* at the periphery of the post-industrial global city.

The Kimbanguist church, the KICC (Francophone branch) and Maman Olangi in London as well in Atlanta are examples of African churches which have territorialized portions of the urban landscape through the occupation of existing, non-religious, buildings. In Atlanta, most Congolese churches I visited occupy former office or commercial units – like the Combat Spirituel church which rents a formerly vacant commercial space located in a small shopping plaza, bordering a very busy highway. In this post-secular suburban space, the church cohabits with other Pentecostal congregations, mainly Hispanic, since the surrounding area contains a large concentration of immigrants from Latin America. The other important Congolese Pentecostal church, the New Jerusalem Church, rents a building located in a suburban business park, also close to a major highway. The site is more spacious than the Atlanta-based average Congolese church and comprises several large rooms, with a warehouse turned into a worshipping space for Sunday services. At the time of fieldwork, the building was undergoing a foreclosure sale while the church was renting the property – its leaders hoping to secure a mortgage deal in order to make an offer on the building in the near future. The importance of the urban regime is salient here as this place-making strategy is embedded in the specific urban economy of the United States at a time of crisis in the real-estate sector, partly triggered by the sub-prime crash of 2006–8. The territorializing of the sacred in the midst of the spatial turmoil generated by this crisis involves a regrounding, a religious and moral reappropriation and repurposing of undifferentiated and devalued space that fills the voids created by urban change and economic decline. Anonymous and barren spaces now become particular places, anchors for meaningful and meaning-making activities, in a 'spatial fix' (Harvey 2001b) recurrent across the 'Pentecoscapes' of the Global North and the Global South (see Adeboye 2012, Krause 2008a).

While churches' spatial trajectories are diverse and shaped by a range of factors (including being part of a wider network like Combat Spirituel or RCCG, which can have an impact on the availability of capital), many Afro-Christian migrant churches follow a similar trajectory of growth (Dejean 2020), from home prayer cell to increasingly larger rented spaces and/or longer-term leases, before being able, in some cases, to purchase a dedicated building or site.

An over-emphasis on this linearity may conceal, however, the synchronicity of diverse spatial scenarios observable across a single denomination. To take the Kimbanguists as an example, one parish rents the main worshipping space of a United Reformed Church in East London, another parish organizes its services in a West London Methodist church, while the Edmonton parish occupies a former industrial/warehouse space, as already mentioned. Another parish occupies a small multi-use community hall on the Isle of Dogs (East London), which is also used for weddings or birthday parties and also by local Muslim worshippers for Friday prayers. This juxtaposition of uses within the same site points not only to the blurred boundary between religious and secular, sacred and profane but also to the religious super-diversity, the 'common place multiculturalism' (Wessendorf 2014) of East London's community landscape. Every Sunday afternoon, with the praying mats of the local Muslim worshippers stashed in a large cupboard and some paper glasses left in bins, betraying a party take took place the day before, Kimbanguists take possession of the space, without adding any material iconography apart perhaps from a green and white cloth (Kimbanguist sacred colours) put on the table used as a preaching pulpit on the room's small stage. The spatial appropriation occurs – like the case with other Afro-Christian groups – when they cleanse the room with the power of their prayers at the beginning of the service, but in contrast to Pentecostals, they invoke the ancestral, prophetic power of Kimbangu, embedding the community within a larger and deeper time-space.

The spatial trajectories of churches are also contingent on the evolution of urban regimes. In London, place-making is often interstitial, taking place within the gaps of the post-industrial city, with cases of transient occupation and use due to planned demolition and/or redevelopment. Churches may also have difficulties with rents (and thus may downsize or sub-let their spaces) and with planning/'change of use' permission, or they may experience conflicts with local residents, as it happened with KICC following the decision to relocate the church from its Hackney base, a site earmarked by the London Development Agency for the London 2012 Olympics, as mentioned earlier. In an interview on the US-based CBN channel (The Christian Broadcasting Network),[3] Pastor Ashimolowo, founder and leader of the church, commented on this move from Hackney to the converted Walthamstow cinema and on the tensions with local residents and planning authorities regarding the KICC's planned development in Havering, which eventually had to be abandoned:

> We were left high and dry to have to face the wrath of the community. When you have a church of our magnitude, with over 90 percent ethnic minority from about forty-six nations, the first thing that comes to the mind of the neighbourhood is 'Oh my God this large church coming to our neighbourhood!' . . . When the largest church . . . has its property taken from it and [is] made to operate from a small building, that is a form of persecution! KICC is the largest church in Western Europe, and I think that ought to have been celebrated, even though Britain is, in all facets, essentially post-Christian and church-unfriendly. . . . There is the United Kingdom which sent missionaries around the world, now they tore down the largest church building, to permit, just, next door, the largest mosque in Europe [the Tabligh Jamaat so called 'mega-mosque' which, in fact, had not been granted planning permission]. It just potentially makes you understand the magnitude of the spiritual warfare you are involved in and to also make you know that we are facing a clash of kingdoms in the realm of the

spirits and there has to be a change. Light will have to prevail somehow over darkness! (Pastor Ashimolowo, CBN interview)[4]

Pastor Ashimolowo's narrative of a multicultural church being 'persecuted' in a 'post-Christian and church-unfriendly' Britain was echoed by several Congolese KICC members I talked to and who, in addition, criticized the accusation of charity fraud made against Ashimolowo in the mainstream media. Some also argued that the difficulties encountered by the church and the pastor were linked to the influence of evil forces, which were blocking its expansion and therefore represented a powerful and, in fact, *positive* sign that the KICC was 'on the right path'.

In the interview, Ashimolowo also referred to the Tabligh Jamaat's controversial and highly contested plan to build a large mosque next to the Olympic site in Newham, explicitly linking the question of Islamic visibility and territoriality to the idea of 'spiritual warfare' – a 'clash of kingdoms in the realms of the spirit', as he put it. Although some of my respondents expressed anxiety over Islam 'gaining territories' in the West (and also in Africa), other Congolese Christians emphasized how Muslims in Britain were an example to follow, for instance, regarding education and transmission of a religious ethos to second- and third-generation youth through the visible establishment of mosques and Islamic schools.

While much smaller in scale and in terms of political/media exposure, disputes involving Black minority churches have also received some level of public attention in the UK context. For instance, the occupation of a semi-derelict portion of Lawrence Road in Haringey, North London, by several Black-led Pentecostal congregations (including a branch of the RCCG) met with opposition from residents and local authorities. Here, two visions of 'regeneration' came together in confrontation. While church representatives stressed the idea of moral renewal – churches have 'brought life' and stopped 'vandalism and prostitution' – local residents and some local authority officials complained about littering, noise and nocturnal 'bright lights' and developed a vision of urban regeneration more in tune with residential concerns.[5]

Since the creation of their first *paroisse* in the early 1990s, London Kimbanguists have also experienced an unstable territorial trajectory. This instability was caused mostly by internal conflicts, but there have also been some disagreements with landlords (over time allocation, rent, building damages or cleanliness) and some level of external hostility, mainly tensions with neighbours and local authorities complaining over the loud music of the church brass band. In Atlanta, Congolese Kimbanguists used to pray in a chapel within Morehouse

College, where Martin Luther King studied. However, as a result of tensions and a split within the congregation, and following a change of administration within the College, Kimbanguists stopped using the chapel and were left with no other options than to organize private services at the home of one of the leaders while looking for another venue.

Kimbanguists deplore the impact of these internal conflicts, but they also link this fragmented experience of place and space, combined with a lack of visibility within the cityscape, to their minority status and, to some extent, to being a 'minority within a minority', as non-Anglophone Africans and with no historical colonial ties to the UK like Ghanaians and Nigerians. Interestingly, they also draw a parallel between the experience of precarious and relatively invisible place-making in diaspora and the early age of Kimbanguism, during colonial times, when the believers had to pray clandestinely and when access to Nkamba, the Holy City of Kimbanguism, was almost impossible. For some, investing in Nkamba should be the priority, while others, mostly second-generation, argue that a stronger base in Europe is not incompatible with the sacred duty of developing the holy city. In truth, Kimbanguist religious community life, including weekly *nsinsani* (money collection ritual) as well as choir and brass band rehearsals, requires space and thus some level of stability and certainty.

Marching for God: public religion as counter-narrative

Occupying a space, in peripheral and isolated areas can, however, offer some benefits. For instance, the Kimbanguists who worship in the remote industrial park in Edmonton (North London) underscored the advantages of such a spatial location, often mentioning the issue of music associated with their brass band, known as 'Fanfare Kimbanguiste' or FAKI. Indeed, religious music entails a spatial boundary-crossing, which can, in turn, result in tensions within what de Witte (2008) calls the sphere of 'sonic politics' of religion and public space. For Kimbanguists, brass band music represents a powerful way of 'glorifying God', away from residential areas where, as one pastor put it, 'white people don't like noise'.

The brass band plays a key part in Kimbanguist church services, and, given its role in early evangelization campaigns, it occupies a prestigious place in the Kimbanguist historiography and collective memory. For Kimbanguists, FAKI acts as a connector to the outside world. In the homeland, and increasingly in diaspora, the band regularly performs for a wide range of private, public and official events. Thus, French and Belgian Kimbanguist musicians have taken part in many local cultural festivals or events such as the *Fête de la Musique*, the annual music festival organized annually on the 21st June all over France. In the UK, British Kimbanguists have also participated in several cultural and public events, including the Black History Month in Woolwich and Islington, the Hackney Carnival, and in more traditional Congolese weddings or funerals (*matanga*). Since 2010, they have participated almost annually in the London New Year's parade (in 2020 because of Covid restrictions all performances were recorded in a studio and broadcast online), alongside international brass bands and cheerleader groups as well as Punjabi Dhol musicians, Samba troupes and Chinese drummers, showcasing the multicultural diversity of London.

For Kimbanguist brass band musicians, performing outside the church and making their presence felt in public space provide a counter-story to the anonymous, peripheral position occupied by their churches in the post-industrial interstices of the global city. After FAKI's participation in the London New Year's parade, a musician commented on the move from the urban periphery to the urban centre, highlighting the importance of being visible on such a 'stage':

> The warehouse where we pray is very anonymous. Who get[s] to know us or to hear our music? The [New Year's] parade increased the visibility of the church, and the fact that it went on YouTube and the comments that people left. It was very important for us to reach that audience after being here [in the UK] for such a long time. And in the essence of Kimbanguism, it exists to be spread – it's the message of God. We can't spread it if we just stick to a small place in Docklands or in Edmonton. We have never been on that stage before. We stood up and we did it! (Interview with a young British Congolese Kimbanguist, brass band member)

The sonic architecture created by Kimbanguist hymns – and also the marching, when Kimbanguists are parading – temporarily territorializes the sacred. For Kimbanguists, the power of the Holy Spirit 'incarnated' in the figure of the spiritual leader of the church was felt by many when parading in Central London. On the day of the New Year's Parade, musicians felt a sense of duty, that it was part of their sacred 'work' (*misala*) to play in such a central public space. For them, it was important that the name 'Kimbangu' could simply be heard and read publicly, so that the prophet could be introduced within the textual and audible sphere of the city, as a first step towards the greater visibility of Kimbanguism as a religious institution (Figures 2 and 3).

Such performances operating as temporary sacralization of space have been interpreted as practices that blur the boundaries between secular and religious and illustrate the deprivatization of religion (Casanova 1994) through an increasing visible (and audible) engagement onto the public sphere. While the

Figure 2 During the New Year's Parade, London. Credit: author.

range of public religious performances and the way they mediate urbanity is wide-ranging, these performances can be viewed, especially when related to minority groups, as public expressions and claims for public recognition.[6] As religious public displays, such as chariot festivals, become more established and firmly rooted in particular locales, they may increasingly be incorporated – alongside diasporic secular events like carnivals or melas – within institutional narratives celebrating multiculturalism through the spectacle of the ethnic 'Other' (Jacobsen 2008) or through the 'eventization' of public religious performances intertwined with the dynamics of branding or heritage (Bramadat et al. 2021).

Through outdoor marching and processing, religious minority groups cross an 'ontological barrier' (Werbner 1996: 332), becoming visible in host society environments. While these spatial enactments of minority presence could be seen as part of a claim for a 'right to the city' (see Chapter 4), there is a complex and at times paradoxical relationship between visibility and urban public recognition, as noted by Griera and Burchardt (2021). Drawing upon Goffman's notion of 'civil inattention', they argue that, in a context where dominant imaginaries of city life foreground indifference, visibility cannot simply be equated with recognition, acceptance or even the legitimacy of an urban presence. A connected argument is

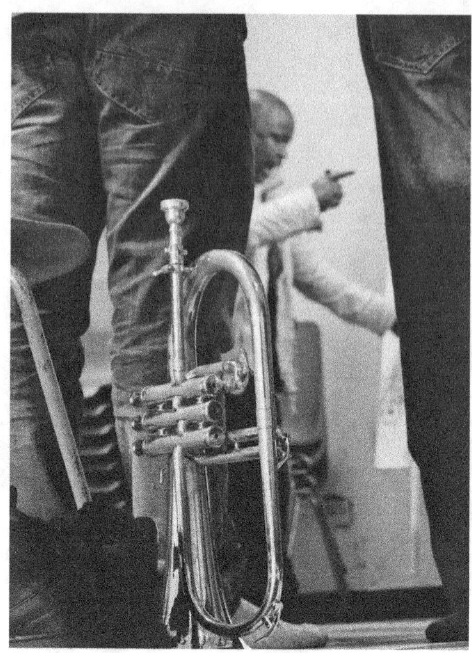

Figure 3 FAKI rehearsal in a London Kimbanguist parish. Credit: Salem Wazaki.

linked to the ways in which cityscapes, in the Simmelian tradition, are construed as spaces of impersonal flows, anonymity and non-interference. Accordingly, as religious public events act as disruptive 'urban manoeuvres' by interrupting the rhythms of urbanity (Strhan 2013), they can have invisibilizing effects, 'making minority religions something fascinating but outside of everyday life' (Giorgi and Giorda 2021: 56) and prevent their normalization within the very fabric of the urbanity they are engaging with. Furthermore, visibility can also of course mean exposing oneself to an orientalist/othering gaze and can also easily turn into 'hypervisibility', 'fostering more intensive forms of surveillance and governance' (Griera and Burchardt 2021: 1729). On the other hand, invisibility, as in the case of Muslim communities in urban Europe, can also appear suspicious (e.g. synonymous with clandestine or underground activities) or a threat to normative understanding of 'integration' (as shown by the whole debate in France about *l'islam des caves*, 'basement cellar Islam', see Bruce 2019).

One way to address this apparent paradoxical tension between (in)visibility and recognition is to acknowledge that first, urbanity is multi-layered, and the potential normalizing/legitimization of particular urban ontologies remains a contested process, and second, that *both* spectacles of difference and the indifference to spectacles can be constitutive of everyday urbanity. Another approach is to consider how the negotiation of tensions between religiosity and everyday life is not consequential but productive, linked to this 'search for coherence' that Strhan (2015) analyses in her study of Evangelical Christians in London.

Similarly, and perhaps empirically closer to the FAKI case study, Elisha (2017) examines how the participation of the members of the Redentor neo-Pentecostal church in the New York Dance Parade is shaped by what he calls 'proximation', a process through which public religious activities become 'entangled with secular categories that they simultaneously resist, resignify, or disavow' (2017: 76). Latino Redentor dancers participating in a non-religious parade adopt a form of urban engagement which is 'at once immersive and dissociative': they are stressing their unique sense of purpose – 'ministering and not performing' – and are empowered by creating differentiating boundaries with other participants, drawing on the mapping of their own moral geography. Both Kimbanguists and Redentor dancers can be objectified in different ways by urban audiences. However, despite the constraint over overt proselytization, both groups view their movement across space as part of a wider spiritual fight.

Sacralizing process through parades – 'suspended moments' (Abdullah 2009: 203) – relates to the visible and aural appropriation of space and to a symbolic remoralizing of the (profane) urban landscape. The religious appropriation of urban and *sonic* space is intimately bound up with the idea of spiritual warfare: Kimbanguists believe that the aural world is populated by evil tendencies or 'traps' as contemporary 'worldly' music can influence people to lead immoral lives or exert negative power in a more covert way through 'hidden' or ambivalent messages, especially within the saturated, 'overcrowded' sonic environment of large cities (Garbin 2012). As a Kimbanguist musician told me, 'we are spreading God's vibes really all around where the Devil has settled all his negativity'.

Another important aspect of the politics and poetics of FAKI procession relates to the ways in which the enactment of ethnic and racial differences on urban public space and the move from the periphery to the centre – from (static) invisibility to (kinetic) visibility – were connected to the prophetic theology of inversion:

> Who could have said that one day we would march in front of all these *mindele* [white people] in Central London. . . . Papa [Simon Kimbangu] told us this: 'The Blacks will become white and the whites will become Black'. This was the prophecy of Papa Simon! And we are his ambassadors in Europe'. (Joe, church member, 39)

In addition, younger marchers also interpreted their participation against a wider political backdrop and debates over racism and multiculturalism. This backdrop affords and delimits a range of categories – Kimbanguist, Londoner, Black British, Congolese, African or even masculine identities – that migrants and minorities can deploy and enact. Kimbanguists see themselves as simultaneously disrupting the dominant discourse associated with Congo and Congolese people and those attributed to Black youth (masculinities) and culture. These discourses operate through negative stereotypes about inner-city Black male youth, associating them with urban violence, aggressive rap/grime music or knife crime. Kimbanguism's counter-discourse functions through the ('shocking') appropriation of a musical tradition, which is habitually viewed as the domain of 'white people':

> Brass Band – people just think white people. This one was just different. It was only Black people. They see just gun and knife crime, that we are doing this, but actually even though there are stereotypes, we are trying hard to take the stereotypes away, like playing music. And there are those who think that we just do rapping, Bashment, I don't know Hip Hop and all them type of music. But Black people actually do classical music and that's what makes them shocked, like: 'Wow! Is this an army?' And because we are disciplined – we are just different'. (Ella, Kimbanguist youth member, eighteen)

During religious processions, the power invested in sacralized kinetics leads to the production of an alternative multisensorial landscape. For Kimbanguists, the chronotopes of prophetic religion are mobilized to reinterpret the physical move from the periphery to the centre against the wider postcolonial backdrop of the diaspora and also to symbolically reposition the group within a multicultural urban assemblage. In a secular context, FAKI plays on the ambiguity of potential external objectifications – 'we can't be too religious or people would be put off' (FAKI senior member) – a process which has to be understood at the same time in relation to Kimbanguist modes of evangelization, eschewing overt proselytizing and more based on the embodiment of an exemplary and convincing virtuous behaviour. The challenge is also of course to negotiate the ambivalent reality of an urban stage, such as during the 'Hackney multicultural carnival',[7] when it was crucial to preserve a sense of moral purity by maintaining a spatial distance with the perceived 'amoral' bodies of the Brazilian-oriented Samba groups.[8]

Pilgrimage as performance of extended territoriality

Public processions may expose believers to the immorality of secular urbanity. In contrast, pilgrimage is performed within a more protective collective space and is particularly key for Kimbanguists and Catholics, for whom it is embedded within a cyclical, ritualized temporality. Kimbanguists engage in transnational pilgrimages to Nkamba often as part of small church groups – FAKI musicians, choir singers, women's or youth associations, drama groups and so on – to attend celebrations dedicated to their sections. Travelling to these annual celebrations in Nkamba reinforces the bonds between members, and, for many, in particular for youth, it is also a way to construct a meaningful relationship with the homeland outside of an extended kinship sphere which can be seen as a source of overwhelming (financial or social) pressure (see Chapter 5). Nkamba, is a very remote place and difficult to access, especially during the rainy season, when even the most powerful jeeps can get stuck for hours in the muddy road leading to it. This isolation is actually part of a narrative constructing the prophetic, mystical and sacred power of Nkamba: 'there is no highway to Heaven' Kimbanguists would often reply when asked why the road to Nkamba had not yet been 'fixed', despite the apparent willingness of the Congolese authorities to do so (since Mobutu, I was told). Pilgrimages to Nkamba, in that sense, embody a spirit of sacrifice, which, as Peña (2011) suggests in her ethnography of the pilgrimages of Latino migrants to the shrine of Our Lady of Guadalupe, can be key to the accumulation of 'devotional capital'.

Recent scholarship on pilgrimages has stressed a need to make sense of the complexity of pilgrimages through a wider 'landscape of connection, communication, competition, fractal-like replication, networking, mobility, infrastructure and governance' (Coleman and Eade 2018: 4). While the pilgrimage as emotionally charged embodiment of the sacred is part and parcel of the experience of religious urbanity, Nkamba is more than a site of worship and devotion and considered to be a highly political space where factional conflicts and rivalries between members of diasporic parishes are regularly played out during holy celebrations. Not unlike Touba for the Senegalese Mourides (Kingsbury 2023), the case of Nkamba shows how pilgrimage place-making constitutes complex assemblages of formal and informal, religious and non-religious practices that can connect a 'holy city' to publics situated beyond its immediate urban boundaries. Since local parish dynamics, including tensions between individuals and groups, find resonance across the Kimbanguist transnational public sphere and are projected often intensively in Nkamba, travel to the holy city constitutes an expanded form of territorialization while reinforcing the idea of a powerfully meaningful centre.

With the large number and growing popularity of Catholic shrines in Europe (Eade 2017), dynamics are clearly different among Congolese Catholics, even if the idea of a (unique) strong historical ecclesiastic centre remains associated with the Vatican. Congolese Catholics are thus embedded in a wider pilgrimage – polycentric – landscape, while keeping a strong connection with African Catholicism's liturgies and frame of references to *le rite Zairois* (adopted after the Second Vatican Council). UK-based Congolese Catholics have organized trips to the Holy Land and regularly undertake group journeys to holy sites and shrines – especially the Marian shrines of Lourdes in France, Banneux in Belgium or Walsingham in England.

The Virgin Mary is said to have appeared to a local noblewoman in the eleventh century in the Norfolk village of Walsingham, instructing her to build a sacred house modelled on Christ childhood's home in Nazareth. After the reformation, the shrine of Walsingham was almost destroyed, but in the early twentieth century the medieval pilgrimage tradition was revived by both Anglican and Roman Catholic churches. As a result, different shrines have been established and parallel pilgrimages have emerged, including multicultural celebrations like the 'Dowry of Mary' pilgrimage to which I accompanied a large group of Congolese Catholics in 2017. After a three-hour coach journey from London punctuated by prayers and songs in Lingala, we joined dozens of groups representing a large cross-section of (mostly London-based) Catholic ethnic/migrant parishes or chaplaincies from Nigerian, Zambian, India/Keralan, Tamil, Chinese, Lithuanian or Cambodian communities at the Slipper Chapel, the official Catholic shrine. Built in 1325, the Slipper Chapel was the last and most important chapel that pilgrims would stop at en route to the pre-reformation shrine in Walsingham. After the Mass in English, each group performed their Hail Marys in their community language to the whole assembly, before joining a march, the 'Holy Mile', to the ruin of the twelfth-century Augustine priory (adjacent to the site where the replica of the Holy House is said to have been built). With its multitude of national flags, its prayers and singing in a wide range of community languages, the 'Holy Mile' procession was a spectacular, multicultural display of diasporic Catholicism solemnly parading within the landscape of a traditionally white English countryside, a landscape greatly contrasting with the dense (hyper-) urbanity within which some of the London African churches are located (Figures 4–6).

The Congolese pilgrims I spoke to had limited knowledge of (and have had a limited exposure to) the long and complex history of the 'England's Nazareth' and its multivocality (Coleman and Elsner 2004). However, all stressed the possibility of a personal, meaningful relationship with God in a space they recognized to be 'authentically' connected to the figure and tradition of Mary,

Figure 4 During the multicultural Mass at Walsingham. Credit: author.

a space where they can get 'spiritual blessings', to quote Rose, a thirty-year-old Congolese pilgrim I interviewed in Walsingham:

> What I get from coming to Walsingham – it is for me a time for prayer, to get spiritual blessings. At home, we have busy lives, we don't really have time to pray and sing – we say singing is like praying twice. But on the coach, during the journey, we spent several hours doing just that: praying and singing. Actually, I do more here than at church or at home! Every year I come here. It's a holy place, where the Virgin appeared. I either ask something to the Virgin or I give thanks. I write messages in the petition box and I go to confession before Mass.

Rose's narrative evokes the alternative time-space afforded by the pilgrimage as both sacred journey and ritual, conforming, in a way, to the classical Turnerian view of pilgrimage as separated from the constraints and demands of everyday life (Turner and Turner 1978). But for Rose and many other Congolese participants, it was clear that their presence in Walsingham was also the symbol of a multifaceted collective positionality. The pilgrimage allows them to be located within a transnational Catholic religioscape which has been increasingly defined by the expansion and interconnection of pilgrimage sites, in particular Marian shrines, across Europe. Their presence alongside other migrant groups also included them in the performance of cultural difference, enacted through a range of multisensorial boundaries – spoken and written language, the material culture of clothing, flags

Figures 5 and 6 Congolese Catholics during the pilgrimage procession of the 'Holy Mile' (Walsingham). Credit: author.

and music instruments or the food consumed (each group brought and consumed collectively their own meals for lunch). Even if there was limited engagement across ethnic boundaries and although the performance of multiculturalism played out through a set of rigidly orchestrated rituals, Congolese Catholics could perceive themselves as rightful contributors to a cosmopolitan religious field in a multicultural British context. Like Kimbanguists, parading in the streets of London, they could claim a place in the host society while territorializing the sacred through the temporary appropriation of space. Even if the Central London brass band parade and the pilgrimage in the deep English countryside differ in many ways, I want to argue that both practices have gradually become embedded in 'parish life' and represent instances of extended territorialization. They reflect the affordances of a diasporic horizon (Johnson 2007), the possibility of stretching outwards the boundaries of an anchoring space.

As we discussed previously, being visible and potentially recognized in the host context is not incompatible with a desire to carve up a protective space in an environment, which is at times perceived as hostile and immoral, and to sustain multiple relations and affective connections with the homeland through religious networks. Moreover, for Catholics this expanded territorialization which, in the case of the Walsingham pilgrimage, brings multicultural urbanity to a rural space, is often constrained by the centralized structure and bureaucracy of the Catholic Church. Despite the postcolonial 'Africanization' of Congolese Catholicism, the Congolese Abbé who led the group deplored a sort of uneven power-geometry in the making of a Catholic pilgrimage landscape, lacking in recognition for sites in the homeland:

> In the Congo, in Africa we have a history of apparitions and many sites with miracles. We have African martyrs. But there are limited means [*moyens limités*] to follow all the procedures so that these sites with miracles are recognised, through an official process of institutionalisation.

Translocal intimacy, sacred mediation and the rise of 'digital religion'

Despite this type of power asymmetries, parading, processing and pilgrimage demonstrate the creative agency of immigrants in diaspora, who, drawing from religious discourses, practices and institutions, reground themselves, carving out places of meaningful livelihood, representing important, albeit ambivalent, forms of territorialization operating in the specific context of multicultural Britain. However, these practices should not be seen in isolation; they interact with others operating at multiple scales, from the personal and local to the transnational and global. Two warrant further exploration: home and cyberspace.

For the three groups studied in this book, homeplace is a 'micro-public' providing its own affordances and connecting possibilities, a sphere of action and interaction that is more than an initial stage of religious territorial expansion. Coexisting with large places of worship and/or transnational architecture, home remains a vital space allowing for small prayer gatherings or biblical discussions bringing people together on the basis of locality, kinship and/or membership to particular church groups (in particular in the case of Kimbanguists).

As Maskens (2013) shows in her study of African and Latino Pentecostals in Brussels, home is also a space for the cultivation of intimacy and spontaneity, central components of a born-again habitus. The possibility of regular, iterative performances in small-group settings, which are more interactive than the space of the church, also constitutes a core element of the Pentecostal 'body pedagogics' (Shilling 2017). For Catholics in diaspora, home prayer groups are linked to the activities of 'Basic Ecclesial Communities' known as CEVB (*Communautés Ecclesiales Vivantes de Base*), which, in the homeland, operate also as neighbourhood mutual aid networks for Catholics, fulfilling a range of social and community purposes (see Chapter 6). In the UK context, a CEVB network covers a wider area – several London boroughs as opposed to the local streets of a Kinshasa *quartier*. As this Congolese Catholic suggests, it is a space of collective learning:

> In our CEVB, we meet and discuss the Bible. We comment a passage, or we discuss the Homily heard at church, we discuss issues of our communities. We also learn together. Someone reads the Bible, comments on a passage. We discuss, everyone contributes something. But there has to be someone who has a little better knowledge of the Bible [*qui maîtrise un peu mieux la Bible*]. It brings confidence and better knowledge of Biblical teachings, it brings experience and self-confidence to people. For instance if you are in a *matanga* [funeral wake] and there is no priest, someone can officiate, even if the priest is not there . . . if you go to an event, if the priest is there, he will pray, that's for sure, but if he's not there, you'll be able to replace him . . Saying a prayer for example to start the event, it's in this sense . . . to implore the Lord and sometimes people weren't able to do it . . . unlike *église de réveil* people [Pentecostals] who are more experienced.

Home space acts as a mediation between smaller groups and often very large congregations, just as Pentecostal megachurches rely on a multiscalar, expanding model in a competitive religious field. For these churches, the use of home spaces is a way to seamlessly blend religious identities and practices into the daily routines and rhythms of members, foster loyalty, form a potential entry point to the congregation or allow the enforcing of norms or social control (see Klaver 2021, Wilford 2012). Despite being one of the key scales of diasporic religious territorialization, providing coherence, continuity and consistency as well as 'achieving an emplaced sense of security, familiarity, and control over space in the present' (Bertolani and Boccagni 2022: 2), the religious use and sacralization of private home space by migrants have been scantily researched. I found the domestic space of Kimbanguist particularly expressive of this desire for continuity with a sacralized homeland and prophetic tradition (Figure 7). For instance, portraits of spiritual leaders (including the Prophet Kimbangu, his son Diangienda and his grandson Kiangani) or framed posters of Nkamba's temple were common in the living rooms of Kimbanguist homes I visited in the United Kingdom and the United States. In addition, Kimbanguists often keep some sacred earth and holy water from Nkamba at home or with them for healing and cleansing purposes, reflecting the portability of their holy city.

For Congolese Kimbanguists, Catholics and Pentecostals, the use of media, in particular digital media, constitutes yet another form of religious regrounding. The interplay of globalization, migration and religion has been dramatically intensified by rapid innovations in computer-mediated communications, particularly by the expansion of the internet and, more recently, the rise of social media. The religious mediascape is fluid and mutable, and religious groups and individuals are able to access increasingly affordable and technically accessible tools, allowing 'instantaneous and simultaneous consumption of the sacrality across multiple sites and scales' (Garbin and Vásquez 2012: 168). In

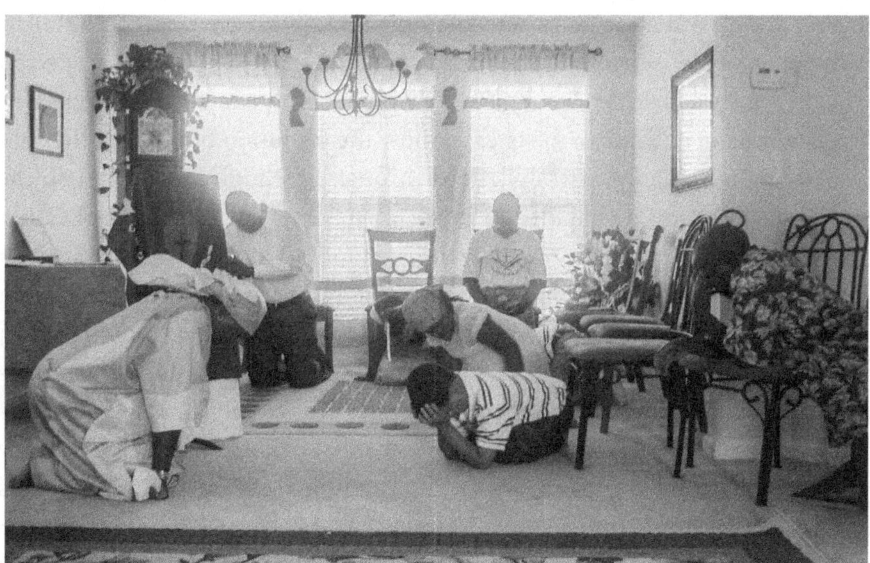

Figure 7 Small service in a Kimbanguist home in Atlanta. Credit: author.

turn, this consumption shapes and is shaped by religious practices, institutions, identities and affects. While in the late 1990s and early 2000s costs of producing and circulating audio-visual footage meant that only a larger, transnational religious organization could technically, logistically and financially afford it, it is now considerably easier to broadcast and stream content, including live events through, for example, YouTube or Facebook Live, with a minimum of hardware or software equipment and technical knowledge, and even with limited digital infrastructure. That said, TV remains important, with many Congolese watching African diasporic channels or religious/Christian channels available for free on satellite networks like SKY from the comfort of their living rooms. Here it is important to acknowledge that contemporary electronic and audio-visual tools stand in continuity with the long-standing tradition of using (mass) media to extend the scope and collective appeal of religion. Morgan (2011) shows how, among nineteenth-century European and American evangelicals, the 'remediation of oral discourse in mass print' was integral to the ambitious, renewed imaginary of an extended Christian 'community of feeling' in the context of intense competition with 'profane' print.

In an era when 'digital religion' (Campbell 2013, Isetti et al. 2021) represents a crucial vector in the politics and poetics of the sacred, we need to pay attention to how 'religious individuals form communities, articulate identities, and negotiate authorities through practices that happen in between online and offline venues' (Campbell and Evolvi 2019: 2). For all three groups studied in this book, mediation (and remediation) though internet-based platforms includes a wide range of practices: Maman Olangi believers dispersed globally can watch church members' testimonies uploaded on a dedicated YouTube channel; Kimbanguists can follow the evolution of projects they are sponsoring in the holy city of Nkamba through Facebook posts or watch the videos of the parades uploaded by FAKI members; Congolese Catholics can attend their parish's Masses remotely or listen to Radio Maria[9] on the internet; Pentecostal pastors from London, Johannesburg, Brussels or Paris engage in political debates, invectives and *polemiques* on YouTube; and, more recently, many have discovered the connecting potential of Zoom prayer meetings and discussion groups in a time of pandemics. These are just a few examples illustrating how the politics of presence can be connected to the capacity of religious actors to generate virtual worlds transcending national borders and crossing 'electronic frontiers' (Vásquez and Marquardt 2003) but also to project global(ized) visions across networked cartographies linking emplaced urban religious worlds.

Figure 8 In a Kimbanguist parish. Credit: author.

Some digital religious practices among Congolese rely heavily on reformatting and remediating, reflecting the overall participatory character of digital cultures based on the 'spreadability' of content and convergence of media forms (Jenkins, Ford and Green 2013). This convergence takes place through interconnection among 'older' forms of mediation like radio and TV and emerging digital media, with the TV content of religious channels recirculated as clips (re-edited and commented) uploaded online, for instance. In that sense, diasporic media dynamics are shaped by the media landscape of Kinshasa whose emergence, evolution and gradual 'Pentecostalization' have been aptly analysed by Pype (2012). She described how the 'key scenario' of Charismatic Christianity, the fight between godly forces over evil forces, the spiritual warfare against the world of *féticheurs* and *magiciens*, has been established as a dominant plot – for instance, in the popular *maboke* (theatre/TV dramas) – with, at its core, *pasteurs* and *prophètes* as 'cultural heroes' of the new moral economy of the city. The competition is fierce in the charismatic/religious sphere of the DRC, and the religious mediascape (of Kinshasa in particular) is a privileged site of struggle for recognition between churches. With the increase in smartphone use and the proliferation of social media and various internet platforms, this competition has intensified, leading to a saturated religious cyberscape. Social media are used by some, in particular Pentecostals, to stage the struggle between good and evil. At the same time, material exposing the supposed immorality or excesses of Pentecostal pastors also circulates widely across the three groups and has become a genre in itself. These critical vignettes are extensively shared, 'liked' and commented, and they often have transnational trajectories since they also feature pastors from Nigerian or Ghanaian churches, and/or practices or rituals performed in these churches, such as spectacular/extreme exorcisms, 'bogus' miracles or prophecies.

Interrogating religious diasporic territorialization and modalities of presence through the production and consumption of religious media – in particular digital media – involves paying attention to the dynamics of offline–online relations. As Heidi Campbell has suggested, digital religion represents 'the technological and cultural space that is evoked when we talk about how online and offline religious spheres have become blended and integrated' (2013: 3–4). Consequently, digital religion acts as a 'bridge that connects and extends online religious practices and spaces with offline religious contexts, and vice versa' (2013: 3–4). Moreover, Coleman (2022) has analysed how regimes of presence mediated by digital infrastructures impact the experience of pilgrimage. He observes that 'cyber-pilgrimages' often rely on multisensorial reconstitution of the experience of shrines and holy sites, which paradoxically suggests that 'online representations can only even be derivative of more experientially powerful, grounded experiences' (2022: 194).

In the context of Covid, questions related to the authenticity of the online experience of worship have been raised. During the height of the pandemic, places of worship both in diaspora and in the homeland remained empty and restrictions on religious gatherings led many to participate remotely in religious services streamed online or broadcast on TV or radio. Taking into consideration the importance of the space-body nexus and the centrality of tactile sensorialities (de Witte 2012), in particular in charismatic practice, we must assess the impact of the pandemic on the physical contact and embodied/emplaced 'collective effervescence' that Durkheim considered essential to religious life. The crisis represented a challenge to forms of religiosity heavily dependent on the performative and spectacular aesthetics of collective intensity and social effervescence, often deployed through the appropriation and transformation of urban space, like is the case for Nigerian megachurches (see Chapter 7). During some follow-up interviews (conducted on the phone during Covid), Maman Josy, a member of a Maman Olangi church, spoke about the potential 'distraction' of online worshipping and noted a clear difference in the performance of offerings:

> When you worship online you can be distracted and tempted to look at other churches, but when you are physically present in the church, you just don't leave the service like that.... Also you tend to be giving less money when worshipping online because not influenced by the heat [*la chaleur*] of the church community.

While pandemic restrictions may have involved the emergence of 'inattentive publics', leading to a volatility of membership and a detrimental loss of capital in the forms of offerings and ritualized donations (see also Kroesbergen-Kamps 2020), they have also led to the creation of alternative spaces of transnational communication. For instance, London-based Kimbanguist youth leaders set up regular Zoom meetings combining praying sessions and discussions on topics related to church life, marriage issues or various moral problems, a novel practice which allowed them to engage with other Kimbanguist youth in Europe and the United States. As one Kimbanguist youth leader told me, these Zoom meetings (but also pre-Pandemic chats on Kimbanguist Facebook groups) allow discussions (for instance, on theological questions, church life or everyday topics) outside the direct social control of community elders. However, while he viewed the possibility of these fora among youth as a positive development, he added that, nonetheless, the virtual world (like the urban world) was full of 'traps' and potentially morally dangerous for young people. Other novel practices adopted during Covid and which remained, even when churches could re-open, include the possibility of transferring donations online for those unable to attend (or even for those attending the service 'offline' – but without cash) and online weekly administrative Zoom meetings which allowed those living far from the parish to save time and money.

In sum, the relation between offline and online is complex and multifaceted. In many ways, the global deployment of digital infrastructure does not erase the relevance of local/physical experience 'under a flood of free-floating signifiers' (Vásquez and Garbin 2016: 695): virtual and physical reality often sustain a relationship of reciprocal influencing. This is further illustrated by the fact that while warehouse churches described earlier are under-communicating the presence of the sacred within the wider urban landscape, they nonetheless contribute to mediated forms of territorialization through an infrastructure of communication and a specific inward-oriented spatial organization. Krause (2008b) thus notes the striking resemblance between the interior decoration of African Pentecostal churches and the furniture arrangement, aesthetics and décor of studios where religious programmes are produced, a similarity that I also observed in churches like KICC, where services were systematically recorded with high-end audio-visual equipment and made quickly available on DVD.

Another notable practice linking place-making and media flows is the viewing, this time, of large recorded or even live religious events or services. This happened several times in my fieldwork, as during some services of the Maman Olangi church in diaspora, when the assembly could worship and react in real time to an important service taking place in the main headquarter of the church, in Kinshasa, and broadcast through the streaming platform of the church TV station (Canal CVV). Finally, while for Kimbanguist FAKI members, the appropriation of centrality through parading in London has deep symbolic and religious meaning, the fact that they could engage with multiple audiences globally through YouTube or Flickr is a great source of pride. In this case, the use of urban space to further claims over recognition and visibility needs to be understood against a digital infrastructure, which has become both an organizational/communicative device and a means to amplify the social impact of public spatialized presence – even if evanescent and transient in character.

The reciprocal entanglement or offline and online worlds, physical and virtual domains points to the multiscalar character of diasporic territorialization and the complex interplay of local and global forces in mediating the sacred. Moreover, mass-mediated communication can globally reinforce the legitimacy of religious power structures and convey notions of sacred authenticity or primordial modes of belonging (Udupa 2015). But it can also open up social spaces of hybridity and alternative tropes, reflecting the difficulty of sacred centres to hold on to their monopoly over the means of production of religious messages and sacred idioms.

For transnational churches with branches dispersed globally – like the Kimbanguist church – the question is often how to address emerging tensions between centripetal and centrifugal forces when it comes to the access and control of the technology linked to the performance and mediation of religious ideologies and global identity. As the diaspora has increasing access to digital knowledge and infrastructure, it can participate more actively in the (re) creation of the tradition, becoming gradually less peripheral in relation to the church headquarters in the Congo (see Garbin and Vásquez 2012). While this suggests a process of decentralization and polycentralization at work within the Kimbanguist public sphere, it is also true that the contents of this digital mediation in diaspora (in particular messages from the spiritual leader and recordings from important festivals held in Nkamba) often tend to reinforce both the legitimacy of the spiritual leader and the 'centring' of Nkamba. This reaffirmation of a strong spiritual and institutional centre is especially important given the existence of both internal schismatic divisions and external criticisms of the evolution of a Kimbanguist 'Christian' theology and politics (see the next chapter). In light of potential heterodoxy, there is growing concern that blogs, websites, discussion forums or DVDs created by Kimbanguists and non-Kimbanguists alike may distort or misrepresent the prophetic message and theology of the church. Debates taking place in the Congo or in diaspora on the Christian or Kongo authenticity of the Kimbanguist church or about its role during Mobutu's or the current regime have found an echo and are amplified on the internet or diasporic African satellite TV networks. This, in turn, leads more and more Kimbanguists to consider the mediascape as an important territory to appropriate, not only to evangelize but also to draw clear-cut boundaries between Kimbanguism and other prophetic traditions or to respond to critiques about the theology or orientation of their church.

Conclusion

This chapter has discussed the various modalities of presence through which diasporic religious practices and identities come to be territorialized. These forms of dwelling and crossing have both constraining and affording attributes, grounding and regrounding actors in particular places, allowing and compelling certain identities and types of belonging, even as they also enable migrants to navigate multiple scales. These forms also reveal the extent to which religious ontologies are spatialized through various modes of collective existence, performances, flows and media. Focusing on these ranges of practices shows the key role of 'grounded theologies' as 'performative practices of place-making informed by understandings of the transcendent' (Tse 2014). Even Kimbanguists and Pentecostals, supposedly influenced by a textualist Protestant ethic that privileges the profession of individual belief unconstrained by tradition and institutions over material, emplaced and collective practices (Keane 2007, Vásquez 2011), deploy these grounded theologies in various ways, negotiating pre-existing or novel constraints and urban regimes, especially when they 'expose' themselves onto the public space as the case of the FAKI 'sonic crusades'.

Moreover, while this process of place-making is intimately bound up with the production of moral cartographies it also reveals how the diasporic regrounding operates through the blurring of lines between sacred and profane, religious and secular. As della Dora (2016) suggests, contemporary infrasecular landscapes of urban religion are interstitial, they represent 'third spaces' where, beyond a simplistic radical Durkheimian separation, secular and sacred do not stand in a zero-sum relation, in which when one triumphs the other fades. Rather, sacred and secular are contested and transitive realms of experience, which often not just coexist or even accommodate each other, but may also blend into each other. For those who mobilize the power of the Holy Spirit or invoke prophetic beliefs to enact the remoralizing (and protecting) of self, community and urban surroundings, religious territorialization is thus often laden with ambiguities.

In any case, practices of place-making operate as resources in a 'quest for coherence' (Strhan 2015). Through parades, pilgrimages, large temples, the inculcation of a habitus of morality or the exhibition of religious materiality at home and mediascapes, the Congolese in diaspora draw from their various religious traditions to (re)localize themselves in the potentially morally dangerous urban ecology, in which they often find themselves in a precarious or invisible condition. Simultaneously, they also establish presence in the national – both the country of origin and settlement – and the transnational and global – presence that is often open to contestation. In the chapter that follows I expand my exploration of these multiscalar processes, focusing on the political diasporic engagement through which the Congolese formulate claims for legitimacy and the 'right to the city'.

4

The 'right to the city' and beyond

Religion, race and diasporic politics

God told the children of Israel to walk and pray outdoors and to suffer for Him. God wants us to pray in the streets and in the avenues. When we pray, God is with us and protects us. Praying on the streets it's to show to God that we are there in His name. It's to glorify God with prayers and music. Prayer has a power. We prayed in front of Downing Street to ask God to intervene, to influence those who lead. (Pasteur Josh)

Pastor Josh is a *pasteur combattant*. He played an active role during the sustained collective protest movement that emerged in the UK and across the Congolese diaspora in opposition to the regime of Joseph Kabila, the president of the DRC who remained in power for nearly twenty years until 2019. The event described in the quote occurred in Central London in 2012 and crystallizes the entanglement of diasporic politics, religion and place-making, the focus of this chapter.

On that day, Pastor Josh was part of a group of Congolese Pentecostal pastors who organized an outdoor prayer service in front of 10 Downing Street, the residence of the British prime minister, David Cameron at the time. The intense preaching of these pastors was accompanied by the sound of drums, guitars and keyboards plugged to a portable electric generator at the foot of a statue of Field Marshall 'Monty' Bernard Montgomery looking towards the guarded gates of Number 10. While many among these participants usually attend 'warehouse churches' at the symbolic and spatial periphery of the global city, they were, on that cold February day, kneeling and praying fervently on the pavement of a Central London street. Turning visibly and audibly a secular street into a temporary place of worship, some were facing the preacher and others were orienting their bodies and prayers in the direction of David Cameron's office, raising their hands, imploring God to intercede for the sake of the Congo.

The period during which the Downing Street prayers took place saw a large and at times spectacular mobilization of the Congolese diaspora in the context of a tense electoral campaign which led to the contested re-election of Joseph Kabila as president of the DRC. While in the UK, the Congolese were particularly active politically, the movement spread across the diaspora. In the United States, Canada, France, Belgium, Germany, Holland and many other countries, Congolese demonstrators opposed to the government of Joseph Kabila organized public demonstrations and pickets in front of Congolese embassies or iconic sites of power such as 10 Downing Street in London or the White House in Washington, DC. In London, some of the largest demonstrations brought together a wider range of community/diasporic actors, including members of the Congolese opposition political parties, women's groups and youth associations, as well as religious actors, mostly Pentecostals and Catholics since Kimbanguists tend to keep a low profile when it comes to politics, as I shall discuss later. Some activists I spoke to during the dozens of demonstrations I attended had plural allegiances, at the intersection of these groups. It was the case, for instance, of 25-year-old Joe who had settled in the UK when he was 14 – thus fluent in Lingala, English and French – and who was a member of the UDPS (Union pour la Démocratie et le Progrès Social, main opposition party at the time) and also a fervent Catholic. As such, he could act as a broker, mediating among the different groups and mobilizing young protesters.

In addition to their anti-Kabila stance, protesters also regularly denounced what was seen as the neocolonial involvement of Western governments in Africa, the role of Congo's neighbours, in particular Rwanda, in fuelling the regional conflict, the exploitation of minerals by armed groups and multinationals, the widespread sexual violence in the east of the country and the relative silence of mainstream media about the situation of the DRC. In the public demonstrations and global online campaigns, activists stressed the link between items such as mobile phones or laptops and the plunder of natural resources in eastern Congo. Their websites, blogs, YouTube channels and email lists were able to reach an audience far beyond the UK.

In this chapter, I explore the differentiated dynamics of diasporic politics linked, in great part, to these public demonstrations. We will see that the mobilization to 'liberate' the Congo is constructed as part of a wider spiritual battle, which, for *pasteurs combattants* like Pastor Josh, relocate the homeland (and those fighting for its renewal/restoration) within a prophetic biblical chronotope. Additionally, I show how these diasporic politics hinge on the deployment of forms of territorialization connecting urbanity, and in particular urban centrality, to political claims – reflecting the importance of a 'right to the city' (Lefebvre 1996). These politics also draw on the performance of ethnic, religious and gendered identities and on the recourse to a collective memory in a 'post-Mobutu' context. These claims are not restricted to the local or national scale. Visibility and recognition within diasporic (counter)publics is as much, if not more, a stake as the city itself. In the second half of the chapter, a focus on the role and experiences of young Congolese activists during these protests will reveal the limitations of the religious field in sustaining widespread and impactful political action and messaging in diaspora.

Before examining the urban performance of young people, I will be first discussing the role of prophetic geo-theologies in framing the (spiritual) long-distance battle to 'save the Congo' among Pentecostal *pasteurs combattants* as well as Kimbanguist and Catholic diasporic actors.

Prophetic politics: 'Bana Israel' and 'Bana Congo'

The *pasteurs combattants* emerged in a context of mobilization and street protests against Kabila in the diaspora; they were also particularly vocal on the internet and Congolese satellite TV channels. They clearly formed a minority, however, as most Congolese Pentecostal religious leaders tended to eschew direct involvement in these diasporic politics, while (not unlike Kimbanguists and Catholics) stressing the need for moral reform as an essential component of collective redemption and spiritual growth.

Pastor Josh's spiritual mobilization for the Congo dates back to several decades. At the end of the 1970s, in Kinshasa, he was a young, active Catholic congregant, involved in the life of his parish through participation in the choir. He was known, as he wrote in his self-published autobiography, to be a *coureur de jupons*, a womanizer, a reputation which gradually led him to feel guilty and question his own morality. His life changed dramatically when one evening, together with three other Catholic friends, he received 'a message', which formed the basis of his calling and subsequent engagement in the Congo and the diaspora:

> That night, the voice spoke for several hours. It told us many secrets, that there was a plan for us and for the Congo, that the Congo got all the diamonds of the Garden of Eden, the diamonds that were hidden in the Garden of Eden. It was the Holy Spirit. Telling us to change, to get rid of all the [Catholic] candles and statues of the Virgin Mary. He told us that the awakening [*réveil*] will happen in the Congo and that from there it will spread across Africa and the world, and that we have a mission to evangelize. (From autobiography, my translation from French)

Most of the revelations were highly prophetic, announcing that the Congo will be 'completely conquered by God', that it will become the 'broadcasting source of God's voice to the world', a 'leading nation' – politically and economically – among all nations. Compiled in several publications, these revelations, and also individual visions received several months after, were often accompanied by Old Testament references to Israel. They also contained a spiritual commentary on the present, for instance, on Mobutu's leadership (described as a transitional phase before a take over by 'servants of God'), on the widespread immorality under his regime or about the localization of sources of evil and occult forces (Matonge's area in Kinshasa, or the then Bas-Congo region, 'capital of witches').

Starting a prayer group, the 'messengers' soon got expelled from their Catholic parish and joined Pastor Ayidini Abala, the key figure of the Kinshasa *réveil* in the 1970s to 1980s, and then started to travel throughout the DRC and beyond to evangelize and share their prophetic message. During the late 1980s, Pastor Josh's calling took him to Paris, where he ended up assisting a Congolese pastor who had migrated there a few years earlier. In his autobiography, Pastor Josh explains how, despite wishing to continue his mission in Europe and North America, he had to return to Congo, following a vision from God enjoining him to evangelize in Kinshasa. 'Being in Europe was the dream of all Zaireans, and returning seen a complete madness, but I had to obey Lord's will', he writes. Here we see how what I have termed 'spiritual infrastructure', which includes prophesizing, revelation and notions of election and mission, shapes mobility even *against* the dominant narrative of migration as the path to progress.

Pastor Josh spent the next few years successfully expanding his ministry and creating church branches across Kinshasa, before, once again been directed by God, during an intense prayer session, to travel to Europe which he reached, thanks in part to the help of Mobutist security staff who were attending his church. He stayed in Belgium for a while, but left for London after he had another revelation through a dream in which God showed him 'England, a country with red brick houses, one with the roof collapsing' and told him 'to go and repair the house'– a sign he had to travel yet again to pursue his mission. In London, he joined other Congolese pastors, like Pasteur T., who had been engaged in the remoralizing of the Congolese migrants during a time of petty crime and *mayuya* (see Chapter 2). Reflecting on his presence in London, he writes that he felt like 'Lot who had chosen to go to Sodom', while Abraham went to Canaan (Gen. 13:1-12). He gradually gained a prominent role within London's Congolese community (navigating various leadership conflicts with other pastors), and after the transition period following the end of Mobutism, he became vocal in his opposition to Kabila's government.

Pastor Josh took a leading role in opposing the Kabila government, linking up with the opposition parties and with a more radical and sometimes violent group of (male) activists known as *les Combattants* ('the fighters'), infamous for their methods of direct action, for instance, occupying Congolese embassies in Europe, preventing the visits of Kinshasa-based pastors or concerts by Congolese musicians seen as supporting Kabila. These spectacular actions and the visibility of the *Combattants* gave the Congolese community in London the reputation of a stronghold of the radical opposition across the Congolese diaspora, a reputation which also travelled to Kinshasa[1] (Figure 9).

Pastor Josh was also instrumental in creating a platform bringing together other – mostly Pentecostal – leaders to liaise with British authority, in particular, through the House of Lords or the Foreign Office, to raise some awareness of the protracted conflict in the east of the country and problems of governance in the DRC. For Pastor Josh, figurehead of the opposition in the diaspora and also for

Figure 9 Protester from *les Combattants* during a Congolese demonstration in Central London. Credit: author.

most *Combattants* and anti-Kabilistes vocal on the internet and social media, travelling to the Congo was deemed too dangerous. In the DRC, I spoke with pastors leading the Kinshasa branches of Pastor Josh's church and who talked about how they had to 'silence' any nationalist, anti-governmental critique because of the risk of being sent to jail (they mentioned high-profile Pasteur Kutino, a staunch opponent of Kabila who was imprisoned for eight years). The following testimony, from a conversation with one of these pastors, points to how, despite the challenges of regrounding oneself in a hostile, secular environment, urban diasporic spaces provide 'agentic' affordances that the homeland does not:

> Here in the Congo, we don't have the freedom to express ourselves, we don't dare to criticize openly. If you do so they can lock you up. So we are silent. We just say: 'this is what God said for our nation' – understand who can. Whereas Pastor Josh has freedom on the other side [*de l'autre côté*, i.e., in the UK]. Here we have to act with a lot of wisdom, in our sermons, our public speeches. . . . The security services [ANR, *Agence Nationale de Renseignements*] are watching us. They can close TV stations, even the Catholic station was shut down in January, Canal Kin also [following a protest movement against the planning of a law to organize a national census which would have delayed the 2016 Presidential elections].

In his internal communication to the Congolese community, Pastor Josh clearly mobilized the political theology of 'Pentecostal nationalism' (Van Klinken 2014), emphasizing the importance of spiritual warfare as an important aspect of the fight to 'liberate' the Congo – a unique God-chosen country both blessed and cursed for its natural resource, a 'martyr' country epitomizing the global and postcolonial plunder of resources. Church sermons, prayer sessions (often displaying a map of the Congo) and broadcast messages via YouTube or satellite TV expressed a longing for a restored and a liberated Congo, outlining a spiritual framework resonating with the idea of a biblical nation associated with the 'children of Israel' (*Bana Israel*). The idioms of mobilization for the sacred homeland and also of return (reinterpreted, for instance, through the figure of Nehemiah returning from the diaspora to rebuild Jerusalem) bestow a powerful religious and divinely sanctioned meaning on the struggle of the 'children of the Congo' (*Bana Congo*) living in Europe and North America.

As Van Klinken (2014) notes, 'Pentecostal nationalism' may seem a contradiction in terms, given the belief in the powerful agency of the Holy Spirit to transcend and transgress a host of boundaries, not least national or ethnic boundaries. (As Paul puts it in Galatians: 'There is neither Jew nor Greek, slave nor free, male nor female, for you are all one in Christ Jesus.')

For Karagiannis and Glick Schiller (2006), African Pentecostal migrants make universalist missionizing claims as part of alternative strategies of incorporation and participation in precarious 'host' contexts, while engaged in the building of local and transnational networks. For these authors, the 'overvaluation' of ethnic and cultural idioms minimizes the significance of transborder, globalizing modes of Pentecostal belongings, expressed, for instance, in 'the rejection of the nation-state as a frame of reference' (2006: 160). But what we see with the Congolese example – and with other African Pentecostals – is the ongoing referential importance of both the nation and the nation-state model for the making of religious ontologies of mapping involving 'dehistoricizing' and 'rehistoricizing' nations through biblical readings (see also Rey 2019). These Pentecostals also affirm political claims by locating a programmatic project of conversion and redemption at the national scale – a least initially (see Marshall 2009).

The 'Congoliness', *la Congolité*, expressed through this Pentecostal nationalism and through a wider diasporic stance is highly *hybrid*, functioning at multiple spatial-identity scales: it draws upon an almost ethnic sense of national identity crystallized around a differentiation with other African diasporic groups and in opposition to Rwanda's regional hegemony, of which Kabila is seen as an accomplice (accused of being Rwandan himself). It is also shaped by pan-ethnic tendencies, that is tropes about the unity of an ethnically diverse Congolese nation, often nostalgic of the Mobutist era when Congo (then Zaire) 'had clear-cut national borders and was not balkanised and plundered by its neighbours like now', as Pastor Josh told me. In addition, while Pentecostal discourses hinge on tropes of ruptures and rebirth, religious leaders like Pastor Josh also mobilize particular forms of ancestral nationalism associated with prophetic figures – in particular Kongo prophetic figures like Simon Kimbangu or Kimpa Vita.[2] Additionally, he spoke about his own ethnic background (Luba) as connected to a unique destiny, again related to the trope of Israel:

> I am Luba and we have many commonalities with the Jews. We have suffered like the nation of Israel. Our language, Tshiluba, it has similarities with Hebrew. My belief is that we will build the third Temple of Israel, with the rich resources of the Congo.

The *mélange* of references and 'floating signifiers' in the making of diasporic political discourse and performance can be illustrated by the visible co-presence, in public protests, of symbols such as Mobutist-era Zairean flags, portraits of Kimbangu or Kimpa Vita, flags of the present-day DRC and attires worn by some protesters, including military camouflage gears (for *les Combattants*) or 'traditional' chief accoutrement.

While this performance of diasporic nationalism is based on a unique combination of elements and mobilizes a range of references to a Congolese/Zairean collective memory, its Pentecostal inflections have parallels with other recent political theologies constructing the sacred and leading character of the nation through biblical/Old Testament tropes, a central element in the discourse of certain American and Brazilian Pentecostals. The Universal Church of the Kingdom of God (UCKG), for instance, has an explicit geo-theology that inverts the core–periphery cartography of the capitalist world system, placing Brazil at the centre of a global project of evangelization (with the United States and Europe as the 'depraved' periphery in need of conversion). The UCKG does this by appropriating Jewish imaginaries of sacred destiny and exceptionalism to claim that it is preaching the most original, authentic and universal Christianity. For example, the church built a replica of the Temple of Solomon, complete with soaring columns and lush gardens, going as far as importing rocks from the Holy Land (Fernandes 2022).

Contested Kimbanguist prophetic politics

The biblical prophetic tropes about Israel have had a powerful effect in framing the construction of the Congo as a unique nation with a divine destiny. They have also constituted a matrix to explain (or even justify) the present. For Pastor Josh, this prophetic geo-theology is central to establishing a clear positioning within a competitive (Congolese) religious field, marking a differentiation, particularly with other Pentecostal churches – in particular prosperity churches (which he rejects as excessively 'fixated' with money) or with those promoting the theologies of ancestral bondage (like Maman Olangi's church which he describes as 'waging a war on the family'). This is done in a context where, with the widespread use of media and the internet, reinterpreted biblical prophetic tropes circulate widely, mentioned in sermons or during meetings, some taking on iconic status like verses of the book of Isaiah (18) mentioning a nation 'beyond the rivers of Ethiopia [Cush]' and 'whose land is divided by rivers' – a nation identified with the DRC.

Another 'message' circulating in the Congolese public sphere relates to the 'map of Congo' appearing clearly on the eroded grounds of the ancient Capernaum[3] synagogue in Israel and which was captured through several photographs and videos (taken by Congolese pilgrims to the Holy Land). Shared by many of my Congolese contacts on Facebook, these materials (sometimes also featuring Congolese pilgrims holding an actual Congolese map and flag and praying fervently[4]) reinforced the idea of an essential link between Israel and the Congo, locating the homeland as the sacred centre within a wider cartography and *longue durée* temporality.

Among Kimbanguists, for whom an identification with the biblical Israel is central, the meaning of the Capernaum 'map' was debated online and interpreted in light of the Kimbanguist prophetic temporality. In fact, for Kimbanguists, the Kingdom of God does not dwell in Israel (i.e. Jerusalem) anymore, it has been 'taken away and given to a nation bearing the fruits of it' (Mt. 21:43) and is now located in Nkamba – the 'New Jerusalem' having *replaced* (the old) 'spiritually empty' Jerusalem:

> A Congolese saw a map of the Congo in Jerusalem [*sic*]. Then more [Congolese] went to see it. They are *bazoba* [stupid]. They haven't read the message properly. Today's Jerusalem is spiritually empty – it is the New Jerusalem that is sacred. They shouldn't be praying there, they should pray in Africa, in Nkamba. What they did was stupid. Those who live in Israel, they don't have the *maponboli* [blessings] anymore, they only have the memory of the blessings. That's why there are so many conflicts in Israel. (Sermon heard during a Kimbanguist church service in London)

This belief in the 'non-sacredness' of Jerusalem in par with the evolution of Kimbanguist doctrine (claiming, for instance, that the three sons of Kimbangu are the embodiment of the Holy Trinity) has met strong rejection from Catholics and Pentecostals (and led to the official exclusion of the church from ecumenical Protestant bodies). However, opposition movements and political activists in the diaspora have also mobilized the anti-colonial, emancipatory and prophetic dimension of Kimbangu. They have viewed Kimbangu as 'the true Congolese prophet', as a charismatic figure whose 'passion' and sacrifice (Chomé 1959) epitomize the collective suffering in the homeland, a figure essential to the construction of an ethnic and/or nationalist identity. In the political field, the prophetic and historical dimension of Kimbangu is often associated to Patrice Lumumba, both seen as anti-colonial figures with strong pan-African resonances. It should be noted that this heroization and the pivotal place occupied by Kimbangu in the Congolese collective memory is not synonymous with support for or even agreement with the church or the cultural and religious reality of contemporary Kimbanguism.

In fact, the tensions between what could be called Christo-centric and Kimbangu-centric tendencies that have shaped the recent theological evolution of the church might explain why, on the one hand, Catholics or Pentecostals/Protestants reject what they view as Kimbanguism's syncretism and deviation from core Christian doctrines, and why, on the other hand, political-religious movements or Kongo-based groups criticize Kimbanguism's 'Christian' origin and orientation.

This is the case of Bundu dia Kongo (BDK), a movement whose central goal is the revitalization of Kongo cultural values and identities. There are in fact many parallels between Kimbanguism and BDK, whose members are mainly based in the Congo with some representatives in the diaspora. Like Kimbangu (and traditional prophetic figures), BDK's Prophet-founder Ne Muanda Nsemi received a divine calling (in the 1960s) which he initially resisted; many Kimbanguists, like BDK members, believe in the sacredness of the Kikongo language; both movements place a central importance in pan-African ideas of 'return' of African Americans to Africa. Some gestures, in particular the *bula makonko* (cupped hand clapping, used in particular as a form of greeting), *dekama* (genuflection) or *fukama,* (kneeling) which are seen as central in the embodied performance of a (precolonial) Kongo identity within the context of the BDK movement (see Covington-Ward 2016) are also important among Kimbanguists (even non-Bakongo Kimbanguists) and during Kimbanguist rituals.[5]

Despite these commonalities, BDK rejects the Kimbanguist use of the Bible, seen as a tool of continued colonial oppression, holding the belief that 'Simon Kimbangu was unable to complete his mission and his work had been deflected from its path' (Demart and Tonda 2016: 207). Moreover, while the BDK, mostly because of secessionist ambitions and sporadic use of violence, has been severely repressed by the Kabila government, many diasporic activists saw the doctrinally 'neutral' political stance of the Kimbanguist church, at odds with the politicization of the prophetic figure of Kimbangu, as providing implicit support for the Kabila regime in the DRC. Just before the 2011 elections, the Kimbanguist spiritual leader did in fact voice his support for Kabila and a widely circulated prophecy attributed to Kimbangu known as the 'Prophecy of the 4 presidents' identified Kabila as the one 'who will save the Congo' (see Mokoko Gampiot 2017: 245)[6] (Figure 10).

This put those diasporic Kimbanguists who were sympathetic to the opposition in a difficult position. Some London Kimbanguists did attend anti-Kabila protests and attempts were even made by some Kimbanguists to organize

Figure 10 Poster of the 'Prophecy of the 4 Presidents' in a Nkamba shop. Credit: author.

opposition meetings in one of the church's premises. Nonetheless, disruptions to Kimbanguist church services did occur in the UK and also in Germany and France, a consequence of the action of small groups of *Combattants* protesting what was seen as pro-Kabila stance by the Kimbanguist church. However, in a context where (Pentecostal) pastors associated with the regime are prevented from travelling and officiating, and where some churches have been occupied and shut down, the Kimbanguists did not face the same level of opprobrium from opposition activists. This, I hypothesize, is due to the ambivalence associated with the Kimbanguist imaginary, whose self-described 'apolitical' character may remain unconvincing, but which, at the same time, is rooted in a collective Congolese postcolonial memory, embodying the martyrdom of the nation and the prophetic hope of renewal and redemption of the homeland.

Another recurrent criticism of Kimbanguists and contemporary Kimbanguism concerns its relation to Mobutu's regime when 'Papa' Joseph Diangienda was the spiritual leader of the church. As suggested earlier and as Mélice (2009) and others (see Mokoko Gampiot 2017) have argued, the official political positioning of the Kimbanguist church as 'apolitical' tends to conceal a more complex reality. This political neutrality is in fact based on a doctrinal attitude of submission to the governing authorities, following the belief that 'the authorities that exist have been established by God' (Rom. 13:1). This attitude took the form, in effect, of an 'institutional contiguity' (Mélice 2009: 63) with the autocratic Mobutu regime and his party, the MPR (Mouvement Populaire de la Révolution). Mobutu also drew upon the figure of Kimbangu as part of his ideology of *authenticité* (authenticity). In a famous discourse, Mobutu questioned why so many Zaireans have no problem accepting the reality of Godly manifestations in Lourdes or Fatima through Mary, whereas Kimbangu's divine status was rejected, and as a 'Black man', Kimbangu was seen as a 'fanatic' and imprisoned (Mokoko Gampiot 2017: 231). The fact that Mobutu banned religious groups and 'dissident sects' loosely identifying with Kimbangu's prophetism also reinforced the official, institutional legitimacy of the (routinized) Kimbanguist church, which, in turn, strengthened a (grateful) compliance from Kimbanguist leaders to the rule of the one-party/ MPR state. This allegiance did not prevent, however, the emergence of anti-MPR voices and tendencies (for instance, those based on ethnic/Bakongo loyalties) among Kimbanguist communities (and some of the clergy). However, these alternative voices were not strong enough to prevent the widespread view that the 'two Josephs' (Joseph Diangienda and Joseph Mobutu) were close allies. On the day of Diangienda's funeral in Kinshasa, in the declining months of the regime, crowds threw projectiles at the procession, shouting insults accusing Diangienda of being a traitor, a witch and a *hibou* (owl), the nickname of the notorious Mobutist secret police often operating covertly, at night (Mélice 2006: 67). The fact that Diangienda banned Kimbanguists to take part in the march bringing together thousands of protesters to reopen the democratic dialogue of National Conference in 1992 was also seen as clear evidence of support to Mobutism.

The protest in question, called *Marche de l'Espoir* ('march of hope'), also known as the 'Marche des Chrétiens', given that it was mostly organized by lay Catholic groups, was violently repressed. It occupies an important place in the post-Mobubu Congolese collective memory. Its thirty-year commemoration in 2012 was one of the key reasons behind the organization of a day of protest when Pastor Josh led street prayers in front of Downing Street.

Diasporic politics and the 'Marche des Chrétiens'

The 2012 'Marche des Chrétiens' was not an isolated event but rather part of a wider transnational movement of public demonstrations and rallies organized across the Congolese diaspora around the time of the election campaigns in the DRC. It took place in many European and North American cities where

Congolese people had settled, including London, Paris, Brussels, Dublin, Washington DC, Montreal and Toronto. While the idea of the march initially emerged in Kinshasa, the city's governor eventually banned it there and the march therefore became a diaspora-only event. It attained its global resonance through Facebook, YouTube and other social media, created a powerful sense of diasporic simultaneity and represented an 'imagined community' united across national borders.

The London-'Marche des Chrétiens' brings to the fore the interplay of diasporic politics, religious identity, place, history and memory that characterizes the transtemporal and translocal dimensions of diasporic religion. However, because two separate religious events – a Catholic service and a Pentecostal gathering – took place that day, it was difficult for the participants to uphold a unified 'Christian vision' for the cause of the homeland. The parallel organization of a Mass celebrated in a church and public street prayers reflected the different ways Catholics and Pentecostals relate to spatial sacralization and religious performance. As we shall see, it also crystallized tensions within the wider Congolese politico-religious landscape between leaders of competing factions who sided with either Catholic priests or Pentecostal pastors.

In London, on the day of the protest, the Congolese Catholic chaplaincy organized a Mass in the prestigious French church of Leicester Square (Notre Dame de France), before the protesters marched across the hyper-centre of the global city to reach Downing Street. During the Mass, which was well attended by Congolese (including many political activists), the political and civic role of the Catholics during the Marche des Chrétiens repressed by the Mobutu regime was praised and the memory of the 'martyrs of 1992' celebrated. As part of his speech, the Congolese Abbé of the chaplaincy talked about the current situation in the Congo and the position of the Catholic Church (which contested the re-election of Joseph Kabila), drawing a clear parallel between 1992 and 2012:

> Life is a gift from God; no one has the right to take it away. Let us pay tribute to the memory of those who died for the cause of democracy during the 1992 protest march. But 20 years after, is the DRC democratic? One of the paths of democracy is elections. What kind of elections did we get? Let us pray to the Lord. Let us give Him a big thank you as He gave us such a beautiful, big and rich country. Let us ask Him the favour of having leaders who love the Congo and Congolese people.

For Catholics, the commemoration forged a temporal connection between the current opposition to Kabila's government and the protest that took place in

Figure 11 Placard, 'Marche des Chrétiens' in Central London. Credit: author.

Kinshasa two decades earlier during Mobutu's declining rule. The commemorative Mass was an occasion to reinforce the significance and legitimate role of the Congolese chaplaincy, linking up, at the same time, with the homeland by echoing the stance of the CENCO (Conférence Épiscopale Nationale du Congo, the Bishop's Conference, the main Catholic body at national level). It also represented an opportunity to demonstrate the chaplaincy's capacity to mobilize the resources of a large (powerful) established institution, through the use of a prestigious space situated at the urban hyper-centre, adjacent to Leicester Square, one of the iconic landmarks of the global city (Figure 11).

For the Abbé, the possibility of using a space in such a central and prestigious location was one of the reasons why the Pentecostal pastors were keen to organize a joint event with the Catholics. In fact, at first, Congolese politicians and pastors asked the Abbé to facilitate access to the Westminster Cathedral, which he deemed logistically impossible. Recounting his meeting with the pastors, he discussed their naivety (in thinking they could easily get access to the seat of the English Catholic Church) and the risk of losing face if Congolese 'come late':

There is a group of people who came to see me: they wanted to use Westminster Cathedral, because it's close to Downing Street, and also because of the grandeur of the church. But the pastors didn't understand that you can't just use the Cathedral as you wish! So many arrangements have to be made. . . . I had suggested Notre Dame de France [near Leicester Square] which was free on the day. . . . In Westminster Cathedral they have 5 Masses a day. . . knowing the Congolese you say Mass at such and such a time and they will come late . . . and it's me who would have problems!

In the end, the Abbé rejected the pastors' suggestion of holding an 'ecumenical Mass' in Notre Dame the France, criticizing them for their tendency to 'disorganization', highlighting, in contrast, the benefit of a clear hierarchical structure and upholding the importance of an established, universal Catholic ritual to be protected from Pentecostal practices:

> They wanted an 'ecumenical Mass' but a Catholic Mass is a Catholic Mass. . . . said by the priest. . . . The Mass has two main parts – the liturgy of the Word and the Eucharist, the consecration. . . . The pastor is not going to come and lay hands on people, that is out of the question! The big problem among these pastors is also disorganization. In the Catholic church, you know who is who. Who was going to speak? They did not agree, for them it is an opportunity for self-promotion. . . . I did the Mass and then, at the end I asked 'is there a pastor here who wants to say anything?' No one. . . . I learnt later the pastors sent [text] messages saying there will be no Mass.

The fact that these text messages were supposedly sent by the pastors to members of the Congolese community telling them that the Mass had been cancelled was a clear cause of discontent. When the main group of protesters arrived in front of Downing Street, where the Pentecostals were praying, clashes erupted as a group of Congolese young people coming from the Catholic service unplugged the instruments and interrupted the prayers and preaching. Pastor Josh was targeted by the young activists as he was leading the prayers. When I asked him about these clashes, he defended his continual politico-spiritual engagement for the Congo and accused the Catholics, 'statue idolizers', of encouraging violence and of being influenced by the Devil:

> The young people do not understand that I have been working for more than 30 years under God's guidance to resolve the crisis, since I had the prophecy of God for the Congo, even during Mobutu I spoke out! I am not here for *monkozi* [power] and money. I sent three pastors to see the Abbé and he refused our intervention because he said that it was against Catholic doctrine. Then in his speech he said: 'where are the pastors?' . . . We are Pentecostals, we do not idolize statues. The young people, why did they do that? . . . They threatened to beat me up. . . . This violence is the influence of the Devil, the Devil of the Catholics.

Pastor Josh's and the Abbé's narratives reflect the existence of clear fault lines between two symbolic and ritual worldviews containing divergent views of authority, doctrine and legitimacy. However, the tensions made legible during the London Marche des Chrétiens should not be seen solely as a confrontation, imported from the homeland, between Pentecostals and Catholics. The fact that two separate events took place on that day also reflected deep fractures within the opposition movement, as leaders from the main opposition party UDPS sided with the Catholics, while other opposition leaders had joined the *pasteurs combattants* in the Downing Street picketing. Some of those who attended the Pentecostal service had been excluded from the UDPS following intense leadership struggles, which had ramifications across the diaspora, mainly in France and Belgium, and in Kinshasa. These struggles should therefore be reinscribed within a wider framework, a larger transnational social field, since an active and visible role in the diaspora can be converted into political capital to help securing positions of power in the homeland, especially in case of victory of the opposition, which many were hoping for during the 'Congolese winter' of demonstrations and intense campaigning.

Intergenerational divides and 'youth' politics

In this second half of the chapter, I focus on the role of young Congolese during the period of intense mobilization. In doing so, I will continue to address some of the issues underlying the whole of this chapter, issues related to the urban performance of diasporic identities and politics, while highlighting some of the divisions operating within the diasporic political field.

For many young people who had been involved in public demonstrations, the conflict during the Marche des Chrétiens was a turning point and led to increasing disengagement and disenchantment. Speaking with some members of the group who disrupted the prayer service in front of Downing Street, it was clear that they saw in this gathering a sign of division, detrimental to the unity of the movement. Other Congolese youth who did not participate in the clash interpreted it as a direct and legitimate reaction to the tensions and leadership struggles. In fact, in a meeting organized by Congolese youth shortly after the Marche des Chrétiens and which took place in a community centre in Tottenham (North London), they directly voiced their concerns to some of the first-generation activists and leaders about these internal divisions. Other grievances included the absence of accountability regarding money collection, general lack of organization or the existence of 'YouTube-only Combattants', seen as more interested in increasing their reputation by uploading videos of themselves on the internet than fighting for the cause of the Congo. Often dismissed by youth as 'YouTube resistance', these performances – measured by 'likes', 'shares' and 'comments' and archived for repeated consumption – are perceived to be motivated by a quest to accumulate personal political capital, not only in a context of competition between those seeking to 'represent' the Congolese community in the UK but also in the internal struggle for leadership within transnationally located opposition parties. As a 25-year-old male activist put it, 'for some of our leaders, it's all about leadership – being filmed so that they can be noticed by people in Kinshasa.'

The organization of a meeting during which young Congolese confronted their elders reflects the increasing willingness of these youth to carve out their own space for political action in a field dominated by first-generation activists. This search for autonomy is linked to the effect of generational divides and gerontocratic power relations, and some activists were very critical of first-generation leaders, politicians and the *Combattants*:

> We are part of the fight for the Congo but our Congolese politicians in the diaspora they don't involve the young people. They don't speak the same language. They disregard young people's opinions. They say: 'I know, you don't know, so shut up!' (Interview with a British Congolese female, twenty-two)

The category 'young people' (*bajeunes*) conceals an internal heterogeneity, encompassing youth and young adults 'born and bred' in the UK and those who came to the UK during their teenage years (the so-called 1.5 generation, see Kasinitz, Mollenkopf and Waters 2004). However, it was recurrently used to mark clear differences in terms of authority and power with those (mostly male) politicians and religious and 'community' leaders (and activists such as *les Combattants*) able to exert social control and monopolize decision-making (for instance, deciding the organization and timing of protests).

Among the group of 'young people' I followed to document the urban reality of Congolese diasporic politics (participating in about fifteen events and demonstrations, all mostly in Central London), the most active were often students or young educated professionals who created Facebook-based organizations, quickly reaching hundreds of followers and who were keen to get involved in a range of ways. In addition to public protests, they took part in awareness-raising campaigns led by non-profit organizations such as Save the Congo, based in London. Save the Congo and other organizations like the US-based Friends of the Congo have launched advocacy initiatives, among other things stressing the link between armed conflicts, human rights abuse and the exploitation of rare minerals in the east of the DRC and in particular coltan used in mobile phones (Nest 2011). Through these campaigns, they also questioned the role played by Britain and other Western powers and international institutions, like the UN, in maintaining or aggravating the conflictual situation in the wider Central African region. Circulating petitions, writing to MPs or attending forums such as those organized by the UK APPG (All-Party Parliamentary Group) on the Great Lakes Region of Africa, they emphasize not only their attachment to the DRC but also their role as 'British citizens':

> UK taxpayer money is being used in Congo, for development and also for example organising local elections like in 2006, which were a huge waste. So much money has been given to the DRC, with no accountability. If British companies support the rebels in the east of the country, it needs to stop. I am speaking as a British Citizen here: we need to lobby our government to put pressure on Congo and also on Uganda and Rwanda. This is our duty as British citizens. (Female British Congolese youth activist, during an APPG meeting in London, from fieldnotes)

Their engagement was expressed through public protests and online activism and, despite their disenchantment with Congolese diasporic politics, there was a strong symbolic and emotional identification with the DRC, which coexisted with a sense of hybrid belonging combining British, ethnic or religious identities (most of them belonged to Congolese Pentecostal churches or were members of the Congolese Catholic chaplaincy). This diasporic and multi-layered notion of 'home' did not prevent feelings of marginalization and exclusion (as we discussed in Chapter 2) connected to direct experiences of racism, but also to the impact of media stereotypes about DRC, Africa in general, or Black youths in the UK and wider European contexts. Moreover, as Levitt and Waters (2002) and others have argued, the way younger generations from an ethnic minority background identify or engage transnationally (including travel to the homeland) varies over the life cycle or according to particular contexts. For many Congolese youths, the 2011 election represented such a context, and they joined the demonstrations in the hundreds, sharing information about the mobilization through 'BB messages' (free messages sent between Blackberry phones, used by many Congolese youth – before the emergence of WhatsApp) or via Facebook groups, set up at the start of the movement. Many of these British Congolese youth were also exposed to the *Combattants'* political programmes on Shot One, a popular Congolese SKY-satellite channel based in London and watched by their parents. It should be said that some youth who initially rejected the *Combattants'* radicalism (in particular, their stance against Congolese musicians) changed their opinions as the movement gained momentum and the Congolese started to organize and protest in the streets of capital cities all around the world.

The draw of centrality and the 'right to city'

I followed these youth in a diverse range of protests, highlighting the multifaceted character of the mobilization. Most of these protests were in Central London, often in busy, touristic or shopping areas – for instance, in front of the Apple Store in Regent Street (to protest the use of 'blood minerals' in electronics), in front of the Congolese Embassy (near Oxford Street), the Rwanda High Commission (near Regent's Park), in front of Downing Street or in Piccadilly Circus (flash mob protests). In the previous chapter, we discussed how, for FAKI members, parading in Central London was not only a powerful enactment of a theology of prophetic reversal but also a way to collectively gain confidence in the public (secular) realm. Similarly, for the Congolese protesters, assembling in the centre of London with a crowd of like-minded people constituted a thrilling, empowering – almost transcendent – experience:

> When you are in a crowd you don't feel [embarrassed], especially when you're moved by purpose. When you have a group of people, everybody's growing from everybody's strength, we're all moving by a particular cause. You're thinking OK, I'm in central London, that's the best place! (British Congolese protester, female, twenty-five)

> If we do it in central London, it has a bigger impact because there's a lot more people, there's masses up here, so if we have a message it will get people's attention and it will get the government's attention. We just want everyone to hear, so I think that's why we have it [demonstrations] in central London. (British Congolese activist, female, twenty-four)

For many of these Congolese youth, it was their first participation in a public protest movement. They were attracted by the ideal of Central London as a prospective *agora* and site of assembly, as well as a space where they could address the British government. Adopting a hybrid citizenship of Londoners, British and Congolese gave protesters a 'particular right to speak out, an upper hand', as one protester put it, to denounce, in front of Downing Street, the role of the British government in the Congolese crisis (the UK being an important bilateral donor to Kagame's government in Rwanda, accused of fuelling proxy wars in mineral-rich eastern Congo):

> Downing Street -that's where the Prime Minister is. To the Congolese community this is where the Prime Minister lives. This is his home. . . . *Our* home is being disturbed. . . . So we're going to disturb *your* home. You need to understand where we're coming from. It's like being that annoying child. . . . I'm going to keep banging on your door until you let me in. If the Prime Minister is the man who has the final say, who decides on these things and if he's working with Rwanda and so forth – if that's the case – then that's the person we want to deal with. (British Congolese activist, female, twenty-four)

The image of 'banging on the door' and disturbing the Prime Minister in *his* home is interesting with the double sense it carries in terms of the domestic setting and nation. So is also the characterization of Congolese protesters as 'annoying children': this is an acknowledgement of being relatively powerless yet belonging. This dependent belonging enables a voice, as young Congolese can use this tensile status to act in a way, as an irritant, that cannot be ignored. Also, as this quote reveals, claiming a 'right to the city' can be translocal, as protests in London are also about injustices in other cities, other continents. It is also linking sense of responsibility as a Congolese–British citizen to the situation in the homeland: 'our tax money is funding the war in the Congo', as one youth put it.

Let us briefly examine the relevance of this notion of the 'right to the city' to make sense of the Congolese protests. First introduced in the 1970s by Henri Lefebvre, the right to the city denotes a 'superior right' concerned with inhabiting the city in the fullest possible manner, a full and profound participation in democratic urban life free from technocratic and capitalist control. The notion has been evoked routinely in discussions about protests and contemporary urban social movements of the 2000s, ranging from Occupy to the *indignados* anti-austerity movement in Spain and from the Gezi Park protests in Istanbul to even the occupation of Tahrir Square in Cairo during the 'Arab Spring'. A specific imaginary of the 'right to the city' has emerged, implying a sort of translocal connection between diverse centres of political resistance and inferring a strong transtemporal dimension, with links made with urban political moments viewed as foundational such as the Paris Commune and *les évènements* of May 1968 (Merrifield 2011). Building on Lefebvre, Harvey (2012) sees the right to the city as a way to explain how the urban is not only the site but also, increasingly, a stake in these protests.

In a way, a wide range of radical urban social movements have been unproblematically placed under this umbrella banner, and perhaps viewed too readily as part of a wider, almost universal movement, a position lacking sociological nuance (Garbin and Millington 2018). In addition, the distinction between use value and exchange value so central in Lefebvre's quest for 'renewed urban life' (Lefebvre 1996: 158) and neo-Lefebvrian formulations of a right to the city as an act of (re)claiming 'urban commons' (see Harvey 2012) also risks simplifying the status of urban space in the politics of diasporic visibility. I want to argue here that the representational significance of 'cityness' and urban centrality may play an important role in the ways in which value can be extracted and converted from visible urban (collective and/or individual) action.

To supplement and critique Lefebvrian perspectives on the urban, I approach exchange value in a more Bourdieusian sense, as a value deriving from equivalences between symbolic and political capitals. These equivalences 'take place' in a context where acts of protest in highly symbolic locations in London are performed with the aim of reaching beyond the city itself. Indeed, pastors leading prayer groups in front of 10 Downing Street, activists delivering memos addressed to the Prime Minister's office (and being photographed in front of the iconic 'number 10' door) or outspoken first-generation activists in military outfits filmed for YouTube clips on Trafalgar Square are examples of staged, embodied enactments of opposition that help constitute a diasporic economy of images (and sounds). These performances gain credence by their staging in locations rich in historically accumulated symbolic capital and may be seen as attempts to convert symbolic prestige into political capital in both Europe and the DRC, a process made possible by mediatization and transnational circulation, via social media, popular diasporic websites or Congolese satellite TV channels.

While being visible, and above all vocal, in protests endows diasporic actors (in particular, first-generation males) with prestige beyond the local and the immediate, there is a complex relationship between visibility, performance and urban public recognition as we saw in the previous chapter when discussing the poetics and politics of Kimbanguist parades. Congolese diasporic urban protests cannot be disentangled from the (racialized) politics of representation and objectivation. For instance, young Congolese are acutely aware of how their presence in the centre of the city could be interpreted and talked about, and what their urban, masculine *blackness* signifies in the eyes of the police, especially in confrontational situations. They are policed in a way that reminds some of how Black youth were policed during the riots that had erupted across London (and in some parts of urban England) a year earlier:

> The police arrested 149 [Congolese] kids during one of the marches, they took them to the police station telling them if they come back anywhere near Downing Street, they can get arrested. The police had the [2011] riots in mind. (British Congolese activist, male, 25)

Another activist I interviewed after one of the protests also talked about the impact that racialization and structural discrimination have on the relationship with the police, processes that are so entrenched that they seem 'a-historical':

> Race – I mean the darker you are, when you are dealing with the police, it is gonna be a tough time. . . . We are unconsciously conditioned to know that, growing up as a young Black man in London, you just know that the police don't like you and you don't like the police . . . (British Congolese activist, male, thirty-two)

There were other connected debates about the objectivation of public performance, with concerns, for instance, about how using drums, chanting and singing in Lingala may create the impression of a 'joyful carnival' that could be misconstrued through a (white) lens of exoticization. Instead, young protesters justified the use of English in slogans, placards and leaflets in many ways: to reach a wide audience, to be efficient and legible in the public sphere or for the protest to achieve more than 'just chanting in Lingala against Kabila like the elders do'.

Global and postcolonial positionalities

Reading the Congolese protests through the lens of the 'right to the city' allows us to connect urbanity, centrality and collective visibility, but we should not ignore political dynamics within the diasporic community or the fact that demonstrations constitute embodied action (Tyler and Marciniak 2014), for they reveal underlying tensions between objectivation and performance against pre-existing power asymmetries. For Congolese protesters, the body represented at the same time a frontline or channel through which the sacrifice, endurance and pain of collective action are experienced. The body is also a political tool and a way to convey identities/modes of belonging (through dress and appearance). A key issue here was also the display, during demonstrations, of graphic images of wounded bodies, in particular the bodies of female victims of sexual and gender-based violence in the conflict in eastern Congo, images which some young people saw as comforting hegemonic (neo)colonial conceptions of the Congo and Africa.

However, other activists were convinced such images can provoke empathy and 'show a reality that should not be hidden' (British Congolese protester, female, twenty-five). In such instances, the aim is to 'establish an emotional and moral connection with people' (Tyler and Marciniak 2014), while at the same time, being able to reclaim 'our own images' from the Western media and NGO/charity narratives.

Young female protesters and activists were particularly keen to engage in these discussions during public meetings and on various internet fora. Some had close links with Congolese women's groups led by first-generation Congolese women which had, over the years, established connections with non-Congolese feminist advocacy groups and NGOs and mobilized the narratives of 'women's rights as human rights' to engage in 'transversal politics' within and outside the Congolese diaspora (see Godin 2018). In doing so, 'they produced a diagnosis of the situation [in the Congo] as well as a prognosis that potentially could be heard by different audiences (within and beyond the diaspora), at different contentious scales of engagement' (Godin 2018: 1403). Congolese women activists were thus engaged in deconstructing what they saw as 'white saviour' feminism, while addressing masculine domination (and domestic violence) within the Congolese community, as well as dominant discourses linked to enduring colonial representations and 'heart of darkness' tropes. For them, it was particularly important to challenge views constructing sexual violence in the DRC as a 'cultural problem' and the idea of women as 'passive victims' (of African/Congolese male violence), an interpretation, which, in their eyes, also stemmed from a lack of understanding of the global, social and political context of war, exploitation and oppression.

Members of both women's groups and youth groups expressed some forms of opposition to the government of the DRC, but many also criticized members of the Congolese opposition movement for pursuing what they believed to be a limited agenda (supporting the main opposition candidate) rather than addressing the globalized and post/neocolonial dimension of the crisis in the DRC. This form of engagement, which goes beyond supporting the opposition movement in the DRC and the diaspora through political parties such as the UDPS or APARECO (Alliance des Patriotes pour la Refondation du Congo), operates across several scales, from local to global. For instance, one Congolese activist took part in the 'Carnival of Dirt' across the City of London (London's financial district), alongside anti-capitalist campaigners, global environmental organizations and migrant activists. The 'Carnival of Dirt' was a parody of a funeral procession, stopping in front of the headquarters of mining companies and trading institutions, such as the London Metal Exchange. Dressed in black, with ash covering their faces and carrying coffins, the protesters commemorated, in their own symbolic way, the memory of victims of human rights abuses in countries exploited for their natural resources in Latin America, Asia, Africa or the Pacific. A member of a Congolese youth platform commented on his participation in the Carnival of Dirt:

> For some of our leaders, it's all about leadership being filmed so that they can be noticed by people in Kinshasa. They said: 'after Mobutu things will change', then 'after Kabila-the father, things will change', and now: 'if Joseph Kabila goes, it will change'. But the problem of the Congo is bigger than that. It's a global problem. The exploitation is global and that's why we need to explore ways of working with people outside our community.

It is interesting to note that some members of Congolese women's organizations were also present during this event. This illustrates how both young activists and women's groups have adopted, in their own particular way, the strategy of bridging with human rights organization and/or social movements addressing wider causes of injustice and exploitation on a global level.

Moreover, some links were established with the Occupy movement in London in an attempt to highlight the human cost of global capitalist exploitation, using the example of coltan mining. Yet, while many were enthusiastic about bridging with Occupy London,[7] some questioned the capacity of such movements to engage across ethnic/race and class boundaries. In their eyes, the Occupy movement did not do enough to welcome their own attempts to link the injustices of global capitalism with its imperial roots:

> We are happy to build alliances with Occupy [. . .] but we can't wait for them. . . . They have their own concerns about salaries because they have lost their jobs, things like that. . . . Marx says that the proletarians of the world should unite but it's the white working class really that he was talking about! (British Congolese activist, male, twenty-five)

In addition, the act of *occupying* – appropriating public space durably and visibly – ran the unnecessary risk of criminalization:

> If we occupy, we will be criminalized even more. It is not a good strategy for us. . . . We have done stuff with Occupy but we are not middle-class whites with lawyers advising us. If we occupy, we'll just be seen as Black immigrants causing problems and we'll become easy targets for racists and the media . . . like during the riots it was like: 'Black youths again!' (British Congolese activist, male, twenty-seven)

Here we see again how race complicates urban visibility and the possibility of making collective 'right to the city' claims for Congolese, and for that matter African immigrants, in the metropolis. Several years before the debates about 'decolonization', Congolese activists were engaged in an act of connecting the colonial past and a present of global – late capitalist – exploitation. For instance, they have sought to, in a way, 'repostcolonize' London, to relocate this global city within a postcolonial framework of intertwining places, spaces, relations and histories, not limited to the DRC-Belgium binary. In doing so, they have engaged with the inherent multidimensionality of the postcolonial city in a context of neoliberal (and post-political) globalization, recreating connections between old and new forms of domination, between historic and emerging centres and peripheries of a wider European/global colonial and postcolonial project.

One participant in a 'flash mob' in Piccadilly Circus ('Don't Be Blind'), organized to raise awareness about the situation in the Congo, highlighted the continuity between colonial exploitation and the contemporary plunder of minerals for the electronic industry:

> Many people are blind to the fact that we are carrying blood in our laptops and mobile phones, that coltan is being plundered in the Congo. . . . Hundred years ago, Congo produced 60% of the total production of rubber before Latin America and Asia were able to grow trees and took over the production. Congolese people were massively killed during that period of mass production, for financial reasons. So we have decided that we are not letting our history be erased. (British Congolese activist, male, thirty-two)

Rejecting the idea that conflict in the Congo/Great Lakes region was driven by ethnicity or 'tribalism', activists are concerned with restating or creating other spatial and temporal connections, using slogans such as 'the real cost of your iPhone is genocide in the Congo', or through the symbolic resonance of sites chosen for protests such as the Apple Store in Regent Street. Raising awareness of how consumers fetishize 'blood mobiles' and 'blood laptops' reflects a diasporic engagement, and represents, at the same time, a way of locating the country on a global map of injustice and human rights abuses (Figures 12–14).

For the Congolese, excavating and recovering a postcolonial reality means challenging the 'bundle of silences' (Trouillot 1995) inherent in the narrative of post-imperial Britain. Congolese youth react angrily when told that, since Congo is not a former British colony, their claims and protest have no place in London:

> Some people even said 'well you guys weren't colonized by the British, you were colonized by Belgium, why don't you go and do something over there?' (British Congolese activist, female, twenty-two)

Figure 12 Flash mob 'Don't Be Blind', Picadilly Circus, Central London.

Figure 13 Small protest in front of the Apple Store, Central London.

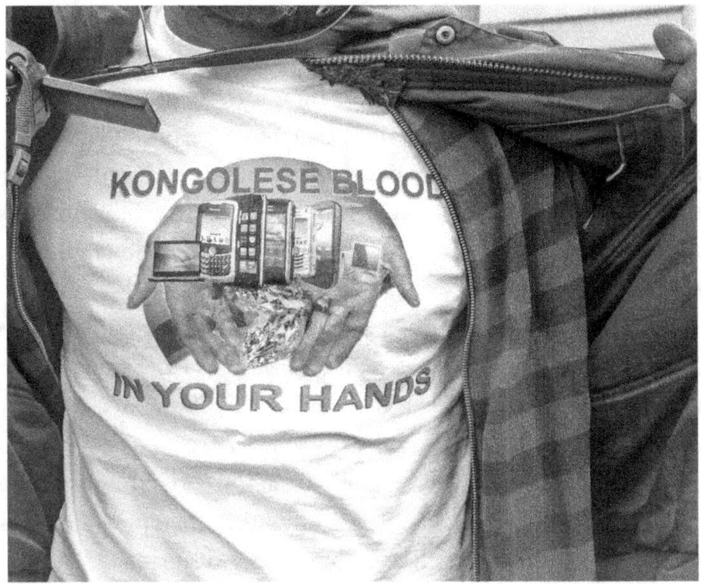

Figure 14 T-shirt of young Congolese protester. All credit: author.

This double Othering – combining a temporal dimension ('your diasporic history is not part of our national history') with a spatial distancing ('your protests don't belong here') – was vigorously contested. As one interviewee put it, 'The British have always had their hands in the Congo since the colonial period, but then that's not talked about.' These political/urban performances and discourses thus had a diasporic reach that foregrounds the 'present pasts' (Huyssen 2003), while, at the same time, deconstructing them.

Conclusion: *Pasteurs te*! Religion and diasporic publics in postcolonial times

This chapter began by examining how the mobilization to 'liberate' the Congo was constructed as part of a wider spiritual battle which, for *pasteurs combattants* like Pasteur Josh, can be expressed by forms of territorialization through the use of power prayers. We saw that these prayers reappropriate urban spaces by remoralizing them in the midst of a hostile and secularized environment. The Marche des Chrétiens also showed two parallel – if not competing – religious performances as well as internal political/factional divisions among Congolese activists. Despite tensions and divisions, those who participated in these protests saw the formulations of political claims and the visible enactment of collective presence through the appropriation of urban centrality as indissociable. Religion is a medium to express and reinforce that tight intertwining.

Beyond that, the Congolese involvement in these protests raises the issue of the type of urban diasporic publics that are being produced and performed. Two questions are particularly important: the perceived efficacy of these urban – 'grounded'– political performances and the role of religious publics in these processes.

The experience of assembling in the centre of London constituted an empowering enactment of collective mobilization. For young protesters in particular, 'the right to the city' echoes 'a global struggle for citizenship that needs to be *grounded* in the city' (Merrifield 2011: 476), as the city serves to anchor and unify (rather than just contain) political action operating across a variety of scales. But with divisions and factionalism within the opposition movement, these young people grew disenchanted and many disengaged. At the heart of their disenchantment was also a clear contradiction between being *visible*, in the sense of being identified and policed as 'Black youth', and frustrations with their *invisibility*, relating to the lack of media, political and public recognition with protests performed in such strategic locations – even in front of the BBC. As a young Congolese activist explained,

> we were outraged at the fact that we were protesting for three months in central London, Oxford Circus, in Regent Street and even outside the door of the BBC, and yet there was almost no coverage in the mainstream news. And the couple of articles were focusing . . . on misrepresenting or demonizing the protests by telling that they were causing a lot of disruptions to the public order, rather than stating the outcry that was going on.

This perception also explains why these activists have used the internet and social media to create alternative publics to convey their political voice, to 'replace the BBC', as one Congolese youth put it (quoted in Godin and Dona 2016: 63). The ability to create such publics outside of the direct control of first-generation activists and religious leaders has led young Congolese activists to initiate new campaigns which, while they emerged from the anti-Kabila movement of the mid-2010s, have continued long after the end of the street protests and the 2019 regime change. Such campaigns have thrown into relief the connection between colonial and postcolonial dynamics. This is the case of the 'Geno-cost' campaign, which includes 'offline' commemorations and virtual campaigns to raise awareness of the 'economic root/aspect of the genocide in DRC . . . [to challenge] the misleading discourse, often led by certain media, that tribal or ethnic conflicts are the root cause of the genocide and instability in Congo'.[8] Through this campaign, durable links have been created across the Congolese diaspora, with collaborations also established with youth in eastern Congo, leading to regular online meetings and the shared production of media outputs.

Most of the Congolese youth – including 'generation 1.5' ones and young adults – I followed during these protests were members of churches or religious groups, mostly Pentecostals (attending Congolese churches or more mixed churches) or Catholics. However, this belonging did rarely translate into support and resources to generate efficacious counter-publics, where these young Congolese could gain a voice and act upon their claims. A handful of *pasteurs combattants* and members of the Catholic Church and some of its clergy were certainly vocal in condemning the Congolese autocratic government. But these religious spaces remain constraining and limiting in their affordances, for they tend to be dominated by first-generation (male) migrants and regulated by rigid sets of rules and ritualistic constraints that discourage the formation of new leadership and the incorporation of broader politico-cultural agendas. These limits are evident in the fact that religious actors, like Pentecostal pastors, eschew political activity or avoid references to politics in their preaching. More militant activists such as *les Combattants* see this avoidance as tacitly reinforcing the political status quo, sometimes even betraying the cause of the homeland in the name of political expediency and church growth. At a high-profile diasporic political meeting in London which took place during the visit of Etienne Tshisekedi, one of the main DRC opposition leaders, members of the audience interrupted a pastor's speech and prayers with shouts of 'pasteurs te!' ('no pastors!'). In an interview, a 28-year-old Congolese activist explained that

> they said 'no pastors!' during that meeting because people don't trust them . . . 'cos they say, the *églises de réveil* have been putting a blindfold in front of people's eyes. Telling them to pray, pray, pray but they are not addressing the real issues. . . . They want to stay neutral. Even Jesus used to take sides against evil and injustice. Why are the pastors saying 'on reste au milieu du village' [we remain in the middle of the village]. Why do you have to be in the middle of the village? You are a man of God, you have to stand for what's right.

In the eyes of some opposition leaders (in particular, those affiliated with Catholics and *pasteurs combattants*), Kimbanguists were also sometimes accused of betraying the cause of the homeland by 'remaining in the middle of the village', in continuity with the Mobutu period. However, as we discussed before, the figure of Kimbangu could be reinterpreted and mobilized as a powerful nationalist symbol of liberation and emancipation. In fact, Kimbanguists themselves keep this heritage alive by connecting the liberation of the Black race, diasporic Africanity and prophetic promises (*bilaka*) as part of their own understanding of the Bible (see Mokoko Gampiot 2017) and in their practices and urban performances. This connection was demonstrated when parading in Central London was reinterpreted as part of a postcolonial theology of messianic reversal, as we saw in the previous chapter. A similar example here includes a Kimbanguist festival in the streets of Lisbon, which took on a special meaning, linking the postcolonial geography of the Portuguese capital to a cosmology of messianic reversal, as Kimbanguist worshippers (local Angolans and Congolese coming from all over Europe, including from London parishes[9]) paraded proudly on a centrally located square where, many remarked, 'slaves were sold'. It should also be noted here that Kimbanguists in the diaspora have formulated several claims over the years about the colonial oppression under the Belgium rule. Requests are continually made to the Belgian government to officially rehabilitate Kimbangu (who was rehabilitated by the Congolese state 'but not by the Belgians', Kimbanguists often insist) to access the documents related to the arrest and death of the prophet and also the internment of thousands of Kimbanguists during the colonial rule in the Congo. In Belgium, these requests have become part of wider discussions about the role of colonial memory and heritage, including the legacy of Leopold II, and of more recent calls to 'decolonize public space' – for instance, by removing statues of Leopold – especially after the Black Lives Matter (BLM) movement.

Black Lives Matter and its related decolonizing movements emerged after my period of fieldwork. Nonetheless, I conducted some follow-up digital research on the online discussions about them. For instance, as part of a series of Zoom meetings set during the Covid lockdown in the UK in 2020, Kimbanguist *bajeunes* (youth) discussed the BLM movement and the connected themes of identity, race and racism. Several participants had joined BLM meetings/demonstrations in London and clearly made a link between race and colonialism, bringing to the fore the memory of its often-forgotten victims in the Congo. Others talked about how the 'liberation of Africa' and resisting systemic racism was indissociable from being a 'better Kimbanguist', also suggesting the importance of a wider pan-African vision linking the experience of Black communities across three continents:

> If you are angry about racism, if you are angry about Black oppression, then go home and think about how you can better yourself as a Kimbanguist individual because that's how you can be better for your community. Because the liberation of Africa is in our hands and if you cannot do it for yourself, then do it for Eric Gardner, do it for George Floyd, do it for Trevor Martin, do it for all the people who are suffering due to this racist system. It is in our hands for us Kimbanguist people to lead African people to liberation.

This is a powerful example of the way in which young Congolese are bringing a more expansive, inclusive and dynamic engagement in politics, bridging the domestic with the public, the personal with the social, history with the present, religious faith with politics, the ethical with the prophetic and the local and national with the global and transnational, all under a compelling theology and ethos of liberation. We have seen, however, that while the diaspora affords certain freedoms to craft alternative forms of transformative thinking and action, divisions and hierarchies among the Congolese – along fault lines of class, religion, gender and age – constrain the emergence, development and effectiveness of these alternative politics.

I have also shown in this chapter the importance of spatial matters, including the centrality of urban spaces, and the multiple representations, including religious representations, that accompany public performances. The 'right to the city' approach is relevant here to link centrality and collective claims; the danger, however, is that it may overlook the 'micro-physics' of power and romanticize protests. Race has been an important dimension in the transformation of these (diasporic) politics, especially among young Congolese, who have been inspired by more wide-ranging and militant protests that seek to challenge institutionalized racism at various levels. Their engagement with global movements like Black Lives Matter through online and virtual social platforms is enabling them to construct alternative identities and counter-publics, offering a way to build more inclusive politics that can transcend the still hierarchical and segmentary nature of traditional diasporic politics.

5

'Painful choices'

The moral economies of remittances

I am at the Sunday service in the New Jerusalem Church, in a former office building typical of Atlanta's exurban landscape. Performed in French, but simultaneously and very skilfully translated into English by a young church member, today's sermon is about 'productivity'. 'It's God's will for us to be productive', Pastor André starts. 'God created us with a goal, we have to be fruitful and at the end time God will assess whether we were profitable', he adds. 'What are the conditions required in order to be fruitful and productive?' he directly asks the congregation, while a PowerPoint slide quoting Psalm 128 is being beamed on the large screen behind him. 'Walk in the path of God and fear Him, and you will rejoice the fruits of you labour. Invest in Him. God never closes, He doesn't know bankruptcy.'

After a long pause, the pastor leaves his position at the church pulpit and starts pacing in front of the audience. 'But some work hard without rejoicing the fruits of their labour', he adds, breaking the silence. 'For them, money comes in but they are left with nothing, because they have to support two families, one here and one in Africa. In fact, in Africa, you often support a whole tribe.' Many in the audience nod in agreement. They know just exactly what Pastor André means. While 'tribe' in this context seems to be used pejoratively, the pastor is not advocating a radical break with the family and community in the homeland. 'Home is Congo', he is quick to say, 'I rejoice when I am in the Congo, when I am under a tree, eating with family and friends, it's relaxing, I enjoy myself.'

Of course, not all diasporic Congolese pastors would depict homeland visits in this romanticized and idealized way since, in some Pentecostal circles, there is a tendency to construct the ancestral land of the village – and its 'traditions' –as a dangerous and risky spiritual environment (Pype 2012, Piot 2010). Despite this, I found that many diasporic Congolese, like Pastor André, have kept ties with their kin. They long for family visits 'back home' and send money (more or less) regularly, a practice often associated, in their narratives, with a sense of 'duty' inherent in 'African culture', to use the expression of many of my respondents. Some have also expanded the family house or invested in a new property in Kinshasa, expressing a desire for continuity with the homeland. Others, especially those who are politically active in diaspora, aspire to a more peaceful and stable *mboka* (homeland) to which, one day, they can safely return even for a short period of time.

Implicit in the pastor's 'tribal' reference are unsolicited financial demands by a great number of kin – some so distant that they are barely known. Many migrants feel that these demands add to the hardship of life in the United States. In that sense, Pastor André directly addressed the challenges and dilemmas of many of his congregants when he also said:

> We have to help our families, help the country [Congo] to develop and grow, but it is not an easy task. In our community, we constantly talk about money. Why? That's because we don't have money. We are in America, but it feels like we're not really here.

Helping kin in the homeland, an important yet 'not easy' task, can thus hinder the fulfilment of the God-given goal of 'productivity' and prevent a full integration in the United States. Indeed, re-evaluating financial obligations towards one's extended family has become integral to the diasporic condition for many migrants. This renegotiation of financial ties with kin in the homeland often expresses a 'reconfiguration of relatedness', as Leslie Fesenmyer (2016: 215) found among Kenyan Pentecostals in London. The Congolese members of New Jerusalem Church in Atlanta, like the Kenyan migrants she studied, have to strike a fine balance between the natal family in the homeland and nuclear/conjugal family in diasporic settings, sometimes reworking transnational familial relations on newly defined terms, a process also influenced by conjugal domestic ideals promoted by Pentecostal Christian theologies.

In this chapter, I want to explore how these moral economies of remittances are played out transnationally. In doing so, I move from an exploration of diasporic politics and religious territorialization to a study of the social and symbolic spaces that have been (re)produced through connections but also disconnections, since remittances, as global money, operate not only as 'currency of care' (Singh 2016) but also involve relations of dependency, debt or even (spiritual) alienation. Congolese also send funds collectively to the homeland through religious groups, such as the Kimbanguist church or the New Jerusalem Church, as we shall see in the next two chapters, and to a lesser extent, through non-religious institutions and NGOs. However, I am choosing here to focus on the social universe of *family remittances* because they represent a key medium to understand how migrants and their family reimagine their attachments to both social/kinship networks and emplaced categories of belonging. In any case, in all my years of fieldwork among the Congolese communities in Europe and the United States, I did not find that sending funds through Hometown Associations (HTAs) or their equivalent is a significant practice. In the Congolese context, these groups are mostly neighbourhood associations known as *bana quartiers* that lack the strength of ethnic and kinship ties of rural communities as the basis of 'long-distance villageness' (Lacroix 2016). They do not typically embark on the type of development/infrastructural projects documented in the literature on migrant transnationalism.[1]

The financial challenges in diaspora discussed by Pastor André at New Jerusalem Church are not limited to a congregation or even to the Congolese. In recent years, migrants have sent between $500 and $600 billion annually in remittances to their family members in developing countries (Ratha et al. 2022). Given the sheer scale and volume of this monetary flow (whose growth has been sustained even despite Covid),[2] remittances have come to play an important part in debates about transnationalism, migration and development (de Haas 2005, Kapur 2004, Kelegama 2011, more recently see Adekunle, Tella and Ogunjobi 2022, Erdal 2022). As discussed earlier, remittances represent much more than financial transfers though. Remittances have a social life; they tell stories of connections, belonging and continuities. They also reveal stories of hard choices, dilemmas, power relations and ruptures. In short, they are at the heart of 'affective transnational circuits' (Cole and Groes 2016), which I will be exploring in all their complexity, ambivalences and spiritual/religious resonances in this chapter.

Relational asymmetry

In Kinshasa, regular remittances from family members abroad constitute an important and often unique source of income for many households in a context of endemic unemployment (Mangalu 2011, Sumata, Trefon and Cogels 2004). Remittances offer a 'life buoy' (*bouée de sauvetage* – a lifeline) for many Kinois, as an interviewee put it. Congolese abroad deplore this situation and frequently express the view that Kinshasa, or even the entire country, would 'collapse' without the financial contribution of its diaspora. I was often told how it was the diaspora which 'saved Kinshasa', when the breakdown of the Mobutist state in the 1990s led to the widespread bankruptcy of public transport companies. Migrants stepped in to fill the gap by shipping second-hand cars bought in Europe, which are now often used as private taxis in the Congolese capital.[3] Here, it is easy to see how the role of diasporic Congolese with their buying and investing power, their easy (or easier) access to commodities, technologies, equipment and infrastructures can be reframed within a power-geometry of uneven centre–periphery relations which has strongly influenced migration in the first place (Waldinger 2015: 170–1). This imbalance between groups divided by migration is often reflected by a discourse of economic *dependency* which stresses the dominating position of those located in the diaspora, in particular when it comes to influencing the voting behaviour of their kin in times of election. A young ('1.5 generation') activist talked about the power of those in the diaspora who control the 'money tap' and can refuse to provide the '*dix* [10] *chiffres*', the ten-digit code used to withdraw the remitted cash at Western Union outlets in the homeland:

> Diaspora is important for the Congo. Politicians from Kin come here [in London] because we dictate what is happening in a way. We tell our family on the phone, 'you should vote for him, if not we cut the money tap, you can't ask for your *dix chiffres*'. Without us, no Western Union money, we have influence. We send clothes and money.

It is clear that these remittance transfers typically operate in contexts of structural and material inequality, and this salient 'asymmetrical reciprocity' (Carling 2014: 245) has been widely observed in many transnational domestic configurations (Thai 2014, Eckstein 2010). However, as Carling (2014) argues, power relations associated with this relational asymmetry of remittances are multifaceted, rarely fixed and cannot be reduced to economic factors. Taking into consideration, for instance, the important role of moral, spiritual or symbolic economies challenges a neat dichotomy between a powerful diasporic 'core' and a peripheral, structurally dependent homeland space. In her classic Bangladesh ethnography, Gardner showed that, while access to *bidesh* ('foreign lands') is locally synonymous with the 'miracle' of wealth and material prosperity, migrants (and their kin left behind) also depend on the sacred and spiritual power of the *desh* (homeland) to assert their prestige and strengthen their sense of diasporic identity, in a context where the morality of *bidesh* is questioned and *bideshi*/ Western way of life devalued. Similarly, Nkamba is a powerful sacred centre and, while power asymmetries structure the relations between Kimbanguists in the

Congo and those in the diasporic 'peripheries', the holy city is the place diasporic Kimbanguists value above all to get spiritual resourcing and religious meaning. This pivotal role of Nkamba as *axis mundi* and spiritual centre is reflected by the widespread practice among Kimbanguist migrants of collecting Nkamba water and soil which then become portable, sacred fragments of the holy city that they carry with them for healing and protection in diaspora.

Here, I concur with Cole and Groes (2016: 6) when they argue that the use of *flow* as a metaphor for the transnational transfer of remittances implies a one-way movement from sending to receiving contexts which overlooks the bidirectional circulation of material and immaterial resources within a transnational kinship space. The *circuit* metaphor, they argue, may be more apt at capturing the complex, overlapping and changing dynamics of reciprocal relationality inherent in migrant transnationalism, while also drawing attention to the fact that transnational social networks can be subject to slowdowns, disconnections and reconnections.

Changing roles within transnational kinship structures can be shaped by life cycles, shifting family arrangements or social/spatial mobility. While the great majority of Catholics, Pentecostals and Kimbanguists I interviewed in the diaspora send money to their family in the DRC – either regularly or occasionally – I did come across alternative scenarios. Several interviewees told me, for instance, that they had stopped sending money to their kin in the DRC, since the latter were financially autonomous, expressing at the same time satisfaction or even pride on having maintained good relations despite having severed regular financial ties and sending money only exceptionally (e.g. participating in funeral expenses). Like for Kenyan Pentecostals in Fesenmyer's (2016) ethnography, some Congolese in diaspora have thus managed to 'disentangle the material and the moral in affective circuits without dismantling the wider moral economy of relatedness' (2016: 142–3).

There were also a few cases when the financial flow had been reversed. For instance, the son of a Kimbanguist widow I met in Atlanta, born in the DRC and who grew up in the United States, returned to Kinshasa in the 2000s, after his divorce. There he started a painting business, which soon became very profitable, allowing him to regularly send money to his mother – to pay for healthcare and other major expenses – as well as for the education of his two children who had remained in the United States (which created some tensions with his second wife with whom he was raising another child).

In addition, as demonstrated by Mazzucato (2011) in her study of Ghanaian transnationalism, remittances from migrants are embedded in a system of reciprocal exchange within which services provided, in the homeland, by non-migrant kin to migrants are common. Congolese migrants and returnees benefit from services that are often time-intensive and demanding (housing construction, business supervision, childcare or education of children sent to the homeland), services which form a key component of the relational reciprocity bound up with the moral economy of remittances. In that sense, while remittances may crystallize a set of asymmetrical transnational relations, these relations are in flux and constantly renegotiated and they cannot be simply reduced to a structural economic dependency between donors and recipients. As we shall now discuss, remittances sending and receiving practices are both embedded in moral frames shaped by tensions between the quest for belonging and autonomy, reflecting, as Lacroix aptly puts it, a 'complex communicational field in which transnationalism bears the simultaneous and paradoxical mark of allegiance and emancipation, of reproduction and change' (2016: 79).

Moral frames and the ambivalence of *Poto*

In the literature on migrant transnationalism, remittances are seen to express the moral, emotional and affective dimensions of familial ties, revealing to what extent personhood is constructed and realized socially and 'emerges at the intersection between individual ambitions, on the one hand, and obligations to wider social networks, on the other' (Cole and Groes 2016: 11). Often framed morally and culturally, the trope of 'duty' was particularly recurrent among my informants. It was the case, for instance, for Lionel (thirty-eight), who lives in Atlanta and goes to a Pentecostal church:

> Family members in Africa, they depend on us. On the money we send. Being here in the US we have a responsibility, a duty to help them. . . . . So what we do here is to try our best: how can I contribute so that I change people's lives in the Congo? People suffer, here we are ok. We see on the news how the state of the country is – it's a struggle there.

London-based Celestin, a man in his mid-forties and the eldest of four siblings, sends money every month to his widowed mum and two of his cousins. He also discusses remittances in terms of 'responsibility':

> There is a saying: *Nalia mbongo nayo* – 'I have to eat your money'. Like I have to taste the money you are earning, a share of it – your family, your uncles, cousins and so on. Family is sacred for us, in African culture. Plus, I am the eldest, so there is a sense of duty, responsibility. . . . Those who are 'lucky' – I say lucky in

inverted commas – to be in Europe, they cannot neglect those who are 'unlucky' [does the inverted comma sign] to still be in Africa. . . . It is about duty. If you don't send them money, people in your family say, 'Why are you neglecting us?'. 'You are happy in Europe and you are neglecting us here in Africa, where it is poor' [*où c'est la misère*]. They think you are selfish if you don't send money.

This quote encapsulates many of the contradictions and moral dilemmas experienced by Congolese migrants when it comes to negotiating and managing ties – especially financial ties – with their kin in the homeland. On the one hand, Celestin stresses his position in the kinship hierarchy, and his sense of duty linked to the 'sacredness' of kinship in 'African culture'. On the other hand, he notes that migrants are subject to strong familial pressure and the moral scrutiny of kin who expect those abroad to fulfil their obligations or risk social sanctions, shame and dishonour. The image of 'eating the money' links remittances to a corporeal, essential 'need' for nourishment, reinforcing the idea of the transnational family as one organic social body. However, there are also strongly negative connotations at play, since the expression 'eating money' (*kolia, manger/bouffer*) is also often used to designate selfish, irresponsible use of money and is also synonymous with embezzling and corrupt practices in politics and business.

Furthermore, discussing the asymmetrical reality of migration Celestin relies on multiple dichotomies – 'lucky' versus 'unlucky', 'happiness' versus 'poverty' – highlighting the importance of what Carling (2014: 237–8) calls the 'obligation and entitlement remittance script'. This script is defined to a great extent by the 'structural parameters of migration' and by the mere fact of being positioned on a particular side of the migration divide, creating a sense of debt among migrant donors and a sense of entitlement on the part of recipients. However, Celestin's use of quotation marks suggests a gap in the narrative, an alternative, overlapping register in the language – a semantic distance within the dominant social script. When asked about this nuance, he replied:

I put quotes [*des guillemets*] because it's a cliché . . . because in spite of appearances, a lot of Congolese are in Europe but they suffer. It's to show the stereotype, like saying 'America is the country of opportunities'. In the eyes of Africans, Europe is the country [*sic*] of opportunities and success. But some really struggled here, for them it was *la galère*, they should have stayed in Africa. . . . I put the quotes to refer to the cliché, in Africa some people manage really well. . . . In Africa, you eat well with little money. The ones that are in Europe do not earn much and live a stressful life – daily problems, pressure from relatives – whereas in Africa, they are relaxed!

Challenging the trope of opposition between the poverty of the homeland and the wealth/abundance of the host societies (the so-called 'money tree syndrome', see Singh 2013) is frequently accompanied by comments on the differentiated value of remittances:

> You have this duty to send money; however, if you tell them about your debts, your financial problems, they don't understand. Earning money is hard work in Europe. In Kinshasa, people who have been to Europe, they understand. My mum understands. (Interview with a French Kimbanguist, in his forties)

A French Congolese (in his thirties) I interviewed in Kinshasa also equated money-as-remittances and 'hard work':

> People I don't know give me lists of requirements – Can you pay my 5 children's *minervals* [school fees]? One time my cousin asked for 250 [dollars] to pay part of a bill of 600. I sent the money to my uncle because I didn't trust this cousin. He was mad because I didn't send him the money directly. He said that anyway this 250 was nothing. But 250 dollars is work, it's not nothing! You have to work hard to earn it.

As Singh (2013: 178) notes, in the context of transnational migration, 'the value of money is interpreted rather than calculated'. In other words, senders often feel that some of their kin in the homeland idealize the availability of money in host societies and/or underestimate the cost of earning it – 'the dollar sent is not the dollar received' (2013: 178). The labour, sacrifices and hardship crystallized in migrants' earnings are obscured by their transformation on the other side of the migration divide into remittances outside the context of its accumulation. This can create intra-familial conflicts; but, of course, migrants are often complicit in this process and can become caught between the image of success and accomplishment they (sometimes actively) convey and the expectations of non-migrants which they deem inappropriate, demanding or burdensome. This tension was vividly illustrated by an exchange I had with Marcel, a Kimbanguist from the United States visiting the DRC for a major pilgrimage. It happened during one of our walks around the Kimbanguist compound in Kinshasa (*le centre d'accueil* in the Kasa Vubu district), after he was asked for some 'taxi money' ('*pona transport*') by a local Kimbanguist 'he barely knew':

> (Marcel) See, people see I am American, the way I dress, the way I walk and they always ask me for money.

(DG) But then why do always you introduce yourself to people here saying 'I am American' and also you are planning to do the *defilé* [church procession at the end of a Kimbanguist service] with an American flag?

(Marcel) Because so that they know who I am, so that they respect me that I am not at their level, I am different.

In the Congolese context, there is a strong social pressure to conform to the image of a mythologized West. As De Boeck (2004: 47) argues,

> admitting that life in the West often is a life of poverty does not invalidate the topos of the Western Paradise for those who remained behind on the home front. Instead it is interpreted as a sign of personal failure and weakness of the *mikiliste* [successful migrant] who followed the trail of the diaspora.

Thus, the 'real' value of remittances can be concealed by the powerful fetishization of *Poto* ('the West') whose imaginary has, for decades, fed fantasies and dreams of glory, success and sophistication, producing the idea of a 'wonderland of modernity' (De Boeck 2004: 46) among Kinshasa's urban youth, particularly in popular culture and in Congolese music (White 2008). Thus, the returning or visiting (male) migrant from *Poto* is expected to give generously to fulfil his role as *mikiliste* or lose credibility.

In Kinshasa and in the diaspora, I was often told about the *moscovitch* a (male) character in a *maboke* (TV Serial), a figure of ridicule, a kind of anti-*mikiliste*. Coming back from Russia, he returns with a large chest full of books and offers them to his kin who have a hard time believing he did not bring them 'proper' gifts – cash in foreign currency, designer clothes, jewellery, perfume, electronics and so on. If the *moscovitch* is the anti-*mikiliste*, Russia is the anti-*Poto*, a place associated, in this narrative with failure and austere life, miles away from the fantasy of a Western land of plenty. The fact the character is dressed in winter clothes (presumably the clothes he was wearing in Russia) in the scorching heat of Kinshasa reinforces even further this contrast.[4] As a Congolese American I met in the DRC put it: 'if you come from Europe or America without gifts . . . they will call you *moscovitch* . . . that means you are not giving, like . . . shame on you!'

In spite of the enduring material and symbolic power of *Poto* in the minds of Kinois, it should be noted that some of my informants were keen to offer a counter-discourse about the West to their non-migrant kin. For instance, Mike a young British Congolese I travelled with for a large pilgrimage in Nkamba commented on the potent symbolic reality of *Poto*, describing an interaction with his cousin:

> I come from Europe. They see me with my belly and my clothes, they read: *Poto*, they read: paradise! [laughs]. This cousin asked me if I was to leave my tracksuit behind – I said 'no way!' They think we get things for free. But they are not free! Things are not available for free. I did explain to him that it was 200 dollars. They don't know we have worked hard for it! They don't understand! I told him that money is not given to us, it's not free money! It doesn't mean the same thing to them. (British Congolese Kimbanguist, male, in his thirties, from field notes in Kinshasa).

Just after another request (which I witnessed) from a soldier, an acquaintance from his Kinshasa extended family, he also told me:

> This *soldat* who asked me 100 dollars. If we lend to him and then we don't see him anymore. He doesn't know we don't have much money and that we came in that crappy flight! [London-Kinshasa via Casablanca with the airline Royal Air Maroc]

Another time I was walking with Marcel in Nkamba when a teenager came to us and told us that he 'wanted to go to *Poto*'. He obviously saw that as, a *mundele* (white) it was almost certain I was indeed from *Poto*, but he could also have, in addition, recognized Marcel from the greetings (*les salutations*) during the morning church service when Marcel had been introduced to the congregation as coming from *la paroisse d'Atlanta*, the parish of Atlanta. Marcel replied to the teenager, asking him why he wanted to go to *Poto*, since '*Lola* – [paradise] – was right here, in Nkamba'. Pointing at me, Marcel added: 'Look kid, *mindele* [whites] come here too – God lives here.' When the young Kimbanguist left, Marcel told me: 'they think it's *Lola*, it's paradise, but nothing comes for free in the US.'

While in this short encounter Marcel did not, in contrast to Mike, explicitly challenge the myth of *Poto*'s 'freely' available commodities, the use of the term *Lola* to refer to Nkamba was a clear attempt to offer a counter-narrative to what he saw as a naive fascination with the West – a fascination which for him translated into incessant (and rather annoying, as he told me) demands for cash and help. *Lola* ('paradise/heaven') is indeed often used as a synonym of *Poto*, the West, but by reprioritizing its religious meaning, Marcel wanted to express the 'authentic' force of Nkamba, a spiritually powerful place which even a fantasized *Poto* was no match for.

This is not to say, as mentioned before, that Marcel's identity as 'American' – at the time of fieldwork he was a Green Card holder and applying for US citizenship – is not used as a symbolic resource in the homeland context, as we saw earlier. Indeed, when he arrived in Nkamba, he was also quick to show me all the designer clothes he had bought in the United States and that he was planning to give to important members of the spiritual leader's family. Ironically, there cannot be any greater contrast between the place where he bought the gifts, a suburban Atlanta shopping mall with designer outlet stores (to which he took me during my fieldwork there), and Nkamba, the holy city 'where God lives'. But these gifts were nonetheless important: not only were they a commentary on his *mikiliste* status, but also a message about the global reach and scope of the church, a scope acquired for the most part thanks to the expanding diaspora of Congolese and Angolan Kimbanguists in Europe and North America. In a way, *Poto* is here associated with authenticity through the material culture of Western designer clothes which, as Newell writes in his ethnography of Ivorian youth, becomes 'transparent indicator of modernity' (Newell 2012: 161). Thus, it was crucial for Marcel to keep the clothes in their original packaging, as further evidence 'they were not *Guanzou*' as he told me. In Kinshasa, goods and consumer items that are called pejoratively *Guanzou* are deemed to be low quality and often fake, Guanzou (Canton) being the manufacturing Chinese city from where a lot of the cheap clothes and electronics sold in Kinshasa's markets and shops originate.

In the discourse of migrants like Marcel, Mike and others I talked to, the repeated emphasis on the fact that earning money is 'hard work' suggested to what extent they felt that (financial) help was often not 'valued' by non-migrant kin. Moreover, while the practice of sending remittances may initially denote young migrants' ability to successfully take care of their kin – and allowing to reach social maturity (Kankonde 2010: 235) – it can increasingly be construed as straining, as debts accumulate and financial pressure grows with the evolution of the family life cycle in diaspora. Blood ties with the homeland are important I was often told, yet difficult choices have to be made:

As members of a family, we are linked by blood [*on est lié par le sang*]. This tie is important, as Africans, as Congolese, family is who we are. If they suffer, it's also a part of you that is suffering. But the weight is enormous [*c'est un poids qui est énorme*] and we would like it to end, we want solutions for our country. Congo needs to develop; people need to have decent salaries. It is a duty for us to send money but we are limited by our budget. For example, I get a phone call, it's my nephew. His wife is in hospital after having giving birth. But it's also my daughter's birthday and she wanted something. You can't satisfy everyone; painful choices have to be made. I said no to them, I can't give right now. (British Kimbanguist, male, in his fifties, interviewed in London)

We can see here how conflicted feelings –familial pride, moral obligations, duty of care and guilt– are intrinsic to migrant transnationalism when it comes to the social construction of kinship relations through financial and material linkages. However, some like Papa Claude, a respected Catholic leader in his late sixties, appeared to deal with these affective and emotional contradictions in a more straightforward way. He has established clear 'red lines' – whom to give, for what purpose and when – a process which also signals his authority and position within the transnational extended family:

> Family life in Europe is expensive but if you don't send money this creates conflicts. . . . But I am in a position where I can decide what I can do or not do and I said it clearly. And people know it. They tend not to bother me. For example, [I say] 'don't call me for a baptism' 'We are going to baptise our child, we need money', I say 'don't call me for that'. Call me if someone is seriously ill, when they need care or when someone passed away. But don't call me: 'we haven't eaten'. My financial capacity is not unlimited. I tell people: 'if you want to study, I will help you'. Those who listened are now in a position where they can take care of themselves and actually now help others. But those who didn't study. . . . If you are dying (*mourant*) yes, I will help, but if you are not ill and you want a new shirt, it's not my problem.

As noted by Carling (2014), helping kin so that 'they can take care of themselves' (and others) through education or small projects and become ultimately more independent, reducing in turn future needs to remit, is a recurrent 'script' in remittances sending practices and discourses. Diaspora investment in the homeland – in small- or medium-size business ventures, land or real estate – is often seen as a way to offset the increasing irregularity of remittances in line with shifting financial priorities in the host society context. Such investments are nonetheless dependent on the accumulation of capital enabled by family savings, involving 'sacrifice':

> We bought some [agricultural] land on the outskirt of Kin a few years back. . . . For us, getting that land, it was a lot [of] sacrifice in terms of savings and so on, but it was a long-term investment, and we see like, we can produce to benefit us as a people, for future projects, trying to grow food. Our family is dealing with this back home . . . it works well. . . . To a certain degree it helps my family back home to become more independent . . . because sending money

regularly depends on priorities . . . money also has to be paid for school, housing, healthcare, education and so on here in the UK. (British Congolese, late thirties, interviewed in London)

However, such stories of investment 'working well' were far less frequent than narratives which emphasized tensions, misunderstandings, growing mistrust and sometimes ruptures and disconnections. For instance, Gerard (London, in his early fifties) had a major dispute with his wife's brother for whom he bought a car to start a taxi business. It was 'a project to help him', as Gerard put it, but instead of turning the gift into a profitable business, his brother-in-law used the car exclusively for his personal use. For Gerard, his brother-in-law demonstrated a clear 'lack of vision', reflecting a growing cultural gap about the (acceptable) use of the remitted gift intended as a 'productive' investment:

> For projects to work, family members have to be educated. My brother-in-law wanted the car, that's it. We said: 'start a business with it', that was the idea we had. With this taxi business, he can make money, then he can buy another car. . . . But he is just keeping it for himself, it is not productive! I don't have billions here, I made a sacrifice buying the car. But one day the car breaks down, he calls me, says he needs more money to fix it. . . . Did he plan this? – no! Who was to pay for the maintenance of the car? They have another way of seeing things, it's a vision they don't have.

Mistrust and disconnections

Gerard story points to issues linked to the earmarking of remittances and the micro-management of the 'investment' by senders, encouraging us to examine 'at what point and on which terms do migrants relinquish ownership of what they sent' (Carling 2014: S244). Another key trope in remittance stories was the question of trust, especially when it came to the construction of a house, a highly valued practice among migrants (Lopez 2015). On this topic, I was frequently told a rather sombre story about a Congolese from the diaspora who ended up committing suicide after realizing that the money remitted to his family had been 'eaten' (*mangé*). He was sending money home regularly, receiving photographic updates about the progress of the construction, the story goes, but the photos were of a different house. He discovered the deception when, suspicious, he flew to Kinshasa unannounced to visit a near-empty construction site, before taking his own life (with a knife).

I found some references to this story on social media and YouTube,[5] but it is difficult – and beyond my scope – to comment on its veracity. However, this story struck a sensitive nerve in the Congolese diaspora, in part due to the large financial commitment, for many a sacrifice, required for such an investment. In addition, as Lacroix (2016) and others have noted, the migrant house is a symbolic and communicational act, a marker of prestige, heralding a successful migration project, even if left empty for most of the year (and thus a signifier of both absence and 'proxy' presence, see Dalakoglou 2010). While in (rural) homeland context the migrant house is often construed in terms of allegiance and continued membership to a (spatially distant) community/village of origin (Lacroix 2016), I would argue that an increased status and prestige, the search for autonomy, increased material comfort and convenience during short stays or holidays are also key motives for Congolese from the diaspora to build their own houses or flats as *pieds a terre* in Kinshasa.

It is true, of course, that house-building by migrants also reflects a longing for a return to the homeland, at the time of retirement for instance. This was the case for Julie, a divorced London Kimbanguist who was sending money regularly to her sister and her sister's husband. They were both in charge of supervising the construction of her house. Like in the tragic story mentioned earlier, some of her kin were misappropriating the remittances earmarked for her house project. Julie came unannounced to Kinshasa one summer and quickly realized that the money had been 'eaten' and all the electronics and furniture she had sent to equip the house were nowhere to be seen. While she severed all ties with her sister's family as a result, she did not give up on her project. Instead, through an acquaintance, she found a contractor whom she put in charge of the construction. These types of stories circulate within the Congolese diasporic sphere through networks of acquaintances, online and in social media – the *radio-trottoir* (lit. 'radio-pavement/sidewalk'). They were particularly commented among Kimbanguists, not only because they are essentially about trust and (changing) relations with family members in the homeland but also because the trope of return is so pivotal in the Kimbanguist prophetic grammar of belonging. Securing a stable home in what is often seen as an unstable context – Kinshasa and/or Congo – is highly valued, and a breach of trust with family members over this is always painful. However, while trust is charged with moral values, I found that forgiveness is often presented as integral to 'good Christian' behaviour and a key mediator of social relations within the Kimbanguist church, especially when it comes to relations involving money or trust-based financial exchange (such as remittances management, loan or participation in *likelemba/tontine*, rotating credit groups).

A Kimbanguist with whom I was discussing Julie's story clearly illustrated this importance of forgiveness:

> Getting scammed by your own family, it hurts ['*ça fait mal*']. . . . But you cannot hurt them back. You can break the tie [*casser le lien*] but you must forgive. But it's true that we trust people more when it's outside the family. When it's with someone you don't know very well, it is more reliable in a way, more serious. People tend to trust more when it is outside the family, to do business.

While the option of working with 'more reliable' outsiders is here chosen to avoid potential conflicts between kin, the social control exerted by family members in the homeland can be highly compelling, restricting the possibility of such strategies, as suggested by the work of Kankonde (2010) among Congolese migrants in Johannesburg. His study shows that because of strong familial pressure and the risk of stigma attached to unsuccessful migration, migrants feel compelled to send money home even though they consider remittances to be a major 'setback to the realization of their initial migration projects', restricting their social mobility and economic integration in the host society context (2010: 225). The threat of social sanctions – even exclusion from the kinship group, akin to 'social death' – is a potent factor, but dynamics inherent to the spiritual world have also a role to play, in particular the belief in the risk of malevolent attacks by kin – through curse or bewitchment (Kankonde 2010: 239; MacGaffey and Bazenguissa-Ganga 2000: 130–1). As we shall now see, this 'dark side of kinship' (Geschiere 2003) impacts on the moral economies of remittances and shapes the ways in which individuals and groups position themselves in the transnational field.

'The debt has already been repaid': Spiritual world and the dark side of kinship

As Congolese Catholic Lucien put it when discussing the familial 'duty' to remit money home: 'Kinship is a sacred chain: one must play its role. If you don't, you are exposing yourself spiritually.' This came up regularly when discussing the themes of remittances and family with my Congolese informants. For instance, Papa Charles, a Paris-based Kimbanguist interviewed in Kinshasa, made a link between the tradition of kinship solidarity, indebtedness, and conflicts potentially leading to *attaques mystiques*:

The African tradition, the African system is a bit strange. Any of your relatives, even the distant ones, can say that they have the right to have their share of what you earn in Europe. You owe them. Now if they don't get this share, they start accusing you or your parents for being selfish. It causes problems. There is a lot of jealousy. Curses [*malédictions*]. And then those who can attack you *mystiquement*, they do it.

In many different cultural contexts, witchcraft accusations are often interpreted as a consequence of rapid or economic and social transformation. In a broader perspective, it is argued that the resurgence of witchcraft tropes constitutes a commentary on capitalist modernity and its contradictions and is intimately linked to the wealth accumulation of 'occult economies' (Comaroff and Comaroff 1999). In her study of Sylhet, a high emigration region of Bangladesh, Callan (2007) is critical of this idea that witchcraft accusations can simply be read as 'metaphor of modernity'. Rather, she argues that one should consider the role of local cultural dynamics in 'mediating the specific effects of global material forces' (2007: 332) and she suggests that, in fact, through narratives linking affliction and sorcery, individuals reposition themselves dialogically in a context where economic change is shaping existing hierarchies – particularly in the kinship sphere. Her ethnography shows how overseas migration (of which the influx of remittances is one aspect) impacts on local belief systems with the emergence of new social inequalities leading to intra-familial tensions and increase in witchcraft accusations, which people partly blame on rivalry and envy (see also Gardner 1995).

In African contexts, the connection between witchcraft tropes and socio-economic and material change has been well documented, with some studies stressing the ubiquity of witchcraft in urban environments (De Boeck 2004: 203). Others have firmly located the perceived dangers and use of malevolent forces more specifically within the kinship structure (Geschiere 2013). The family, including the transnational family with its global 'stretching of intimacy' (Geschiere 2013: 62), thus becomes 'the domain of both primary attachment and primary fear' (Van Dijk 2002: 181 see also Geschiere 2013). In that sense, African Pentecostal discourses on family are ambivalent and address this contradiction, offering spiritual protection and solutions to deal with the risks of evil forces from kinship sources.

Between Geschiere arguing that witchcraft is exclusively internal to the kinship structure and De Boeck pointing to deep changes of dynamics and the ubiquity of witchcraft in the everyday lives of Kinois, I would take a middle-ground position and would argue that while attacks by non-related people and strangers are strongly feared, the discourse of parental affliction and witchcraft attacks by family members is also pervasive in some Pentecostal circles, as we shall see. De Boeck is right to argue that Pentecostal churches 'imposed a restricting redefinition of lineage and clan relations' (2004: 203) and that the spiritual dangers of the outside world 'penetrat[e] the intimate circle of the nuclear family' (2004: 203), but tropes associating witchcraft with family members as sources of attack are the central component of the spiritual (defensive) infrastructure of churches like Maman Olangi and circulate through testimonies.

Among my research participants, there was a general ambivalence about the importance of family relations, as many stressed the prominence of blood ties while deploring the pressure to send money exerted by kin back home. Some held more deep-seated, radical views, for instance, those attending Maman Olangi's Combat Spirituel church, whose preaching and sermons often demonize lineage affiliation and ancestral, *longue durée*, social temporalities. As explained previously, the path to deliverance according to the vision of Combat Spirituel is a constant re-examining of kinship as a source of evil bondage, 'limitations' and blockage for the individual. Here debt is a powerful, perhaps the most powerful, tie between the (born-again) individual and its 'exploitative' family, as Meiers (2013: 127) shows in her study of Olangistes in Belgium. Freeing yourself from *la coutume*, breaking with the past (of sins, polygamy, ancestor worship, etc.), means, in this perspective, rejecting the traditional indebtedness of kinship as a basis of a 'collective subject-formation' (De Boeck 2013: 197).

According to this theology, an individual can be entrapped, 'spiritually tied' through the social mechanism of familial debt in a number of ways. Thus, in Atlanta, I sat through a Combat Spirituel church service during which all the testimonies that day centred on the notion of *héritage* – inheritance. Several church members took turns behind the altar to share a past experience of inheriting a responsibility in the family, a property or a sum of money from the homeland. They talked about how it was only through the teachings of the church – and similar testimonies – that they came to realize, after intense self-examination, that this inheritance was indeed what was 'blocking' them in their lives. These *combattants spirituels*' testimonies stressed the extent to which inheritance was a powerful tool for family back home to control their lives at a distance, creating a sense of debt and affecting them spiritually. Not only was the inheritance seen as a form of dependency to the extended family, but it was also tying them to ancestral curses as a result of past contracts indebting ancestors to witches, taking the form of 'blood covenants' with agents of the Devil, to gain their favour. It is only by following a path of deliverance through spiritual warfare and after the tie was severed – the money was rejected/returned, the gift destroyed and the offer eventually rejected – that progress could be made in one's life in relation to various misfortunes – in the spheres of marriage, immigration status or employment for instance.[6] Here while the trope of debt revolved around the act of receiving and not giving/sending (remittances), both practices are in fact understood to be at the heart of a moral economy of reciprocity from which the born-again individual needs to move away in order to achieve salvation, attain material success and be part of a modern 'global ecumene' (De Boeck 2013: 197).

In the following quote, from an interview with Tony (thirty-five), a Combat Spirituel youth leader I met in Kinshasa, indebtedness to one's extended family is presented as a submission to *la coutume*, placing the individual under 'total control'. Kinship-as-debt as a central organizing principle is rejected as an 'evil practice' and contrasted to the debt Jesus already repaid by shedding his blood, redeeming humanity of its sins:

> A lot of our *chrétiens combattants* they want to be autonomous . . . responsible. The young people who want to get married, they don't want to be helped.[7] 'I will fight, I will work and find money by myself, to marry my wife'. If your family helps, you become indebted, they can mistreat your wife. You won't be able to say a word, they will remind you: 'you got our money so that you could marry her'. They will have a say over your wife, the children. [. . .] There is a debt here. But the debt has been repaid already . . . the debt has been repaid by Jesus himself [. . .] Inheritance – it's the same. . . . In my family they are polygamist, my uncles, those in my lineage, they have girlfriends here and there. For *Batetela* people, it's *la coutume*. My father was not like that. But when he passed away, his brothers came to me, wanting to give me money. I said 'no thanks, I am not taking it'. I rejected the money. They wanted to become my new parents. I didn't want this, they are not Christians like me, they are polygamists, they live double lives. . . . But if you say yes, they have a right over you, total control, even spiritual control [. . .] These practices are evil, this is why people prefer to withdraw [*se retirer*] from the extended family to concentrate on the nuclear family [*proche famille*].

Tony, working as a civil servant in a government ministry, travels regularly to France where his wife, also a follower of Combat Spirituel, currently lives. Exposed to the social dynamics on both sides of the transnational divide, he also had a lot to say about remittances and the role of financial bonds (*liens*) in the moral and spiritual economy of the Congolese diaspora:

> Those in Europe who have followed the message of Papa and Maman Olangi, they send money to their brothers here, but only if their brothers, their cousins share the same vision, the same spirit. Let me give you an example – hypothetically. My brother is not Christian, he drinks alcohol, he lives his life and all that. He finds himself in a situation: he needs money. He asks me. But I won't give him money because I know he will drink the money with his friends. I won't give money to him. We hold opposite visions. If I give him some money, it will destroy him! Some also are afraid of witchcraft: 'my cousin from the village, I don't trust him, he can block me'. So, he doesn't send him any money because he is afraid he will block him through witchcraft. [. . .] At church, we had some testimonies: some have sent money, families had asked for money from the person, so that they can block that person afterwards. Sending money creates a point of contact. It is a bond [*un lien*], which can be used to destroy you. Through this bond they can block you.
>
> DG: If you give they can block you? But if you don't give?
>
> If you don't give, you will be hated, and there will be no contact. And then they will start to speculate about you, saying you are selfish. . . . They may start attacking you spiritually, trying to block you . . . but you pray the Lord and you protect yourself. He protects you.

Such discourses about the potential malevolent power of financial bondage are recurrent among Olangistes. In fact, in the leader's autobiography (Olangi and Olangi 1999), they constitute a core part of the foundational story of the church, in particular in the first few chapters describing the couple's return to the Congo after a decade or so spent in Belgium during the 1970s. The reintegration was hard for the Olangis: they write that, in Europe, they had 'adopted a conception of life in general and marriage in particular which had nothing to do with African traditions' (1999: 36), but in Congo they had to confront a world where one is indebted to the wider kinship group and where the 'yoke of la *coutume*' is too powerful. In this new life, Papa Olangi was 'in charge of more than 20 people', had 'to be productive to serve his clan' (1999: 37) and the couple had lost total control of the household budget – now being 'controlled from the village' (1999: 37). This familial pressure, defined as oppressive and exploitative, and which was negatively affecting their relationship, was at the heart of a negative spiritual economy producing only conflict, limitations, blockages and ultimately bondage to evil forces. The fightback involved a 'real' process of deliverance.[8]

While money is here a medium of dependency and spiritual alienation and a vehicle through which familial/ancestral debt is 'realized' (Graeber 2001), at another level, it can also support a host of practices deemed immoral and be injected into the circuits of the occult economy – by paying for the services of a *nganga*, marabout or *sorcier*, for instance. As one of Maman Olangi's sons told me when we met in Kinshasa, money given to untrustworthy, 'irresponsible' – non-born-again – kin 'can do the work of the Devil', paying for drinking, gambling or prostitution. Here what is also suggested is an implicit but ever-present need to break away with a Mobutist symbolic economy of excess (and its legacy, see Pype 2010), when, in the political circles of the kleptocratic regime, masculine prestige was measured by potlatch-type practices and the ability to support several mistresses/lovers, also known as *bureaux* (lit. 'offices').

Finally, if we return to Tony's narrative we can see how, while the rejection of financial demands can lead to spiritual reprisals, giving money, even transnationally, can also create *points de contact* allowing spiritual attacks. In that sense, money, like clothes, or body elements such as hair or nails (collected during certain rituals, for instance, funerals) are considered to be an extension of the person. In other words, even if they are separated, physically 'cut', from a person, they can still act as a material and spiritual connection for a bewitcher to do harm. Here, considering money as an extension of the person, as a way to 'connect' with her, challenges the traditional Maussian distinction made between the sphere of cash exchange and the gift economy (Mauss 2012[1925]) – a separation which defines gifts as inalienable, imbued with part of the donor's identity, and money as a seal of value, alienable, impersonal and generic.

Conclusion

This chapter has shown that remittances are charged with a range of emotional qualities and are imbued with affective and also moral attributes. In that sense, remittances as 'global money' (Singh 2016) are *personal* and personalized, encouraging us to reevaluate the role and meaning of money beyond its pure market functions (Zelizer 1997), beyond its totemic status as a signifier of disenchanted modernity, characterized, in classical social theory, by a *depersonalizing* power, a 'merciless objectivity', as Simmel once famously wrote.

What this chapter has also suggested is that, while few diasporic Congolese would deny being attached to their homeland, often expressing a longing for a return to a more peaceful and 'developed' *mboka*, a focus on remittance-sending practices and discourses revealed a deep sense of ambivalence, especially in terms of familial attachment and trust. We saw that the moral economy of financial links is bound up with the structuration, evolution and meaning of kinship networks on both sides of the transnational divide. Remittances tell stories of moral obligations, (be)longing, entitlements, conflicted feelings, 'painful choices' and dilemmas. They tell stories of guilt and oftentimes of mistrust and intense frustrations. As such, then, remittances can be understood as 'a form of communicative action' (Lacroix 2016: 172) which, while (re)creating proximity, can, and often do, also produce and express social and symbolic distance.

Moreover, in spiritual terms, remittances also appear to crystalize a set of tensions at the heart of a globalized, diasporic relational economy. For Pentecostals such as Olangistes, discourses about money are in part shaped by a powerful theology of bondage involving a critical reassessment of past ancestrality (through a process of 'uprooting', *déracinement*, see Meiers 2013) and contemporary indebtedness and dependency. For them, debt is at the heart of an 'economy of subordination' (Marshall 2009: 175), leading to both entrapment and sin, and as such should be fiercely resisted. Spiritual fight – *combat spirituel* – has a concrete translation in the everyday discipline of separating oneself from evil practices, influences and temptations. However, while an individual born-again embodied subjectivity (Marshall 2009) is seen to go hand in hand with processes of 'de-parentalization' and entails a radical rupture with traditional gift-giving systems, the logic of debt has not been totally evacuated – far from it. Works on Pentecostals show that debt relations get rescripted in many different ways – within the community of the church, in the conjugal sphere, in relation to God or the charismatic pastor.[9] One of the key messages of these churches is that they offer the strong ties needed to protect the individual from the dangers of a sinful (spatial, social and temporal) 'outside' and the instability/uncertainty of a born-again status under 'constant stress' (Pype 2011: 281). In a way, the church becomes the new relevant kinship structure with its own system of gift exchange, reciprocity and, ultimately, dependency, operating through money practices (i.e. giving of offerings and tithes) and the emotional and social labour of membership. This new structure functions as *groupe de la sortie du groupe* (Meiers 2013: 54), perhaps 'reintroducing the kinds of social pressures and exclusionist communitarianisms one is trying to escape from in the first place', as De Boeck and Plissart (2004: 112) state when writing about Kinshasa's Charismatic churches.

What is certain is that this quest for autonomy – generating new forms of dependencies – is shaping the landscape of transnational relations and the meaning diasporic actors attribute to remittances in particular. The Pentecostal rupture, as an act of reimagination of the ancestral and 'traditional' space of the homeland, entails a symbolic and physical distanciation, in particular with 'the village', metaphor of all things demonic (Coleman and Maier 2013, Ukah 2004, Piot 2010). However, as Piot noted (2010: 60–1), this demonization of the village as a core element of Pentecostal spiritual mapping also entails a continuous flow of images, signs and commentaries about the rural world, rendering its imaginary even more present, relevant and full of efficacy – especially in the urban popular culture. This distanciation with the rural world does not exclude the homeland altogether from a wider spiritual and socio-spatial cartography. Organizations such as Maman Olangi – or even non-Pentecostal ones such as the Kimbanguist church – have truly become transnational movements and they rely on a global geography connecting people and places, linking homeland territories and diasporic peripheries, a relation influenced by both centrifugal and centripetal forces. Visits to church headquarters, for special church events, religious conventions or 'crusades' – or simply for more individual spiritual renewal – take on the form of urban pilgrimages[10] which, more often than not, enact a 'reconfiguration of relatedness' when it comes to family relations (Fesenmyer 2016: 125). Thus, choosing to visit only a selected few, evading the pressure and obligations of one's extended family or avoiding all kin (and 'friends'/past acquaintances) altogether is now made easier by the availability of cheap and convenient 'flathotels' which have mushroomed in recent years in Kinshasa. For diasporic visitors, there is also the possibility of staying in residential infrastructure built by religious groups themselves – a nascent phenomenon in Kinshasa but well underway among large Pentecostal churches in Nigeria (see Ukah 2016a). These recent infrastructural developments are not limited to residential accommodation and include health and educational facilities, for instance. This will be explored in greater detail in the next two chapters which will be focusing on the discourses, practices and understanding of 'development' and on the various dimensions of religious territorialization/urbanization in the homeland and the transnational social networks facilitating it.

6

Developing and (re)moralizing the homeland

Narratives and interventions

We saw in Chapter 4 that the level of transformative political engagement varies for religious actors. However, most of these actors shared the idea that *le sous-développement* ('underdevelopment') of the homeland has spiritual roots and thus requires spiritual – often radically redemptive – answers. Particularly for Pentecostals, these interventions take place at multiple social and moral scales, from the individual to the global. In fact, and as Piot (2010) notes, African Pentecostal discourses often mirror dominant development tropes by promoting a state of constant crisis that calls for (radical) intervention, involving the idea of an active and continual rupture not only with sins but also with locality, ancestrality, rurality and 'traditional' forms of community. In this chapter, I explore several case studies of developmental interventions and infrastructures in the homeland, an environment which Catholics, Pentecostals and Kimbanguists alike perceive as dysfunctional, encouraging immoral and corrupt tendencies – what Congolese sometimes coin 'anti-valeurs'.[1]

Of all the interventions I encountered in the field, I chose to focus on religious schools and health infrastructures because they have become central to how religious actors link the 'moral body' to the wider 'social body' against a wider (post)colonial temporality but also because they are deeply embedded in differentiated transnational configurations and moral economies. As I shall show, this embeddedness has a direct implication on the kind of moral, financial and symbolic resources religious actors can deploy to realize their own developmental vision for the homeland and its future. Smaller infrastructures like the New Jerusalem's Miséricorde hospital, for instance, are almost entirely dependent on the donations of members from the diaspora. In comparison, the Kimbanguist hospital, also in Kinshasa, is larger and more established. Nevertheless, it suffers from chronic under-investment due to the prioritization of Nkamba, the Kimbanguist holy city (see the next chapter). These entanglements of religion and development are also shaped by the history of religious organizations. For instance, despite the Pentecostalization of the public sphere in the Congo, Catholicism retains a degree of prestige as an older, more established church, while displaying an impressive capacity for adaptation, as it extricates itself from associations with Belgian colonialism and eventually comes to be seen as promoting post-Independence forms of Africanization.

Obvious differences between these institutions notwithstanding, the developmental actions they undertake raise a number of common questions related to the moral underpinnings of development, their capacity to transcend secular/religious boundaries and the extent to which their theologies, ecclesiologies and missionary activities foster inclusion or exclusion, making economic and sanctioned religious goods differentially available to their members and those they serve. Some of these wider questions have been addressed by a growing literature on religion and development, particularly in African contexts, where, in addition to shaping and regulating individual conducts and norms of behaviour, religious groups have been at the forefront of initiatives providing key services in welfare, sanitation, healthcare or education (Burchardt 2015, ter Haar and Ellis 2006, ter Haar 2011, Deneulin 2009, Freeman 2012, Jones 2012). Some of this literature has begun to remedy development theory's 'blind spot' in relation to religion (ter Haar 2011: 5; see also Freeman 2012: 1) and points to the promotion and implementation of holistic religious models connecting individual remoralization and personal empowerment to wider notions of societal progress and well-being, as well as to interventions in education and health.

Today, these interventions need to be situated vis-à-vis the rolling back of the state and the global diffusion of neoliberal governance agendas encouraging the involvement of 'third sector' actors and the increasing recognition of a legitimate developmental role for 'Faith-Based Organisations'. The rise of FBOs and increasing religious developmental ambition can be seen as reflections of the increasing dominance of NGOs and other non-state actors in the wider development sector, especially from the 1990s onwards. In the African context, the fiscal discipline imposed by neoliberal policies and the structural adjustment programmes advanced by multilateral organizations such as the IMF and the World Bank in order to have access to loans led to the privatization of state services, a process which paralleled the promotion of NGOs as efficient channels of development aid for international donors. Presented as better – more responsive and grassroots – models of 'good governance', NGOs filled the gap opened by a rolling back of the state in the name of 'market liberalization', often a shorthand for deep cuts in civil service and welfare budgets, with often disastrous consequences in terms of socio-economic inequalities (Ferguson 2006). In Mobutu's Zaire, IMF structural adjustment programmes in response to the mounting foreign debt had devastating effects: a dramatic informalization of the economy, a spiralling inflation and a general decline of living standards, despite the country's mineral riches (MacGaffey and Bazenguissa-Ganga 2000, Renton, Seddon and Zeilig 2007).

Within the development landscape, 'FBO-ization' and 'NGO-ization' are thus processes that often follow parallel or even overlapping trajectories. For instance, in his ethnography of HIV/AIDS-related Christian activism in South Africa, Burchardt (2015) observes that 'FBO-ization' was largely driven by the availability of international funding, which led religious groups to adopt the technocratic templates governing global development models. The centrality of an 'FBO model' influenced by the possibility and distribution of external funding from foreign donors and partners should, however, be nuanced. While there is a clear tendency for 'NGO-ization' on multiple levels in the DRC, most religious organizations in the Congo rely on internal resources (including tithes, offerings and donations) to expand and orient some of their activities and infrastructural development towards education, healthcare or other welfare goals. Of course, partnerships do exist, but they have not always significantly impacted on organizational dynamics nor on the ways in which these groups see themselves. Moreover, as we shall see in the case of the Kimbanguist church, religious actors can downplay the existence of (and need for) external financial support/partnership because it may contradict the strong emphasis on self-reliance and financial autonomy that is central to theology or church identity.

What most African Christian religious groups – in particular Pentecostal, 'FBO-ized' or not – have in common is a clear totalizing tendency, a 'religious holism' described by Jean Comaroff (2012: 48) as working 'to imbue the profane reaches of everyday life with divine purpose'. This vision is linked to a quest for 'integral development' and moralization which is key in the legitimation of educational interventions, as I shall now discuss drawing upon the case studies of Catholics and 'Maman Olangi' (Pentecostal) educational infrastructures.

The moral quest for 'integral' development in education

Catholic education

Historically, in the Congo like in many parts of Africa, Catholic missionaries played an integral part in the colonial project. During Leopold II's brutal regime of resource extraction in the late nineteenth century, Catholic missions were supported by the Belgian king who provided capital and allocated them vast portions of land, tasked to evangelize the natives to 'fight paganism', in the name of Western superiority, in part through the creation of a school system (Demart 2010: 85). Education during the Leopoldian rule and subsequently during Belgian Congo[2] was not meant to emancipate. It was largely a tool for reproducing colonial segregation and legitimizing a system of racialized boundaries and power relations (Mokoko Gampiot 2014: 122–3). While most key figures of the independence movement had received a Catholic education, and while there existed an extensive network of thousands of Catholic primary schools, when Congo became independent in 1960, there were virtually no Congolese academics or *cadres militaires* – military cadres (Demart 2017: 140).

Congolese Catholics I talked to recognize the exploitative and segregationist character of colonialism of the Congo, but they expressed some degree of ambivalence over the role of Catholic institutions. Several were keen to emphasize the legacy and social benefits of missionary activities in terms of education and healthcare provision, especially among the most educated, who, like many Congolese political elites today, went through the Catholic school system.[3] One interlocutor in the diaspora commented that 'if the church was on the side of the colonial power, it is not because it was the Catholic church, it was because it was the *Belgian* church (emphasis added)'. The sense of pride I perceived from some of my interviewees in relation to Catholic education – reflecting the importance of education for class distinction– went hand in hand with a discourse about the role played by the church for the 'development' of the country and its civic/opposition role, including during Mobutu's regime and the contested Kabila presidency, as we saw in Chapter 4.

In light of their perceptions of the homeland as a dysfunctional place, my Catholic interlocutors also highlighted Catholicism's organizational contributions. The point they made is that, since Catholic institutions are well established and (historically) organized through a clear bureaucratic and hierarchical order, they constitute reliable vehicles for the development and progress of the nation, unlike Pentecostal churches, which are often accused of being businesses led by entrepreneurial, opportunistic pastors, without proper religious training and prioritizing short-term gains over the common good.

It must be said here that Catholicism in the DRC exhibits a certain degree of internal pluralism, with a multitude of religious orders (most of them internationally organized) running parishes and associated institutions, which, in the case of schools, can enjoy some degree of autonomy in terms of ethos, management styles or pedagogical approaches. Despite this pluralization, as well as the existence of tensions between the different orders and the socio-economic inequality between parishes, the organization of the Catholic network remains strongly centralized in its coordination and hierarchical structure (Titeca, De Herdt and Wagemakers 2013). This was seen as a clear marker of difference with Pentecostals, evidence of the legitimacy of the Catholic church for religious (but also social and political) governance by most of my Catholic interlocutors. To some extent, there was a comparable narrative among Kimbanguist followers who emphasized their organizational discipline based on a strictly centralized hierarchical structure and their wide-ranging network of institutions, mostly schools, established in a context of marginalization and exclusion of Kimbanguists from the mainstream – mostly Catholic – schools after independence (Mokoko Gampiot 2017).

The research in Kinshasa suggests that morality was another important aspect of the narratives linking religion, development and education. The idea that morality is transmitted through religious education, especially through embodied practices and norms of behaviour, was here recurrent. As stated by the rector of a Catholic high school interviewed in Kinshasa, this proved particularly attractive to parents:

> What attracts parents who bring their children here is, first of all, the morality that we have. We try to inculcate morality to the children. The way they dress: we also take this into account and also the behaviour of our students. We need to prepare the integral development of students. . . . It is with us that students prepare this and through work we show their achievements to the people [*au peuple*] and to the nation.

In connection to this notion of integral development, there was a repeated stress on the role of religious education in the making of exemplary 'moral citizens'. For instance, the deputy director of a Catholic primary school in a Limete parish (northeast of Kinshasa) talked about the importance of honesty as a core principle of the school whose ambition is to train *des bons citoyens* ('good citizens'):

> This is a Catholic school and we have norms for a good discipline. We accept all children including those who are not Catholics. But there is no discrimination, everyone must come on time for the prayer. The school has designed a code of conduct [*ligne de conduite*] that all children must follow. . . . Our school's core principle is that we must train good citizens, good citizens, and honest people. Since a good citizen, an honest citizen, must be honest everywhere,

be they Catholic, Muslim, Protestant, of from Nzambe Malamu [well-known Pentecostal church], they must be honest citizen, wherever they go. Not only in our school but also outside, when they will be working in the wider society. They won't always stay here, in the Catholic school.

Attended by Catholic and non-Catholic pupils (including a small number of children from Muslim families), the school ethos is based on a strict discipline, a *ligne de conduite*, enjoining pupils to observe norms of punctuality and order, and on the incorporation of moral values through religious education. While all pupils must attend religious classes, morning assemblies – *le mot du matin* (led by a priest if available) – and a Saturday Mass, non-Catholic pupils are not obliged to partake in certain rituals such as communion or Ash Wednesday. Preparing children for life outside of the school is what drives the quest for excellence and is a central element of the vision of the school, whose achievement is partly measured by the academic performance of pupils, many of them moving on to some of the most selective Catholic secondary schools in Kinshasa. While the school has benefited from the support of the Order of Salesians of Don Bosco, which took over the parish from the Scheut Missionaries[4] in the 1990s, former pupils who became politicians or civil servants have also contributed to the renovation and maintenance of the school through philanthropic donations. In addition to academic achievements, the good reputation of the school is evidenced by these high-profile connections, an important marker of distinction in the educational market, but also, and perhaps more importantly, in the context of a diversified and competitive urban religious landscape, increasingly dominated by Pentecostal churches. The fact that a former pupil who became a TV presenter and is now a well-known Pentecostal pastor publicly praised the education he received was seen as a sign of recognition of the esteem and value of the school and, more widely, of Catholic education.

In an interview with the academic director of a Catholic high school (*lycée*) for girls, a similar point was raised about the popularity of Catholic education among Pentecostal leaders:

If you do a census, you'll find that 60% of our students come from Pentecostal churches, maybe 30% come from Catholic churches and 10% from Protestant and Kimbanguist churches. It is because these Pentecostal churches are very weak in the field of development. These people, even their pastors, prefer to send their children to study in Catholic schools and not in their own schools. I am a Catholic. All my children have studied in Catholic schools, but children of [Pentecostal] pastors and some of their followers study in Catholic schools.

> During the preaching pastors chastise [*fustigent*] the Catholics, the statues, this
> and that, but then they tell their children to go to study in Catholic schools!

This all-girl Catholic *lycée*, initially set up by a Belgian missionary order and now run by the Kinshasa-based chapter of a French sisterhood congregation, enjoys a very good reputation in Kinshasa and beyond. The school attracts students whose parents are from the wealthier end of the socio-economic spectrum, who can afford higher than average annual fees. Here the stress on Catholic morality dovetails with the reproduction of class identities that transcend religious differences, as pupils (and their families) forge networks that may serve them later in life. One of the school's coordinators emphasized how the idea of a 'complete education' was linked to the need to uphold virtue and morality in the context of a 'corrupt society':

> What we want in this school is to train girls who will be able to defend themselves
> in society, on all levels – intellectual level, but especially moral level. It is not
> only about education, instruction: we want to train a complete man, a complete
> woman. And today there are people who complain about the Catholic Church,
> they say it has failed because the majority of people who lead us have studied in
> Catholic schools, and we can see what these people are doing at the level of the
> government and so on. . . . But society too can corrupt them and you look at their
> curriculum [*cursus*], what they were taught is not what they are applying. Society
> has corrupted them. That's why we, along with our alumni society, want to follow
> where our girls go, where they work and if there are any problems to talk with
> them so that they can go back on the right track [*rentrer dans le droit chemin*],
> following the moral principles that the school had taught them in religious
> classes. . . . We want to make sure that they don't let themselves influenced by
> other people. This is why we provide a complete education, we want to train
> girls with good morals, so that she avoids the corruption rampant in our society.
> When I talk about morality it means for example that when a girl goes and look
> for work, she doesn't offer her body [*donne son corps*] to get the job.

This quote is interesting for several reasons. First, the mention of 'complete education' echoes what we tend to hear repeatedly when it comes to religious education and the centrality of ethical frameworks incorporated through learning and appropriation of values. As shown by Dilger (2017: 514) in his ethnography of Christian and Muslim schools in Dar es Salaam, the formation of a 'moral habitus' can be mediated both explicitly, through the curriculum, for instance, and implicitly, through informal interactions in everyday school settings. This habitus reveals that the embodiment of moral personhood is co-constructed by teachers and students in a fluid and sometimes fragmented process. Children are not passively reproducing moral values simply by being exposed to them and, additionally, there are observable discrepancies between promoted moral ethos and actual attitudes and practices. Nevertheless, this habitus 'establishes specific relationships between individual actors and their socio-economic and religious environments' (2017: 514).

Dilger's study is of real value to our understanding of how the moral habitus operates in a plural educational environment. A major difference between the Congolese and Tanzanian contexts lies in the fact that Catholic actors must address a powerful tension between, on the one hand, a claim for moral rigour and legitimacy, and, on the other hand, what they see as the reality of a society 'rampant with corruption', especially in the political and the civil service spheres which comprise leaders who have received a 'good' Catholic education. Here there is an implicit recognition that Catholics have both succeeded (in forming elites, including in the early post-Independence period) and failed (to equip them morally to govern society). Catholics attempt to reconcile this contradiction by presenting 'society' as a corrupting force and a 'complete Catholic education' as the remedy. Such an attempt reflects the importance of principles, values and embodied ethical frameworks and expresses an ideal and visionary trope, a quest to establish a moral citizenship capable of carving out a project for the nation.

This trope is contingent and gendered and cannot be understood outside the Christian-inflected construction of women's role and position in a society where gender relations have been shaped by the greater economic autonomy of women and the overall increasing influence of Pentecostal domestic models centred around the nuclear family (Meiers 2013, Ayimpam 2012). In the scenario described by the school coordinator as an example of the need to 'follow up' on former students, a young woman is 'offering her body' as a strategy to gain employment. She is the only actor of the hypothetical story, a one-sided interaction with an implicit but absent (supposedly male) employer and, as a result, the situation is read solely through the prism of her moral agency (or lack thereof). Echoing Ruth Marshall's (2009) influential Foucauldian reading of Pentecostal/born-again governmentality in Nigeria, I found that this Christian understanding of womanhood does not redefine the uneven power-geometry of gender relations. Rather, it fulfills a 'programmatic' moral regime that provides believers with resources to avoid sinful and corrupt practices. But unlike Catholicism, African Pentecostalism is, for the most part, a regime of spiritual warfare and rupture revolving around a continuous spiritually embodied engagement (prayers and fasting), which is essential to the maintenance of a born-again subject-formation (Daswani 2015). However, Catholic 'complete education' is in some ways similar to the unstable born-again condition (Engelke 2010, Marshall 2009), because it is never really 'complete'. There is a perception that this 'incompleteness' is rendered ever more legible by what is seen as the corruption among Catholic-educated leaders and politicians – an idiom of the failed congruence between the Catholic moral habitus and the processes of state-formation and governance.

Pentecostal orientations: Maman Olangi's educational ethos of 'transformation'

While Pentecostalism's mode of governance draws upon holistic models of moral formation that are particularly relevant in the educational sphere, in Kinshasa, schools set up by Pentecostal churches/FBOs represent a small minority within a religious-oriented educational field largely dominated by Catholic and to a lesser extent (mainline) Protestant institutions (Titeca, De Herdt and Wagemakers 2013). Among the Pentecostal schools in Kinshasa, the Bérée school, *l'Ecole Bérée,* established by the 'Maman Olangi' Ministère du Combat Spirituel church is one of the most well known. There are two Bérée schools in Kinshasa, one in the Limete commune founded in 2001 and one in the Ngaliema commune, which contains pockets of more affluent, middle-class population, created in 1997. In addition, the church has set up three schools outside the Congolese capital in the towns of Matadi (Kongo Central province) and Mbandaka (Equateur province) and near Tshikapa (Kasai province) through its Olangi Wosho Foundation. The school in Limete is located within the main Maman Olangi church complex, developed on a formerly industrial site. It also comprises a large place of worship, a bookshop, a cooperative and various administrative buildings. With around 1,400 pupils across pre-school (*maternelle*), primary and secondary sections, this school is by far the largest school of the emerging Ecole Bérée network. The school benefits from being centrally located, a stone's throw from strategic avenues connecting the local neighbourhood to the important urban communes of Lemba and Matete, from where a significant number of the school's students come. At around $350–380 a year, the fees are higher than most Kinshasa's schools, which explains why the school caters mostly to children of middle- to high-income families. High-profile politicians, businessmen and army officers connected to the church are known to send their children to Bérée. However, school administrators and managers interviewed in Kinshasa were keen to paint a picture of class diversity and stressed the existence of a scheme for so-called *cas sociaux*, that is providing assistance to poorer children and orphans.[5]

Just as for the Catholic schools I studied, the notion of 'complete education' is central to the ethos of Ecole Bérée, whose motto written very visibly on its outside wall reads 'informer, former, transformer' ('to inform, train [and] transform'). The motto is adapted from the church's slogan 'nous informons, nous formons et nous transformons' (Ndaya Tshiteku 2007: 3). According to the head, Ecole Bérée is a place where pupils benefit from *un encadrement intégral* and where education targets 'body, soul and spirit [*corps, âme et esprit*]'. Like in the case of the Catholic educational dynamics examined earlier, 'training good citizens' is part and parcel of a trope constructing religious education as a project for the wider society, through the promotion of core values and the rejection of practices deemed corrupt and immoral. For Bérée, however, this ethical framework reflects the centrality of a Pentecostal moral habitus, produced and reproduced through a regime of intensive spiritual embodiment, as this excerpt from an interview with a female teacher, Maman M., suggests:

> Here, what we want for each child is that they have good morals [*des bonnes moeurs*]. We want them to be mature, complete and honest citizens, with integrity. This is why we are working hard, despite adolescence, despite difficulties, to educate, to educate and to educate more. In prayers, in wakes [*veillées*], in fasting sessions, we exhort children to be role models, to be good citizens, to reject unfruitful works [*oeuvres infructueuses*] like corruption, cheating [*la tricherie*], things like that. In Ecole Bérée, we train children to be good citizens. To be serious in all things, in their lives. And to love God and to serve Him, so that when they are grown-ups, they remember.

The distinction with other non-Pentecostal educational cultures, especially Catholic ones, is an important aspect of the ways in which the school is defined. This is particularly salient in narratives about the origin of the school. Its creation responded to a need identified by the Olangi couple, the need for a spiritual environment allowing children to be educated according to the vision of the church. In fact, the school was designed to be an extension of the ministry, allowing parents attending Combat Spirituel to withdraw their children from educational environments deemed contradictory to the church's orientation or even 'influenced by occultism and Freemasonry', as a member of the Ministère and parent interviewed put it. The distinction with Catholic schools seemed to be the most significant and it operated at several levels. For instance, during an interview, the director accused some Catholic schools of using their connections with civil servants to obtain and then pass on exam questions to their pupils. Bérée students, he commented, 'have been taught not to cheat and that cheating is an *anti-valeur*'. In the narratives, the other salient difference revolved around the 'aesthetic regime' of Catholic socio-material and ritualistic world (Butticci 2016), deemed to be promoting idolatry and adoration. By contrast, the director of the school stressed how, in Ecole Bérée, children could be educated 'according to the Word of God' in an environment prioritizing spiritual deliverance and transformation:

> This school has been created by our shepherds [*bergers*], Maman and Papa Olangi. They noticed that our children, the children of the Ministère, when they were attending other schools, they would see things that were contrary to the vision of the Ministry. So they decided: 'No! we need to create our own school, we will see our children get deliverance, because there is not only science, there is also the spirit and the soul'. . . . There are schools where they do the sign of the cross, where they adore statues. Whereas for us, this is contrary to the Bible. So we and the parents decided to create a school where children can be educated according to the vision of the Ministère du Combat Spirituel, according to the Word of God [*la parole de Dieu*].

In the discourses collected, the idiom of transformation was central not only with regard to the ethos of the school and its impact on children but also when it came to the individual spiritual journeys of teachers and other staff members, all actively involved in the Ministère and regularly getting together for spiritual retreats and prayer wakes. Maman M., for instance, talked at length about changes in her life as a result of her encounter with the Ministère. Initially, she was attending a Pentecostal church 'with a good pastor, good teachings', but 'something was missing', as she put it. Suffering from anxiety attacks, insomnia and bouts of depression, she claimed that it is only when she started to follow Maman Olangi's teachings and to submit to an intensive regime of deliverance prayers that her health improved. Through Maman Olangi's preaching and a deep spiritual introspection, she also came to understand why there were 'blockages' in her life, such as her fiancée leaving her and her struggle to find employment. She recalled how she uncovered that curses from kin, especially from her grandmother, were the origin of these blockages (echoing the experience of Papa Marcel and Maman Betty in Chapter 2 for whom family curses were hindering mobility and migration). Equipped with the new knowledge about the negative role of past ancestral *malédictions*, she joined a 'spiritual warfare of renouncement', her transformation expressing itself through more stability and a newfound respect towards herself and others. The school is here presented as an agent of personal transformation but also upward social mobility:

> I fought, I started to pray, to renounce, fighting all these spirits. Spirits of the family, family bondage, condemnation, curses. Fighting with prayers, through fasting and even through seeding [*les semences*, i.e. money offerings]. And one day I thought about Ecole Bérée, about being a teacher. . . . I started low, 45 dollars [a month], but I moved up, 60, 100, 130 and now I live normally. God gave me victory. . . . In the *Ministère* I got to learn to respect myself, first of all, to respect my body, my life and how to dress, and to respect others, to respect the country and the public good [*le bien public*]. . . . Before, I was always ill, always feverish . . . I started to reject this, to renounce all the problems that I had . . . I managed really good results.

Like the community of the Ministère, a space of deliverance where one can learn about and act upon the power of ancestral bondage, the school is where pupils can become autonomous and detach themselves from what is seen as a detrimental spiritual environment. This was, in essence, the message heard during a prayer service which was held at the back of the school building. In front of an assembly of fifty or so older children (twelve- to fifteen-year-olds), a Combat Spirituel pastor encouraged them to reject the negative judgements of family members who are telling them that they 'will never succeed'. Instead, pupils were told to trust God and challenge the spoken curse of their family by responding 'in the name of Jesus I will succeed', a counter-performative utterance of individual spiritual empowerment consistent with the overall theology of the Ministère. Of course, it is not really in the interest of the school to alienate parents, so it is presented as an environment of spiritual transformation, empowerment and remoralization. Teachers talked about how the priority given to order and discipline was attractive to parents but above all how the cultivation of Christian principles was integral to upholding moral values among youth in the context of a 'sinful city' like Kinshasa. As one teacher stated, by inculcating in them 'the fear of God', pupils think twice about 'committing wrongdoings like stealing, cheating or being lustful and indecent'. For parents who are affiliated with the Ministère, the school offers a continuity with the home environment and with religious family practices. According to the director, all parents, including those who are not part of the Ministère, must sign an agreement and accept the vision of the school and its principles and methods. The school is recurrently portrayed as creating an environment through which children 'with problems' will noticeably change, will be 'calmer and respectful' and also will be more religiously committed in their behaviour and attitude at home. Several times, Ecole Bérée staff mentioned the situation of children who, thanks to their transformation, triggered changes in their families, even the conversion of their parents. Maman M. described such a situation using the example of a pre-school boy:

> We have parents who are not in the Combat [i.e., Ministère du Combat Spirituel], but when they send their children to our school, they integrate [to the Ministère] because they see how their children change. Stubborn children now start praying and this makes parents really happy. I can give the example of a boy in pre-school [*maternelle*]. His parents put him in the pre-school section because they just lived next door. The parents didn't pray, they were pagans [*paiens*], the father and the mother. . . . After his first week, during family dinner the parents asked how school went and the child said: 'the teacher said before eating we need to pray, don't eat, we need to pray and give grace to God'. The child prayed and everyone ate and the parents were wondering 'why is this happening?'. At night, before bed, the child came to his dad: 'dad, we need to pray'. . . . Before going to bed he tells his mum, 'mum, we must pray'. The mum and the dad, they then came to us, to our teachings [*enseignements*] with the child. He accompanied them. Now they themselves have joined the Ministère. They gave a testimony about it.

This story of conversion constructs the school as a vector of transformation not only for the child but also for the parents. The pupil, who has incorporated the intensive praying regime of the school, manages to dramatically shape the everyday life of his parents, introducing a religious rhythm to the domestic space, 'accompanying' them to the Ministère and its teachings. The pupil pushes outward the boundary of the school environment; he becomes an outpost of the 'God of Maman Olangi' (Meiers 2013) into the 'pagan' world. The Ecole Bérée constitutes an environment where pupils must obey a rigid teaching and religious schedule and submit to a regime of constant spiritual overseeing (*encadrement spirituel*). To quote the director, it is a school where 'pupils must fear God' and where teachers 'do not teach without mentioning and elevating the name of Jesus'. Life in the school should be in a sense a reflection of a life of *combattants spirituels,* who display an undivided commitment to the vision and mission of the Ministère. The Ministère and school are both strongly integrative environments but the agency of the pupil, a very young, pre-school-aged pupil, is at the centre of a narrative which has become constructed as an exemplary story, conveyed and circulated in the form of a testimony.

There is another side to this story of children evangelizing and transforming the 'pagan' world: the figure of the possessed or spiritually afflicted child. For those who are thought to exhibit symptoms of afflictions, Ecole Bérée provides an *encadrement spirituel* consisting of praying and fasting. If deemed appropriate, a *cure d'âme*, 'soul healing', is performed by the *cureurs*, the 'healers' of the Ministère. The *cure d'âme* is a long process, I was told. It involves a 'research' to locate 'clues' so as to understand the origin of an affliction, for instance, an event in the child's personal history (like a curse by an elder kin). Because children are deemed 'too young to understand', as one teacher put it, there is dialogue, consultation and agreement with the parents on diagnostic and healing methods, with a strong focus on 'targeted prayers',[6] including in the home environment.

One of the Bérée school teachers spoke about a variety of scenarios of spiritual affliction caused by the detrimental power of ancestral bondage, possession by evil spirits or even 'conscious witchcraft' (*sorcellerie consciente*), citing the case of a pupil 'having astral projections and visions of killing and eating [people]'.[7] 'Behavioural problems' – examples cited ranged from stealing, being rebellious or rude to adults – that 'cannot be explained' are often read through the prism of spiritual affliction and witchcraft (*kindoki*), a process constructing and legitimizing the school as a space of moral disciplining but also, and above all, a therapeutic space of intervention – part and parcel of a spiritual warfare spearheaded by the Ministère through its vision and mission of renewal and transformation. In parallel, the Ministère has set up an organization – *les rachetés* (the redeemed) – supporting street children who have been accused of being witches (*bandoki*) and who had been abandoned by their kin. Some of these children attend the Bérée school for free and here the stress is again on treating witchcraft and possession as an illness – 'some say the Ministère tell people to abandon *enfants sorciers* [child witches], that is not true, they should not be abandoned, they should be healed', as one teacher told me.

The association between witchcraft and childhood is relatively recent in African contexts (La Fontaine 2016), and most of those who have studied the phenomenon in the DRC argue that it has to be understood against the backdrop of rapid societal change and transformation in the moral economy of kinship. De Boeck (2009), in particular, mentions the complex interplay of factors linked to the restructuring of kinship models, including the vulnerable positions of 'adopted' children (nieces, nephews, step children, etc.) amidst restricted networks of care, or the often fragile situation of children born of what he coins 'short-circuit marriages', romantic cohabitation without the consent of lineage members, mostly because of the increasingly unaffordable cost of the traditional bridewealth for the male spouse. In both cases, the redefining of kinship recentred on the nuclear family in the context of generalized economic strain negatively impacts on the status of children. In some of these situations, children can become a burden, no longer a marker of symbolic capital within lineage groups (2009: 137). The striking change in the valuation of childhood is also apparent in De Boeck's discussion of the increasing association between violence and childhood through the figure of child soldiers and the *bashegue*, street children, often sleeping in cemeteries or markets, who are depicted by In Koli Jean Bofane in his 2014 novel *Congo Inc.* Because youth and children have become prominently visible in the urban public landscape of Kinshasa, they are increasingly the source of new anxieties, as traditional gerontocratic hierarchies are challenged, fuelling intergenerational tensions. These intergenerational conflicts are being relocated to and negotiated in the (therapeutic) space of the church, with pastors competing for followers instrumentalizing the idiom of witchcraft, staging and performing the spiritual warfare as a necessary enterprise to counteract the ubiquity of evil. As Demart (2017: 183) aptly argues, Pentecostal churches are not merely interpreting signs of witchcraft but have been instead actively *producing* them, constructing the occult as source of all crises and promoting spiritual solutions through individual and collective deliverance, involving, in the case of *bana bandoki* (child witches) a process of 'reparentalisation within the global family in Christ' (Tonda 2008: 339).

A discussion with Sylvie, a member of the Ministère du Combat Spirituel and a spiritual overseer (*encadreuse spirituelle*) in Ecole Bérée, brought some nuance to a narrative identifying all things 'deviant' among children as purely witchcraft, however. Sylvie happened to reside and work in Europe but has taken some extended leave to be in Kinshasa with her husband (who does not have yet his legal residency status to live in Europe permanently). She spoke about the need to listen to children as essential to her therapeutic approach:

We see witchcraft like an illness, a problem, that we can get rid of. . . . You can cure it. . . . And it's not about money, it's not because you come to school in a Jeep and your father is a general that you are safe from it! Sometimes parents come and see us 'my child has a problem, he's 17 he still wets the bed at night' – so how do you explain this type of behaviour? So we speak with the child, we can spend even 4 hours, just with one child. Because in Africa, the child is not listened to. I come from Europe, where children speak, we listen to children there. We need to listen and pay attention [*tendre l'oreille*] to try to understand their dreams and worries . . . and this requires establishing a climate of trust, enabling the child to speak. And the child speaks, we understand that maybe what one calls witchcraft, maybe it's not witchcraft. Maybe it's just an internal wound [*blessure intérieure*], or maybe something that happens at home, an injustice, the way his dad treats his mum. . . . Maybe there are other treatments. . . . We try to listen to the children, to give them time. Little by little, each case at a time, we manage to help these children.

There is an implicit recognition here of the influence of other models (of 'treatment') to engage with 'problematic' behaviours. Diagnostics about witchcraft may not be straightforward and rather could be seen as contingent on individual assessments – in this case, the judgement of someone who has been exposed to an environment where 'children are listened to'. In support of her approach, that some of her Bérée colleagues at school criticized for being 'too European', Sylvie also argued that Maman Olangi herself warned against quick diagnostics and advocated sustained periods of observation and communication with the child, instead of rushing to the 'cure d'âme' therapy.

The fact that witchcraft diagnostics may be open to internal debate does hardly change the reputation of the Ministère and the Ecole Bérée, in particular among some sections of the Kinshasa population. After the death of Maman Olangi, for instance, there were many critical voices on social media accusing the Ministère of 'dividing families' (in both diaspora and DRC contexts) and the Ecole Bérée of being a 'school for the rich', with a harsh discipline revolving around practices deemed tough like repeated fasting. Because of the state's inability to properly regulate the religious field and thanks to the Ministère benefiting from high-profile connections with Congolese politicians, the school is also largely evading any external or state scrutiny regarding its (strict) methods.

Health interventions in pluralized therapeutic landscapes

Besides education, health is another major sector of involvement for Kimbanguists, Catholics and, to a lesser extent, large Pentecostal organizations like the Maman Olangi church. Here again, Catholics are important religious providers, another legacy of their role during the Belgian colonial rule. Kimbanguists have also developed their network of small health centres in Kinshasa and across the country with a main hospital in Kimbanseke, Kinshasa. While these actors acknowledge the inability of the state to fully meet its role in terms of healthcare provision, there was no real claim or aspiration about *replacing* the state in its mission, especially among Catholics and Kimbanguists. As one of the senior staff of the Kimbanguist hospital puts it:

> The primary role of the church is to bring souls to the Lord [*amener les âmes vers le Seigneur*] – the salvation of souls. The church also needs to deal with the

welfare aspect of its followers' lives but I think development is the role of the state, generally speaking. Churches have seen how the state has failed [*l'Etat a failli*], how it does not do its job correctly. This is why there is this support from churches. It is not the role of the churches, but they are accompanying the state in its role.

While the Congolese state is often seen as hostile and predatory in its everyday incarnation (Trefon 2011: 87–100), some narratives underlined the need for relations of complementarity or even partnership with state agencies. These particular relations are reflected by the existence of contractual institutional linkages with the state through structures that are *conventionées* (in contract with the state) which is the case, for instance, of the Kimbanseke Kimbanguist hospital.

The Kimbanguist hospital in Kimbanseke (Kinshasa)

Opened in 1974, the hospital was originally a smaller medical centre born out of the need of members of the church to create their own healthcare infrastructures in a context of exclusion of Kimbanguists from state and Catholic health facilities. It was converted into a hospital in 1988 with the financial support of Israeli and American development agencies and with some Belgian assistance. The institution is contractually a partner of the Congolese state, which supports the salaries and bonuses of most of the staff and is integrated into the overall DPS (Département Provincial de Santé, Provincial Health Zone) management structure. In addition to the salaries, the electricity and water bills are directly paid by the state, but the institution does not benefit from any other public subsidies – for instance, to purchase equipment, pharmaceuticals and other medical products or consumables, or, perhaps more importantly, to improve/maintain the building as Doctor A. describes:

> We have serious difficulties to operate. Maintaining a hospital in a good state requires a lot of resources. There are no subsidies from the state, the church does not support us, so it is a daily struggle. The hospital was last rehabilitated in 1988, more than 30 years ago and since then, nothing. Equipment dating from 1988 has not been replaced and we work with outdated infrastructure and equipment. With whatever means at hand [*avec les moyens du bord*], we try to replace the smaller pieces of equipment so that we can continue to work. But we have almost no financial resources also because many patients struggle to pay their medical bills.

The partnership with the state, while deemed crucial since it enables the day-to-day running of the hospital and staff presence, is clearly not sufficient to address the chronic overall under-investment in the infrastructure. As suggested by Doctor A., the lack of state subsidies is made worse by the overall lack of support from the Kimbanguist church, which puts more emphasis and investment on the development of Nkamba. Moreover, among Kimbanguists, the spiritual and cultural importance of customary donations during service (*nsinsani*) is bound up with the construction of a collective identity promoting autonomy as a central value. This trope of self-reliance is also connected to the collective memory of a 'golden age' of solidarity, during the colonial repression, when Kimbanguists were forced to worship underground. While a particular Kimbanguist moral economy explains the church's reluctance to solicit (at least officially and visibly) external financial support and partnership, it is also clear that divisions and conflicts within the church, a history of financial malpractice and the existence of a rigid, centralized bureaucracy have had a negative impact on the church's attractiveness to potential donors and NGO/FBO partners (Rich 2019). This helps to explain why the initial support received from USAID and other government agencies was not repeated.

The hospital has benefited and still benefits from occasional support from the diaspora. For instance, Papa Laurent, a Kimbanguist based in Atlanta, was instrumental in obtaining medical supplies and second-hand equipment, including a CT scanner and an ultrasound machine, for the Kimbanseke hospital. This was accomplished with the support of a prominent African American former civil rights activist who is a Methodist deacon and founder of an NGO with projects in Africa and Brazil. Papa Laurent had met him through a common (Sierra Leonean) acquaintance in Atlanta and, after hearing about Kimbanguism and the life of Simon Kimbangu, this African American activist developed a keen interest in the church and travelled to the DRC with Papa Laurent in 2015. They went to Nkamba and visited various other Kimbanguist sites, including the Kimbanseke hospital where he was reportedly 'shocked' at the sight of its neglected state. This example illustrates how the 'horizon' of the diaspora can be a site for new connections and possibilities (Johnson 2007). It also shows how the figure and story of Kimbangu can find some resonance with a wider pan-African imaginary, whose relevance and potency in the United States and especially in the Atlantan/New South context, where there is a long-standing history of racism and anti-racist activism, has the potential to create diasporic affinities across a transnational 'Black Atlantic' space (Gilroy 1993, Covington-Ward 2016). Here we again see how, while being in diaspora may generate displacement, intra-family tension, financial hardship, moral dilemmas and deep longing for the homeland, it is also a potential source of empowering solidarity and transformative engagement.

Unlike the current spiritual leader who has been putting more emphasis on the development of Nkamba, Papa Diangienda, the first leader of the (officially recognized) church, invested a great deal in the expansion of Kimbanguist infrastructures in Kinshasa – mostly health and educational facilities. Today, many Kimbanguists see the Kimbanseke hospital as a testimony to Diangienda's charitable 'vision and philosophy', to quote one of the administrators of the hospital:

> It's true that we need money to operate, but human life is at the heart of what we do. This was the vision of Papa Diangienda, who had the idea of the hospital, here in the periphery [of Kinshasa], where it was semi-rural and where people didn't have access to good health care. He said: 'we must develop here [in Kimbanseke] because it is a poor environment, why should we do it in La Gombe where people are wealthy? It's not going to help people there'. That was his vision, his philosophy.

Kimbanguists see healthcare as part and parcel of an 'integral approach to development' (Cochrane 2011), alongside education or initiatives of rural development through agricultural cooperatives. This approach is seen as contributing to a wider and collective aspirational quest for welfare and change (for Kimbanguists and non-Kimbanguists alike). Resonating with some of the narratives examined earlier about religious education as a 'moral citizenship' project (Dilger 2017), this vision ties the betterment of the individual to the 'developmental' aim of impacting society as a whole:

> We accept patients who are often insolvent, even for 1,000 Congolese Francs [0.60 Dollars]! So our contribution is really significant. When we talk about development, you don't develop a nation if people are sick. Healthy people bring about development. So the Kimbanguist church contributes greatly to society and its development. Here people are destitute, the *commune* is semi-rural, and you have a lot of unemployed people. If you are unemployed and you fall sick, it's catastrophic. (Hospital senior manager)

The trope of work (*misala*), a key Kimbanguist precept (alongside mutual love – *bolingo* – and the obedience of divine laws, *mibeko*), is here particularly significant in the ways in which healthcare and the notion of development are articulated – 'a healthy individual is able to work and is productive for society', as one doctor argued. It is true that this notion of work among Kimbanguist is usually understood as 'working for the church', that is, mostly for the development of Nkamba through *nsinsani* donation. In that sense, it echoes the Mouride conception of work as a sacred practice (Kingsbury 2023). While, in theory, *misala* primarily relates to the moral community of the church and is shaped by a prophetic aspiration; it is metonymic of a wider attitude to society as a whole, in part due to the belief that Kimbanguism is the redemptive solution to society's ills and true 'hope of the world' – *espoir du monde*, one of the mottos of the church. By 'working' for the church, one works for universal emancipation and the salvation of all.

Another core element of the Kimbanguist triad, the *bolingo* (love) value, also plays a key role in the group's understanding of healthcare. The place occupied by compassion, humanitarianism and care for everybody regardless of their financial means was often held as a unique Kimbanguist 'added value':

> Spirituality has a role to play for us. What is spirituality? We have a triad in our church which goes: Love, the Law [i.e., divine law] and Works [*les oeuvres*]. We preach and advocate love, and in the health sector, love is almost a vocation. We have spiritual values which help us to fulfill this vocation, the teachings of our church really help us to better care for the sick. We are not here for profit [*le lucre*], for our own interest, no. Our only joy is to see someone cured.

The ethos and environment of Kimbanguist healthcare was sometimes contrasted to state institutions, which are seen as badly managed and where 'harassing' patients to extract revenues 'on the side' is rife:

> We are trying to make sure that all the bad practices that happen in other hospitals are not replicated here. In other hospitals, state hospitals, as soon as you get to the door, they start ransoming you [*ils vous rançonnent*]. You have to give money to a guard; the nurse will ask you 2,000 Congolese Francs before an injection or will sell you medicines on the side. This harassment does not exist in our hospital! We make every effort for the well-being of our patient. And state institutions are not financially managed properly – it is dysfunctional, disorderly. But us, we respect the sick and our management is rigorous.

While all types of patients are accepted, regardless of their economic status or religious affiliation, the Kimbanseke hospital remains a Kimbanguist institution above all. The Kimbanguist bodily regime is enforced within its space. For instance, women wearing trousers or not covering their hair are denied access by the security staff guarding the entrance. There is a chaplaincy, a prayer room and a Kimbanguist religious service organized every morning and open to staff and patients. Kimbanguist prayer times are observed and patients throughout the day can request the assistance of a Kimbanguist pastor for spiritual support. Interestingly, Kimbanguist patients, I was told, are exempted from paying consultation fees, since they are considered to have already contributed through their *nsinsani*, their church offerings.

Among the staff, there was a widespread critique of patients who delayed urgent care 'to consult Pentecostal pastors with the risk of worsening their condition', as one doctor put it. However, there was no rejection of the recourse to spiritual therapy or *tradipraticiens* (herbalists) in the name of biomedicine. That said, the use of fetishes or visits to *sorciers* and *féticheurs* (witch doctors) was disapproved outright as sinful and evil. The hospital also allows religious specialists belonging to non-Kimbanguist groups to assist patients, should they request it. In that sense, there is a recognition and acceptance that patients navigate a pluralized space of therapeutic possibilities.

Miséricorde hospital

The Miséricorde hospital, whose creation in 2006 was financially supported by the diasporic members of the New Jerusalem Church, offers another example of an institution set up by a transnational religious organization. Unlike the Kimbanguist hospital, it is not *conventioné* and is also smaller in capacity and size. While there are obvious differences in terms of religious orientation and theology between the two churches, the Miséricorde and Kimbanguist hospitals share several characteristics. Both are established in peri-urban areas, both reach the poorer segments of the Kinshasa population and have adopted comparable visions of development and charitable mission. The Miséricorde hospital is situated in an area containing low-income populations (including fishermen and their families) and, given its proximity to the Congo River, the area has a higher prevalence of malarial transmission. Its consultation fees are kept low, around $2, and treatments are also cheaper than in other (private or even public) hospitals. The members of the church living in Kinshasa do not pay for treatment and consultation, just as for the Kimbanguist case described earlier. Here religious membership and participation (mediated by offerings and donations) can thus be seen to create affordances through an implicit and exclusive system of redistribution and 'social security' outside any other formal (public or private) structures (Leutloff-Grandits, Peleikis and Thelen 2009). Despite the relevance of boundaries between members and non-members linked to this practice, one hospital doctor made it clear that 'Christian values' were at the heart of the hospital's charitable mission, drawing a distinction with 'other hospitals', which are more profit-driven, according to him:

> The state doesn't do much in terms of health care. It doesn't do what it is supposed to do like in Europe or other African countries. The main difference between our hospital and other private hospitals is that in other hospitals the main goal is profit, but not us. For us, it's care first, money is secondary. . . . Here we have values that we need to convey – charity [*la charité*], love of others [*l'amour du prochain*] – this is our plus. And it's not me who is saying this – it's the Bible.

This distinction becomes even more relevant in a context where the state is seen to have failed in its mandate to provide decent welfare to its citizens. Given the limited revenues from patients, there is a quasi-total financial dependency on the diasporic members of New Jerusalem, who, in effect, pay for the equipment, salaries and general running costs of the hospital. This dependency is a source of anxiety for hospital staff, especially after the founder of the church in Belgium passed away in 2019 when, I was told, financial contributions from the diaspora started to become less regular. One doctor pointed out that, since the creation of the hospital was the vision of the church founder, a lot relied on his personal involvement, including plans for future development. Even prior to the leader's death, the doctor and other staff talked of a need for more help from external partners, NGOs and donors, including state health authorities (currently providing limited logistical and organizational support). Hope was also expressed that the church members in the United States and Belgium would, in the near future, be able to create and mobilize new networks in host countries to allow greater access to external resources or even funding.

Like is the case with the Kimbanguist hospital, the Miséricorde hospital does not restrict patients on the basis of their religious affiliation, and the dominant view was that faith and spirituality were part of an integral approach to individual health and well-being. 'Sinful' practices – drinking or polygamy – were also described as 'unhealthy'. The medical staff see moralizing patients about these when possible as part of their normal therapeutic role. Every morning, there is a short collective prayer and before each operation a prayer is also performed, providing a spiritual 'insurance', protecting and guiding the practitioner:

> The role of the spiritual is important. We always pray before an intervention because we want the supreme being [*l'être suprême*] to be among us and to help us, so that the intervention goes well. We seek the spiritual because we want to succeed in what we are doing. When a doctor prays, it brings them comfort:

'now I have prayed, things will be alright'. They will not panic. Even if blood
flows, they will not panic: 'I have prayed, God will help me'. That means God has
given an insurance. (Senior doctor)

A similar view was expressed during an interview with a junior doctor:

We are a religious hospital. In the morning, we have a short 20-minute prayer
when we pray for the sick. We implore the Lord to help us and to help our
patients. Our intelligence also comes from God. We have studied medicine, we
have read books and studied, but this intelligence comes from God.

Moreover, and echoing some of the narratives heard among Maman Olangi's
Bérée school staff, certain symptoms and health problems are made legible
through the prism of spiritual affliction. For example, a doctor told me the story
of Maman Monique, a woman who had intense lower abdominal pain and who
claimed to have been spiritually attacked by her own father. The pain started after
she dreamt that her father stabbed her in the chest and stomach while she was
defending her elder sister from being attacked by him. Her cousin, a member
of New Jerusalem living in Belgium, urged her to visit the Miséricorde hospital.
After an echography was performed, she was diagnosed with a benign myoma.
The spiritual attacks continued, mostly expressed by the dreams of Maman
Monique being 'eaten like a chicken' by her father and aunt. An operation was
planned to remove her myoma, but prior to this, she went through deliverance
at the hospital, with a *cure d'âme* specifically targeted to fight what was seen
as a family curse affecting her. The deliverance took the form of three days of
intense prayers and isolation in one of the hospital rooms, led by one of the
(non-medical) staff members, who happened to be *intercesseur* in the New
Jerusalem Kinshasa branch. Following the deliverance, Maman Monique had
another dream: this time she saw a knife being removed from her stomach as she
climbed a set of stairs 'out of a dark hole'. Shortly after, further medical analyses
were conducted, revealing another related and underlying condition requiring
her transfer to a more specialized health centre in Kinshasa. The deliverance was
nevertheless held as a success: Maman Monique's pain receded with a significant
reduction of her initial abdominal problem, and the deliverance 'unblocked', in
a certain way, the identification of the physical root cause of her ill health. The
deliverance brought a literal *revelation*.

This example shows how spiritual and biomedical solutions can be entwined
within a therapeutic mode of intervention and also how individual narratives
of spiritual affliction and attacks can form part of a health diagnostic. While
doctors insisted that their therapeutic mission was essentially 'medical', they also

recognized that faith guides and drives their work. As a doctor put it, 'patients often come with two files [*dossiers*] – a medical file and a spiritual file'. In Monique's case, the spiritual intervention which led to the removal of the knife in the 'second world' played an important role – in a way mimicking a medical intervention in the 'first world'. Through intense prayers and deliverance work, the Holy Spirit filled a body-space which had been colonized by evil forces and expelled them out of the afflicted body.

In her work among Pentecostals in Ghana, Krause (2006) suggests that this absence of conflict between spiritual and biomedical reflects a broader Pentecostal ideology of healing and a response to affliction which rests upon a discursive affinity between Charismatic Christian subjectivity and notions of development and progress. She points out that the 'Holy Spirit is seen as a spiritual force of modernisation . . . and is called to fight against obstacles which have been on the biomedical and development cooperation agenda for a long time' (2006: 60). Here the emergence of a Christian 'modernization paradigm' expressed by a combined recourse to biomedical solutions and spiritual treatment mobilizing the potency of the Holy Spirit has to be understood against the perceived failure of Western/postcolonial modernity to empower individuals against the destructive and evil – thus re-enchanted – influence of ancestral curses and witchcraft as sources of poverty and sickness (Meiers 2013: 55, see also Marshall 2009). The Pentecostal 'body politics' of healing and revitalization (Krause 2006) thus engages with both the social and physical bodies through the power of the Holy Spirit channelled within a wider sphere encompassing patients and staff and also a diverse range of material objects, medicines, instruments and so on.

In the recent literature on health in Africa, there is a strong focus on medical pluralism and the ways in which people navigate and/or combine therapeutic possibilities. Frictions and tensions often characterize the existence of these plural regimes of diagnostics, support and care, often shaped by both local and transnational forces (Dilger, Kane and Langwick 2012). In the case of Miséricorde hospital – and this applies to the Kimbanguist case too – the medical staff were consistently critical of the over-reliance on 'spiritual diagnostics' to treat physical problems. When recalling the different stages of his career, a Miséricorde doctor talked about his experience in several religious health institutions in Kinshasa that he had left because 'the spiritual was taking over the medical'. He deplored the 'weakness' of doctors who, despite 'having received their intelligence from God', were risking the lives of patients by 'totally surrendering to the will of pastors'. Another doctor interviewed underlined the necessary complementarity between spiritual and medical modes of intervention but similarly rejected the therapeutic monopoly of pastors in some Pentecostal churches. Here the image of the pastor/praying community 'following' the sick to the hospital illustrated a more desirable model of intervention:

> The physical is the physical. . . . If you have malaria you need to be treated medically. In certain [Pentecostal] churches you are sick and you only see the pastor – that's not good. In our church, if one brother or sister falls sick, our pastor says: go see a doctor first, we will follow you to the hospital to pray for you and be with you. Even if the problem is spiritual, the implications can be physical and need to be treated.

By criticizing the potential curative monopoly of pastors, both doctors expressed their anxiety about the rejection of biomedical options and perhaps articulated some level of insecurity over their own position and legitimacy in a wider and plural field of competing therapeutic interventions. While they seem to indicate a critique of an 'irrational' choice linked to a blind trust in the healing capacity of religious experts, these narratives reinforce the sense of a religious therapeutic pluralism rather than pointing to a religious/secular dichotomy in regard to the understanding of healing possibilities. In this framework, the paradigm of 'healing through conversion' which 'forecloses adopting a positive attitude toward biomedicine' (Burchardt 2015: 155) constitutes a more radical form of Pentecostal investment in the power of the Holy Spirit. For Burchardt (2015), it is part of an available cultural repertoire within which individuals can mobilize specific social resources to make sense of the impact of illness and affliction on their changing selves. What is suggested by the emphasis on the entanglement of spiritual and biomedical is that religion has a legitimate role to play in the transformation and 'development' of society in great part through a moral project of fashioning individual subjects and through the legitimizing of a set of values and 'responsibilized behaviours' (Burchardt 2015: 127).

Conclusion

In this chapter, I placed side by side the development narratives from three different Congolese transnational religious groups to highlight convergences and divergences in their visions of what kind of society the homeland should be, and in their strategies, particularly as they relate to the key fields of education and health, to achieve these visions.

Kimbanguists, Pentecostals and Catholics share a number of beliefs regarding the role of the occult and witchcraft and its impact on people's health and well-being. They tend to view the world as full of insecurity, an everyday reality requiring divine protection and active religious engagement and commitment through prayers and rituals to minimize and address spiritual risks. In all cases, there is also a core belief about the body as being porous and potentially full of entries for evil forces to penetrate. The religious groups diverge, however, in the way they treat afflictions, with Kimbanguists placing a lot of emphasis on the therapeutic power of their spiritual leader – an *inherited* prophetic power which is also contained in sacred substances such as the Nkamba water and earth. Pilgrimages to Nkamba or a visit to the spiritual leader when he is in Kinshasa – which has become less frequent with the 'recentring' of the holy city – is vital for those in need of physical and/or spiritual healing. Pentecostals, in contrast, favour the trope of spiritual warfare, as they seek to deliver the faithful from the bondage of evil spirits and curses that produce sickness, strife and suffering. Cleansing, protecting and fortifying the autonomous (vis-à-vis traditional bonds) and productive body are key in this cosmic struggle.

While actors at both hospitals I discussed stress the importance of an overall vision driven by Christian values of charity and care for the poor, defining them as purely 'religious spaces' would minimize the productive role played by the entwinement – and at times interaction – between biomedical and spiritual domains. These institutions should not be considered purely as 'secular' spaces either, given how religious norms organize their internal spatial and temporal environments and given how they are part of wider religious networks extending far beyond their local environments. While falling outside the scope of this book, this ambivalence deserves more attention, especially considering how most of the literature on religion and health tends to focus on the role of religious healers and religious/spiritual everyday therapies rather than on medical spaces developed and/or run by religious organizations (Janzen 2019).

When it comes to education, all three groups share a deep concern with cultivating honest, reliable and upright citizens, a concern that is not surprising given the widespread perception that the DRC is a disorderly, dysfunctional and unsafe society. All groups would like their schools to advance the 'integral development' of the person, infusing religion and morality into the formation of their students. This is, again, a response to a pluralized society in which traditional structures of authority have increasingly lost their grip, due to a rapid social change which has resulted in dramatic urbanization and the migration to the metropole.

Despite these significant similarities, the ways in which each group implements its vision of integral development vary. Because of its imbrication with colonialism, Catholic education benefits from a vast network of institutions that, notwithstanding their diversity, are embedded in a hierarchical and centralized church. This established, durable mode of organization is appealing in a society that is experienced as fragmented and precarious. Catholic institutions have also been educating Congolese elites for some time, a fact that gives them a certain degree of status and prestige. However, these comparative advantages may also result in the reproduction of class inequalities, a process that stands in tension with the notion of the common good that is at the heart of the idea of 'integral development'.

As we saw in the case of the school run by Maman Olangi's church, Pentecostal education in the DRC sees the construction of moral citizens as closely tied with spiritual warfare. This connection makes sense in a society that is felt as inhabited by a plethora of evil forces bent on doing harm to and blocking the paths of believers. The only way to transform a society of this sort is to create disciplined Christian soldiers who 'put on the full armour of God' (Eph. 6:11) and will join the battle on Jesus's side. We have seen that because of changes in kinship structures, children may be sometimes considered a burden and a potential threat, a threat that is read by seeing them as being both vulnerable to and the potential source of witchcraft. Thus, disciplining them is central to the process of creating a moral, Christian Congo. While we saw that Pentecostal educators, just like doctors working in Pentecostal hospitals, often nuance the narrative of spiritual warfare, introducing scientific and pedagogical considerations in a mix of religious and secular worldviews, this approach can lead to serious abuses of children (La Fontaine 2009). Spiritual warfare may be echoing and sanctifying in the religious and symbolic planes the violence that many Congolese confront in everyday life.

In the following and final empirical chapter, I want to continue exploring these developmental dimensions of religious modalities of presence, turning more specifically to the spatial aspects of religious-driven changes. The aim will be to address how the construction of health and education infrastructure contributes to a process of religious urbanization, signalling and enacting religious visions, while occupying an important place in discourses and theologies of social change.

Building the 'alter-city'

Religious urbanization in the homeland

On a hot summer day in 2015, I embarked on a transnational pilgrimage journey with three members of the Kimbanguist brass band, planning to attend the sacred festivities dedicated to Kimbanguist musicians held in Nkamba. We were flying from London to Kinshasa, where we planned to stay for a few days, allowing for short family visits, before heading to Nkamba, which we eventually reached after what turned out to be a long and tortuous eight-hour drive in a cramped and overloaded Jeep.

That day, I arrived at Gatwick Airport well in advance, following the instructions of my co-pilgrims who were eager to find out how much of my allocated 46-kilogram luggage weight I could potentially 'share' with the group. Since I travelled light I was given a medium-size suitcase to check in which contained various items, mostly gifts, including clothes (shirts, trousers and shoes), medicines, beauty products, toiletries, perfume and, much to my surprise, even foodstuff like pasta or biscuits which I knew to be widely available in Kinshasa's growing range of supermarkets. 'It doesn't matter if you can also find this in Kinshasa, it is written in English, it's from *Poto*, that's what counts!', said Maman Josy, one of the church members present at the airport to help us packing (and repacking). However, not all suitcases were filled with items conveying the power and prestige of *Poto*, the West, to family members. One in particular, and which caught my attention, was to be delivered to church members working on a construction site in Nkamba, where a guest house was being built, one among many other 'sacred works' being carried out to 'develop' the holy city over the years. It was part of a collective effort to increase Nkamba's accommodation capacity and to eventually prepare for its prophetic advent as the New Jerusalem where 'all nations will gather' (Isaiah 66).

The suitcase in question mostly contained equipment for the construction workers: small tools, working clothes and also high-visibility vests and helmets –

'they don't have a health and safety culture in the Congo and we want to change that', I was told when attending the church service during which these items had been donated by church members. The suitcase was actually only a small part of what London diasporic Kimbanguists were contributing to this guest house project; other larger equipment and materials and even a second-hand truck (bought in France through a French Kimbanguist) had been or were to be shipped to the Congo. Before passing through security and as we were saying our goodbyes, Maman Josy was keen to praise the 'development' of Nkamba, and, like most Kimbanguists when describing their holy city, she stressed its peacefulness and sacred power, contrasting it with Kinshasa:

> Papa David, let me tell you: you will return from Nkamba with blessings – for you and your family. In Nkamba you will feel the power of the Holy Spirit. Nkamba is much better than Kinshasa. Kinshasa is too dirty, overcrowded, full of witchcraft. You'll see how peaceful and how developed Nkamba is!

∗   ∗   ∗

This introductory vignette brings up several themes which I wish to develop in this chapter in relation to the making of sacred geographies and the interplay of religion and urbanization. As briefly hinted, the suitcases and their contents suggest the importance of a cross-border gift economy, a sphere encompassing migrants and their kin in the homeland, and they also point to the role of a transnational space of circulation within which religious actors are embedded. The tools and equipment sent to contribute to the expansion of the Kimbanguist holy city illustrate this 'flow-oriented materiality' of the contemporary religious movement that Bruno Reinhardt (2014) aptly documented in his study on Pentecostalism in Ghana. They belong to a particular repertoire of socio-materiality, the one that ties religious place-making to the active *work* of building and constructing. The connection between work and religious attitudes is of course well established in the Weberian tradition and Kimbanguists, as self-identified Protestant Christians would not deny the intrinsic moral value of work. In fact, in Kimbanguist theology, the notion of work (*misala*) encompasses in fact a wide range of sacred duties – which can include praying and church activities like choir singing or brass band performance (Garbin 2012). The most sacred task of all is the work to erect and develop Nkamba and is mostly expressed by donation in cash and kind during the ritual of *nsinsani*, taking place at the end of the service in all Kimbanguist parishes (*paroisses*) in Congo and the diaspora.

While in the previous two chapters I discussed the place of money within the transnational domestic sphere and the religious involvement in health and education, respectively, in this chapter, I want to return to some of the themes of Chapter 3, which explored place-making and the production of spiritual geography in the diasporic contexts of London and Atlanta. In this chapter, I also, however, continue to interrogate the tropes of development and change in particular through the collective work of material and urban transformation but, this time, in homeland contexts. As I suggested in Chapter 3, urban religion's key dialogical ambition is to foreground the way in which city's socio-spatial landscapes affect, transform, hinder or facilitate the deployment of religious ethos and practices, revealing how, in turn, religious cultures refashion, adapt or reproduce particular modes of urbanity. While the 'spatial turn' (Knott 2008) has shaped the study of urban religion with a strong emphasis on the material fabric, iconicity and 'texture' of religion, the process of religious urbanization has been somehow neglected in this growing scholarship. While religious urbanization is of course only partly realized through the physical production of religious space and built environment, there is a risk of approaching 'urban religion' simply through the prism of a collective relation to 'the city', construed as a neutral 'space' pre-existing any form of socio-religious presence, intervention or imagination. Moreover, if urbanity has historically reshaped religious ethos and practices (Rüpke 2020) there is also a need to challenge reductive dichotomies and the positioning of 'religious actors' at the receiving end of particular regimes of urban governance and regulation, denying their capacity to not only conceive and envision the urban on their own terms but also to mobilize an urbanizing socio-spatial agency potentially affecting wider society. Place-making through building or infrastructural development, urban planning and projection, urban aspirations (Burchardt and Westendorp 2018) and also anticipation and expectation constitute key processes and time-spaces of religious urbanization, which, because they create affordances, also need to be foregrounded.

The other relevant theme flagged up by this vignette and which I will address in this chapter is the production and performance of a sacred urban *imaginaire* itself bound up with the overall process of religious urbanization. Like Maman Josy, Kimbanguists make sense of their 'New Jerusalem' according to a prophetic vision of future redemption (Mokoko Gampiot 2017). Nkamba is thus a divine city-yet-to-come, relocated within a temporality of hope (Sarró 2015) and depicted as an eminently sacred and ordered space in clear contrast with the chaotic, syncopated and urban world of Kinshasa and its pervasive 'spiritual insecurity' (De Boeck 2013). We shall see throughout this chapter that the desire to establish an alternative moral (urban) order is a key driver of religious territorialization seen as a project of (re)appropriation and redemption through the urbanizing, infrastructural and material ambition of building an 'alter-city' or 'heteropolis' following Wariboko (2014). An important component of this quest for moral and spatial regeneration lies in the idea of frontier development, as a way to realize expansionist visions and strategies and to position oneself in the wider society.

Development and the urban frontier

Studies about social and economic change brought about by Pentecostal and Charismatic Christianity generally link idioms of transformation with personal moral reform and search for greater individual autonomy, expressed as a rupture – with the past (Meyer 1998) or alternatively as 'realignments' (Engelke 2010) or acts of 'taking control' (Van Dijk 2002; 2010) – especially in relation to the influence of kinship and ancestrality, like in Maman Olangi's spiritual warfare. Pentecostals are also said to operate within a this-worldly, 'new economy of affect', the born-again project of individual moralized transformation correlating 'with new forms of subject-formation under neoliberalism' (Kirby 2019: 16).

In her work on Pentecostalism and development in Ethiopia, Freeman (2012) notes that this Pentecostal project of transformation 'start[s] with the self' before 'moving out to the social and material' (2012: 164). This idea of an ego-initiated, outward movement propelling collective change was indeed recurrent among most of my Pentecostal interlocutors when discussing 'development' and societal transformation. For instance, it was the case of a Ministère du Combat Spirituel interviewee who underlined the centrality of 'integral development' for the individual, echoing the narratives on religious education and health we discussed in the previous chapter. This holistic yet person-centred approach to 'development' takes clear precedence and here has the potential to drive the transformation of a wider 'environment':

> Something that differentiate us from NGOs: we put more emphasis on the person, the being [*l'être*]. The person is composed of body, soul and spirit and we focus on his or her integral development. We believe that development, as far as the person is concerned, does not begin with the environment. Just as in anthropology it is said that Man [*sic, l'Homme*] conditions the environment and the environment makes the person what they become. Before the environment can influence Man, it is Man who first influences

the environment. So the development starts with the being, the person, their interior and we focus on that.

However, it is clear that for Pentecostals the production of an 'environment' by reformed individuals resonates with a quest for regenerating and remoralizing space and the process of religious urbanization linked to the presence of the Combat Spirituel church in Limete can also be seen as part of this logic. The Combat Spirituel church complex is a cluster of buildings which includes a large prayer auditorium, the Bérée school, a book shop, a business cooperative and several other edifices serving administrative or residential functions. It was once a *friche industrielle*, an industrial wasteland, a place which was 'abandoned, dirty, where *sheges* [gangs of street children] were roaming and prostitution was rife', as one Combat Spirituel leader recalls. In fact, the de-industrialization of this large urban area of Kinshasa formerly known for its small workshops and food processing factories had been in great part caused by two waves of military-led looting sprees which took place across Kinshasa in 1991 and 1993 and destroyed most of its economic infrastructure (Nzongola-Ntalaja 2002, De Boeck 2005). The gradual territorial takeover of the area by the Combat Spirituel and a dozen of other Pentecostal churches can be seen as part of a wider vision aimed at the conversion (and redemption) of a sinful, immoral society, with a territorial reconquest 'filling the gaps' of the post-Mobutu era – the frenzied looting incidents of the 1990s personifying the unpredictability of a chaotic and dysfunctional urbanity. In that sense, religious urbanization does not operate here merely through the 'filling up' of neutral, empty spaces devoid of meaning, as already discussed in Chapter 3, but rather through an active transformation and taming of an environment perceived to be already 'full' of wilderness, crime, sins, disorder and so on (Coleman and Vásquez 2015: 42). This is the case of the appropriation of not only post-industrial, declining urban spaces like the Limete neighbourhood but also peripheral, peri-urban spaces, whose growth and densification have pushed outwards the boundaries of many African metropolises, with sprawling megacities like Kinshasa or Lagos inexorably extending into their hinterlands (Trefon 2009, Simone and Pieterse 2017, Gandy 2006).

In Lagos, religious peri-urbanization often operates on a large – if not spectacular – scale. It is driven by churches like the Redeemed Christian Church of God (RCCG) which has built a self-sufficient and rapidly growing urban enclave – 'Redemption Camp' – surrounding 'bush' land where mass prayer gatherings often attract million-strong crowds (Ukah 2016, Osinulu 2014). In addition to church auditoria and preaching grounds, these 'prayer cities' also often contain banks, shops, schools, hospitals and electricity and water infrastructure and are hailed as ordered, safe and crimeless. In other words, such spaces have taken on the ideal features of an 'alter-city' in opposition to what is perceived as the chaos and immorality of the adjacent metropolis. While the peri-urban prayer camp model and, in particular, the RCCG Redemption camp, because of its size and exemplarity, has attracted growing academic attention over the years (Coleman and Vásquez 2015, Butticci 2013, Janson and Akinleye 2015, Katsaura 2019, Osinulu 2014, Ukah 2014, 2016a), it is also a religious spatial form which circulates transnationally within the wider Pentecostal world and even beyond, across religious boundaries.[1] Leaders of Combat Spirituel I met praised the RCCG's vision and its strategy of urbanization through the development of suburban enclaves and have adopted the praying city model with the creation of 'Mahanaim City'[2] on the periphery of Kinshasa. While Mahanaim City, the Combat Spirituel's compound, is visibly more modest in terms of size and infrastructure compared to the suburban Nigerian 'prayer camps', it includes a school, cooperative, health centre and praying facilities. In addition, the project of building a university on the site also reflects the ambition of Combat Spirituel to emulate the holistic approach of the RCCG. The Ministère du Combat Spirituel, like most of its Nigerian counterparts – RCCG, Mountain of Fire and Miracles Ministries (MFM), Winner's Chapel, etc. – has, in the last two decades or so, considerably extended its reach globally through transnational connections and migration. The availability of peri-urban spaces to be appropriated allows the fulfilment of an expansionist aspiration, driven by an eschatological desire to create a boundless sacred city, defined in opposition (yet connected) to the adjacent megacity. In the case of the RCCG, it is striking that this process draws on representations of a 'pagan land', echoing older references to the 'evil bush', central to nineteenth-century missionaries (Coleman and Vásquez 2015).

Not all Pentecostal churches have the resources to acquire tracks of suburban land to enable mass prayer gatherings and realize their aspirations for expansion and autonomy through the creation of large 'moral enclaves' (Dilger and Janson 2022). Yet peri-urban locations can crystallize the idea of what could be called *frontier development* for smaller churches lacking the capacity to embark on large-scale (sub)urbanization. For instance, the Miséricorde hospital, developed by the transnational church New Jerusalem, was established in a so-called *commune urbano-rurale*, a fringe area which lies both at the edge of Kinshasa and at the boundary of the rural hinterland (Trefon 2009). With the growing scarcity and inflation of land and housing within the city, these peri-urban spaces have attracted both Kinois, leaving expensive and cramped city neighbourhoods and populations migrating from outlying, poorer rural areas. The availability of cheaper plots and the possibility of providing care to lower-income populations lacking affordable health facilities were, for church leaders, among the key reasons for planting a religious hospital in this peripheral, remote area.

In addition, church members and hospital staff were keen to point out how they had contributed to the general improvement and urbanization of the area – 'the hospital brought development locally' to quote a hospital manager. This idea of 'pioneering' urbanization at the city frontier is reinforced by the fact that the road where the hospital is located took on the name of the leader of the church, who had the vision for the hospital in the first place. The local impact of this religious urbanization can be perceived in many ways, for instance, with the arrival of a small-scale informal economy – food and drink, stalls and mobile phone credit sellers – in the immediate vicinity of the hospital. It has also had some significant consequences in terms of local infrastructure. Since the area lacks access to piped water, the local hospital set up a borehole which some local residents are also using. To be connected to the electric grid, the hospital had to spend thousands of dollars on equipment and material, including cables, circuit boxes, posts and so on and even had to privately pay an engineer from the SNEL (Société Nationale d'Électricité), the national electricity company, to set up the connection. Soon, local residents started (most of them, illegally) to get electricity from this newly created connection entirely financed by the hospital, which in turn weakened the intensity of its own power supply. It has also left the hospital more exposed to *délestage*, 'load shedding', the irregular rotating supply of electricity across the urban region. As De Boeck (2016: 99) notes, *délestage* is a perfect illustration of the 'syncopated' rhythms of infrastructures in Kinshasa and is metonymic of the volatility and unpredictability of urban life in the megacity. To respond to this infrastructural instability, the church – thanks to the financial contribution from its members in Belgium and the United States – purchased diesel generators and solar panels, but with high running and maintenance costs, the hospital struggles to ensure that power is available during important medical procedures and operations.

A question of scales

The construction of the Miséricorde hospital at the frontier of the city highlights a process of pioneering urbanization bound up with a wider aspiration for territorial presence and legitimation. While the plan to create a church parish on the land where the hospital stands is part and parcel of this aspirational process of place-making, the process of religious urbanization is not merely a by-product of an ambition to refashion individual subjectivities, redeem (urban) society or carve up protective spaces within it. Rather it shows to what extent religious experience – and in this context I mean a range of practices, vision and aspiration for growth – is inherently spatial. The idea of 'development' at various scales (from the individual to the family, the city, the nation and beyond) can be seen as a spatial-urban process in a significant way for all religious groups and actors studied in this book, including for Catholics who also often point to the (frontier) urbanization and infrastructural modernization linked to religious missionization in the Congo:

> Things that work today in Congo it is thanks to the Catholic church and it has always been like that! I was born in a small village in Congo and I was able to reach the university in Kinshasa because there was this system of missionaries and I am grateful for the church. . . . If you go deep into the interior of Congo today, and there is electrical lighting, there is 90% chance that it is the parish that put it there. (Maurice, member of the London Congolese Catholic Chaplaincy, in his sixties)

> It's thanks to religion and the Church that things are working back home. If you go to the deep Bandundu [province], you'll find the mission Ngi, or another mission. You will find that there is light, there is everything you want to have. People leave distant villages to form new villages around missions. This means that the Church has always brought something new to the social life of the people. (Papa Firmin, fifty-five, member of the London Congolese Catholic Chaplaincy)

In addition to such accounts opposing the darkness of the bush, of the 'deep' Congo, and the 'light' brought about by Catholic developmental presence (echoing colonial *mission civilisatrice* tropes), there is also a strong emphasis on the idea and importance of *locality*, especially in urban contexts. The parish system is of course a central organizational principle which anchors the lived experience of Catholics to a territorial, hierarchical and ritualized time-space. Parish community life creates a space of involvement and recognition at the local level, a scale connected to other scales – the city, the region, the nation and beyond – through a range of networks (hierarchical or ecclesiastical but also financial).

Localized forms of 'parochial' belonging in the Congolese Catholic context take various forms, including participation in 'Basic Ecclesial Communities' known as Communauté Ecclesiales Vivantes de Base (CEVB) and which started emerging in the DRC after the first post-Independence Episcopal Conference (1961). In Kinshasa and under the impetus of Cardinal Malula, the CEVBs responded to a need to reaffirm pastoral care at a grassroots level, instil a Christian/moral ethos in the everyday life and promote the decentralized involvement and leadership of lay Catholics (see Maduku 2012). CEVBs operate today as neighbourhood groupings for Catholics, fulfilling a range of purposes and criss-crossing the entirety of the city, as a kind of 'network of networks' to borrow Hannerz's (1980) classic characterization of the 'urban order'. Members of CEVBs met in Kinshasa cited as main activities prayers and Bible reading/ discussions but also charitable assistance for the poor and the sick or funeral needs through regular money collection and rotating credit – *tontine*. Mentioned were also small and targeted initiatives to maintain the street environment (potholes, cleaning of drains and flood protection) or address infrastructural issues (waste collection, electricity or water provision). However, these interventions on the urban landscapes are said to often drive tensions with local/state authorities, the latter blaming religious actors for infringing on their domain of responsibility. Papa Tony, a CEVB leader in Lemba, recalled how, when the CEVB tried to fix one of the parish roads, the local *commune* (council) officers intervened to block the work, demanding instead funds to undertake the repairs themselves. Here again, the *fonctionnaires* (civil servants/public agents) blamed for being 'blind and deaf to people's problems', as Papa Tony put it, were seen to be actively pursuing a predatory mode of governance, to be using every possible opportunity to capture private resources rather than ensuring the public good.

In the Kinshasa context, for Catholics, Kimbanguists and large Pentecostal churches alike, local embeddedness is combined with a networked assemblage of neighbourhood or area groupings, prayer cells and *paroisses* across the city (and beyond). There is a dynamic and dialogical ecology at work here: religious urbanization in the megacity Kinshasa is shaped by demographic growth, sprawling and densification, but as mentioned earlier it can be at the same time 'pioneering' through urban and infrastructural *frontier* transformations spearheading wider changes. The traditional mainline Protestant or Catholic parish-based organizational model establishes local churches as focal points of geographically bounded communities, but for Pentecostal actors there is also a clear emphasis on the idea of expansive, conquering territorial coverage with 'church planting' as its core. This is a paradigm influential in the Nigerian Pentecostal sphere, and churches like Maman Olangi are attempting to emulate strategies adopted by large Nigerian congregations, in particular the RCCG – albeit with significantly less resources. The RCCG ambitious vision for church planting relies on a 'temporal and spatial grid' that is both 'global in ambition and adaptable to local circumstances' (Coleman and Vásquez 2015: 38). It expands through diffusion, missionization and subdivision, for example, breaking and expanding larger congregations into smaller ones – a form of 'rhizomatic geo-spirituality', as Coleman and Vásquez (2015: 38) coined it. Thus the 'prayer camp' model of peripheral enclaving mentioned earlier and with a capacity to attract million-strong crowds is just one aspect of this process of religious urbanization. While paying attention to the monumentality of such urban religious spaces, in particular their centrifugal potency and their mass 'sensational appeal' (Meyer 2010) is key to an understanding of the Pentecostal take on space and materiality – one should therefore not overlook the importance of smaller, local anchoring and its role in terms of both evangelical outreach and 'social saturation of Pentecostalism' in the urban landscape (Ukah 2016b: 532). As Wilford (2012) suggests in his study of evangelism in California, megachurches have successfully adapted to the polynucleated and sprawling geography of suburbia and 'rescaled' the 'expansive, world-conquering image of the conversionary evangelicalism' (2012: 164) by productively connecting the 'authenticity' of home prayer cells to the collective worshipping experience in the mall-like megachurch. There are of course obvious differences between the suburban (post)secular fragmented landscape of Orange County and the urbanity of Lagos or Kinshasa. However, one could argue that one of the keys to the success of churches like the RCCG is to have managed to create a fruitful coexistence between the intimacy of parish-based membership on the one hand and the 'aesthetics of persuasion' (Meyer 2010) of its imposing sites of worship on the other hand, offering the punctual experience of mass collective effervescences and also providing the more permanent affordance of living within a self-contained, ever-expanding 'sacred city'.

Religious urbanization is thus polymorphic and occurs at different scales simultaneously, linking local (often embodied) dynamics of territorialization to aspirations for global reach. This scalar perspective encourages us to think about the wide range of ways religion 'takes place' and 'makes place' (Knott 2005: 43), revealing how the production of religious space (or the production of space by religiously driven actors) is not solely the reflection or the iconic expression of collective beliefs and ethos. Additionally, while the emergence of a new religious subject is key to tropes of reform and renewal, in particular among Pentecostals, the process of religious urbanization is more than just an 'expansion outward' of individual transformations, produced through the ripple effect of an increasingly encompassing force spreading across society. Socio-spatial scales, in this perspective, do not merely 'contain' each other – like Russian dolls – nor should they be viewed through the prism of a fixed territorial hierarchization. Scales are interdependent, often complementary, as well as dynamic and changing. Such a perspective is at the heart of recent theorizations of 'planetary urbanization', largely inspired by the work of Henri Lefebvre (1991, 2003) – in particular his paradigm of expansive urban 'implosion/explosion'[3] – aiming to provide an analysis of 'relationally multiscalar, variegated, and uneven geographies of the capitalist urban fabric' (Brenner 2019: 27).

Planetary urbanization and the religious 'spatial fix'

In most policy, developmental and planning discourses, the challenges of urbanization, in particular in Global South contexts, are predominantly linked to demographic factors, that is, the growth of urban populations. A recent United Nations report indicates, for instance, that 55 per cent of the world's population is now living in urban areas, with this population expected to increase to 68 per cent by 2050 (UN 2018) – an urban growth particularly salient in Global South megacities and set against a backdrop of inadequate urban infrastructural development and weak state or municipal planning capacity and governance (see UN-Habitat 2016). The dominant discourse in the policy literature is that these challenges are particularly acute in African urban environments where there is an increasing prevalence of informality – the growth of 'slums' being the most tangible manifestation of these issues (see Amin and Thrift 2017: 136–40 for a critical discussion of the dominant trope of the slum in urban policy). In the urban policy literature addressing the challenge of mega-urbanization, in particular in the Global South, religious urbanization does not constitute a 'legitimate' (or even problematic) example of infrastructural development, while a host of non-state 'informal' urban dynamics, social business-led development or community-based projects are recurrently discussed and sometimes hailed as innovative models (see RUA 2017).

Baker (2015) in his preface to a volume on religious urbanism in South Asia, while rightly addressing the secular blindspot of urban policy but also of critical urban theory, talks about 'the saturation of religion as a lived identity marker and embedded cultural and political reality *within* the very nation states *in which* planetary urbanisation is taking place' (Baker 2015: xvii, emphasis added). However, there is a risk here of minimizing religious actors' capacity to operate as (planetary) 'urbanizers', given how religious and urban dynamics reciprocally produce one another as 'urban-religious configurations' (Lanz 2014). In fact, as Becker et al. (2014) have clearly shown in a diversity of national/transnational contexts (and at various scales), urban religious actors can be key drivers of forms of socio-spatial change and urbanizing practices which could easily fit within the conceptual purview of planetary urbanization and 'splintering urbanism' (Graham and Marvin 2001) – gated enclaving, property-led investments, large infrastructural developments or polycentred and suburban territorialization. Work on these politics of religious urbanization suggests how religious actors are often driven by a desire to exert control over urban space with an aspiration to generate segregated/autonomous forms of religious enclaving. These shape particular geographies of socio-spatial fragmentation and competing sovereignties which AlSayyad and Roy (2006) have theorized as 'medieval' urban modernity because of their tendencies to rely on the imposition of prescriptive norms and rules within what they call 'quasi-feudal enclaves'.

Applying a similar political economy approach to the study of religious urbanization in Nigeria, Ukah (2014, 2016a) argues that the suburban-enclaved prayer camp of the RCCG, with its sizeable residential and infrastructural developments and its commercial and banking outlets, 'is no longer simply a ritual site; it represents a formidable strategy of spatial and territorial domination and resource capture' (Ukah 2014: 179). In that sense, the creative deployment of entrepreneurial neoliberal practices in the production of 'urban-religious configurations' spurs the integration of evangelism with business, real estate and market logic (Lanz and Oosterbaan 2016).

Given the volume of capital some religious groups have invested in land and buildings, it is tempting to link more explicitly these processes of 'entrepreneurial' religious urbanization to the theorization of the (uneven) geographies of late capitalism under globalization, and I am thinking here more particularly of the idea of 'spatial fix' conceptualized by David Harvey (2001a). Harvey argues that cyclical crises linked to overaccumulation are partly solved through 'fixing' investments spatially, creating, in turn, new urban landscapes for capital accumulation, often through geographic expansion and global restructuring. The notion of 'fix', Harvey notes, should be understood according to its multiple meanings in the English language – at the same time an operation of spatial embeddedness and immobilization, a 'solution' to a tendential problem and a possible response to an 'insatiable drive' (i.e. 'fix' being related here to the trope of drug addiction). Under capitalism there is a necessary tension between flow and *statis*, mobility and immobility, a tension materialized and territorialized at a global scale and shaped by the evolution of 'scalar patterns' involving crisis-induced socio-spatial rescaling (Brenner 2019: 51).

While there are clear limitations to foreground the idea of *cyclical* crisis as a driver of religious urbanization (since what predominates, for instance, among Pentecostals is the idea of constant crisis), one could argue that the expansionist drive of Pentecostal Christianity is its raison d'être and is projected onto the symbolic and social space of a moral community inherently 'called' to grow and transcend a whole range of earthly boundaries. The circulation-investment nexus is also a key aspect of the dynamics of 'sacred capital', as Simon Coleman (2000) shows in his study of globalized Pentecostalism. Thus, the creation of sacred value is inherently tied to the idea of 'keeping the flow going' – a rejection of hoarding as unproductive and 'sterile' (Coleman 2000: 189). In many cases, however, while religious infrastructures' efficacy in creating and managing publics lies in their capacity to act as 'spatial fix', the conversion of resources (both church donations and religious surplus capital) into physical spaces also becomes a testimony to the entwining of human action and divine vision, as illustrated by the case of Nkamba for Kimbanguists.

Infrastructures

Before examining the dynamics of (transnational) place-making in Nkamba, it is important to say a few additional words about the role and significance of infrastructures in the overall process of religious urbanization. Urban infrastructures – as the 'banal material of population management' (Amin and Thrift 2017: 122) – are indeed key components of religious urbanization and they *matter* in many different ways. Directing, accommodating and also ordering and sorting praying bodies – and the praying masses of faithful and pilgrims – would be challenging if not impossible without the deployment of spatial and infrastructural systems connecting buildings to road, water or energy networks, for instance. This question of infrastructure cannot be separated from a discussion about the role of space and materiality in the Protestant/evangelical experience and theology of place-making, a role often ambivalent given the existence of a permanent tension between materialization and de-materialization (Hovland 2016, see also Vásquez 2009 on the idea of 'pneumatic materialism').

As suggested earlier, religious infrastructures are integral to the operation of spatial fix and materialization of sacred capital while creating affordances allowing the collective experience of religious life, even if some religious subjectivities – like Pentecostal ones – rely heavily on individualized tropes of conversion and deliverance. The need for communal space of worship is also strategic when it comes to donations and offerings, whose collection often ritualized, staged, emotionally and spiritually charged, brings the intensity of collective effervescence into being (as the Kimbanguist *nsinsani* ritual does). As discussed in Chapter 3, during Covid lockdowns there was widespread anxiety building up among Congolese pastors and religious leaders about the difficulty of churches to 'fix', in a way, their members (and their financial capital), with online worship also representing a challenge to the performative and spectacular aesthetics of collective intensity and social effervescence.

Pentecostal worship is also a time-space within which believers 'commune with God alone while in the presence of others', encouraging us to identify the 'productive dynamic between the individual and the group' (Hovland 2016: 341). In that sense, churches can be considered spaces of intersubjectivity and also of social control through mutual gaze, as Simon Coleman (2000) pointed out in his study of Swedish evangelicals. Additionally, they constitute spaces of embodied learning, where individuals internalize the performativity of charismatic *techniques du corps* and can develop an introspective habitus by being exposed to the emotionally charged testimonies and public confessions of others. As discussed in Chapter 1, while Charismatics and Catholics each rely on their own distinctive aesthetic regime, we should nuance a radical opposition between, on the one hand, a supposedly dematerialized, disincarnated Protestant/evangelical tradition and a 'grounded', materialized Catholic ritualistic universe. Despite their particularities, the different groups studied in this book share a 'longing for real presence' (Butticci 2016: 9) which cannot be separated from strategies of urban visibility and territorialization, afforded in great part by the production of infrastructures required not only for everyday functioning but also for connection and expansion.

These 'basic' urban infrastructures, such as roads, water and electricity systems, are often said to form the invisible backdrop of urban life, paradoxically often solely 'felt' through their absence, dysfunction or syncopation (Graham and Marvin 2001, De Boeck and Baloji 2016, Gupta 2018). Additionally, they raise a range of questions related to governance, sovereignty and the power-geometries of urban citizenship rights as they can play a role in creating and reinforcing divisions and inequalities, in a way unevenly binding the city together (Graham and Marvin 2001, Simone and Pieterse 2017). However, while it has been increasingly argued that urbanization is unevenly shaped by neoliberalization, alongside other forces (see Ong 2006, Parnell and Robinson 2012), there have also been suggestions that the question of infrastructure cannot be reduced to the 'inherent' logics of capital immobilization (Amin 2014, Bennet 2010, Larkin 2013, Tonkiss 2013). For instance, some, like Amin, have prioritized the need to 'foreground the urban backstage' to reveal the vitality of socio-assemblages and lively infrastructures (Amin 2014: 139) or have focussed on the 'poetics and politics' of 'ambient' infrastructural environments, like Brian Larkin (2013).

For Larkin (2013), the stress on the 'invisibility' of (functioning) infrastructures – that is, the fact that their ontology is only revealed in the events of breakdowns – conceals the fact that they are 'metapragmatic objects, signs of themselves deployed in particular circulatory regimes to establish sets of effects' (2013: 336). Accordingly, infrastructures exist separately from their purely technical functioning and need to be analysed as concrete semiotic and aesthetic 'vehicles'. Similarly, Birgit Meyer argues that the 'sensational appeal' of Charismatic 'aesthetics of persuasion' is revealed in embodied experiences, in a rich material culture, as well as through highly perceptible spatial and architectural deployments, in particular religious mega-structures, signs of divine presence, blessings and success (Meyer 2014: 757). While these aesthetic landscapes of sensational forms are bound up with the 'sign-value' of infrastructures and constitute affective and embodied experience, Larkin (2013: 328) points out that infrastructures also produce the ambient conditions of everyday life.

Thus we should be mindful not to reduce urban and religious infrastructures to their material, sensorial, ethical or affective dimensions. They matter in many different ways simultaneously, creating aesthetic landscapes and structure, realizing aspirations and revealing a wide range of relations between people and things (and 'relation between things', as Larkin 2013 suggests). Here I want to focus on two additional aspects of 'infrastructural' religious urbanization crystallizing this diversity, in particular when it comes to the process of enclaved territorialization or place-making linked to the development of a sacred city like Nkamba. The first aspect is the fact that strong emphasis is put on autonomy and self-sufficiency, in a context where dysfunctional/unpredictable connections to (public) infrastructural systems are part and parcel of everyday life in megacities like Kinshasa. Investment in alternative sources of water and power supply, for instance, is seen as a prerequisite for the production and management of enclaved religious space but also for the functioning of educational and above all health facilities to compensate for the irregular energy and water provision from the 'syncopated' and incomplete 'grid'. The religious 'alter-city' reimagines itself as a model of moral order, and it is also a *city that works* and can ideally function independently of the socio-technical vicissitudes of the wider/surrounding urban society.

The second aspect lies in the idea of connection and assemblage in the making of urban religious spaces. When Amin and Thrift argue that 'cities are above all, constellations of entwined infrastructures' (2017: 106), they indicate the potency of infrastructures 'to hold the urban together', to create agglomeration, entanglement and meshwork urbanism. In terms of religious urbanization, what infrastructural development does is create networks solidifying an internal structure, while providing coherence and ease of interlinkages, flow and access (often bypassing state/public infrastructural grids). Yet, as I discussed, urban infrastructures remain 'biased in their affordances and allocations' (2017: 120), an idea central to neo-Lefebvrian readings of the roles played by infrastructure in the globalization and uneven rescaling of the capitalist urban fabric (see Brenner 2019: 376–9).

Similarly, while they may incarnate (or aim to incarnate) the biopolitical power of a centralized authority (e.g. the state), infrastructural systems can produce hybrid assemblages of improvisions, diversions and innovations (Amin and Thrift 2017: 122). I mentioned earlier the examples of the Miséricorde hospital and how the question of infrastructural access and provision can become a zone of tension and constant friction with the state. Here discourses about the infrastructures needed for the running of the hospital conjure images of the state seen as a threatening, predatory force, failing in its mission of welfare and care for populations:

> When there is a *mouvement associatif* [charity group] which wants to intervene in the social life of people that the state should be in charge of, the state should help, giving them subsidies and exonerating them, to encourage their work. But the state demands a lot of money from us, and we are helping the state to take care of its population. They are taxing us all the time, even to drill for the water, for the borehole. We even had to stop, we want to serve the population but they are threatening us with fines because we 'made do' [*on s'est debrouillé*, i.e. we did it by ourselves] and the state doesn't have the capacity to bring drinkable water here because their pumping system doesn't have enough pressure to bring water up to here. So we chose the borehole option but the state is not nice with us . . . threatening us with fines and disconnections. Electricity same thing, we suffered so much, the state agents [*fonctionnaires*] coming and threatening us.

Here, it is clear that not only are nodes and connections in infrastructural networks important to apprehend but also, in the context of religious urbanization, relations (and ruptures) between religion, state, economy and citizens. As we shall now see in the case of the urbanization of Nkamba 'New Jerusalem', this question of infrastructure and infrastructural networks also reveals multiple dynamics of frictions and tensions, while hinging on powerful tropes of connectivity and autonomy relocated in the prophetic temporality of a sacred 'city-yet-to-come'.

A sacred city-yet-to-come: Kimbanguist religious urbanization as materialization of 'sacred remittances'

In terms of religious urbanization and infrastructure, the case study of Nkamba is heuristic in several ways, in particular because it reveals the important linkages between the collective production of an 'alternative' city, transnational financial networks and the idea of 'sacralized' work. Kimbanguists in diaspora play an important role in the urbanization of Nkamba by collecting offerings and donations to fund or co-fund projects to develop their holy city. Here, parallels can be drawn between Kimbanguists and members of the Sufi Mouride order, who contribute transnationally to the development of their ever-growing holy city, Touba, in Senegal, attaining salvation 'not through accumulated wealth but by constantly divesting themselves of money' (Buggenhagen 2012: 88). For both Mourides and Kimbanguists, the spatial expansion of their holy city is thus an objectivation of an entire process of capital circulation which, in turn, delineates the boundaries of a globalized moral community.

Money collection aimed at funding the development of Nkamba usually takes place after the main religious service, during the ritual called *nsinsani*, which can last several hours, in particular when funds are needed for significant or iconic projects, such as the large, multi-story museum planned to mark the centenary of Kimbanguism in 2021. During the *nsinsani* (lit. 'competition') groups (church sections, such as youth, elders, choir or brass band members, etc.) compete with one another, often in a festive atmosphere full of singing, teasing and laughter and stimulated by the *animateur* who encourages individuals to come to the front to bring their donations on behalf on their section. The value of donations is then publicly announced, triggering congratulations and applauses. Here cash then becomes a crucial relational and social medium which is made very visible during this ritual. However, while there is an intense sociality within and between church groups trying to collect as much as possible, church members in diaspora (and the DRC) challenge the idea that is money in itself that is bringing them together. Rather they stress that it is the collective effort to build their church and their work (*misala*) for the common good that is enacting a spirit of solidarity which can be traced back to the time when Kimbanguists, seen as a threat to the Belgian colonial order, had to worship underground.

I have shown in more detail elsewhere (Garbin 2018) how cash donations among Kimbanguists could be seen as 'gifts' in the Maussian sense, since they are inscribed within a wider moral economy of blessings which, in this case, rewards trustful aspirations and the belief both in the divine promise (*bilaka*) of redemption and in the inherited vision of the current spiritual leader linking a prophetic past, a sacred and 'active' present and a future of possibilities. The mission of building and expanding Nkamba, 'our debt to God' as stated by the spiritual leader, forms the essential component of this temporal chain (Figures 15 and 16).

Diasporic Kimbanguists who travel to the homeland, like the FAKI members described in the opening vignette of this chapter, can measure first-hand the 'realized' value of their offerings through the visible spatial transformation of their holy city, and the hospitality (free food and accommodation) offered to visitors and non-Kimbanguist (sometimes prestigious) guests and, of course, to the thousands of pilgrims who flock there for major celebrations. Moreover, work on Nkamba's building sites is often filmed and documented, with videos and photos regularly posted on social media, in particular Facebook, so that Kimbanguists in diaspora can also see (and comment on) the evolution of the projects they have contributed to. With its collective discipline, the church, Kimbanguists often stress, is a social and economic model for the whole nation:

Figure 15 Nkamba Temple. Credit: author.

Figure 16 One of the many building sites in Nkamba.

it is presented as resilient, financially autonomous and based upon an inspired and incarnated prophetic vision, which projects a whole moral community into a social future.

Besides from the centrality of (sacralized) work in the building of Nkamba, one of the most important aspects of Kimbanguist place-making is the tension between presence and absence. While this tension is to some extent related to what Engelke (2007) calls the 'problem of presence' – namely the problem of how to make an invisible God present (and thus how to materialize and make sensible the divine) – it can also be appropriately captured through the prism of temporality. At an experiential level, Nkamba is saturated with time and this 'thick' Kimbanguist temporality is produced by the rhythms of daily prayers, rituals, annual festivals, pilgrimages and weekly religious services held in the holy city. Nkamba's sacred and predictable temporality is frequently heralded as an alternative to the uncertain, volatile and insecure temporality of Kinshasa where residents' lives unfold around truncated or absent infrastructures, where, as De Boeck argues, they have to adopt daily strategies of survival far removed from 'the teleological time-frames of the nation-state or the Pentecostal churches and the futures they propose' (2013: 544). De Boeck writes that Kinois are instead anchored in an everlasting present and are 'continuously seizing and capturing the opportunity of the moment to reinvent and reimagine their lives in different ways' and, as a result, 'in these urban lives there is never a straight line between today and tomorrow, or between here and there, between possibility and the impossible, success and failure, life and death' (2013: 544).[4]

The aspiration to become an 'alter-city' is materialized for a large part through the infrastructural development of Nkamba. However, if the prophetic advent of the Nkamba-New Jerusalem hinges on the ideal of a 'city that works', that is, with constant electricity, reliable water supply and appropriate (road) access, then Nkamba is not ready as yet to become the city where 'all nations will gather' (Isaiah 66). This question of infrastructural connections, for instance, through road or electricity access, is central to consider because it reveals the coexistence of multiple narratives and a profound ambivalence, hinging on a relation to prophetic territoriality, development and tensions between a range of actors. Improving electricity provision by replacing the small diesel-powered generators operating across Nkamba by a connection to the national grid is seen by many I spoke to as an aspiration to urbanize in tune with developmental modernity. The desire to eventually overcome Nkamba's 'off-grid-ness' and marginality locates the church within an aspirational assemblage through which investment in infrastructure is shaped by 'linear teleologies of developmental time' (Appel 2018: 54). However, there was also some scepticism among some Kimbanguists about replacing one form of dependency (on oil for generators) by another one (the national electric company with the ever-present risk of malfunction and syncopation) even if, I was told, there were opportunities to benefit from new sources of hydro-electric power in the surrounding region.

The issue of infrastructural development to fulfil the prophesized advent of Nkamba also reveals the complex politics of relations with the state. For instance, during the democratic transition, the then Minister of Finance Bemba is said to have blocked the possible electrification of Nkamba, since it would have benefited his main rival, the former president Kabila, who could have then been able to appeal more favourably to Kimbanguists (since they form a significant potential reservoir of votes in the DRC). Other narratives pointed to issues of financial mismanagement associated with the running of infrastructures. For instance, some spoke about the fact that in case of electrification those who are currently in charge of the main diesel generator (operating only in the evening and at night) may 'lose out', since their livelihood is contingent on their position in a chain of dependency, linking the infrastructure with a network of suppliers and intermediaries. While, as De Boeck observes, infrastructural deficit and syncopations are not merely lived obstacles but can create gaps which open up a range of possibilities and urban engagements, in this context, the infrastructural (under)development of the holy city is read through a spiritual grammar of evil blockages and slowdowns:

> Witches are slowing down the development of the church and Nkamba. Some people don't want electricity here, because they would lose a source of regular income. They over-invoice [*surfacture*], they steal petrol for the generators. If electricity comes here, it's a loss of money for them! Our leader knows all of this. But he says: 'better for the witches to eat money than to eat my followers'. (Interview with a Kimbanguist youth leader in Nkamba)

These 'blockages' are said to be detrimental to the overall development of Nkamba and are expressed by building projects getting delayed or abandoned, thus becoming 'ruins of the future', to borrow from Gupta (2018: 69). The causes of these blockages – 'unproductive' rivalries between churches/sections in charge of delivering particular projects or mismanagement of funds – are relocated within a moral and spiritual sphere and shape the ways in which the transnational economy of sacred remittances operate, with diasporic Kimbanguists often preferring to send material and equipment (via container shipping) to Nkamba rather than money. In fact, most diasporic Kimbanguists I spoke to expressed little trust in the local construction material and, more importantly, in the expertise, experience, integrity and reliability of teams of architects and contractors in Nkamba. If those in charge of managing funds are 'eating some of the money', it is because, some in diaspora argue, those working for the church in the DRC receive little or no payment, reflecting the wider logic of predation and lack of accountability among the underpaid, disillusioned agents of the Congolese state. That said, accusations of mal-governance and financial malpractices are also notable among church members in diasporic context, adding to conflicts over ecclesiastic legitimacy and authority (see Garbin 2011).

Moreover, in her study of the 'remittance landscape' in Mexico – spatial changes in the homeland driven by US-based Mexican migrants – Lopez (2015) argues that transnational material investment practices are embedded in power relations and patronage dynamics. This process is also observable within the Kimbanguist global public sphere with groups competing for prestige at various scales (national level, local parishes or church-based groups) through the realization of projects, which can also bring more legitimacy to individual

Figure 17 The Kimbanguist Brass Band (FAKI) performing sacred hymns to help spiritually 'unblock' the progress of a major building site in Nkamba. Credit: author.

church members or leaders. Practices of gift-giving linking diasporic actors and homeland-based clergy members – not formally located within the moral economy of 'sacred remittances'/*nsinsani* though at times connected to it[5] – are also shaping the politics of this transnational social field.

In Nkamba, tensions over newly introduced practices by diasporic Kimbanguists – for instance, the use of corrugated iron fences to secure building sites, seen as 'waste' by locals who would rather use them as roofing material – and the exclusion of local experts also reveal the existence of frictions over knowledge and norms. The fact that diasporic actors are in a position to reclaim some autonomy vis-à-vis existing power structures and deploy significant material, financial and symbolic resources and social capital to that effect, reinforces what could be called an uneven geography of remittances replicating the dynamics of 'asymmetrical reciprocity' (Carling 2014) observable among transnational families and examined in Chapter 5.

Conclusion

I suggested in this chapter that religious urbanization should not simply be read as the corollary, the by-product of religious transformation, or be reduced to the sole materialization of faith expressed through place-making. Religious urbanization implies changes at multiple scales, linking the embodied subject to aspirations for local–global territorialization. Religious urbanization also drives the transformation of the city through the collective experience but also the production and consumption of resources and urban infrastructures. In some cases, 'entrepreneurial religion' (Lanz and Oosterbaan 2016) spearheaded by Pentecostal churches willing to establish autonomous and functioning enclaved spaces is not a challenge to (or a protection against) a retreating state but clearly a constitutive force of a particular type of urban modernity.

In this sense, religious transformations do not operate simply against a backdrop of 'planetary urbanization' and a better perspective sees religion as an active agent of urbanization processes as well as 'reacting and adapting' to changing urban conditions (Rüpke 2020: 61). In addition, the link between religious city-building and these wider processes of urbanization also deserves some attention. Drawing upon the work of Henri Lefebvre, theorists of planetary urbanization argue that it is reductive to equate this process to the worldwide proliferation and diffusion of a unique type of urban form – the city – rejecting what they call 'methodological cityism' (see Angelo and Wachsmuth 2015). However, the city – its ambivalent imaginaries and counter-imaginaries – has not lost its relevance with the 'implosion-explosion' (Lefebvre 1996: 70–1) inherent in processes of urbanization, be they religious or not. In truth, Lefebvre pointed out that the city has, in a way, survived, the generalized urbanization of society (*'le tissu urbain'*), its 'image' creating affordances – its representations having 'real effects' (Millington 2016: 4). Here I would agree with Walker (2015) who argues that the proponents of the planetary urbanization thesis have extended 'the concept of the urban as far as it will stretch' (2015: 186) in their crusade against 'methodological cityism' and 'empiricism', mostly justified by the arbitrariness of demographic attempts at 'defining' where the city starts and ends. After all, while the political, cultural and economic influence of contemporary urbanization is tentacular, intense and overwhelming, its social production and lived experience also operate through categories embedded in wider moral cartographies, imaginaries and 'representational spaces' (Lefebvre 1991), including socio-spatial spiritual mapping and moralized models of divine cities-yet-to come.

Despite clear differences between Catholics, Kimbanguists and Pentecostals in terms of theological orientation or embodied and emplaced experience of the sacred, there are commonalities when it comes to processes of religious urbanization. For all three groups I noted the importance of a process of pioneering urbanization, with the idea of frontier development quite central in the narratives about religious territorialization, and taking the metonymic form of a project of (re)appropriation and redemption of either the chaotic 'fallen city' or the pagan 'bush'. This process is embedded in different politics of locality and socio-spatial temporalities, with, for instance, Catholics often referring to the 'historic' role played by missions (that some were keen to disentangle from colonial Belgian oppression). Among Kimbanguists, the embeddedness of Nkamba within a prophetic territoriality resonates with tropes of continuity, restoration and, ultimately, reversal, while the Pentecostal grammar of rupture, regeneration and renewal leaves little if no space for ancestral memorialization.

I also noted how the conversion of financial flows into urban materiality operates within a transnational sphere, and for diasporic actors, the act of giving money in the form of sacred remittances can be interpreted as a form of proxy presence, the materialization of a collective will to transform the homeland from afar. As the case of Miséricorde hospital or the construction of Nkamba shows, this sphere is fraught with tensions, revealing the ways in which asymmetric relations between people divided by migration as well as difficult if not conflictual interactions with the state or its agents can shape the process of religious urbanization at various scales. Key also is the role of material of infrastructural development in creating what Levitt (2001a) calls an 'alternative cartography of belonging', with the production of a space of connections and circulation superseding established boundaries, be they national borders or social/kinship borders. London Kimbanguists, for instance, were often talking about the ongoing construction of a small airport strip in Nkamba as a way for them, perhaps one day, to avoid the constraints of the extended family in Kinshasa. The 'dream' was, I was told, 'to fly from Europe to Kinshasa Ndjili airport, change to Nkamba [thus] avoiding the stress and pressure of relatives to be able to focus on spiritual matters' (Kimbanguist youth leader, thirty-eight). A similar logic applies to the networks of 'flathotels' (residence with private apartments/rooms to be rented on a short-term basis) developed by the Combat Spirituel church and turned into *bergeries* (lit. 'sheepfolds') hosting diaspora-based pastors or church members keen to circumvent family obligations or who have simply cut ties – *coupé les liens* – with kin in the homeland. Through the adoption of circulating and connecting practices (including financial linkages) – as well as through the production of imaginaries – these religious actors construct transnational religious architectures. This resonates with the work of Coleman and Meier (2013) who argue that, while the city remains for them morally ambivalent, RCCG members locate themselves within a single, continuous space – a stretched 'London-Lagos' – within which they can 'realize their full capacity as both believers and urban citizens committed to achieving successful lives' (2013: 362).

At the heart of the ambivalent construction of the city – as both a vehicle of hope and risk – the 'alter-city' promises to address the insecurity and syncopation of the postcolonial present. Redemption Camp, Nkamba or Mahanaim City have the ambition and aspiration to enact visions of moral and aesthetic order and constitute 'modelling' possibilities for an urban future. Within the discursive landscape of Kimbanguism, Nkamba is the poster child of a sacred centre *à la Eliade* – an axis mundi connected vertically to the ethereal world, detached from its disorganized, immoral, wild and dangerous outside. However, there is another side to this story of prophetic and hierophanic sacredness: Nkamba is thus experienced as a place of *intrigues politiques*, where intense conflicts for leadership are played out, where the fear of evil forces is expressed through anxiety over spiritual permeability and porosity, a place which, in fact, connects horizontally with a host of other places, not least to Kinshasa, but also to Kimbanguist diasporic peripheries increasingly influential within a wider sacred geography. These discrepancies between politics and experience of religious socio-spatiality and more normative accounts of territorial sacrality have been documented elsewhere, for instance, by Kingsbury (2023) in her study of the Mouride holy city of Touba, by Osinulu (2014) in his work on the RCCG's Redemption Camp and who argues that social and status distinction observable within the camp, reflects or even reproduces dynamics operating within wider Nigerian society. The focus on the 'alter-city' suggests to what extent religious urbanization is a process of sacralized place-making relying on a programmatic project of renewal and hope, carving up a material and spiritual 'elsewhere', which does not seem to constitute a challenge to entrenched uneven power-geometries (Marshall 2009). In many ways, my case studies show that the urban offers a particular kind of medium for religious organizations to operate within modernity and for those religious actors capable of both demonizing the city as a den of immorality and celebrating it as a key sphere of opportunity. Despite the global 'stretching' of this urbanization process said to be dissolving the very notion of cityness, the potency of the *city*, its image and ambivalent moral meaning and aesthetic order remain thus central in the ways in which an emerging religious landscape is experienced.

Conclusion

Moral worlds and the global landscapes
of Congolese Christianities

> A lot of good work has been done. Congolese want to be together [*être ensemble*], want to share. We can now express our own identity. . . . Before we were with Ivorians, Cameroonians – a bit of everything – we were trying to adopt an African identity. . . . But now we see more and more a Congolese identity, which is wonderful especially as the country [Congo] is divided. (Father Emile, London-based Congolese Catholic Priest)

Speaking at an event to celebrate the fifth anniversary of the creation of the Catholic chaplaincy in London, Father Emile praised the 'good work' of the Congolese Catholics having succeeded in creating a space for themselves in the diaspora. The move from an African Francophone environment, in multicultural Catholic parishes, where Congolese used to join Masses, to a purely monocultural Congolese one is presented here as a way to express a strong sense of identity and unity against the backdrop of a 'divided' homeland. This sense of identity is constructed through performance and social interaction and relies on an intimate connection between a renewed Congolese Catholic subjectivity and the carving up of a relatively autonomous space of practices and rituals in diaspora, through which affiliation with and belonging to the host society are articulated. This specific universe of performance is perceptible in a range of ways, through the adoption of the Lingala language in sermons and hymns, through the use of particular instruments like drums and through evocations of the ancestors (*bakoko*) at the start of the Mass or the reconstitution of church groups and movements, replicating homeland parishes. It relocates the Congolese Catholics both spatially and temporally, reinforcing – and formalizing – a host of connections with the homeland (in particular with the Kinshasa archdiocese and the CENCO) while operating as a link to an important postcolonial moment, the adoption of the *rite Zairois* which signalled an attempt to Africanize Congolese Catholicism and disentangle it from its colonial origin.

In certain ways, for the different groups I described in this book, the making of a religious space in diaspora can be seen as a way to perform (and reassemble) a sense of Congolese identity that is often both translocative and transtemporal. However, it is also true, as we saw in our introductory discussion on attitudes to death and ancestrality, and throughout this book, that the ways in which Congolese define and project a collective sense of self through religion is plural and inflected by a range of worldviews, attitudes and understandings of time and space. Despite the existence of a Congolese Christian 'collective habitus' – *collusio* (Rey and Stepick 2013) – revolving around the shared belief in the (harmful or protective) potency of ancestors or, to a lesser extent, in the sacredness of the homeland, there are many ways of being – or acting as – a (urban and/or 'diasporic') Congolese Christian. Perhaps more importantly, and this is very evident in the case of Pentecostal interventions and narratives, there is a marked tendency to make the formulation of a Congolese Christian identity an important stake in the conduct of religious life, in particular in the plural landscape of the diaspora, which is also a horizon of new negotiations, encounters and reflexivity (Johnson 2007). In this sense, since 'identity is performatively constituted by the very "expressions" that are said to be its results' (Butler 2007: 34), the enactment of the Pentecostal self has become a strategic way of projecting what an authentic Congolese Christian identity is or, more importantly, should be.

In this concluding section, I want to return to this overarching theme of (religious) performance in the homeland and diaspora. Key to my argument is that religious practices and discourses enable us to identify how categories of social life are articulated in the making of moral worlds. Here I want first to consider the highly performative process of mapping, as it reveals the production of ambivalent urbanity not only as a site of multiplicity (of identity, belonging and religio-political mobilization) but also as a site of intervention, projection, categorization and recategorization. These 'interventions', while they recurrently draw upon tropes of spiritual warfare or are often less confrontational than they claim and may appear to be, involve a lot of (protective) boundary-making labour, in particular in the diaspora context.

The performance of ambivalent landscapes

We saw how the performance of ambivalence is made apparent in the ways in which 'the city' is morally foregrounded by my Congolese interlocutors in diaspora. In truth, both the city (as a socio-spatial form and imaginary) and the urban (as a matrix of expansion and modernity) have traditionally had an ambivalent status in the contemporary moral geographies of Christian piety. In *Gods of the City*, a now classical exploration of the entanglements of lived religion with everyday city life and place-making, Orsi (1999: 18) shows that for nineteenth-century American Christian reformers, the mission of remoralizing working-class neighbourhoods initially entailed 'distinctly Protestant anti-urban poetics in which the pre- or anti-urban became the moral and aesthetic ideal' (1999: 18). Long before the spatial takeover of urban Pentecostalism and the urban monumentalism of megachurches, the emergence of evangelical forms of Pentecostal Christianity as expressed, for instance, by the iconic Los Angeles Azusa Street Revival (led by the Black preacher William Seymour in 1906) was closely tied to the wider process of modern urbanism, in particular concerns over the fraying moral fabric in the bustling city. As Coleman (2009: 36) argues, the Azusa Street tenement (formerly used as a Methodist church) was converted into a spatial catalyst for the power of the Holy Spirit, an outpost of spiritual regeneration within the urban landscape of the 'de-spiritualized capitalism'. For the pioneers of modern Pentecostal Christianity, the early-twentieth-century city thus became the place 'where God is encountered with special intimacy' (Orsi 1999: 4), a privileged terrain of investment and moral (re)conquest since 'only urban contexts could provide mobile and mass publics to appeal to, combined with the sensation – increasingly crucial to some forms of evangelicalism – of defining the faith against a proximate and dangerous other' (Coleman 2009: 37). As we saw in this book, addressing the 'proximate other' – the immorality of secular urban societies – is also key to many of the religious actors we discussed, although the re-spiritualization of capitalist (post)modernity can, in truth, be pursued by some as part of a theology of prosperity, recasting moral valorization against God-sanctioned and God-driven economic success.

Many Congolese religious actors I met in the diaspora see their presence in the city in terms of potential for transformation, growth, prosperity, new connections and new possibilities. But they also recurrently talk about moral risks associated with sexual freedom, the culture of alcohol and drug consumption or the need to maintain strong boundaries to challenge what they perceive to be the disempowering attitude of the state regarding the education and the disciplining of children. I showed in this book that the religious registers of mapping remain overall quite flexible and multiscalar – concerned with a range of places and spaces often vaguely defined, lacking nuances – reflecting in a sense the fact that religious space is often understood as 'nondefinitive, protean, multivalent, temporally ambiguous, irregular, and by definition ultimately unchartable'

(Corrigan 2008: 160). However, it is clear that the process of identifying and categorizing particular environments and spaces in terms of moral risks is highly performative as it justifies and legitimizes a range of actions, moral stances and claims – as well as place-making practices.

Moral mapping may have its limits and contradictions, but it is also efficacious. It provides a sense of agency by (often symbolically or discursively) inserting diasporic lives as legitimate actors at the heart of the city, circumventing various regimes of closure that produce exclusion, discrimination and othering. A spiritual landscape is brought into being and invites – requires – intervention and creates a vision of a desired, idealized future. The world can be mapped, or rather remapped, to plant churches, orient spiritual warfare, deploy moral cartographies, separate good from evil and also re-narrate migration and exile in a biblical or prophetic way.

But performativity is not only about the property of *enunciation as enactment*. It is also, at the same time, and as pointed by Bourdieu (1992) in his reading of Austin's speech-acts theory, about reproducing particular modes and positions of authority. By connecting mapping and territorialization, religious actors, in particular Pentecostal pastors, regain an ascendance over 'human' space and time, and, driven by what they claim to be divine election or inspiration, they locate with some level of certitude the battlefronts where the spiritual warfare needs to be staged. In parallel to this, moral claims may contribute to a sense of 'virtuous citizenship' (Fumanti 2017), in order to assert a legitimate presence in a context of precarity and marginalisation. I acknowledge the transformative power of these claims, even as I recognize that they are also embedded in politics of authority and control. As I discussed in Chapter 3, conflating Christian and 'African' values, for instance, can be a way to reaffirm parental authority in a context of intergenerational tensions and against the fear that youth might evade social control in a global city remapped as a moral 'black hole', to paraphrase a Kimbanguist youth leader. The morally inflected attitudes to family life, sexuality, sexual orientations, femininity and masculinity contribute to a gendered division of the world, oftentimes shaping and shaped by forms of patriarchal domination, though, of course, women are never passive and do regain some form of pious agency and autonomy through religious life – which is the case, for instance, of the women 'spiritual warriors' of the Maman Olangi church (Meiers 2013).[1]

This question of authority and control is also important in the idea of mapping as a symbolic technique of moral distinction and differentiation. Mapping is about power. Mapping has been key to Western colonial spatialization and expansion and often entails imagining and projecting particular spaces as culturally or morally 'empty' before rendering them 'familiar and knowable, thus controllable' (McEwan 2009: 87). Securing colonial territorial ownership has operated through various processes of mapping – and also often relied on acts of erasing or *unmapping*, processes of reconfiguration and 'reduction' essential to the exercise of power and the exploitative control of population (Tremlett 2012). So, what are the power effects of the forms of mapping deployed by the religious actors I discussed? Are they forms of domination and/or are they part of dynamics of counter-memory and resistance? The answer defies facile dichotomies. Pentecostals invoke the superior power of the Holy Spirit to 'take territories', involving a radical vision of both transformation and control, claiming a legitimacy that they may present as undisputable (because divinely inspired) and thus superior. This legitimacy also draws upon a powerful sense of belonging to a global moral Christian community involving a process of 'scale jumping', taking the form of a transcendent supralocal, supranational identification 'viewed as being intelligible at every scale', as Fesenmyer (2022) notes in her study of Kenyan Pentecostals in London. This universal optic remaps the world according to a vision of global territorial conquest and ownership (Coleman 2010), 'unmapping' the nationalism that still dominates politics (and the methodology of the social sciences). However, this erasing of existing environments and active reappropriation of them may remain largely symbolic, partial and/or non-confrontational at least in the environments of the diaspora, due to a lack of resources or in a context of disadvantaging postcolonial entanglement of race and belonging (particularly since the Congolese are twice minoritized as Francophone Africans in the UK for instance). In other words, even when they help migrants carve out moral and meaningful spaces of livelihood, Congolese Christian churches are limited in the remapping they can do, especially when compared to their influence in the homeland, where they do not have to operate in a super-diverse environment in which racial discrimination and secular forces are not as prominent and constraining as in the metropoles in Europe and North America.

But what maps often do is simplify as they communicate a simple, distilled message. In 1989, in the Kimbanguist holy city what (clearly) looks like a large 'map of Africa' appeared after a landslide in the form of a hardened mud formation close to the main temple. This 'map' was soon after enshrined (and remains so to this day) in a covered monument, becoming yet another prophetic hierophany within the landscape of Nkamba. The map has been interpreted as a clear indication that Africa is the 'cradle of humanity' (Mokoko

Gampiot 2004: 348) and that God, through Papa Simon Kimbangu, had chosen Nkamba as a place from where the salvation of the Africans and then the whole world will start. Nkamba's 'map of Africa' echoes another map evoked in this book, the 'map of the DRC' which appeared on the eroded grounds of the ancient Capernaum synagogue in Israel, reinforcing the idea of an essential link between Israel and the Congo for those who shared it widely on social media. This map of the DRC (which after all is a representation of the outcome of colonial bordering) is an image of a nation that has been endowed with an exceptional, sacred destiny for Congolese Christians. Interpretations may differ though, with Kimbanguists arguing that the sacred has completely 'abandoned' the Holy Land and, thus, the 'map' is an indication of a *transfer*, a new covenant, rather than simply a connection. In any case, and across religious lines, this map remains a powerful way for Congolese Christians to relocate themselves within a longer and deeper history. The revealed map provides a spiritual resource to create a transcending and alternative form of territorial cartography where a peripheral nation that was once the personal domain of a Belgian king can occupy a central place in universal sacred history (with Belgium and the whole of Europe, in effect, becoming the wicked periphery that will be redeemed by Congolese Christians).

By remapping space, operating as an enactment of sacred or inspired vision(s), Congolese in diaspora can narrate a story and begin to reposition themselves outside the rigid regimes of closure and exclusion, retain or regain some form of agency and carve out a collective future through forms of moral citizenship often articulated to spiritual tropes of redemption and ethics of renewal. In doing so, they also unveil the ambivalence and contradictions of the diaspora condition partly expressed through urban life in the global city, as the locus of relevant relations gradually shifts from the homeland to host society. But connections to the homeland – often expressed as material, socio-religious or emotional investments – do endure, though they may take on new meanings as linkages and bonds can be reassessed or renegotiated alongside religious, social and domestic affective circuits. Here again, as we saw in our study of remittances, the moral economies of ties can be shaped by the coexistence of variegated attitudes to family connections, revealing a plural affective repertoire. Just as transnational religious networks are the source of not only bonding, collective identity and empowerment but also sectarian and intra-church conflicts, remittances are too marked by tensions: money can be associated with debt and conflicted feelings of guilt, envy and the heavy burden of care. Money may even be spiritually laden, creating possible linkages to the occult and the cursed.

In the homeland, in particular in Kinshasa, the creation of urban forms of religious territorialities reveals the extent to which urbanity, by mediating actions and strategies of development, offers a space of evangelical possibility and opportunity for radical change, or at least a horizon of hopes or remoralization of a space perceived as chaotic and corrupt. But this moral and physical remapping is also ambivalent in its performativity. Processes of religious urbanization, as we saw in Chapter 7, often tell a story of the need to fill the metaphorical, moral and spatial gaps of a postcolonial society shaped by a range of contradictions and paradoxes, as De Boeck has shown in his extensive work on Kinshasa. Kinshasa, in his view, is a sprawling metropolis where the urban is reimagined as born-again *cosmopolis* breaking with the occult, detrimental ancestrality of the village, yet it is shaped by forms of ruralization (in relation to food production, for instance) and peripheralization, entailing increasingly elusive boundaries between rural and urban. Kinshasa is where neoliberal fantasies of urban development coexist with the persistent potency and prestige of traditional forms of authority such as land chiefs, remaining key players in a process of rapid urban growth (De Boeck and Baloji 2016: 289).

In this context, for some of the churches studied in this book, attempts at building alternative socio-spatial and moral enclaves become a way to stage both a moral and societal project: the possibility of offering some kind of infrastructural security and predictability against the contradictions, disorder and volatility of Kinshasa, constructing crucial spaces to heal the individual and the social body, to build morally superior citizens and/or to train them as 'spiritual warriors'. Thus, these spaces are also performative in their own ways, as implicit critiques of the dysfunctional megacity and immoral society and they work as a matrix of simplification and reassemblage of a cultural and political reality of fragmented governance.

However, these churches themselves crystallize a host of contradictions and ambivalences. Christian churches – Kimbanguist, Catholic or Pentecostal – reframe their interventions as a mission in the way they pursue or seek to pursue health, educational or basic infrastructural development, with the ambition and aspiration to address the gaps of a retreating, postcolonial and also post-Mobutu state. But overall, rejecting the idea that their motivation is to 'replace' the state, religious groups in the homeland have to 'play the game' and engage with a hybrid assemblage of governance perceived to embody the corrupt nature of an obstructing, if not predatory, state. Autonomy is here a quest associated with a vision for a future of liberation, but these actors can never escape the (constraining) reality of fragmented governance.

As we have seen in the case of Nkamba whose urbanization powerfully remains a sacred duty for Kimbanguists, this duality of the 'alter-city' is also salient in spiritual terms. On the one hand, Nkamba is a divine city-yet-to-come, a space of order and spiritual certainty contrasted with the morally chaotic and spiritually insecure Kinshasa. On the other hand, it is highly porous and always susceptible to blockages and slowdowns – often caused by the corrupt or immoral practices of members or even leaders. This immorality and also interpersonal conflicts seen as part of it are reinterpreted as spiritual attacks which can then be confronted more explicitly through prayers, spiritual retreats or the sonic power of the brass band playing sacred hymns directly 'received' from God. Thus, when large construction projects are repeatedly delayed – by a lack of materials or equipment, because of conflicts or financial issues – the Nkamba Kimbanguist brass band (joined by diaspora FAKI pilgrims if present) regularly performs within the actual space of the building site, fighting the evil energies to unlock and unblock the sacred work (*misala*). All these blockages are signs that evil forces are operating and thus that Nkamba-as-a-target can be confirmed as a holy city. The spiritual struggle is a race against the 'Devil who is also building his own city in the second world', as a Kimbanguist leader once told me, saying that not only the Devil was actively corrupting men and women, but that he was stealing bricks and cement to urbanize and expand his dominion. Both the forces of good and evil are here locked into a battle through urbanization and territorialization across the physical/ethereal boundary. In a way, delays and blockages – expressing the Devil's incursion into the 'first world' of an urbanizing Nkamba – contribute to a sense of incompleteness, that is also salient among Catholics and Pentecostals – a sense of incompleteness as a message about the need for active waithood, endurance and continuous vigilance and commitment.

Thus, at the risk of appearing functionalist, we can conclude that one of the most important common things that Congolese Christianities do is provide a chastened-yet-always-hopeful sense of futurity and will to transcend. These Christianities mark rupture from the chaotic and sinful here and now, but this rupture is invariably incomplete, since churches themselves often reproduce the asymmetrical dynamics and structures they seek to transform and moralize, and since the goal is always frustrated and postponed – the DRC (through its government, as a state) is corrupt despite the governance of Catholic elites and Nkamba is unfinished. Still, in spite of all this 'fallenness', Congolese Christians persevere, not just in spirit and imagination, but also in action, as they carve out meaningful spaces of livelihood. There are always new projects, new goals and new milestones which keep the faithful engaged, active and hopeful, especially when the going gets tough. As they respond to the challenges of dislocation and relocation, we have seen how diasporic horizons shape and are shaped by this efficacious religious projectivity.

Global landscapes – frictions and (dis)connections

The case study of Nkamba is particularly heuristic for an understanding of how global landscapes of religion are made and remade and how the entanglement of diasporic consciousness and transnational networks can shape the way people relate to religious and sacred places over time. Despite the 'diasporization' of Kimbanguism from the 1980s, a process which has accelerated in the late 1990s and early 2000s, the centrality of Nkamba in the DRC has strengthened and not dissipated for those who have made their lives in Europe and the United States, even among second generations, some of whom may not have first-hand experience of the holy city, let alone of the country where their 'roots' are.

This 'recentring' has grown on a par with forms of 'retraditionalization' that reaffirm the linkages between the prophetic figure of Kimbangu, the holy city and an ancestral imaginary of the former Kongo Kingdom spanning present DRC, Congo-Brazzaville and Angola. This can be illustrated by a range of practices and orientations, including the approach taken by the current spiritual leader, in sharp contrast to his predecessor, Papa Diangienda (1918-1992). Papa Diangienda regularly visited diasporic branches in Europe as part of his international travels, while the current spiritual leader is much less internationally mobile and mostly travels regionally to Angola or Congo-Brazzaville – the other 'two Kongos'. This process needs to be understood in relation to the configuration of the religious field in the Congo, as discussed in Chapter 1, in particular the sustained significance of religious or politico-religious organizations drawing upon Kongo ethnic identity and heritage or mobilizing the figure of Kimbangu. In addition, internal divisions within the church have played a part in the evolution of the status and position of Nkamba, in particular a conflict between Kimbangu's grandchildren. These disputes resulted in a schism in 2001 with the 'official' branch retaining control of the holy city and prioritizing its development over an institutional and infrastructural presence in Kinshasa, where the other group, seen as the 'dissident' church, is headquartered with no access to Nkamba.[2]

In many ways, Nkamba 'stabilizes' the diasporic religious experience, which, as we have seen in Chapter 3, can entail some forms of precarious place-making or spatial trajectory reflecting a position of minority at the symbolic margins of the 'global city'. In that sense, Nkamba is an immense source of hope, regeneration and a pivotal, ancestral place channelling Kimbanguist theologies of return and prophetic reversal. Pilgrimages to Nkamba, which I also discussed in this book, constantly confirm and reactualize the sacredness and authority of the holy city. They also contribute to a sense of expanding territorialization for the pilgrims collectively engaged in cross-border journeys, representing their parish, their church group or even their diasporic country of residence while worshipping and taking part in various rituals (or even performing music or drama) in Nkamba. These pilgrimage journeys are often demanding in terms of resources and time, and they can also be impacted negatively by various regimes of mobility, in particular for those whose immigration status prevents them from travelling. On this note, not being able to travel to the major pilgrimage of *Le Centenaire* in 2021 – marking the 100 years since the start of Kimbangu's ministry in 1921 – was particularly devastating for many of my London Kimbanguist interlocutors and friends (some had saved for years for the occasion) as the DRC was put on a 'red list' of countries during the Covid pandemic.[3]

Given the interplay of tropes of return and exile, global expansion through transnational networks and the diasporic regrounding of Kimbanguism abroad, the dialectics of centrifugal and centripetal dynamics is crucial for an understanding of the global cartography of Kimbanguism (Sarró and Mélice 2010). Despite the idea of a strong centre embodied in the sacredness and authority of Nkamba (and a relatively 'fixed' spiritual leader), the diaspora, through their financial resources and their access to technology and media, has become gradually less 'peripheral'. Consequently, the process of sacred prophetic (re)centring of Nkamba here coexists dialogically with processes of decentralization and polycentralization at work within the Kimbanguist diasporic public sphere.

The global architecture of churches described in this book often relies on the deployment of cross-border networks and the transnational circulation of people and things and also of ideas, symbols and values. In some ways, because these networks strongly connect places and local diasporic contexts with local homeland environments, it may be more apt to stress the *translocal* characters of this global cartography (Brickell and Datta 2011). While this is implied in the book, as I zoomed in on the social and religious role of particular places – schools, hospitals, places of worships, holy city or even infrastructures – within a wider landscape of relations, the transnational perspective is also germane here as it indicates the continual relevance of nation-state borders and regimes in framing mobility and a host of relations between individuals and groups separated by migration. That both translocalism and transnationalism help make sense of the experience of Congolese migrants attests to the need to adopt a multiscalar approach to diaspora.

What is certain is that the configuration of the global landscape of Congolese Christianities is plural and shaped by a range of centre–periphery dynamics. The Congolese Catholic landscape can be both defined by a rigid and hierarchical ecclesiastical structure and also by its repertoire of institutional connections to the homeland, the host society and the Vatican. Beyond these institutional linkages, I described a process of postcolonial 'Africanization' of Congolese Catholicism. This Africanization has resulted not only in transcultural liturgies that incorporate some of the rich and dynamic histories and cultures in the region but also in a cornucopia of 'hybrid' beliefs and practices at the grassroots level, just like other diasporic Catholicisms have shown, for instance, among US Latinos (Peña 2011, Matovina 2011). However, just as in the case of Latinos, the global institution is ambivalent about these local, popular beliefs and practices, at best ignoring them and at worst labelling them heterodoxic. In Chapter 3, we encountered a diaspora-based Congolese priest who deplored the fact that the Vatican does not give sufficient recognition to the myriad of miracles and sacred sites that dot the African continent.

In that sense, the global landscape of Congolese Christianities is also shaped by power-geometries, and this was also particularly evident in the Kimbanguist case. Among Kimbanguists, as I have suggested, relations between members of the church in the DRC and those in diaspora operate in contexts of structural and material inequality, involving the kind of 'asymmetrical reciprocity' (Carling 2014) observable in the transnational domestic sphere. With their better access to equipment and technology, diasporic Kimbanguists have played an increasingly strategic role in providing the expertise and material resources needed for the city's infrastructural development, creating tensions with local actors who have felt 'displaced'. Moreover, not unlike within extended families, the imaginary of *Poto*, 'the West', also impacts the relations between church members in the Congo and their diasporic counterparts. For instance, one youth leader from London deplored the lack of 'depth' in his relationship with some Nkamba clergy members from whom he wanted guidance but who, according to him, only considered diasporic Kimbanguists as 'endless source of money'.

The 'Maman Olangi' church has adopted a model closest to the Kimbanguist one – with the idea of a strong centre in Kinshasa – the headquarters complex 'Cité de Triomphe' – where faithful from all over the diaspora converge for large church events and prayer meetings. Centripetal forces also play a role here as migration is seen as key to the expansion of the *ministère*, though this encouragement can nonetheless coexist with an explicit critique of the potential immoral risk of life in *Poto*, and the idea that an eventual return with skills/resources acquired in diaspora can benefit the (church in the) homeland (following the examples set by the late leaders, Maman and Papa Olangi). Churches like Maman Olangi headquartered in Kinshasa operate in an urban context where international migration is valued as a promise of (individual and collective) betterment and social mobility. Among Pentecostals, a lot of spiritual investment is directed at the possibility of joining a kin in Europe or 'trying one's luck' – *tenter l'aventure* – in *Poto*, and thus migration is highly aspirational and embedded within a moral economy of blessings – alongside professional, monetary or matrimonial success. As we saw, in Kinshasa, these Pentecostal theologies operate against a reconfigured system of gift exchange (recentred around the individual and the nuclear family). These theologies also recast waithood as *productive* by requiring a deep and enduring commitment through an intense spiritual and embodied praxis of fasting and prayers and, above all, through donations and tithes with the hope of a (highly superior) 'counter-gift' from God. This spiritual infrastructure also operates in conjunction with the possibility, the promise, of connecting church members in the DRC to global circuits – which are made legible by various performances of a global deployment – through the visits of members or pastors from the diaspora or the use of TV or social media, like it is the case in Maman Olangi's church.

Some Pentecostal churches which emerged in the diaspora, linking Congolese hubs in Europe and North America, have later sought to establish branches and/or projects in the homeland where interventions in health and education can be part and parcel of a vision for development in the pursuit of a charitable mission, as we saw with the New Jerusalem Church. While not revolving around a process of ancestral sacralization like for the Kimbanguist church, this reflects the sustained importance and meaning that the homeland maintains for those in diaspora. Here it is clear that establishing or maintaining a branch in Kinshasa can provide some form of legitimacy and authenticity for diasporic churches – another way of linking everyday religious life in diaspora to the performance of a Congolese identity. Moreover, the presence in Kinshasa of diaspora-based pastors (through a branch, projects or regular public visits) can be validating, perhaps similarly to the ways in which the credibility of Congolese musicians and bands can be acquired through their success, or at least recognition and visibility, in the Congolese capital.

Among Pentecostals, it is also true that the prestige of a connection to *Poto* is seen as a resource to mobilize in Kinshasa, a guarantee to attract a large following, which, in turn, increases the reputation of the pastor and/or church in diaspora. As the Atlanta-based pastor Josh told me when discussing his project of setting up a branch in Kinshasa:

> We are sending money to rent a *parcelle* [land plot] in Kinshasa for people to come and pray. We will support them and they will come in high numbers. When they will hear that the pastor come[s] from America, they will come. They will provide powerful prayers, with high energy – as we can have a lot of people there, they can pray, they can fast. The energy will flow to us in Atlanta.

Here the making of a global religious landscape hinges on a translocal configuration, through which members in the United States provide financial capital while those in the Congo produce 'spiritual energy' that can flow back to the diaspora. This is, again, another example of the centre–periphery religious cartography we have encountered at several moments throughout the book, with a clear division of financial and spiritual labour, where the United States provides capital and the DRC the praying bodies. From the optic of a prosperity gospel, this is a fair, taken-for-granted exchange. Still, underlying asymmetries persist, since the praying individuals in Congo are also likely to provide donations, which though small may be numerous, helping in the diasporic church's accumulation process. This type of connection is not without problems, especially when groups in the DRC are dependent on their diasporic counterparts for financial support like in the case of the Miséricorde hospital discussed in Chapters 6 and 7, and whose future was becoming uncertain after the death of the pastor-founder of the church in Belgium.

In a competitive religious market or in a context of conflicts or political tensions, connections to Kinshasa can also be detrimental to pastors. This is related to the potential suspicion that a successful pastor in the diaspora may have used occult means, for instance, through the use of fetishes from the homeland, to 'seduce' and attract followers. In addition, some pastors have also been accused, in particular by the opposition movement, of cultivating ties with the Kabila government when visiting Kinshasa, and this has led to some violent altercations or disruption of Sunday services.

The actions of the opposition movement, in particular the group known as *les Combattants*, have had a significant impact on the circulation of religious leaders and musicians seen as complicit or associated with the regime. Using the affordances provided by the internet and social media, which amplify the power of *radio-trottoir*, these opposition groups have circulated rumours, shamings and threats to successfully regulate the movement of people across transnational political and religious networks, creating as it were, an alternative, yet impactful regime of (im)mobility 'from below'. This phenomenon, while contingent on a combination of political factors embedded in a post-Mobutu collective history, points to a need to consider how obstructions and slowdowns have an impact on the transnational circuits of global religious landscapes. Ironically, this 'frictional' dimension (Tsing 2005), contrasting with the usual emphasis on flows and circulations in transnational studies or on the fluidity of religioscapes (Tweed 2006), is notable in a context where religious actors – especially Pentecostal actors – stress the power of the Holy Spirit to address immobility and blockages, to open up paths of progress and transformation.

*   *   *

In this book, I have followed multiple paths – obstructed or not – to explore how the production of moral worlds operates across a range of boundaries and scales. While my case studies point to a selective range of configurations of lived or institutional religion (and how these are acted out through diasporic and/ or urban presence and interventions), I have shown that the making of these moral worlds both results from and facilitates a process of 'regrounding' for Congolese Christians. By creating, recreating or defending the existence of these moral (or remoralized) worlds, Congolese Christians performatively reveal how ambivalent and ambiguous their social and cultural environments can be and also how contingent they themselves are on their location across the migration divide, even if the homeland and diaspora could be seen in many ways as part of the same wider encompassing public sphere.

But religion is of course more than the performative mapping of moral worlds across scales and boundaries. And while religious actors, especially Pentecostals, stress the legitimacy and superiority of an all-encompassing moral vision, alternative formulations of progress and change are produced outside the religious sphere, even when Pentecostal aesthetics and 'key scenario' (Pype 2012) have become a dominant force in the Congolese public/media space. When discussing diasporic politics, we showed how religious actors could be contested by anti-Kabila activists – and this applies to Kimbanguists, Pentecostals and even Catholics, who, despite their engagement for civil liberties and democracy in the Congo, have been criticized at various times for being too accommodating with some practices of the regime in place. The act of challenging religious leaders, especially (but not only) Pentecostal pastors, is also linked to a widespread rejection of deviant/immoral behaviours to do with scandals about sexual misconduct, financial misappropriation or 'bogus miracles' regularly erupting in the public sphere in the homeland and the diaspora.[4] As we discussed earlier, the impact of these alternative and critical voices interrogating the sincerity of religious actors should not be minimized, both in the diaspora and the homeland, as they reconfigure the lines of moral legitimacy and generate 'anxieties about how to assess genuine spiritual power through pastors' public performances' raising the 'specter of spiritual trickery', as Shipley (2015: 176) describes in the context of urban Ghana.

Beyond issues of morality, the question of the 'promise' of change brought about by religious practice and affiliation is also important here. In the Congo, the critique of this promised societal and individual transformation is powerfully encapsulated by the song *Nini to sali te?* ('What have we not done?'), produced in 2021 by the Hip Hop group MPR (acronym of 'Musique Populaire de la Revolution' and which ironically echoes the name of the Mobutu's autocratic party MPR – 'Mouvement Populaire de la Revolution'). The clip of *Nini to sali te?*[5] which at the time of writing counted more than 2.9 million views on YouTube depicts the predicament of youth in contemporary Kinshasa and lists the (betrayed) promises they have received over the years – for instance, the promise that, with an education, they would find employment, the promise that, after Mobutu, peace and stability will emerge or that, after Kabila, things will improve. In the clip, the critique of religion – especially Pentecostalism – is explicit: we see the main character nodding in disagreement when faced with a preacher evangelizing in a public bus, a scene reflecting the omnipresence of Pentecostal actors in the urban landscape of Kinshasa. Born-again modes of worshipping and theologies of rupture are also deemed pointless: 'we have prayed and fasted, we have severed family ties, what have we not done?'.

It is important to highlight these contestations, as they illustrate that, while religious life provides affordances and resources, people also exercise – whether outside or within religious institutions – a high level of agency by critically reflecting on the morality, truthfulness or sincerity of religious discourses and those generating them. This is not to minimize the significance of religious life, beliefs and practices to Congolese both in diaspora and the homeland and the capacity for religious groups, in particular Pentecostals, to maintain or even expand their influence on public and private domains. Here, one could argue that temporality – at multiple scales, near future included – has also been invested and appropriated by religious actors, who, drawing upon the powerful trope that divine time transcends human-made expectations and constraints, are both filling spatial and temporal gaps by meaningfully linking enduring commitment and hopeful waithood to possible horizons of redemption and change.

Notes

Introduction

1   All the names used in this book are pseudonyms.
2   See De Boeck (2014).
3   formerly Bas-Congo, Kongo Central is one of the 26 provinces of the Democratic Republic of the Congo.
4   The official national languages of the DRC aside from French are Lingala, Tshiluba, Kikongo and Swahili.
5   The 'Matonge' area of Brussels (Porte de Namur) is the cultural, commercial and social hub of Belgian Congolese and is named after the famous Matonge quartier in Kinshasa, renowned for its nightlife during the heyday of Congolese rumba.
6   O'Neill's argument is that these disciplined subjects serve the interests of the neoliberal project advanced by the Guatemalan and US states.
7   'Revival churches', as Pentecostal churches are also known in Congo and its diaspora, due to their focus on the gifts of the Holy Spirit: glossolalia, divine cure and prophesizing.
8   Joseph Kabila was the president of the DRC at the time of fieldwork.
9   As we shall discuss in the book (see Chapter 4 in particular), while many Kimbanguists see themselves as Protestant Christians, Protestant bodies, including the World Council of Church (WCC, that the Kimbanguist church joined as a member in 1969), have criticized the Kimbanguists for their interpretation of the Trinity, and for their perceived 'syncretism'. The WCC withdrew the Kimbanguist church's membership in 2021 mostly on theological grounds.

Chapter 1

1   In this sense I agree with Baumann (1996) who argues in his now classic ethnography of multiculturalism in South London, *Contesting Culture*, that people navigate and make sense of plurality by often drawing upon fixed notions of identity and 'community' even if 'practicing' hybridity in their everyday urban lives. See also the debates in postcolonial studies and gender studies about the notion of 'strategic essentialism' (Spivak 1984).

2 Combining ethnographic observations in multiple contexts, semi-structured and informal interviews (more than eighty in total) and focus group discussions with members of Congolese youth organizations and Kimbanguist youth groups in London and the United States. Most of the interviews were conducted in French and translated in English, with the exception of the interviews with young activists in Chapter 4 (mostly conducted in English).

3 'The religious lives of migrant minorities: a transnational and multi-sited perspective'. A project of the Social Science Research Council (SSRC) funded by the Ford Foundation, 2006–9.

4 Some in the church believed that the reason why a Nigerian pastor was leading the French Connection branch was to maintain a tighter control from the mother church and linked to fear of a Congolese taking some members out of the Francophone branch to create his own church (which eventually happened).

5 This trip led to the production of a project book and a small film, see https://vimeo .com/161746817.

6 As in 'système débrouille': from 'se débrouiller' meaning 'to make do', 'to manage' and the ability of being resourceful (sometimes in illegal ways) in often challenging contexts.

7 See 'Migrations between Africa and Europe – MAFE' project: https://mafeproject .site.ined.fr.

8 See Schoumaker et al. (2013).

9 The American Academy of Religion and the international research network 'Global Prayers' (see http://globalprayers.info/) supported this fieldwork during the summers of 2008 and 2011.

10 During Kabila's rule, and in part because of the reputation of London for anti-Kabila opposition, obtaining a visa from the DRC embassy was difficult if not impossible without sponsorship and/or strong connections, in particular with embassy staff.

11 As 'Mobutu's dystopian dictatorship deployed its tentacles to bring all cultural activities into the fold' (Gondola 2016: 14), state propaganda constructed Mobutu as a quasi-divine figure, encouraging various forms of collective 'worship' through public performances and dances.

12 This was an official Mobutist state ideology originated in the late 1960s and early 1970s centred around the affirmation of a 'purified', authentic national identity, with policies banning, for instance, the use of Christian names or encouraging non-Western style of clothing, in addition to new Zairean symbols and names.

Chapter 2

1 This is also recurrent in the narratives collected among African migrants in transit countries as shown by the work of Berriane (2021) in Morocco, Den Boer (2015) or

Gusman (2021) in Uganda. Gusman describes, for instance, how the biblical trope of the exodus is invoked by Congolese refugees in Kampala 'try[ing] to make sense of suffering as part of God's plan for them' (Gusman 2021: 133), nourishing hope of reaching the 'Promised Land' of a stable, prosperous and peaceful destination through resettlement in the West, while often attributing their immobility to 'spiritual "blockages" attributed to witchcraft' (Gusman 2021: 133).

2 The Home Office is the ministerial department responsible for immigration, security and policing in the UK.

3 This reverse missionizing has also attracted media attention, see Adogame (2013: 171–3).

4 https://www.flickr.com/photos/catholicwestminster/albums/72177720298581088/page2.

5 See debates surrounding the 2021 UK Borders and Nationality Bill.

Chapter 3

1 http://www.kicc.org.uk/ accessed May 2018.

2 See also the work of Klaver (2021) on the Hillsong megachurch.

3 Created by famous televangelist Pat Robertson.

4 http://www.youtube.com/watch?v=Nnr7kl9qBQQ accessed May 2015

5 'Need a spiritual boost? You could try living there', *Metro*, 15/10/2010; 'Opposition to plans for eight churches in Lawrence Road', *Tottenham and Wood Green Journal*, 14/10/2010.

6 Among a growing literature, some of the key works on migrant/diasporic urban religious performance include studies of Hindu Chariot festivals (David 2012, Knott 2016) Sikh, Vaisakhi or Ashura processions (Griera and Burchardt 2021), Christian or Easter parades (Saint-Blancat and Cancellieri 2014) or Sufi parades (Abdullah 2009, Werbner 2003). For a recent cross-religious and comparative overview, see Bramadat et al. (2021).

7 The brass band had been invited by a local Congolese organization to 'represent the Congolese community'.

8 To maintain this distance, the leaders of the church made a request (which was granted) to lead the parade, so as to leave enough space behind the musicians.

9 Catholic radio station streamed online and broadcast from more than sixty countries (including the DRC) and in many different languages.

Chapter 4

1 One of their most emblematic faits d'armes was when, during a short stay in London in October 2006, She Okitundu, the then head of Kabila's cabinet, was assaulted and

stripped naked ('mutukalisé'). Pictures related to the attack were later posted on the internet.

2   See Thornton (1998).

3   Town cited in the Bible, in particular in the Gospels of Matthew, Mark, Luke and John. It is mentioned also that Jesus taught and performed healing miracles in the synagogue (including healing evil possession, as in Lk. 4:31-36).

4   See, for instance, this clip posted on YouTube featuring a group of Congolese pilgrims to the Holy Land praying and singing around the 'map': https://www .youtube.com/watch?v=4X8tr3uzmQs (accessed April 2021).

5   At the end of a FAKI rehearsal, I witnessed a Kimbanguist leader teaching youth how to appropriately perform the *bula makonko,* telling them that the flat hand clapping was for *mindele* – white people.

6   This prophecy predicted the independence of the Congo and described the succession of four post-independence presidents, and their length of time in power, the fourth president predicted to 'save the country . . . bring[ing] happiness and real independence' (Mokoko Gampiot 2017: 245).

7   Congolese youth participated in several Occupy meetings, and several Occupy activists also attended some Congolese demonstrations.

8   https://www.genocost.org/about/what-is-the-geno-cost/.

9   In 2009, Kimbanguists from all over Europe gathered in Lisbon as the spiritual leader's visit had been announced there (his first visit to Europe). The visit was cancelled at the last minute, but the gathering and public procession still took place.

Chapter 5

1   For example, see Orozco (2013), Sørensen (2016) or Lopez (2015).

2   https://www.worldbank.org/en/news/press-release/2021/05/12/defying-predictions-remittance-flows-remain-strong-during-covid-19-crisis (accessed January 2022) on the resilience of remittance flows during Covid.

3   See Eriksson Baaz (2013) for the importance of import/export of vehicles and spare parts as an economic activity/investment among Congolese return migrants.

4   There is also here a subtle social critique of superficial demands made by Kinois, who are depicted are not seeing the value of books and by extension education.

5   'Escroquer [*sic*] par sa famille, un Congolais de la diaspora se suicide a Kinshasa', https://www.youtube.com/watch?v=38QixLOrrSk (accessed February 2018). See also https://www.youtube.com/watch?v=O5KizPY6vyo.

6   As Van Dijk notes, 'the Pentecostal ideology, therefore, informs people of the ambiguities of the gift, exposes its history, its intentions and messages and prepares it for alienation so that it can be returned, disposed of or destroyed, which is often seen as an act of contestation' (2002: 188).

7 To finance the dowry/brideprice, for instance.
8 The 'real' deliverance came after the revelation of the need for spiritual warfare (which is a continual process).
9 See Marshall (2009), Meiers (2013), Ndaya Tshiteku (2007), Zimango Ngama (2016).
10 While trips to Nkamba may not constitute urban pilgrimages per se, the city is urbanizing and the rural (including the immediate surroundings) is constructed negatively, as we discuss in Chapter 7.

Chapter 6

1 Pype (2017: 123) defines 'anti-valeurs' in the Congolese context as referring to 'asocial actions like corruption, immodesty, and loose-ness, and are connected to the quality of one's personal relationships, be they with the nuclear and extended family, friends, neighbours, and business partners'.
2 Belgium took over from King Leopold II in 1908.
3 That is, before going to university in the Congo – mostly Kinshasa – or abroad, in France or Belgium, for instance.
4 Originating from Scheut, Anderlecht, a suburb of Brussels, also known as the CICM Missionaries (Latin: Congregatio Immaculati Cordis Mariae or the Congregation of the Immaculate Heart of Mary), it is a Roman Catholic missionary congregation established in 1862 by the Belgian priest Theophiel Verbist (1823–68).
5 This ties in with the idea that charity among Pentecostals is seen as the right moral response to economic inequality and poverty, rather than engaging in an explicit critique of the system as some Catholics may do, like in the case in some Latin American countries.
6 Targeted at the particular origin/cause, once identified. The same process takes place among adults.
7 This corroborates De Boeck's findings in his Kinshasa ethnography. See in particular De Boeck and Plissart (2004: 139–55 and 173–83) and De Boeck (2009).

Chapter 7

1 See Janson and Akinleye (2015) on Muslim and Christian 'prayer camps' along a stretch of the Lagos-Ibadan expressway – a 'spiritual highway' as they have coined it.
2 Mahanaim is a place mentioned several times in the Bible, where Jacob met the Angels (Gen. 32:2-10).
3 As a set of processes expanding the urban fabric to the extent where there is no longer a clearly identifiable non-urban elsewhere against which the city can be defined.

4 If Nkamba's temporality is shaped by a predictable sacralized rhythm, it is also bound up with power dynamics which at times may affect the mobility of church members, especially those with ecclesial responsibility and thus may introduce some elements of unpredictability. The spiritual leader has indeed a lot of influence on people's decision to leave the holy city, which has to be authorized, spiritually validated so to speak. I met several diasporic Kimbanguists who were planning to leave Nkamba but some have missed flights to Europe and had to extend their stay because the spiritual leader 'had other plans for them' and told them to stay put. Some even had to leave their jobs in Europe.

5 In the case of gifts purchased with money collected though *nsinsani* rituals, for instance.

Conclusion

1 See also, among a growing literature on patriarchy and gender in Evangelical Christianity, Griffith (1997, 2017), Burdick (2013) or Sanchez-Walsh (2018).

2 See Garbin (2011) for an exploration of schismatic dynamics within the Kimbanguist church.

3 At the time of the centenary, travelling (back) from 'red list countries' required a compulsory quarantine (costing several thousand pounds) in designated private hotels on UK territory.

4 See the work of Gez et al. (2021), especially Chapter 4, about similar observations in the Kenyan context. See also Shipley (2015) about how religious/Pentecostal performance relates to notions of sincerity or fakery in Ghana. Pype (2012) explores this issue in Kinshasa.

5 https://www.youtube.com/watch?v=KqzEwuvVvYs.

References

Abdullah, Z. (2009), 'Sufis on Parade: The Performance of Black, African, and Muslim Identities', *Journal of the American Academy of Religion*, 77 (2): 199–237.

Adeboye, O. (2012), '"A Church in a Cinema Hall?" Pentecostal Appropriation of Public Space in Nigeria', *Journal of Religion in Africa*, 42: 145–71.

Adekunle, I. A., S. A. Tella and F. O. Ogunjobi (2022), 'Remittances and the Future of African Economies', *International Migration*, 60: 252–70.

Adogame, A. (2013), *The African Christian Diaspora: New Currents and Emerging Trends in World Christianity*, London: Bloomsbury.

Agamben, G. (2005), *The Time that Remains: A Commentary on the Letters to the Romans*, Stanford: Stanford University Press.

Alsayyad, N. and A. Roy (2006), 'Medieval Modernity: On Citizenship and Urbanism in a Global Era', *Space and Polity*, 10 (1): 1–20.

Amin, A. (2014), 'Lively Infrastructure', *Theory, Culture & Society*, 31 (7–8): 137–61.

Amin, A. and N. Thrift (2017), *Seeing Like A City*, Cambridge: Cambridge University Press.

Angelo, H. and D. Wachsmuth (2015), 'Urbanizing Urban Political Ecology: A Critique of Methodological Cityism', *International Journal of Urban and Regional Research*, 39 (1): 16–27.

Appadurai, A. (1996), 'Disjuncture and Difference in the Global Cultural Economy', in *Modernity at Large: Cultural Dimensions of Globalisation*, 27–47, Minneapolis: University of Minnesota Press.

Appadurai, A. (2013), *The Future as Cultural Fact: Essays on the Global Condition*, London: Verso Books.

Ayimpam, S. (2012), 'Violence et sorcellerie. Prolifération normative et incohérence statutaire à Kinshasa', in J. Bouju and B. Martinelli (eds), *Sorcellerie et violence en Afrique*, Paris: Karthala.

Ayimpam S. (2014), *Economie de la débrouille à Kinshasa. Informalité, commerce et réseaux sociaux*, Paris: Karthala.

Baker, C. (2015), 'Preface', in Y. Narayanan (ed.), *Religion and Urbanism, Reconceptualising Sustainable Cities for South Asia*, London: Routledge.

Basch, L., N. Glick Schiller and C. Szanton Blanc (1994), *Nations Unbound: Transnational Migration, Postcolonial Predicaments, and the Deterritorialized Nation-State*, Langhorne: Gordon and Breach.

Baumann, G. (1996), *Contesting Culture: Discourses of Identity in Multi-Ethnic London*, Cambridge and New York: Cambridge University Press.

Becker, J., K. Klingan, S. Lanz and K. Wildner, eds (2014), *Global Prayers Contemporary Manifestations of the Religious in the City*, Zurich: Lars Mueller Publishers.

Benjamin, R. (2009), *Searching for Whitopia: An Improbable Journey to the Heart of White America*, New York: Hyperion.

Bennett, J. (2010), *Vibrant Matter: A Political Ecology of Things*, New York: Duke University Press.

Bertolani, B. and P. Boccagni (2022), 'Domestic Religion and the Migrant Home: The Private, the Diasporic and the Public in the Sacralization of Sikh Dwellings in Italy', *Ethnicities*, https://doi.org/10.1177/14687968211069376

Berriane, J. (2021), '"Conquering New Territory for Jesus?": The Transience and Local Presence of African Pentecostal Migrants in Morocco', in B. Meyer and P. Van der Veer (eds), *Refugees and Religion*, 143–59, London: Bloomsbury Academic.

Boccagni, P. (2014), 'From the Multi-Sited to the In-between: Ethnography as a Way of Delving into Migrants' Transnational Relationships', *International Journal of Social Research Methodology*, 19 (1): 1–16.

Bourdieu, P. (1992), *Language and Symbolic Power*, Cambridge: Polity Press.

Bourdieu, P. (2000), *Pascalian Meditations*, Cambridge: Polity Press. Orig.

Brah, A. (1996), *Cartographies of Diaspora: Contesting Identities*, London: Routledge.

Bramadat, P., M. Griera, J. Martínez-Ariño and M. Burchardt, eds (2021), *Urban Religious Events: Public Spirituality in Contested Spaces*, London: Bloomsbury.

Brenner, N. (2019), *New Urban Spaces: Urban Theory and the Scale Question*, Oxford: Oxford University Press.

Brickell, K. and A. Datta, eds (2011), *Translocal Geographies: Spaces, Places and Connections*, Burlington: Ashgate.

Brown, W. (2010), *Walled States, Waning Sovereignty*, New York: Zone Books.

Brubaker, R. (2005), 'The "diaspora" diaspora', *Ethnic and Racial Studies*, 28 (1): 1–19.

Bruce, B. (2019), *Governing Islam Abroad: Turkish and Moroccan Muslims in Western Europe*, London: Palgrave Macmillan.

Buggenhagen, B. A. (2012), *Muslim Families in Global Senegal: Money Takes Care of Shame*, Indiana: Indiana University Press.

Burchardt, M. (2015), *Faith in the Time of AIDS: Religion, Biopolitics and Modernity in South Africa*, Basingstoke: Palgrave Macmillan.

Burchardt, M. (2017), 'Pentecostal Productions of Locality: Urban Risks and Spiritual Protection in Cape Town', in D. Garbin and A. Strhan (eds), *Religion and the Global City*, London: Bloomsbury.

Burchardt, M. and M. Westendorp (2018), 'The Im-Materiality of Urban Religion: Towards an Ethnography of Urban Religious Aspirations', *Culture and Religion*, 19 (2): 160–76.

Burdick, J. (2013), *Blessed Anastácia: Women, Race and Popular Christianity in Brazil*, London: Routledge.

Butler, J. (2007), *Gender Trouble: Feminism and the Subversion of Identity*, New York: Routledge.

Butticci, A. (2013), 'Crazy World, Crazy Faith! Prayer, Power and Transformation in a Nigerian Prayer City', *Annual Review of the Sociology of Religion*, 243–61. DOI: https:// doi.org/10.1163/9789004260498.

Butticci, A. (2016), *African Pentecostals in Catholic Europe, the Politics of Presence in the Twenty-First Century*. Cambridge, MA: Harvard University Press.

Burgess, R. (2009), 'African Pentecostal Spirituality and Civic Engagement: The Case of the Redeemed Christian Church of God in Britain', *Journal of Beliefs & Values*, 30 (3): 255–73.

Byrne, B. (2014), *Making Citizens: Public Rituals and Personal Journeys to Citizenship*, Basingstoke: Palgrave.

Callan, A. (2007), '"What else do we Bengalis do?" Sorcery, Overseas Migration, and the New Inequalities in Sylhet, Bangladesh', *Journal of the Royal Anthropological Institute*, 13: 331–43.

Campbell, H. A. (ed.) (2013), *Digital Religion: Understanding Religious Practice in New Media Worlds*, London: Routledge.

Campbell, H. A. and G. Evolvi (2019), 'Contextualizing Current Digital Religion Research on Emerging Technologies', *Human Behavior & Emerging Technologies*, 2019: 1–13.

Carling, J. (2014), 'Scripting Remittances: Making Sense of Money Transfers in Transnational Relationships', *International Migration Review*, 42: 3.

Cartledge, M. J. S. Dunlop, H. Buckingham and S. Bremner (2019), *Megachurches and Social Engagement: Public Theology in Practice*, Leiden: Brill.

Casanova, J. (1994), *Public Religions in the Modern World*, Chicago: University of Chicago Press.

Chomé, J. (1959), *La passion de Simon Kimbangu*, Paris: Présence Africaine.

Chu, J. Y. (2010), *Cosmologies of Credit: Transnational Mobility and the Politics of Destination in China*, Durham: Duke University Press.

Clifford, J. (1994), 'Diasporas', *Cultural Anthropology*, 9 (3): 302–38.

Cochrane, J. (2011), 'A Model of Integral Development. Assessing and Working with Religious Health Assets', in G. ter Haar (ed.) *Religion and Development: Ways of Transforming the World*, 231–52, London: C. Hurst & Co Press.

Comaroff, J. (2012), 'Pentecostalism, Populism and the New Politics of Affect', in D. Freeman (ed.), *Pentecostalism and Development: Churches, NGOs and Social Change in Africa*, 41–66, Basingstoke: Palgrave Macmillan.

Comaroff, J. and J. Comaroff (1999), 'Occult Economies and the Violence of Abstraction', *American Ethnologist*, 26 (2): 279–303.

Comaroff, J. and J. L. Comaroff (1997), *Of Revelation and Revolution: The Dialectics of Modernity on a South African Frontier Vol. II*, Chicago: Chicago University Press.

Cole, J. and C. Groes (2016), *Affective Circuits: African Migrations to Europe and the Pursuit of Social Regeneration*. Chicago: University of Chicago Press.

Coleman, S. (2000), *The Globalisation of Charismatic Christianity: Spreading the Gospel of Prosperity*, Cambridge: Cambridge University Press.

Coleman, S. (2009), 'The Protestant Ethic and the Spirit of Urbanism', in R. Pinxten and L. Dikomitis (eds), *When God Comes to Town: Religious Traditions in Urban Contexts*, 33–44, London: Berghahn.

Coleman, S. (2010), 'Constructing the Globe: A Charismatic Sublime?', in G. Hüwelmeier and K. Krause (eds), *Traveling Spirits: Migrants, Markets and Mobilities*, 186–202, New York: Routledge.

Coleman, S. (2019), 'Satan on the Old Kent Road: Articulations of Evil in a Pentecostal Diaspora', in W. C. Olsen and T. J. Csordas (eds), *Engaging Evil: A Moral Anthropology*, New York: Berghahn Books.

Coleman, S. (2022), *Powers of Pilgrimage: Religion in a World of Movement*, New York: New York University Press.

Coleman, S. and J. Elsner (2004) 'Tradition as Play: Pilgrimage to "England's Nazareth"', *History and Anthropology*, 15 (3): 273–88.

Coleman, S. and K. Maier (2013), 'Redeeming the City: Creating and Traversing "London-Lagos"', *Religion*, 43: 353–64.

Coleman, S. and M. Vásquez (2015), 'On the Road: Pentecostal Pathways through the Mega-City', in D. Garbin and A. Strhan (eds), *Religion and the Global City*, London: Bloomsbury.

Coleman, S. and S. Chattoo (2020), 'Megachurches and Popular Culture: On Enclaving and Encroaching', in S. J. Hunt (ed), *Handbook of Megachurches*, 84–102, Leiden: Brill.

Coleman, S. and J. Eade, eds (2018), *Pilgrimage and Political Economy: Translating the Sacred*, Oxford, New York: Berghahn Books.

Corrigan, J. (2008), 'Spatiality and Religion', in B. Warf and S. Arias (eds), *The Spatial Turn: Interdisciplinary Perspectives*, London and New York: Routledge.

Covington-Ward, Y. (2016), *Gesture and Power: Religion, Nationalism, and Everyday Performance in Congo*, Durham and London: Duke University Press.

Creese, G. and B. Wiebe (2012), '"Survival Employment": Gender and Deskilling among African Immigrants in Canada', *International Migration*, 50 (5): 56–76.

Dalakoglou, D. (2010), 'Migrating-Remitting-"Building"-Dwelling: House-Making as "Proxy" Presence in Postsocialist Albania', *Journal of the Royal Anthropological Institute*, 16 (4): 761–77.

Daswani, G. (2015), *Looking Back, Moving Forward: Transformation and Ethical Practice in the Ghanaian Church of Pentecost*, Toronto: University of Toronto Press.

David, A. (2012), 'Sacralising the City: Sound, Space and Performance in Hindu Ritual Practices in London', *Culture and Religion*, 13 (4): 449–67.

De Boeck, F. (2005), 'The Apocalyptic Interlude: Revealing Death in Kinshasa', *African Studies Review*, 48 (2): 11–32.

De Boeck, F. (2009), 'At Risk, As Risk. Abandonment and Care in a World of Spiritual Insecurity', in J. La Fontaine (ed.), *The Devil's Children: From Spirit Possession to Witchcraft: New Allegations that Affect Children*, 129–50, London: Routledge.

De Boeck, F. (2013), 'The Sacred and the City: Modernity, Religion, and the Urban Form in Central Africa', in Lambek, M. and Boddy, J. (eds), *A Companion to the Anthropology of Religion*, London: Wiley.

De Boeck, F. (2014), 'Cemetery State', in J. Becker, K. Klingan, S. Lanz and K. Wildner (eds), *Global Prayers. Contemporary Manifestations of the Religious in the City*, Zurich: Lars Mueller Publishers.

De Boeck, F. and M.-F. Plissart (2004), *Kinshasa. Tales of the Invisible City*, Ghent: Ludion.

De Boeck, F. and S. Baloji (2016), *Suturing the City: Living Together in Congo's Urban Worlds*, London: Autograph ABP.

De Haas, H. (2005), 'International Migration, Remittances and Development: Myths and Facts', *Third World Quarterly*, 26 (8): 1269–84.

De Haas, H., S. Castles and M. J. Miller (2019), *The Age of Migration International Population Movements in the Modern World*, London: Bloomsbury.

DeHanas, D. N. (2016), *London Youth, Religion, and Politics: Engagement and Activism form Brixton to Brick Lane*, Oxford: Oxford University Press.

de Witte, M. (2008), 'Accra's Sounds and Sacred Spaces', *International Journal of Urban and Regional Research*, 32 (3): 690–709.

de Witte, M. (2012), 'The Electric Touch Machine Miracle Scam: Body, Technology, and the (Dis)authentication of the Pentecostal Supernatural', in Jeremy Stolow (ed.), *Deus in Machina: Religion, Technology, and the Things in Between*, 61–82, New York: Fordham University Press.

Dejean, F. (2020), '*It Was a Cinema; It Is Now the House of God!* Les Églises sans église ou le renversement des contraintes spatiales en opportunités', *Annales de géographie*, 731: 113–33.

Della Dora, V. (2016) 'Infrasecular Geographies: Making, Unmaking and Remaking Sacred Space', *Progress in Human Geography*, 42 (1): 44–71.

Demart, S. (2017), *Les territoires de la délivrance: Le réveil congolais en situation postcoloniale (RDC et diaspora)*, Paris: Karthala.

Demart, S. (2010), 'Les territoires de la délivrance : Mises en perspectives historique et plurilocalisée du Réveil congolais (Bruxelles, Kinshasa, Paris, Toulouse)', PhD thesis, University of Toulouse.

Demart, S. and J. Tonda (2016), '"Mboka Mundele": Africanity, Religious Pluralism and the Militarization of Prophets in Brazzaville and Kinshasa', *Africa*, 86 (2) 2016: 195–214.

Den Boer, R. (2015), 'Liminal Space in Protracted Exile: The Meaning of Place in Congolese Refugees' Narratives of Home and Belonging in Kampala', *Journal of Refugee Studies*, 28 (4): 486–504.

Deneulin, S. (2009), *Religion in Development: Rewriting the Secular Script*, London: Zed Books.

Dilger, H. (2017), 'Embodying Values and Socio-Religious Difference: New Markets of Moral Learning in Christian and Muslim Schools in Urban Tanzania', *Africa: Journal of the International African Institute*, 87 (3): 513–36.

Dilger H. and M. Janson (2022), 'Religiously-Motivated Schools and Universities as "Moral Enclaves": Reforming Urban Youths in Tanzania and Nigeria', in David Garbin, S. Coleman and G. Millington (eds), *Ideologies and Infrastructures of Religious Urbanization in Africa: Remaking the City*, London: Bloomsbury.

Dilger, H., A. Kane and S. A. Langwick, eds (2012), *Medicine, Mobility, and Power in Global Africa: Transnational Health and Healing*, 1–27. Bloomimgton: Indiana University Press.

Dilger, H. O. Kasmani, D. Mattes. (2018), 'Spatialities of Belonging: Affective Place-making Among Diasporic Neo-Pentecostal and Sufi Groups in Berlin's Cityscape', in B. Röttger-Rössler and J. Slaby (eds), *Affect in Relation Families, Places, Technologies*, London: Routledge.

Eade, J. (2012), 'Religion, Home-Making and Migration across a Globalising City', *Culture and Religion*, 13 (4): 469–83.

Eade, P. J. (2017), 'Parish and Pilgrimage in a Changing Europe', in D. Pasura and M. B. Erdal (eds), *Migration, Transnationalism and Catholicism: Global Perspectives*, London: Palgrave.

Echtler, M. and A. Ukah (2016), 'Introduction: Exploring the Dynamics of Religious Fields in Africa', in M. Echtler and A. Ukah (eds), *Bourdieu in Africa: Exploring the Dynamics of Religious Fields*, 1–32, Leiden: Brill.

Eckstein, S. (2010), 'Immigration, Remittances, and Transnational Social Capital Formation: A Cuban Case Study', *Ethnic and Racial Studies*, 33 (9): 1648–67.

Eckstein, S. E. and A. Najam, eds (2013), *How Immigrants Impact Their Homelands*. Durham: Duke University Press.

Eiesland, N. (2000), *A Particular Place: Urban Restructuring and Religious Ecology in a Southern Exurb*, New Brunswick: Rutgers University Press.

Elden, S. (2013), *The Birth of Territory*, Chicago: Chicago University Press.

Elias, N. (2000 [1939]), *The Civilizing Process*, Oxford: Blackwell.

Elisha, O. (2017), 'Proximations of Public Religion: Worship, Spiritual Warfare, and the Ritualization of Christian Dance', *American Anthropologist*, 119 (1): 73–85.

Engelke, M. (2007), *A Problem of Presence: Beyond Scripture in an African Church*. University of California Press.

Engelke, M. (2010), 'Past Pentecostalism: Notes on Rupture, Realignment, and Everyday Life in Pentecostal and African Independent Churches', *Africa*, 80 (2), May 2010: 177–99.

Erdal, B. M. (2022), 'Migrant Transnationalism, Remittances and Development', in B. S. A. Yeoh and F. L. Collins, *Handbook on Transnationalism*, 356–70, Cheltenham: Edward Elgar Publishing.

Eriksson Baaz, M. (2013), 'Successive Flops and Occasional Feats: Development Contributions and Thorny Social Navigation Among Congolese Return Migrants', in L. Åkesson and M. Erikssson Baaz (eds), *Africa's Return Migrants: The New Developers?* London: Bloomsbury, 22–43.

Ferguson, J. (2006), *Global Shadows: Africa in the Neoliberal World Order*, Durham: Duke University Press.

Fernandes, S. (2022), *Christianity in Brazil: An Introduction from a Global Perspective*, London: Bloomsbury.

Fesenmyer, L. (2022), 'Ambivalent Belonging: Born-again Christians between Africa and Europe', *Journal of Religion in Africa*, 52 (1–2): 119–45.

Fesenmyer, L. (2016), '"Assistance but not Support": Pentecostalism and the Reconfiguring of Relatedness Between Kenya and the United Kingdom', in J. Coles and C. Groes (eds), *Affective Circuits: African Journeys to Europe and the Pursuit of Social Regeneration*, Chicago: University of Chicago Press.

Flahaux M.-L., B. Schoumaker, A. González-Ferrer and O. Obucina (2013), *Determinants of Migration between Africa and Europe: The DR Congo Case*, MAFE Working Paper n°23, Paris, INED.

Foucault, M. (2007), *Security, Territory, Population*, New York: Picador.

Freeman, D. (2012), 'The Pentecostal Ethic and the Spirit of Development', in D. Freeman, D. (ed.), *Pentecostalism and Development: Churches, NGOs and Social Change in Africa*, Basingstoke: Palgrave Macmillan.

Fumanti, M. (2010), 'Virtuous Citizenship, Ethnicity and Encapsulation among Akan Speaking Ghanaian Methodists in London', *African Diaspora*, 2 (1/2): 1–30.

Fumanti, M. (2017), 'Interdisciplinary Approaches to Cultural Citizenship and Migration', in S. Coleman, S. Hyatt and A. Kingsolver (eds), *The Routledge Companion to Contemporary Anthropology*, London and New York: Routledge.

Gandy, M. (2006), 'Planning, Anti-planning and the Infrastructure Crisis Facing Metropolitan Lagos', *Urban Studies*, 43 (2): 371–96.

Garbin, D. (2010), 'Embodied Spirit(s) and Charismatic Power among Congolese Migrants in London', in A. Dawson (ed.), *Summoning the Spirits: Possession and Invocation in Contemporary Religion*, 40–57, New York: I.B.Tauris.

Garbin, D. (2011), 'Symbolic Geographies of the Sacred: Diasporic Territorialization and Charismatic Power in a Transnational Congolese Prophetic Church', in G. Huwelmeier and K. Krause (eds), *Traveling Spirits: Migrants, Markets and Mobilities*, London: Routledge.

Garbin, D. (2012), 'Marching for God in the Global City: Public Space, Religion and Diasporic Identities in a Transnational African Church', *Culture and Religion*, 13 (40): 425–44.

Garbin, D. (2013), 'Visibility and Invisibility of Migrant Faith in the City: Diaspora Religion and the Politics of Emplacement of Afro-Christian Churches', *Journal of Ethnic and Migration Studies*, 39: 677–96.

Garbin, D. (2014), 'Regrounding the Sacred: Transnational Religion, Place Making and the Politics of Diaspora among the Congolese in London and Atlanta'. *Global Networks*, 14: 363–82.

Garbin, D. and A. Strhan (2017), *Religion and the Global City*, London: Bloomsbury.

Garbin, D. (2018), 'Sacred Remittances: Money, Migration and the Moral Economy of Development in a Transnational African Church', *Journal of Ethnic and Migration Studies*, 45 (11): 2045–61.

Garbin, D. and G. Millington (2018), '"Central London under siege": Diaspora, "race" and the Right to the (global) City', *The Sociological Review*, 66 (1): 138–54.

Garbin, D. and A. Mokoko Gampiot (2022), 'Territorialized Visions of Development and Urban Christianities in the Congo', in D. Garbin, S. Coleman and G. Millington (eds), *Ideologies and Infrastructures of Religious Urbanization in Africa: Remaking the City*, 35–54, London: Bloomsbury.

Garbin, D. and M. A. Vásquez (2012), '"God is Technology": Mediating the Sacred in the Congolese Diaspora', in L. Fortunati, R. Pertierra and J. Vincent (eds), *Migration, Diaspora, and Information Technology in Global Societies*, 157–71, London: Routledge.

Gardner, K. (1995), *Global Migrants, Local Lives: Travel and Transformation in Rural Bangladesh*, Oxford: Clarendon Press.

Geschiere, P. (2003), 'Witchcraft as the Dark Side of Kinship: Dilemmas of Social Security in New Contexts', *Etnofoor*, 16 (1): 43–61.

Geschiere, P. (2013), *Witchcraft, Intimacy, and Trust: Africa in Comparison*, Chicago: The University of Chicago Press.

Gez, Y., Y. Droz, J. Rey and E. Soares (2021), *Butinage: The Art of Religious Mobility*, Toronto: Toronto University Press.

Giles, L. (1995), 'Sociocultural Change and Spirit Possession on the Swahili Coast of East Africa', *Anthropological Quarterly*, 68 (2): 89–106.

Gilroy, P. (1993), *The Black Atlantic: Modernity and Double Consciousness*, London: Verso.

Gondola, D. (2016), *Tropical Cowboys: Westerns, Violence, and Masculinity in Kinshasa*, Bloomington: Indiana University Press.

Giorgi, A. and M. C. Giorda (2021), 'Festivals of Religions and Religious Festivals: Heritigized Heterotopias', in P. Bramadat, M. Griera, J. Martínez-Ariño and M. Burchardt (eds), *Urban Religious Events: Public Spirituality in Contested Spaces*, London: Bloomsbury.

Godin, M. (2018), 'Breaking the Silences, Breaking the Frames: A Gendered Diasporic Analysis of Sexual Violence in the DRC', *Journal of Ethnic and Migration Studies*, 44 (8): 1390–407.

Godin, M. and G. Dona (2016), '"Refugee Voices", New Social Media and Politics of Representation: Young Congolese in the Diaspora and Beyond', *Refuge*, 32 (1): 60–71.

Graeber, D. (2001), *Toward An Anthropological Theory of Value: The False Coin of Our Own Dreams*, New York: Palgrave.

Graham, S. and S. Marvin (2001), *Splintering Urbanism: Networked Infrastructures, Technological Mobilities, and the Urban Condition*, London: Routledge.

Griera, M. and M. Burchardt (2021) 'Urban Regimes and the Interaction Order of Religious Minority Rituals', *Ethnic and Racial Studies*, 44 (10): 1712–33.

Griffith, R. M. (1997), *God's Daughters – Evangelical Women and the Power of Submission*, Berkeley: University of California Press.

Griffith, R. M. (2017), *Moral Combat: Sex, Politics, and the Fracturing of American Christianity*, New York: Basic Books.

Gupta, A. (2018), 'The Future in Ruins: Thoughts on the Temporality of Infrastructure', in H. Appel, N. Anand and A. Gupta (eds), *The Promise of Infrastructure*, 62–79, Durham: Duke University Press.

Gusman, A. (2021), '"Are We an Elected People?": Religion and the Everyday Experience of Young Congolese Refugees in Kampala', in B. Meyer and P. van der Veer (eds), *Refugees and Religion*, 125–42, London: Bloomsbury.

Hagan, J. (2008), *Migration Miracle: Faith, Hope, and Meaning on the Undocumented Journey*. Cambridge, MA: Harvard University Press.

Hall, S. (1990), 'Cultural Identity and Diaspora', in J. Rutherford (ed.), *Identity: Community, Culture, Difference*, 222–37, London: Lawrence & Wishart.

Hannerz, U. (1980), *Exploring the City: Inquiries Toward an Urban Anthropology*, New York: Columbia University Press.

Harvey, D. (2001a), 'Globalization and the "Spatial Fix"', *Geographische Revue*, 2: 23–30.

Harvey, D. (2001b), *Spaces of Capital: Towards a Critical Geography*, Edinburgh: Edinburgh University Press.

Harvey, D. (2012), *Rebel Cities: From the Right to the City to the Urban Revolution*, New York: Verso.

Herberg, W. (1955), *Protestant, Catholic, Jew: An Essay in American Religious Sociology*, Garden City: Doubleday.

Hirschkind, C. (2006), *The Ethical Soundscape: Cassette Sermons and Islamic Counterpublics*, New York: Columbia University Press.

Hirschman, C. (2004), 'The Role of Religion in the Origins and Adaptation of Immigrant Groups in the United States', *International Migration Review*, 38 (3): 1206–33.

Hovland, I. (2016), 'Christianity, Place/Space, and Anthropology: Thinking Across Recent Research on Evangelical Place-making', *Religion*, 46 (3): 331–58.

Hsu, A. Y. (2006), *The Suburban Christian: Finding Spiritual Vitality in the Land of Plenty*, Downers Grove: InterVarsity Press.

Hunt, S. (2002), '"Neither Here nor There": The Construction of Identities and Boundary Maintenance of West African Pentecostals', *Sociology*, 36 (1): 147–69.

Huwelmeier, G. and K. Krause, eds (2011), *Traveling Spirits: Migrants, Markets and Mobilities*, London: Routledge.

Imoagene, O. (2017), *Beyond Expectations: Second-Generation Nigerians in the United States and Britain*, Oakland: University of California Press.

Isetti, G., E. Innerhofer, H. Pechlaner and M. de Rachewiltz, eds (2021), *Religion in the Age of Digitalization: From New Media to Spiritual Machines*. London: Routledge.

Jacobsen, K. A. (2008), *South Asian Religions on Display: Religious Processions in South Asia and in the diaspora*. London: Routledge.

Janson, M. (2021), *Crossing Religious Boundaries: Islam, Christianity, and 'Yoruba Religion' in Lagos, Nigeria*, Cambridge: Cambridge University Press.

Janson, M. and A. Akinleye (2015), 'The Spiritual Highway: Religious World Making in Megacity Lagos (Nigeria)', *Material Religion*, 11 (4): 550–62.

Janzen, J. M. (2019), *Health in a Fragile State: Science, Sorcery, and Spirit in the Lower Congo*, Madison: University of Wisconsin Press.

Jenkins, H., S. Ford and J. Green (2013), *Spreadable Media: Creating Value and Meaning in a Networked Culture*, New York: New York University Press.

Johnson, P. C. (2007), *Diaspora Conversions: Black Carib Religion and the Recovery of Africa*, Berkeley: University of California Press.

Jones, B. (2012), 'Pentecostalism, Development NGOs and Meaning in Eastern Uganda', in D. Freeman (ed.), *Pentecostalism and Development: Churches, NGOs and Social Change in Africa*, 181–202, Basingstoke: Palgrave Macmillan.

Kalu, O. U. (2008), *African Pentecostalism: An Introduction*, Oxford: Oxford University Press.

Kankonde, P. (2010), 'Transnational Family Ties, Remittance Motives, and Social Death among Congolese Migrants: A Socio-Anthropological Analysis', *Journal of Comparative Family Studies*, 41: 225–43.

Kapur, D. (2004), *Remittances: The New Development Mantra? – UN discussion Paper*: http://www.cities-localgovernments.org/committees/fccd/Upload/library/ gdsmdpbg2420045_en_en.pdf

Karagiannis, E. and N. G. Schiller. (2006), 'Contesting Claims to the Land: Pentecostalism as a Challenge to Migration Theory and Policy', *Sociologus*, 56 (2): 137–71.

Katsaura, O. (2019), 'Pentecosmopolis: On the Pentecostal cosmopolitanism of Lagos', *Religion*, 50 (4): 504–28.

Kasinitz, P., J. H. Mollenkopf and M. C. Waters (2004), *Becoming New-Yorkers: Ethnographies of the New Second Generation*, New York: Russel Sage.

Keane, W. (2007), *Christian Moderns: Freedom and Fetish in the Mission Encounter*, Berkeley: University of California Press.

Keating, L. (2001), *Atlanta: Race, Class, and Urban Expansion*, Philadelphia: Temple University Press.

Kelegama, S. (2011), *Migration, Remittances and Development in South Asia*, London: Sage.

Khan, A. (2022), 'Pious Publicity, Moral Ambivalence and the Making of Religious Authority in the Tablighi Jamaat in Pakistan', *History and Anthropology*, DOI: 10.1080/02757206.2022.2119231

Kingsbury, K. (2023), 'Mouride Imaginaries of the Sacred and the Time-Spaces of Religious Urbanization in Touba, Senegal', in D. Garbin, S. Coleman and G. Millington (eds), *Ideologies and Infrastructures of Religious Urbanization in Africa: Remaking the City*, 75–91, London: Bloomsbury.

Kirby, B. (2017), 'Occupying the Global City: Spatial Politics and Spiritual Warfare among African Pentecostals in Hong Kong', in D. Garbin and A. Strhan (eds), *Religion and the Global City*, 62–77, London: Bloomsbury.

Kirby, B. (2019), 'Pentecostalism, Economics, Capitalism: Putting the *Protestant Ethic* to Work', *Religion*, 49 (4): 571–91.

Klaver, M. (2021), *Hillsong Church: Expansive Pentecostalism, Media, and the Global City*, London: Palgrave.

Knibbe, K. (2009), '"We Did Not Come Here as Tenants, but as Landlords": Nigerian Pentecostals and the Power of Maps', *African Diaspora*, 2 (2): 133–58.

Knott, K. (2005), *The Location of Religion: A Spatial Analysis*. London: Equinox.

Knott, K. (2008), 'Spatial Theory and the Study of Religion', *Religion Compass*, 2 (6): 1102–16.

Knott, K. (2016), 'Living Religious Practices', in *Intersections of Religion and Migration. Religion and Global Migrations*, 71–90, London: Palgrave Macmillan.

Koser, K., ed. (2003), *New Africans Diasporas*, London: New York. Routledge.

Krause, K. (2006), '"The Double Face of Subjectivity": A Case Study in a Psychiatric Hospital (Ghana)', in H. Johannessen and I. Lazar (eds), *Multiple Medical Realities. Patients and Healers in Biomedicine, Alternative and Traditional Medicine*, 54–71, New York and Oxford: Berghahn Books.

Krause, K. (2008a), 'Spiritual Spaces in Post-industrial Places: Transnational Churches in North East London', in M. P. Smith and J. Eade (eds), *Transnational Ties: Cities, Identities and Migrations*, 109–30, New Brunswick: Transaction Publishers.

Krause, K. (2008b), 'Transnational Therapy Networks among Ghanaians in London', *Journal of Ethnic and Migration Studies*, 34 (2): 235–51.

Kroesbergen-Kamps, J. (2020), 'Horizontal and Vertical Dimensions in Zambian Sermons about the COVID-19 Pandemic', *Journal of Religion in Africa*, 49 (1): 73–99.

Kruse, K. M. (2007), *White Flight: Atlanta and the Making of Modern Conservatism*, Oxford and Princeton: Princeton University Press.

Lacroix T. (2016), *Hometown Transnationalism: Long Distance Villageness among Indian Punjabis and North African Berbers*, London: Palgrave.

La Fontaine, J. (2009), *The Devil's Children: From Spirit Possession to Witchcraft: New Allegations that Affect Children*, London: Routledge.

La Fontaine, J. (2016), *Witches and Demons: A Comparative Perspective on Witchcraft and Satanism*, Oxford: Berghahn.

Lanz, S. (2014), 'Assembling Global Prayers in the City: An Attempt to Repopulate Urban Theory with Religion', in J. Becker, K. Klingan, S. Lanz and K. Wildner (eds), *Global Prayers: Contemporary Manifestations of the Religious in the City*, 17–43, Zürich: Lars Müller.

Lanz, S. and M. Oosterbaan (2016), 'Entrepreneurial Religion in the Age of Neoliberal Urbanism', *International Journal of Urban and Regional Research*, 40 (3): 487–506.

Larkin, B. (2013), 'The Politics and Poetics of Infrastructure', *Annual Review of Anthropology*, 42: 327–43.

Lefebvre, H. (1991), *The Production of Space*, Oxford: Blackwell.

Lefebvre, H. (1996), *Writings on Cities*, Oxford: Blackwell.

Lefebvre, H. (2003), *The Urban Revolution*, Minneapolis: University of Minnesota Press.

Leutloff-Grandits, C. A. Peleikis and T. Thelen (2009), *Social Security in Religious Networks: Anthropological Perspectives on New Risks and Ambivalences*, Oxford and New York: Berghahn.

Levitt, P. (2001a), 'Between God, Ethnicity, and Country: An Approach to the Study of Transnational Religion', Paper presented at Social Science Research Council workshop, "Transnational Migration: Comparative Perspectives," June 29–July 1, Princeton.

Levitt, P. (2001b), *The Transnational Villagers*, Berkeley and Los Angeles: University of California Press.

Levitt, P. and C. M. Waters, eds (2002), *The Changing Face of Home: The Transnational Lives of the Second Generation*, New York: Russell Sage Foundation.

Levitt, P. (2008), 'Religion as a Path to Civic Engagement', *Ethnic and Racial Studies*, 31 (4): 766–91.

Lopez S. L. (2015), *The Remittance Landscape: Spaces of Migration in Rural Mexico and Urban USA*, Chicago: Chicago University Press.

MacGaffey, J. and R. Bazenguissa-Ganga (2000), *Congo-Paris: Transnational Traders on the Margins of the Law*, Oxford: James Currey.

Maduku, I. N. (2012), "Religious Socialisation and Political Involvement of Christians: The Experience of Basic Ecclesial Communities in Kinshasa', in K. Krämer and K. Vellguth (ed.), *Mission and Dialogue. Approaches to a Communicative Understanding of Mission, (One world Theology 1)*, 129–43, Freiburg im Brisgau: Herder.

Matovina, T. M. (2011), *Latino Catholicism: Transformation in America's Largest Church*, Princeton: Princeton University Press.

Maguire, M. and F. Murphy (2012), *Integration in Ireland: The Everyday Lives of African Migrants*, Manchester: Manchester University Press.

Mahmood, S. (2005), *Politics of Piety: The Islamic Revival and the Feminist Subject*, Princeton: Princeton University Press.

Maier, K. M. (2011), *Redeeming London: Gender, Self and Mobility among Nigerian Pentecostals*, Unpublished PhD Thesis, University of Sussex.

Mangalu, A. M. (2011), *Migrations Internationales, transferts des migrants et conditions de vie des ménages d'origine. Cas de la ville de Kinshasa*, Louvain La Neuve: Presses Universitaires de Louvain.

Marshall, R. (2009), *Political Spiritualities. The Pentecostal Revolution in Nigeria*, Chicago: University of Chicago Press.

Maskens, M. (2013), *Cheminer avec Dieu: Pentecôtismes et migrations à Bruxelles*, Brussels: Éditions de l'Université de Bruxelles.

Mauss, M. (2012 [1925]), 'Essai sur le don. Forme et raison de l'échange dans les sociétés archaïques', Paris: PUF, Quadrige.

Mazzucato, V. (2011), 'Reverse Remittances in the Migration–Development Nexus: Two-Way Flows between Ghana and the Netherlands', *Population, Space and Place*, 17 (5): 454–68.

McEwan, C. (2009), *Postcolonialism and Development*, London: Routledge.

McGuire, J. (2008), *Lived Religion: Faith and Practice in Everyday Life*, Oxford: Oxford University Press.

McRoberts, O. (2003), *Streets of Glory: Church and Community in Black Urban Neighborhood*, Chicago: University of Chicago Press.

Meiers, B. (2013), *Le Dieu de Maman Olangi. Ethnographie d'un combat spirituel transnational*, Louvain-la-Neuve: Academia-Bruylant, Coll. Anthropologie prospective vol. 12.

Mélice, A. (2006), 'Un Terrain Fragmenté: Le Kimbanguisme et ses Ramifications', *Civilisations*, 49 (1–2): 67–76.

Mélice, A. (2009), 'Le kimbanguisme et le pouvoir en RDC', *Civilisations*, 58–2: 59–80.

Merrifield, A. (2011), 'The Right to the City and Beyond: Notes on a Lefebvrian Reconceptualization', *City*, 15: 473–81.

Meyer, B. (1998), 'Make a Complete Break with the Past: Memory and Postcolonial Modernity in Ghanaian Pentecostalist Discourse', *Journal of Religion in Africa*, 28 (3): 316–49.

Meyer, B. (2010), 'Aesthetics of Persuasion: Global Christianity and Pentecostalism's Sensational Forms', *South Atlantic Quarterly*, 109 (4): 741–63.

Meyer, B. (2015), *Sensational Movies. Video, Vision and Christianity in Ghana*, Berkeley: The University of California Press.

Millington, G. (2016), 'The Cosmopolitan Contradictions of Planetary Urbanization', *The British Journal of Sociology*, 67 (3): 476–96.

Mokoko Gampiot, A. (2004), *Kimbanguisme et Identité Noire*, Paris: L'Harmattan.

Mokoko Gampiot, A. (2014), 'L' ethique Kimbanguiste et l'esprit de developpement', in E. M'Bokolo and K. Sabakinu (eds), *Simon Kimbangu: Le prophete de la liberation de l'homme noir*, Paris: L'Harmattan.

Mokoko Gampiot, A. (2017), *Kimbanguism, An African Understanding of the Bible*, University Park: Penn State University Press.

Moore, M. (2015), *A Political Theory of Territory*, Oxford: Oxford University Press.

Morgan, D. (2011), 'Mediation or Mediatisation: The History of Media in the Study of Religion', *Culture and Religion*, 12 (2): 137–52.

Ndaya Tshiteku, J. (2007), *"Prendre le bic": "Le Combat Spirituel" congolais et les transformations sociales*, Leiden: African Studies Centre, African studies collection 7.

Nest, M. (2011), *Coltan*, Cambridge and Malden, MA: Polity Press.

Newell, S. (2012), *The Modernity Bluff: Crime, Consumption, and Citizenship in Côte d'Ivoire*, Chicago: Chicago University Press.

Nzongola-Ntalaja, G. (2002), *The Congo from Leopold to Kabila: A People's History*, London: Zed Books.

Olangi, E. and J. Olangi (1999), *Le Combat spirituel: Combattre et vaincre*, Kinshasa: Patmos.

O'Neill, K. L. (2015), *Secure the Soul: Christian Piety and Gang Prevention in Guatemala*, Oakland: The University of California Press.

Ong, A. (2006), *Neoliberalism as Exception: Mutations in Citizenship and Sovereignty*, Durham: Duke University Press.

Orozco, M. (2013), *Migrant Remittances and Development in the Global Economy*, Boulder: Lynne Rienner Publishers.

Orsi, R. (1999), 'Introduction: Crossing the City Line', in R. Orsi (ed.), *Gods of the City. Religion and the American Urban Landscape*, 1–78, Bloomington: Indianapolis University Press.

Osinulu, A. (2014), 'The Road to Redemption: Performing Pentecostal Citizenship in Lagos', in *The Arts of Citizenship in African Cities: Infrastructures and Spaces of Belonging*, 115–35, New York: Palgrave Macmillan.

Parnell, S. and J. Robinson (2012), '(Re)theorizing Cities from the Global South: Looking Beyond Neoliberalism', *Urban Geography*, 33 (4): 593–617.

Pasura, D. (2012), 'Religious Transnationalism: The Case of Zimbabwean Catholics in Britain', *Journal of Religion in Africa*, 42 (1): 26–53.

Peña, E. A. (2011), *Performing Piety: Making Space Sacred with the Virgin of Guadalupe*, Berkeley: University of California Press.

Piot, C. (2010), *Nostalgia for the Future: West Africa after the Cold War*, Chicago: The University of Chicago Press.

Prabhat, D. (2018), *Britishness, Belonging and Citizenship: Experiencing Nationality Law*. Bristol: Policy Press.

Pype, K. (2007), 'Fighting Boys, Strong Men and Gorillas: Notes on the Imagination of Masculinities in Kinshasa', *Africa*, 77 (02 / May 2007): 250–71.

Pype, K. (2010), 'Of Fools and False Pastors. Tricksters in Kinshasa's TV Fiction', *Visual Anthropology*, 23 (2): 115–35.

Pype, K. (2011), 'Confession cum Deliverance: In/Dividuality of the Subject among Kinshasa's Born-again Christians', *Journal of Religion in Africa*, 41 (3): 280–310.

Pype, K. (2012), *The Making of the Pentecostal Melodrama: Religion, Media, and Gender in Kinshasa*. Oxford and New York: Berghahn Books.

Pype, K. (2017), 'Branhamist Kindoki: Ethnographic Notes on Connectivity, Technology, and Urban Witchcraft in Contemporary Kinshasa', in K. Rio, et al. (eds), *Pentecostalism and Witchcraft: Spiritual Warfare in Africa and Melanesia*, London: Palgrave Macmillan.

Ratha, D. E., J. Kim, S. Plaza, E. J. Riordan, V. Chandra and W. Shaw. (2022), 'Migration and Development Brief 37', Report by KNOMAD-World Bank, Washington, DC.

Renton, D., D. Seddon and L. Zeilig (2007), *The Congo: Plunder and Resistance*, London: Zed Books.

Reinhardt, B. (2014), 'Soaking in Tapes: The Haptic Voice of Global Pentecostal Pedagogy in Ghana', *Journal of the Royal Anthropological Institute*, 20 (2): 315–36.

Rey, J. (2019), *Migration africaine et pentecôtisme en Suisse. Dispositifs rituels, pouvoirs, mobilités*, Paris: Karthala.

Rey, T. (2007), *Bourdieu on Religion: Imposing Faith and Legitimacy*, London: Routledge.

Rey, J. (2015), 'Missing Prosperity: Economies of Blessings in Ghana and the Diaspora', in Heuser, A. (ed.) *'Pastures of Plenty': Tracing Religio-Scapes of Prosperity Gospel in Africa and Beyond*, Brill.

Rey, T. and A. Stepick (2015), *Crossing the Water and Keeping the Faith: Haitan Religion in Miami*, New York: New York University Press.

Rich, J. (2019), 'An African Jerusalem Found and Lost: Ecumenical Churches, Foreign Aid, and the Kimbanguist Church in the Democratic Republic of Congo, 1965–1974', Presentation at the *Greater New York Area African History Workshop*, Princeton University, 5 April 2019.

RUA (2017), *Urbanisation and Development: A Policy Review*. RUA Working Paper No1.

Rüpke, J. (2020), *Urban Religion: A Historical Approach to Urban Growth and Religious Change*, Berlin: deGruyter.

Rutheiser, C. (1996), *Imagineering Atlanta: The Politics of Place in the City of Dreams*, London: Verso.

Saint-Blancat, C. and A. Cancellieri (2014), 'From Invisibility to Visibility? The Appropriation of Public Space Through a Religious Ritual: The Filipino Procession of Santacruzan in Padua, Italy', *Social & Cultural Geography*, 15 (6): 645–63.

Sanchez-Walsh, A. M. (2018), *Pentecostals in America*, New York: Columbia University Press.

Sarró, R. (2015), 'Hope, Margin, Example: The Kimbanguist Diaspora in Lisbon', in Garnett J. and Hausner S. L. (eds), *Religion in Diaspora. Migration, Diasporas and Citizenship*, London: Palgrave Macmillan.

Sarró, R. and A. Mélice (2010), 'Kongo and Lisbon: The Dialectics of Centre and Periphery in the Kimbanguist Church', in S. Fancello and A. Mary (eds), *Chretiens Africains en Europe*, 43–67, Paris: Karthala.

Schoumaker B., E. Castagnone, A. Phongi Kingiala, N. Rakotonarivo and T., Nazio (2013), *Integration of Congolese Migrants in the European Labour Market and Re-integration in DR Congo*, MAFE Working Paper n°27, Paris, INED.

Sharp, L (1995), 'Playboy Princely Spirits of Madagascar: Possession as Youthful Commentary and Social Critique', *Anthropological Quarterly*, 68 (2): 75–88.

Sheringham, O. (2013), *Transnational Religious Spaces: Faith and the Brazilian Migration Experience*, London: Palgrave.

Shipley, J. W. (2015), *Trickster Theatre: The Poetics of Freedom in Urban Africa*, Bloomington and Indianapolis: Indiana University Press.

Shilling, C. (2017), 'Body Pedagogics: Embodiment, Cognition and Cultural Transmission', *Sociology*, 51 (6): 1205–21.

Simmel, G. (2005), *The Philosophy of Money*. ed. D Frisby. London: Taylor & Francis. Electronic version.

Simone, A. and Edgar Pieterse (2017), *New Urban Worlds: Inhabiting Dissonant Times*, Cambridge: Polity Press.

Singh, S. (2013), *Globalization and Money: A Global South Perspective*, New York: Rowman & Littlefield Publishers.

Singh, S. (2016), *Money, Migration and Family: India to Australia*, London: Palgrave.

Sørensen, N. N. (2016), 'Migrants, Remittances and Hometown Associations in Promoting Development', in J. Grugel and D. Hammett (eds), *The Palgrave Handbook of International Development*, 333–345, London: Palgrave Macmillan.

Spivak, G. C. (1984), 'Criticism, Feminism, and the Institution', in S. Harasym (ed.), *The Postcolonial Critic: Interviews, Strategies, Dialogues*, London: Routledge.

Stevenson, D., K. Dunn, A. Possamai and A. Piracha (2010), 'Religious Belief across "Post-secular" Sydney: The Multiple Trends in (de) Secularisation', *Australian Geographer*, 41 (3): 323–50.

Strhan, A. (2013), 'The Metropolis and Evangelical Life: Coherence and Fragmentation in the "Lost City of London"', *Religion*, 43 (3): 331–52.

Strhan, A. (2015), *Aliens and Strangers: The Struggle for Coherence in the Everyday Lives of Evangelicals*, Oxford: Oxford University Press.

Sumata, C., T. Trefon and S. Cogels. (2004), 'Images et usages de l'argent de la diaspora congolaise : Les transferts comme vecteur d'entretien du quotidien à Kinshasa', in Trefon, T. (ed.), *Ordre et désordre à Kinshasa. Réponses populaires à la faillite de l'État*, 61–62, pp. 134–54, Coll. Cahiers Africains.

ter Haar, G. (2011), 'Religion and Development: Introducing a New Debate', in G. ter Haar and J. D. Wolfensohn (eds), *Religion and Development: Ways of Transforming the World*, 3–25, London: Hurst.

ter Haar, G. and S. Ellis (2006), 'The Role of Religion in Development: Towards a New Relationship Between the European Union and Africa', *European Journal of Development Research*, 18 (3): 351–67.

Thai, H. C. (2014), *Insufficient Funds: The Culture of Money in Low-wage Transnational Families*, Stanford: Stanford University Press.

Thornton, J. K. (1998), *The Kongolese Saint Anthony: Dona Beatriz Kimpa Vita and the Antonian Movement, 1684–1706*, Cambridge: Cambridge University Press.

Tipo-Tipo, M. (1995), *Migration Sud/Nord: Levier ou Obstacle?: les Zaïrois en Belgique*, Paris: L'Harmattan.

Titeca, K, T. De Herdt and I. Wagemakers (2013), 'God and Caesar in the Democratic Republic of Congo: Negotiating Church–State Relations Through the Management of School Fees in Kinshasa's Catholic schools', *Review of African Political Economy*, 40 (135): 116–31.

Tonda J. (2008), 'La violence de l'imaginaire des enfants-sorciers', *Cahiers d'études africaines*, 189/190: 325–43.

Tonkiss, F. (2013), *Cities by Design: The Social Life of Urban Forms*, Cambridge: Polity Press.

Trapido, J. (2017), *Breaking Rocks: Music, Ideology and Economic Collapse, from Paris to Kinshasa*, New York: Berghahn Books.

Trefon, T. (2009), 'Hinges and Fringes: Conceptualizing the Peri-urban in Central Africa', in F. Locatelli and P. Nugent (eds), *African Cities: Competing Claims on Urban Spaces*, 15–36, Leiden: Brill.

Trefon, T. (2011), *Congo Masquerade: The Political Culture of Aid Inefficiency and Reform Failure*, London: Zed.

Tremlett, P.-F. (2012), 'Two Shock Doctrines: From Christo-Disciplinary to Neo-Liberal Urbanisms in the Philippines', *Culture and Religion*, 13 (4): 405–23.

Trouillot, M. R. (1995), *Power and the Production of History*, Boston: Beacon Press.

Tse, J. (2014), 'Grounded Theologies: "Religion" and the "Secular" in Human Geography', *Progress in Human Geography*, 38 (2): 201–20.

Tsing, A. L. (2005), *Friction: An Ethnography of Global Connection*, Princeton: Princeton University Press.

Tuckett, A. (2018), *Rules, Paper, Status: Migrants and Precarious Bureaucracy in Contemporary Italy*, Stanford: Stanford University Press.

Turner, V. and E. Turner (1978), *Image and Pilgrimage in Christian Culture: Anthropological Perspectives*, Oxford: Blackwell.

Tweed, T. (1997), *Our Lady of the Exile: Diasporic Religion at a Catholic Shrine in Miami*, New York: Oxford University Press.

Tweed, T. (2006), *Crossing and Dwelling: A Theory of Religion*, Cambridge, MA: Harvard University Press.

Tyler, I. (2013), *Revolting Subjects: Social Abjection and Resistance in Neoliberal Britain*, London: Zed.

Tyler, I. and K. Marciniak (2014), *Protesting Citizenship: Migrant Activisms*, London: Routledge.

Ukah, A. (2004), 'Pentecostalism, Religious Expansion and the City: Lesson from the Nigerian Bible Belt', in P. Probst and G. Spittler (eds), *Resistance and Expansion: Explorations of Local Vitality in Africa*, 415–41, Lit: Münster.

Ukah, A. (2014), 'Redeeming Urban Spaces: The Ambivalence of Building a Pentecostal City in Lagos, Nigeria', in J. Becker, K. Klingan and S. Lanz (eds), *Global Prayers: Contemporary Manifestations of the Religious in the City*, 178–97, Berlin: Lars Müller Publishers.

Ukah, A. (2016a), 'Building God's City: The Political Economy of Prayer Camps in Nigeria', *International Journal of Urban and Regional Research*, 40 (3): 524–40.

Ukah, A. (2016b), 'Re-Imagining the Religious Fields: The Rhetoric of Nigerian Pentecostal Pastors in South Africa', in M. Echtler and A. Ukah (eds), *Bourdieu in Africa: Exploring the Dynamics of Religious Fields*, 70–95, Leiden: Brill.

UN-Habitat (2016), *Habitat III: New Urban Agenda*, New York: United Nations Human Settlements Programme.

United Nations (2018), *World Urbanization Prospects: The 2018 Revision*, New York: United Nations.

Van der Veer, P., ed. (1996), *Conversion to Modernity: The Globalization of Christianity*, New York: Routledge.

Van Dijk, R. (2004), 'Negotiating Marriage: Questions of Morality and Legitimacy in the Ghanaian Pentecostal Diaspora', *Journal of Religion in Africa*, 34 (4): 438–67.

Van Dijk, R. (2002), 'Religion, Reciprocity and Restructuring Family Responsibility in the Ghanaian Pentecostal Diaspora', in D. Bryceson and U. Vuorela (eds), *The Transnational Family: New European Frontiers and Global Networks*, 173–97, Oxford: Berg Press.

Van Dijk, R. (2010), 'Social Catapulting and the Spirit of Entrepreneurialism. Migrants, Private Initiative, and the Pentecostal Ethic in Botswana', in G. Hüwelmeier and K. Krause (eds), *Traveling Spirits: Migrants, Markets and Mobilities*, 101–17, New York: Routledge.

Van Dijk, R. (2012), 'Pentecostalism and Post-Development: Exploring Religion as a Developmental Ideology in Ghanaian Migrant Communities', in D. Freeman (ed.), *Pentecostalism and Development: Churches, NGOs and Social Change in Africa*, Basingstoke: Palgrave Macmillan.

Van Klinken, A. S. (2014), 'Homosexuality, Politics and Pentecostal Nationalism in Zambia', *Studies in World Christianity*, 20 (3): 259 –281. ISSN 1354-9901.

Vásquez, M. A. (2008), 'Studying Religion in Motion: A Networks Approach', *Method and Theory in the Study of Religion*, 20 (2): 151–84.

Vásquez, M. A. (2009), 'The Global Portability of Pneumatic Christianity: Comparing African and Latin American Pentecostalisms', *African Studies*, 68 (2): 273–86.

Vásquez, M. A. (2011), *More Than Belief, A Materialist Theory of Religion*, Oxford: Oxford University Press.

Vásquez, M. A. and D. Garbin (2016). 'Globalization', in M. Stausberg and S. Engler (eds), *The Oxford Handbook of the Study of Religion*, 684–701, Abingdon, Oxfordshire: Oxford University Press.

Vásquez, M. A. and K. Knott (2014), 'Three Dimensions of Religious Place Making in Diaspora', *Global Networks*, 14 (3): 326–47.

Vásquez, M. and M. F. Marquardt (2003), *Globalizing the Sacred: Religion Across the Americas*, New Brunswick: Rutgers University Press.

Vertovec, S. (2007), 'Super-Diversity and its Implications', *Ethnic and Racial Studies*, 30 (6): 1024–54.

Vigh, H. E. (2016), 'Life's Trampoline: On Nullification and Cocaine Migration in Bissau', in J. Cole and C. Groes (eds), *Affective Circuits: African Migrations to Europe and the Pursuit of Social Regeneration*, 223–44, Chicago: University of Chicago Press.

Waldinger, R. D. (2015), *The Cross-border Connection: Immigrants, Emigrants, and Their Homelands*, Cambridge : Harvard University Press.

Walker, R. (2015), 'Building a Better Theory of the Urban: A Response to "Towards A New Epistemology of the Urban?"' *City*, 19 (2–3): 183–91.

Warikobo, N. (2014), *The Charismatic City and the Public Resurgence of Religion: A Pentecostal Social Ethics of Cosmopolitan Urban Life*, New York: Palgrave Macmillan.

Werbner, P. (1990), *The Migration Process: Capital, Gifts and Offerings among British Pakistanis*, London: Routledge.

Werbner, P. (1996), 'Stamping the Earth with the Name of Allah: Zikr and the Sacralizing of Space among British Muslims', in B. Metcalf (ed.), *Making Muslim Space in North America and Europe*, 167–85, Berkeley, CA: University of California Press.

Werbner, P. (2003), *Pilgrims of Love: The Social Anthropology of a Global Sufi Cult*, London: Hurst Publishers.

Wessendorf, S. (2014), *Commonplace Diversity: Social Relations in a Super-diverse Context*, Basingstoke: Palgrave.

White, B. (2008), *Rumba Rules: The Politics of Dance Music in Mobutu's Zaire*, Durham: Duke University Press.

Wilford, J. (2012), *Sacred Subdivisions: The Postsuburban Transformation of American Evangelicalism*, New York: New York University Press.

Wilkens, K. (2020), 'Narrating Spirit Possession', in *Narrative Cultures and the Aesthetics of Religion*, 45–65, Leiden: Brill.

Wimmer, A. and N. Glick Schiller (2003), 'Methodological Nationalism: The Social Sciences and the Study of Migration: An Essay in Historical Epistemology', *International Migration Review*, 37 (3): 576–610.

Zelizer, V. A. (1997), *The Social Meaning of Money: Pin Money, Paychecks, Poor Relief, and Other Currencies*, Princeton: Princeton University Press.

Zimango Ngama, R. (2016), 'Églises de réveil et luttes symboliques: Analyse du processus de déconstruction-reconstruction des rapports de pouvoir au sein des couples à Kinshasa', Unpublished PhD Thesis, University of Kinshasa.

Index